THE CROOKED LADDER

C. R. BRACHER

Disclaimer:
This is a work of fiction. All characters, locations, and businesses are purely products of the author's imagination and are entirely fictitious. Any resemblance to actual people, living or dead, or to businesses, places, or events is completely coincidental.

GELU OCEANUS
RIVER BRUN
TURICUM
COPORTA
FRYX MOUNTAINS
RIVER STOUR
HOBART GAP
HERCYNIAN FOREST
CALOR RIVER
REGILLIUM
BOAR'S TUSK
BERT
VINDIUS MOUNTAINS
THE ACADEMY
EMON
PERGAMON
HOG'S END
BATH
FINCHES FIELD
RIVER GILPIN
CAVERNS OF CARCEREM
TYRUS
BELUM
SINUM OCEANUS
GUARACI

A VISIT

Gray clouds pushed by overhead, dropping occasional bouts of rain as Eldred spied down on the castle and the adjacent city of Boar's Tusk from where he sat on a nearby hill. He frowned as his father's stronghold briefly disappeared behind a veil of mist. The castle was the nearest thing he had left to a home. He would have liked to join his parents down in the keep, he thought as he wiped a spatter of raindrops off his forehead—nice to be warm, nice to be fed. But he knew if he wandered down to the gate, the guards would kill him. It was a certainty. Not for cause, not from malice—they just couldn't help themselves.

The incident at Buxton had made it all clear. The town was the first civilized place he had visited upon returning from the north from the ill-fated expedition to kill the Dragon of Turicum. Oh, the dragon had died along with everyone but Eldred, Lord Kenelm and the vile Lord Ferris. But though he had lived, he had changed. He had taken physical damage—his right cheek was plastered with pallid dead-looking skin, his left hand scarred and ugly. He hated this, but his other problem was of greater concern and greater danger. He had sought the Bond, the mystical link between the invincible Deiran warriors. He had only found the noise, noise which Lord Kenelm had told him had grown more irritating each day they had traveled south through the Eryx mountains.

In Buxton, he learned just how insufferable the noise had become for his fellow citizens. The Deiran warriors in the town had barely waited a minute before setting on him, chasing him into the hills and capturing his pack horse. He had no doubt they would have murdered him on the spot if his mount, Hobbie, hadn't proved himself the faster horse. He reached up and poked his finger through a hole in the back of his leather jacket where a veruta thrown by one of the enraged warriors had caught him in the shoulder. The spear had only caused him minor injury, but the fine blue and gray coat Sammanus had given him was punctured beyond repair.

What if I'm also beyond repair? thought Eldred glumly. But he remained sitting, watching the castle, watching and waiting until finally she appeared riding out of the gate with her escort. "Five blessed days," he grunted, rising to his feet and beckoning Hobbie. Mother used to go riding everyday, or so her letters had said. Those had often been the only words he had received from her during his childhood at the Academy. She had been distant then; now she was nearly unreachable.

Eldred made a quick descent down an overgrown game trail to the location he had scouted along the bank of the River Clyde. He glanced to his right at a long stand of trees, a mile in length; trails ran on both sides. How well would they think, he wondered. He counted on them being mindless with rage. In the worst case, he could just flee. But then the opportunity would be lost. He idly scratched Hobbie's neck. "Just don't lose your footing." That would be the end of both of them.

As he waited, he reached into a saddle bag and pulled out a rumpled green riding hat with purple cloud sparrow feathers—supposedly the finest sort of Maldavian riding hat. She should recognize that even if she didn't recognize him—his face. She had given him the hat on a better day, the day four years ago on his fourteenth birthday when he had passed the Maldavian vision trials.

They were finally coming into view on the left with his mother tucked safely in the midst of her five escorts. Eldred watched them ride, peeking out between two leafy bushes. Of the men, he only recognized Pounder, his favorite of his father's podmen. Pounder rode at the front, wearing his normal genial face. Eldred felt his shoulders growing tense as he waited for Pounder's expression to change.

At two hundred yards, Pounder squinted and started to look around. At one hundred yards, he grimaced; a definite grimace. The question flashed in Eldred's mind. How close should he let them get? Hobbie was amazingly fast, but he would be starting from rest. "Be ready, friend," whispered Eldred. The men looked angrier with every stride.

At fifty yards, Eldred nudged Hobbie and shot out in front of the men waving the hat over his head. "It's me, Mother. Wait here!" he shouted. Hobbie turned right, and the race was on. The men closed the distance quickly as Hobbie started his sprint on the slick wet grass. *Too close, too close,* the thought rattled in Eldred's mind. Pounder was only twenty feet back and screaming with rage. Two of the men had their swords raised, and one of the others threw his veruta, which narrowly missed Hobbie's rear. But the plan was working. The men were in hard pursuit and Ghyslaine had pulled her horse up, watching the chase with a befuddled expression.

Eldred chose the trail to the right of the trees and slowed Hobbie, lest he leave his pursuers too far behind, but he was still charging fast. Pounder chased, shouting obscenities. Two men followed close behind him, then another came on in frenzied haste. Eldred's stomach dropped as the last man went left. Why did he do that? Eldred urged Hobbie on. He could just ride off. He probably should. He wasn't even sure she recognized him. She hadn't called out or waved.

"I'll cut your face off!" shouted Pounder.

"Kill him!" called one of the others.

"Make him bleed!" cried a man waving his sword.

Eldred hunched over Hobbie as the trees flew by, only a minute from the turn. He had to choose. Would it be straight on to safety, or turn left and face a crazed warrior on the other side of the trees. Would she even still be there? He could die for nothing. Turn left or straight on—he could be dead in three minutes. Turn left or straight on. Eldred exhaled a shuddering breath. He needed it. He had to have it. He urged Hobbie left; the horse's hooves slid on the grass, but he kept his footing. Then he was away, letting Hobbie show his speed as he left the screaming riders in the distance.

Eldred spotted the man almost at once, coming to rest on his horse five hundred yards away. The man looked up with anger and confusion dancing across his face. He was out of range of the noise and recovering, but that would change in a moment, change for the worse. Eldred's heart began to thump. Pounder and his crew of maniacs had just made the turn. Eldred was between them now. It all came down to Hobbie.

Hobbie sped towards the man, aiming to pass him on the left, behind his horse. At first, he just stared at Eldred and his pursuers with his mouth open. But then, as the noise filled him, his eyes changed and his lips curled in a snarl. He turned the horse towards Eldred and kicked it hard. The man was coming for Eldred.

Eldred emitted a low groan. He wanted to draw his own sword, to throw his veruta, but the man was senseless because of Eldred's mental noise. To kill him seemed wrong. And the plan, it wouldn't work if this man died. He was sure of that. He urged Hobbie further left, looking for a sliver of room along the tree line. There might be enough. There had to be.

"You Motherless dog!" yelled the man as he closed.

Eldred dodged the low hanging boughs as best he could, knocking one acorn laden branch up over his head. Hobbie was vaulting over the bushes and somehow increasing his pace.

The man shot towards Eldred, brandishing his sword. Eldred's stomach twisted into a knot. The man was there, right there, starting the fatal swing at Eldred's neck. Eldred lurched forward in the saddle, and then the man was gone, both horse and man crashing into the small trees that marked the edge of the stand.

Eldred patted the back of his neck, feeling for blood, but he had only caught the wind of the man's sword, not the steel.

"Curse you! I'll gut you!" shouted the man.

Pounder shouted in the distance as well, but Eldred could not make out the words.

They were all behind him now. Soon they would be out of the noise. What would they do then? In any case, their horses were spent and would never catch him. Eldred laid his hand on Hobbie's neck, and the great horse slowed a step. "You did it," said Eldred.

Now it was up to her. He spied her as he came around the final trees. She was still seated on her horse. Eldred recognized her mount; it was Adelet. Good—one of the younger horses she favored. Some of Mother's mounts were long in tooth and lacked speed.

Eldred waved the feathered hat again, gesturing back towards the castle. "Ride, ride, Mother. We need to talk, and they are coming."

She cringed, looking past him at the distant pursuers.

"Mother, it's me. It's Eldred! Ride with me so we can talk!" shouted Eldred.

She looked back at him, and her blessed eyes changed. She recognized him, but she still looked frightened.

He was closing in, only fifty yards now, slowing lest he just fly past her. "Please, Mother. Ghyslaine! This is our only chance to talk."

She set her chin and turned Adelet, who started off in a canter. Hobbie came alongside on her right.

"What are you doing?" demanded Ghyslaine.

Eldred looked back. His pursuers were out of the noise, but still chasing. "Only what's necessary, Mother. Only what's necessary."

Ghyslaine shifted in her saddle, craning to see the right side of his face. "What happened to you?"

Eldred sighed and shook his head. "No time for that; barely time for anything."

A tear formed in the corner of her eye. "I do not understand."

"I'm cursed, Mother. Cursed to all Deiran warriors who have the Bond. I have what Lord

Kenelm called the noise. It makes warriors go crazy, mad with fury. You just saw its effect. They would have butchered me if they had caught me."

"How did this happen?"

Eldred crinkled up his face. "I don't rightly know. This is—it's my version of the Bond, I think. That's what they said anyway. It came about— it happened when I took some of their medicine."

Ghyslaine frowned. "Who are you talking about?"

Eldred groaned inwardly, trying to avoid that name. "The citizens of Turicum."

Ghyslaine's eyes went wide. "You mean the Wretcheds? They did this to you?"

"They're not"—Eldred gave his head a small shake—"really wretched. They call themselves the Sun People."

Her face grew red. "They must pay for this. This cannot go unanswered. I will tell your father—"

"It's not important," interrupted Eldred. "They only did what they had to do. I was injured, near death. But now, I do need something from you." He trailed off, looking ahead. They were coming up on the castle.

"What is it you need, son?"

Eldred took a breath, phasing his request in his mind. "I'll come back tonight, to the castle gate at nightfall. You must have Father there and convince him to come out to meet me by himself. I'll be out from the wall; you've seen I can't get close. He must come meet me so I can speak to him. He must come alone."

Ghyslaine looked back at her escort, following in ragged pursuit. "Tell me," she said with a note of urgency. "Just tell me now. What is it you need to know from him?"

Eldred pointed ahead. "The castle approaches, Mother. If I get too close, they'll come buzzing out like a swarm of bees. Just do as I ask. It may be the last thing I ever ask of you."

"No, do not say that." She leaned out to put her hand on his side.

"I'll be there tonight, Mother. Make sure Father does as I ask. And have them keep the area clear. If there are any warriors out, they'll kill me."

Her tears were running freely now. "How has it come to this?"

Eldred shook his head and pulled up Hobbie, letting Ghyslaine ride ahead. He did not like upsetting her, but it was necessary. He turned on a side road off to the left headed into the forest. Even if Pounder and his men followed, they could not catch him. He had passed the message. He was that much closer to his goal.

BOAR'S TUSK

The day passed with agonizing slowness. Eldred saw no sign of Pounder and his men, but he took no chances and wound his way up deep into the forest. Eventually, he found a good vantage point and sat, resting Hobbie while he watched for the king's men.

Eldred did not doubt that his mother had passed on his message, but he wondered how his father, King Alfred, would take it. He wasn't even sure his father would be glad to hear he was alive. More than one person on the expedition north had suggested that Alfred had arranged the entire mission to get rid of him. Though that did seem extreme. It should have been easy enough to force him to be a steward, a simple servant. Eldred pressed his hands together and raised them to his lips. Simple enough, but there would be the stench of disgrace, more for him, of course, but some hint of it might cling to the great man, the king.

As shadows fell longer across the forest floor, Eldred called Hobbie and began his way back, retracing his steps to his father's castle. He approached the castle as dusk was fading into night, pausing a mile away for the transition to complete. Darkness was his friend. Thanks to his Maldavian blood, he had both far sight and dark vision. If matters took a bad turn, he would at least have that advantage over his pursuers.

After a measured check for lurking warriors, he continued towards the castle. As he closed the distance, he made out his mother and father standing behind the parapet wall above the closed gate, staring out from the torchlit castle into the darkness. Alfred's podmen stood by his side, including Pounder, who appeared to be locked in conversation with the king and queen. Dozens of men armed with veruta manned the wall. They appeared vigilant, rather than hostile, but that would change if he went too close.

Eldred stopped at a bit more than two hundred yards, straining his eyes to make out the men's faces. But the flickering torch light made it difficult to get a read on their expressions. He dared go no closer. He would stir up the entire castle.

"Father! It's me, Eldred! Come out to me!" shouted Eldred. The sound carried clear in the cold night air.

On the wall, Ghyslaine pointed Alfred towards Eldred.

Alfred leaned on the wall. "Come closer!"

Eldred quickly surveyed the men's faces, still calm as best as he could make out. "No! I dare not. I'm cursed! Did Mother not explain?"

"Are you playing some stupid game?" came his father's booming voice.

Eldred frowned and wished it could be as simple as that. "No! Are you frightened, Father? Does it worry you to come out by yourself?"

There was silence for Eldred as his parents argued up on the wall. Finally, after a minute, Ghyslaine turned and yelled out to Eldred. "Stay put, son! I am coming out."

Alfred raised his palms as she turned and headed for the stairs. After a pause, he grudgingly made his way after her. A few moments later, the gate opened and Ghyslaine strode out, looking regal in an elegant red dress, though worry showed on her face. Alfred and his head steward, Morris, trailed after her, ten yards back. Alfred bore his famed blade, Capito, in a scabbard on his hip. The stubble on his cheeks was almost as thick as the thinning hair on his head. His face showed his age much more than hers did. His hard eyes were not blessed as hers were—him being Deiran and her being half-Maldavian— so Morris carried a torch to light his way.

Eldred gazed upon them as they came, struck for the hundredth time by how different he was in appearance from his parents. He took almost entirely after her other half, her Mercian half. He stood six feet, half a foot taller than the average Maldavian, who would be an inch or two taller than your usual Deiran. Thick and broad, like a Mercian; only his blessed eyes showed any hint of his Maldavian ancestry.

As Ghyslaine approached, Eldred dismounted and looked past her to his father. He was the one to mark. Morris was merely a steward. At a hundred yards, Alfred's face looked red. His eyes narrowed. His mouth was turned into a sneer, but he left Capito in its sheath, the named blade blessed by the Night Mother herself. Eldred swallowed. Out here, away from his pod and battered by the madness of the noise, Alfred would not fight with the skill of a bonded warrior, but he would still swing a deadly sword.

Ghyslaine rushed forward over the final stretch, arms out to embrace Eldred, but he pushed her aside and drew his sword.

Ghyslaine stepped forward and grabbed at Eldred's sword arm. "What are you doing?"

Eldred brushed her away. "Stay back, Mother. I won't hurt him if I can help it."

Ghyslaine looked shocked. "Have you gone mad?"

Alfred's face grew tight as he picked up on the disturbance. He rested his fingers lightly on Capito and picked up his pace. Morris's torch bobbed up and down as he hurried to keep up. At thirty feet, he must have seen the reflection of Eldred's sword and paused only a second before snatching Capito out of its scabbard. He stood, his face red with anger, lit from behind by torchlight.

Eldred took a deep breath and stepped towards Alfred, sword ready.

"You'd better think about that, boy," said Alfred.

Eldred halted and studied Alfred's face. "Are you—angry?"

Alfred leveled Capito at Eldred. "Good guess, son. Do you have some explanation for this pointless charade?"

Eldred gave Alfred a searching look. "But you have your senses? You can think?"

Alfred puffed out his chest. "By the Mother, of course I can think, you dimwit. Why have you summoned us out here in the cold of night?"

Eldred looked back and forth between his parents as he lowered his sword. Where was the curse? "I—I needed to see you before I left."

"You are leaving us?" asked Ghyslaine in surprise.

"Where's the rest of the expedition?" demanded Alfred.

Eldred sheathed his sword, feeling confused. Father was his usual self; it should not be so. "They're all dead, except for Lord Kenelm and possibly Lord Ferris. We killed the dragon."

"And your face?" asked Ghyslaine.

"Dragon venom," said Eldred.

Ghyslaine grabbed Eldred and hugged him.

Alfred took the torch from Morris and moved closer to peer at Eldred's face. "We can do all this in the castle. No need to be out here."

Eldred shook his head violently. "No! I'm cursed, Father. Your men will kill me."

Alfred waved his hand dismissively. "You just have a mark on your face.

It's a simple thing. Come inside." He turned and started back towards the castle, Capito back on his belt.

Eldred felt his legs grow weak as he watched the blade moving away from him.

Ghyslaine tugged at Eldred's arm. "Come along. You must not leave."

Eldred wrinkled his brow. "I'll come, but you walk up with Father. You can't be beside me. They will throw their veruta. You'll see."

Ghyslaine raised an eyebrow. "You are speaking nonsense. You took us by surprise today. You were charging around on your strange mount. But now, everyone knows who you are. You are safe. I guarantee it."

"No, Mother. You don't understand. Walk ahead, please."

She half hugged him, resting her hand lightly over his heart. "You have been through something terrible. I can tell. But do not be like this. Come inside. Your father and I will keep you from harm."

Elderd blew out his breath. "Very well, Mother. But you must walk ahead." He urged her forward. He waited for her to get fifty feet ahead before he mounted Hobbie and slowly paced after her, keeping the distance. He was within two hundred yards now. The men on the wall should be feeling the heat, but they didn't seem perturbed. They looked bored. Was the curse gone?

At a hundred yards, Eldred's neck muscles tightened, but the men on the wall calmly gripped their spears. At one hundred feet, they could see him in the torchlight. Eldred stopped as Ghyslaine entered the gate. He searched the faces on the wall, looking for the rage to which he had grown accustomed, ready to turn and flee. But there was no anger. Eldred took a deep breath and entered the gate, tensing his shoulders as it swung shut behind him. Then he remembered that they never shut the gate, those that fear none having little need for such a barrier. For a moment, he feared the men streaming down the stairs would attack. But they were just lining up to take a look at Eldred, as were some of the castle servants.

Eldred dismounted and handed off Hobbie to a stablehand he recognized. "Take good care of him. Only the best feed."

The stablehand nodded and led Hobbie away.

The crowd pressed in on Eldred. "Where are the others?" "What happened to the dragon?" "Where did you get that horse?" "Why are you wearing those strange clothes?"

An older woman pushed her way to the front and tapped Eldred on the chest. "Where's Yeowars?"

Eldred cleared his throat. It had not been a pretty thing. The young steward had been the first to die, ripped apart by a pack of wolves while relieving himself in the woods. Eldred had barely escaped them himself. "He died," said Eldred blankly.

The woman tugged at her hair. "What? How? How did he die?"

Eldred glanced around. He was surrounded by a hundred folk, many of them bonded warriors. He kept checking their faces to make sure they were calm.

The woman grabbed his hand. "How did he die?" she shouted.

Eldred stepped back, startled. "He was killed by wolves in the Hercynian Forest."

The woman shrieked and turned away in tears.

A warrior stood up on his toes to get in Eldred's face. "What happened to the lords? Why're they not with you?"

Eldred noticed Pounder approaching Alfred and Ghyslaine on the edge of the crowd. A knot worked in Eldred's stomach, but Pounder seemed calm, absent of murderous intent, at least for the moment.

The warrior shook Eldred's shoulder. "The lords?"

Eldred swallowed. "Lord Kenelm lives. He came south with me, but made for Evenwood. Lord Ferris found his own way, whether successfully or not, I do not know. The others are all dead, both lords and squires."

The crowd went silent.

Eldred looked around him, feeling the weight of the silence. "They were each brave in their own way. The other squires fell to wolves at our camp near Turicum. The lords died in battle against the dragon. Lord Vance dispatched it at the cost of his life."

"Lord Vance then; it was he that won the day," said an older warrior.

Alfred curled his lips. "That's enough news for now. Let him through. My wife wants to feed him. For now, let us all just note that the expedition I sent was a success. As I predicted, five Deiran warriors were sufficient. The dragon that terrified the north has been put down!"

Alfred waved to the crowd, who clapped and gave a light cheer. Then he turned and walked with Ghyslaine towards the residence tower. Eldred picked his way through the crowd after them.

REUNION

They settled in Alfred's private dining room, a cozy wood paneled room warmed by a fireplace. Alfred sat at the head of the small table, Ghyslaine at the foot and Eldred on the side. Morris poured wine for Alfred and Ghyslaine and set a goblet of water before Eldred.

"Morris, please have Wilkey send up some hot food for Eldred," said Ghyslaine.

Morris bowed. "Yes, ma'am." He glided from the room.

Alfred peered at Eldred's right cheek and waved his finger in a circle. "Does that hurt?"

Eldred shook his head. "No. It feels fine. It will just take some time to appear more normal. They said the coloring should improve."

Alfred narrowed his eyes. "Who said?"

Eldred gestured weakly; he had to use the name. "The Wretched."

"Well, who cares one bit what they say?" grunted Alfred.

"They are not so bad. They healed me. I would have died without their help," said Eldred.

Alfred took another look at Eldred's cheek. "Is that so?"

"Yes," said Eldred.

Ghyslaine patted the back of Eldred's right hand, his good hand. "If true, I thank them for that."

Alfred set down his wine cup. "We have news here as well. We are at war with the Corporians. It seems they were lurking around Lord Ferris's borders after all."

"A war or just a scrimmage?" asked Eldred.

"A true war. They built a city up in the Vindus mountains. A large city, according to our scouts. And they will fight for it. I sent a silver pod, and the Corporians killed them to the last man."

"So there are hundreds of Corporians up there?"

"Thousands. Many thousands," said Alfred with an air of satisfaction.

"Why would they be there? What is the sense in building a city in our realm?" asked Eldred.

Alfred scratched his cheek. "They must mean to wet our swords with their blood. Well, that's the news. What are your plans? You said you were leaving. Are you taking Benedict up on his offer and becoming his steward?"

Eldred shuddered. "No, not that."

Alfred looked Eldred up and down. "What then?"

Eldred paused and was about to answer when Wilkey came bustling in with a plate of mutton and mashed potatoes, which he set down in front of Eldred.

"For the young man. He must be hungry," said Wilkey with a wide grin.

"Thank you, Wilkey," said Eldred.

Wilkey gave Eldred a nod. "I heard you killed the dragon."

"No," said Alfred in a flat tone. "The lords did. Eldred was merely present."

Eldred looked over at Alfred. "I did lure it out into their trap."

Alfred shrugged.

"Well, it's good to see you return, young Eldred," said Wilkey as he turned and left the room.

Eldred took a fork full of mashed potatoes. It was a great improvement over the trail food he had scrounged since he lost his supplies in Buxton.

Ghyslaine smiled. "So good to have you back, Eldred."

Alfred sighed and drank his wine.

After watching Eldred eat for a few minutes, Alfred set down his wine cup. "So your plans, son? If you're not intending to stay with Benedict, what is your destination?"

Eldred returned Alfred's gaze. "I'm still considering. I did not expect to be able to enter the castle."

"Why not?" asked Alfred.

"I'm cursed, cursed with the noise."

"This again? Your supposed curse," said Alfred mockingly.

Eldred set down his fork and wiped his mouth. "We were in the mountains after we fought the dragon. Lord Kenelm and Lord Ferris said I had the noise, but that it was odd. It made Lord Ferris angry, which is why he split from us. It drained Lord Kenelm and made his head hurt, but he stayed peaceable. But since then—in Buxton and this morning on the road—it has made bonded warriors mad with fury."

Alfred snorted. "Your mother mentioned some nonsense of that sort, some curse. If you really had such a curse, why come here? More bonded warriors to kill you here than just about anywhere and me foremost among them."

Eldred picked up his knife and cut off a hunk of mutton. "Well, that's what they said. They said it was noise like someone might get before manifesting the Bond."

"Alright, hold still a moment then. Let me take a look at you." Alfred stared intently at Eldred's forehead, examining him in silence for a full minute. Then he looked away and blinked. "There's something."

Ghyslaine leaned forward. "What do you mean?"

"But it's cursed, right?" asked Eldred.

Alfred shrugged. "You seem fine to me."

Ghyslaine turned to Eldred. "You have the Bond, the working Bond? This changes everything."

Alfred gave a short laugh. "No, it doesn't. We're at war with the Corporians. This is no time for change. But it's something to ponder for the future."

"It changes things for Eldred. He can be a bonded warrior now, not some trifling steward," said Ghyslaine.

Morris paused in the doorway, holding another bottle of wine.

Alfred gestured at Morris to enter. "Bring it! Don't mind her."

"Oh, I am sorry, Morris," said Ghyslaine.

Morris brought the bottle to the table, scarcely looking up from the floor. "It's nothing, ma'am."

Alfred pointed at Eldred. "He hasn't passed the trial. I can't just declare my son a bonded warrior. And the timing is bad. Harold's raising an army to fight the Corporians. We can't go shifting things every which way now. We can settle this soon enough after the Corporians are put to the sword."

Ghyslaine glared. "If there is a time for you to stand up for your son, this is the time. If there is a war to be fought, Eldred needs a role. Give the greater honors to your nephew, if you must. But your son needs to spill some Corporian blood. That's the only thing you Deirans respect."

Alfred made a face and took another drink of wine. "Fine. Let him practice for the trial." Alfred glanced back at Eldred. "Find someone, some warrior. Practice with the kid swords. I'll make some deal, but I tell you, this will be no easy thing, not with the disgraceful way you left the Academy."

GHYSLAINE

After Alfred retired to his chambers, Eldred and Ghyslaine climbed to the top of the tower to take in the view. They stood in the dark, looking out into the overcast night. Eldred's eyes traced the River Clyde as it snaked its way into Boar's Tusk, just to the north of the castle.

Eldred looked over the town and frowned. Its walls were discolored and had fallen down in a few places. There were no gardens, just patches of weeds where flowers and produce should have been planted. The roof tiles of the buildings were old and broken, patched in some places by discolored lumber.

"It's a wreck."

Ghyslaine stepped next to Eldred. "What is?"

"The whole town. You should see Turicum, or even abandoned Regillium. They're in much better repair."

Ghyslaine gave Eldred a worried look. "How much time did you spend with the Wretched?"

"Some time. I told you, they cured me. That took—a week," said Eldred untruthfully. It had been much longer. He had lived with them. He still would be there if they hadn't kicked him out.

"You would do best to forget them. Don't praise their cities or keep wearing their clothes. No one here will care for that."

Eldred rested his hands on the stone wall. "You have to do something for me. You have to send the count of the Wretched to your brother."

"Julian will send his own expedition for that task when he is ready. He'll deal with it."

Eldred pointed off towards the north. "The dragon took its toll. It killed forty-three Wretched. Uncle Julian has to acknowledge the covenant. It's the Night Mother's decree."

Ghyslaine pursed her lips. "I was going to write to him anyway to let him know you returned. I can include this odd note if you so wish."

Eldred nodded. "I do."

"You should be worrying about more important matters."

"Like what?"

"Your training. You must pass the trial in the next few days if you can."

Eldred narrowed his brows. "That would be very quick."

"You have the Bond. Don't you?"

Eldred crinkled up his face. "I have something. It drives warriors insane, or it did, anyway, until tonight. Lord Ferris said he wanted to kill me. The men in Buxton hunted me when I came through there. And you saw Pounder this morning. I didn't expect I would ever be standing here again, but the trial? I don't know if I should rush it."

"Word of your return will reach Harold shortly. When he hears you are taking the trial, he could do anything. He already struts around as if he were king."

Eldred clenched his fist by his side. "Father is king."

"Your father is an old king. You heard him. Harold is gathering the army. Harold is leading the charge against the Corporians. If Harold succeeds, your father will be king in name only. You must act quickly."

Eldred shook his head. "I don't know. I wasn't thinking about any of this in the morning."

Ghyslaine narrowed her eyes. "What were you thinking? You drew your sword on your father after I led him to you."

Eldred looked away. "I told you to send him out alone."

"He wasn't going to go. He saw no reason to humor your request."

Eldred sighed. "I told you I wouldn't hurt him."

"If you could help it. You said that you wouldn't hurt him—if you could help it. You will explain yourself."

Eldred twisted his lips, looking off into the darkness.

"Well?" asked Ghyslaine.

"I thought I had no place here. I decided to seek the Mercian crown."

Ghyslaine gave a sharp laugh. "This again? King Capuan must have defended his throne at least a dozen times against the fiercest Mercian warriors. He has a named sword. What makes you think you would last a minute against him?"

"I had treatments from the Sun People. I'm stronger now—and faster. If I have Capito to match his sword, I could win."

Ghyslaine stepped back, her expression hard. "So you aimed to rob your father. And you involved me."

Eldred rubbed his hands together and looked out over the town. "I was cursed. I thought I was cursed. How could I not think I was? I wouldn't have kept the sword. I would have only borrowed it."

"Oh, you think King Capuan would have sent it back once he killed you?"

Eldred crossed his arms.

Ghyslaine rested her hand on Eldred's arm. "Well, I'm glad that you ended up here instead. Your future is with us." She pulled him close. "You have the Bond. Your father said so. He would never say it unless it were true. Your Deiran stone has finally worked."

She rustled his hair to show his three fatum lapides running down from his left temple towards his ear—Mercian red, Deiran blue, Maldavian green—and smiled. "And your Wretched curse, such as it was, has been lifted. The future that you should always have had is here, or nearly so. You must be strong. You must finish this. You need to push your father. He is your father, not Harold's. Give him a reason to support you. His vanity will do the rest."

Eldred leaned on the wall. "I saw Noll in the crowd tonight. I know him from the Academy. I could ask him to work with me."

"And you know what to do?"

"I trained for years, Mother. It's almost all I have ever done."

"You don't have years now."

Eldred nodded. "No, I don't. Still, rushing the trial could be a mistake. I probably have only one chance. Right now, I don't even have a partner."

"You could use Noll for that, too"

Eldred shrugged. "Perhaps, but it's all so odd, Mother. I'm not a squire. I'm too old at eighteen. I don't know how any of this works now."

Ghyslaine rested her hand on Eldred's shoulder. "Leave that to your father. He is the king. He can change the rules if need be."

$$ \text{APARTMENT} $$

Apartment

I t was late when Eldred followed Morris to the fourth floor of the residence tower. A smile played on Eldred's lips as they approached the door to his assigned room. He had always stayed in this room during his brief breaks from the Academy. It was well furnished, as were the other rooms in the tower. Still, this room had always felt like his own room and—in any case—it was much nicer than the supply closet Morris had planted him in during his last stay before the expedition.

Eldred noted that his saddle bags were piled up on the dresser against the far wall. "Thank you, Morris."

Morris gave a short bow and gestured towards a stack of clothing on a chair. "Not at all, young master. I also rounded up some proper attire for you. It's likely a bit tight, but your mother thinks it would be a great improvement over your current garments."

Eldred grunted and looked down at his dark blue and gray leather jacket, wound through with red and purple lines. It might be gaudy by Deiran standards, but the tough hide had kept him intact through some unpleasant encounters.

"If that's all, I bid you goodnight," said Morris.

"Oh, Morris, there's one thing. I need to train with Noll tomorrow. Can you find him and let him know? Have him meet me first thing after breakfast in the old barn. And we'll need wooden swords for the training."

Morris nodded. "I will arrange it, young master."

"Thank you, Morris."

Eldred followed Morris to the door and shut it after him, driving in the bolt for privacy. He turned and took a deep breath as he looked around the room—a large poster bed, freshly made up; a small table with two chairs by the window; a sturdy oak armoire next to the dresser against the far wall; a thin red wool carpet along the side of the bed. It made for an enormous improvement over the dew dampened grass that had made his bed the previous night.

Eldred crossed to his saddle bags and dug out the sample bag that held the two packets of Balaur powder that he had taken from the Sun People. They were key to winning his duel against King Capuan, a source of strength when the time came. Eldred examined the packets in his hand. Would he still fight that duel? Did he need to? Eldred tilted his head and stuffed the sample bag back in the saddle bag.

Moments later he was tucked in the bed, wrapped in clean warm blankets. Not the luxurious comfort of his bed in Turicum—these wool blankets were scratchy—but good enough. Eldred smiled. The curse was somehow lifted. Next thing he would be fighting Corporians and killing them by the hundreds. It all seemed possible. He adjusted his head on the straw packed pillow. Perhaps he could be king, king of the Deirans. His lifelong dreams were coming true.

✣

TRAINING SESSION

When Eldred reached the old barn the next morning, he found Morris sitting on a stone and the thirteen-year-old Noll pacing back and forth under the open sky—only the stone walls of the building remained; the roof had fallen in generations ago.

Morris smiled and rose to present Eldred with two wooden swords. "I trust these will serve, young master."

Eldred took the swords and tested their heft. "These are splendid, Morris. Well done."

Morris bowed. "I shall leave you young men to it."

Eldred offered one of the swords to Noll. "Will this one work for you?"

Noll waved the sword away, exuding disdain from his boyish frame. "What is this about, Eldred?"

"Didn't Morris explain it?"

Noll met Eldred's gaze with narrowed eyes, framed beneath his wide forehead and short black hair, which was unusual since most Deirans wore their hair long. "He told me that you are training for the trial, but he did not make much sense. You're not a squire anymore, not since you turned eighteen. And I'm certainly not one. You were there when I ascended. I don't see what any of this has to do with me."

Eldred pressed the sword into Noll's hand. "Well, take this and I'll explain things."

Noll held the sword stiffly and glowered at Eldred.

Eldred raised his sword. "I have the Bond. My father is going to arrange a trial for me at the Academy. But before I go, I need to run through a few practice sessions. I'll also need someone to pair up with for the actual trial at the Academy. I'm thinking that you would be a great partner."

"That is what Morris said, but that is not how any of this works," said

Noll, his voice shrill. "If you were still a squire—which you're not—you would pair up with another squire, but I'm a bonded warrior. I don't play with wooden swords anymore. I don't practice for trials. I fight real battles with real swords. And I'm not going to go back to the Academy and take the trial again. My family already celebrated my ascension."

Eldred stuck out his chest. "I've also seen real fights with real swords. You might not have heard about it, but I just returned from the expedition that battled the dragon. I don't know if there have ever been any battles that were more real than that."

Noll shrugged. "I guess you were a squire then."

"And that battle stirred me to manifest the Bond. I have it, as witnessed by Lord Kenelm and my own father, your king. So you will now lend your assistance as commanded by the king himself."

Noll rolled his eyes. "Fine. We can do a few practice sets. But I'll have to hear the words from King Alfred himself before I go to the Academy with you."

"Very well. Do you wish to lead?"

"Your choice, Eldred. You're the one who wants to play these games."

Eldred huffed. "Fine. I'll lead."

DEMANDS

Eldred marched up to his father's chambers carrying the practice swords tucked under his arm. He encountered two men in the antechamber that led to his father's study, Bate and Wallace. Bate was one of Alfred's four podmen—tall for a Deiran at five and a half feet with a willowy build. He looked up at Eldred with a hard glint in his eye. Wallace had served under Alfred's father, Berdic. An old bent man with only a few threads of hair, he sat on a stool with stooped posture, leaning against the wall.

Wallace grinned when he saw Eldred, showing the remnants of his yellow teeth. "Hello, young master, where're you rushing to?"

"I need to see him."

Wallace gestured to a line of wooden chairs on the opposite wall. "He's meeting with some lords from Bert. It could be a while."

Eldred glanced at the chairs. "This can't wait. Let him know I'm here."

"They just started," said Bate.

Eldred stepped towards the door. "I'll be brief."

Bate blocked Eldred's path and held up his hand. "You'll have to wait."

"Move aside," demanded Eldred.

Bate raised his chin. "No."

Wallace shuffled up onto his feet. "What's this? It's likely just a few hours. Why not visit Wilkey in the kitchen for a bite? Come back after."

Eldred shook his head and pushed past Bate. "I don't have time."

Bate grabbed Eldred's left arm, but couldn't hold him. "Hey!"

Wallace stretched his arms wide. "This won't do."

Eldred carefully scooped up Wallace with his right arm and advanced to the door, pounding it with his left fist. Bate continued to pull ineffectually on Eldred's arm while Eldred released Wallace, who stepped away.

"This is rubbish," complained Wallace.

The door flew open, framing Alfred in the doorway. "What in the Mother's name is going on?"

Eldred shrugged off Bate. "I did what you directed. I met with Noll. Out of twenty practice sets, I did not come close to passing once. You told me I had the Bond."

Alfred raised his brows, glancing at Wallace and Bate. "This is a simple matter. If Noll doesn't match, find someone else. I don't have time to hold your hand."

Eldred stepped forward, looming over Alfred. "There's nobody else to train with. It's a joke to them, Father. Perhaps if you had been drinking less and seeing clearer last night, you wouldn't have sent me on a fool's errand."

Alfred's jaw tightened. "I don't know. Seems like the perfect sort of mission for you."

Eldred's face turned red.

"Fine. Very well. Come in. I'll put the war on hold." Alfred sighed. He stepped back into his study—with Eldred trailing after him—and motioned his four visitors to their feet. "We must continue our discussions after dinner. It seems that I need to attend to a personal matter."

Eldred stood to the side—by a sparsely filled bookshelf—as the lords filed out. Alfred made his way over to his enormous oak desk set before a wall of windows looking down on the courtyard and removed his sword belt, placing Capito on the table. He took a seat and waved Eldred towards one of the chairs arranged in a semi-circle in front of the desk.

"I rule because I have the respect of my men. When you act in a childish manner, you undermine me. When they laugh at you, they're laughing at me," said Alfred.

Eldred sat. "We only had one or two matches each set. On the fourth set, we had three matches, but that was the best we did. Why did you tell me that I have the Bond?"

"Calm yourself. I'll take another look." Alfred solemnly stared at Eldred's forehead for ten seconds, then nodded. "I was right. You have the Bond. It's at a decent level, too. Noll should've had no trouble following you."

Eldred stood up and pressed one of the wooden swords in Alfred's face. "Show me, then. Show me right now."

Alfred pushed the sword away. "These are children's games. Morris will find someone to work with you."

Eldred narrowed his eyes. "I need to see it now. I'll not leave this room until you prove it."

Alfred glared back into Eldred's eyes before stiffly rising to his feet and pulling Capito over. "I'll give you one set, then you go. Do you understand?"

Eldred nodded curtly and stepped back. Alfred rounded the desk and walked to the center of the room, stopping in front of the fireplace where a fire was burning briskly.

Alfred pulled Capito free and frowned. "It's been a while since I have done this. Just a few years. Turn around. I'll lead."

Once they were back to back, Alfred went through the paces—randomly mixing motions of stepping back, stepping forward, swinging left, swinging right and thrusting—calling out each act after he took it. After the set of ten acts, he turned to Eldred. "That was odd."

Eldred's shoulders drooped. "Just two matches." On the fourth act, they had both stepped forward. On the eighth act, they had both swung right.

Alfred tilted his head. "I know. I could feel you taking the wrong step, the wrong swing. I counted the two as we went."

Eldred turned to look at the fire. "I guess I'm too weak. Just noise."

"No, that isn't it. If you were weak, I wouldn't have felt anything. I wouldn't have known that we had a two-count before you told me. Let's go again. You lead."

They got back in position and Eldred started a set, calling it as he went. When he was done, he turned to Alfred. "Well?"

Alfred smiled. "Ten. Ten matches."

Eldred took a shallow breath. "Truly? You're not joking, are you? It was really ten?"

Alfred clapped Eldred on the shoulder. "You don't want to just pass. You should look for at least one arch removed. You just need a decent partner."

"Shall we go again?"

"No point doing another set in here. We need a wall between us, like one of the arches at the Academy. That's where you're going to have to prove yourself." Alfred walked over to the door and opened it. "Bate, go fetch Pounder and Mack. Meet me over at the library and be quick about it. Wallace, you come with me."

Eldred and Wallace chased after Alfred as he hurried through the castle. When they reached the entrance to the library, Alfred opened the door of the adjoining room and peered in. "The wall between the rooms is not quite thick enough, but it will be some sort of test."

Eldred glanced in the library at the mostly empty shelves. "You know they have a huge library in—"

"Ah, here they are," said Alfred as Bate came jogging up with Pounder and Mack. Mack was another of Alfred's podmen—the heavyset man was out of breath.

"Pounder, you conduct the proceedings from the library with Eldred. Wallace, you come with me next door. Bate and Mack—complete the bridge through the hallway. Score it fair, gentlemen, just the way Headmaster Tibbot would score it himself. Well, if he ever bothered to do anything useful, that is."

After they arranged themselves, Eldred stood facing Pounder at the far end of the library—wooden sword in hand—while Alfred's men practiced exchanging hand signals. Eldred frowned. They looked rusty.

Once the men were satisfied, Pounder raised his eyebrow. "Whenever you are ready, Eldred."

Eldred nodded and Pounder started the set. Eldred went through the motions Pounder signaled, stepping forward and back, swinging left and right.

When it was done, Pounder turned to Mack and held up ten fingers. "Perfect at one library removed."

Eldred smiled. It was all so effortless and amazing.

Alfred pushed past Mack into the doorway "Ten! An easy ten. Let's switch. I'll lead."

Alfred returned to the other room, and Wallace called the start of the set. Eldred moved, keeping to the cadence of the trial. He was supposed to mirror whatever Alfred did, but he had no more sense of that than he had in the sets that morning with Noll. As Eldred shifted around—swinging, stepping, thrusting—he couldn't help but notice Pounder wince. He ought to feel something, but he didn't. He never had.

When it was done, Pounder held up one finger. "Sorry, Eldred."

Alfred came racing back around to the door. "Ugh! I could feel it going wrong the whole time! What were you doing? What's wrong with you?"

Eldred held up his hands. "I don't know."

"We will go once more with you leading," said Alfred.

"If it works when I lead, I can pass. That's all that's needed."

Alfred looked Eldred up and down. "True enough."

After the set, Pounder held up ten fingers. Alfred came up behind Mack and leaned on the doorframe with one hand. "Well, that works. Now we have to figure out how to make a test like two arches removed."

Wallace piped up. "The stone alcoves in the wine cellar could do."

Alfred pointed at Wallace. "You're right. Come on, everyone. To the cellar!"

After sending Wallace for some candles, they made their way down the stone steps into the cool darkness of the cellar, Alfred in front with Eldred just behind him.

As Alfred reached the bottommost step, he turned to Eldred. "No cheating in the dark."

Eldred frowned. "I won't cheat."

"Good. That's as it should be."

The far wall of the cellar had five alcoves set apart by stone walls that came out ten feet into the room. The back of each alcove was lined with racks of wine bottles. Barrels and crates were scattered around the floor.

Alfred held up his candle as the men lined up behind him. "Not a bad likeness. These walls are not thick enough, though. Those Academy arches are awfully thick."

Eldred stepped into the middle alcove. "But these alcoves are wide enough. Even a little wider than the arches."

Alfred grunted. "Clear out the leftmost and middle alcoves. We're attempting two arches removed."

After a few minutes spent dragging out all the clutter, Eldred stood in the middle alcove facing Pounder while Alfred was situated in the leftmost alcove with Wallace. Eldred's heart raced. Two arches removed. Harold had only passed at one arch removed. According to how Uncle Benedict had once stated it, Eldred would be king if this worked. Strength in the Bond mattered more than anything.

Eldred took a breath, and Pounder kicked off the set. As before, Eldred went through the motions, taking the actions Pounder signaled. When it was done, Eldred jerked his head around to stare at Mack, standing over a candle at the edge of the alcove. Mack was holding up ten fingers. Pounder clapped his hands. Eldred gave a stuttering laugh.

As Alfred came around the wall of the alcove, Eldred dropped his wooden sword and darted forward to hug him. Alfred held his candle out wide and patted Eldred's back. "All right, all right. That's enough. You made two arches removed. Not bad at all."

Eldred stepped back and looked Alfred in the eye. "I can be king!"

Alfred crinkled up his face. "Let's not get ahead of ourselves. We still have a king. For now, let's try three arches removed."

"No! Four arches. The same as you had, Father."

Alfred waved his hand. "Four arches, then."

Alfred returned to the leftmost alcove, and Eldred moved to the rightmost, leaving three empty alcoves between them.

"Whenever you are ready, Pounder!" called Alfred.

Pounder nodded and started the set. Once done, Pounder held up ten fingers. Eldred shook his head in disbelief.

Alfred walked over carrying a candle. "I trained for two months with my partner when I passed at four arches removed. We just walked down here today and did the same."

"It's strange that I can't follow, though," said Eldred.

Alfred wagged his finger. "To be an effective warrior, you need to be able to listen as well as lead. I'm hearing everything today. I'm even hearing Wallace. Wallace, I don't think I have heard you in five years."

Wallace shrugged. "It comes with age."

"Let's try that. I'm testing with Wallace at four arches removed," said Alfred.

"But I'm not taking the trial," said Wallace.

"No, you're not. But we'll test because I want to. Where did you pass in that distant trial of yours, so many years ago?"

"In the center arch, my liege."

"I'll try you at four alcoves today. I'm swapping Eldred out for Wallace."

Eldred rubbed his knuckles on his chin. "I don't see the need."

Alfred headed back to the leftmost alcove. "I want to try it."

They ran a set with Wallace taking the signals from Pounder. Eldred took Wallace's place, counting Alfred's matched acts. Alfred's steps and swings were clear, concise and without hesitation. When it was done, Eldred held up ten fingers, which passed back through the chain to Pounder.

"Ten again," said Alfred.

Eldred furrowed his brow. "Yes, another ten." Ten that didn't matter.

Alfred walked out into the cellar and picked up a candle. "Bate, Pounder, Mack, what do you hear?"

"I hear you clearer than I have in many a day," said Pounder.

"That's true," said Bate.

Alfred pointed at Wallace. "What about him?"

"Maybe a buzz of something," said Mack.

"He's ancient. It's amazing that you hear anything. And Eldred?"

Alfred's men stood silent.

Alfred raised his hands. "Well?"

"Nothing," said Pounder.

Alfred shook his head. "You should hear a drum. He's loud. Louder than Wallace. That's for sure. He's even louder than you, Pounder. What does it mean?"

Pounder shuddered. "I told you, it was not right yesterday. I'm sorry to say it, but there's something wrong."

Alfred scoffed. "The curse, eh? There is no curse. You were surprised by a large Mercian with a discolored face. He's perfectly fine—except for that—and definitely has the Bond. I just took him and Wallace through the paces at four arches removed. You couldn't do it, Pounder. You try it with Bate or Mack if you disagree."

Pounder sighed. "I still think something's wrong."

Alfred pointed Capito at Pounder. "You lack vision. This is telling. My power stirs. I have been sitting, watching things happen. It's time I started making things happen again. Like today. Wallace and Eldred, you don't even hear them, but they're crystal clear to me."

"Yes, my liege," said Pounder.

"I need my men, my army. I'm the one who should crush the Corporians. They trespassed on my lands. Send for my men, not Harold's. Get the word to Lord Trenth. Get the word to Lord Hargraves. Get the word to all of my loyal subjects. I want them here within three days."

"You plan to lead the attack?" asked Pounder.

"I just said it. Now let's go. I need a new plan. This changes everything."

Alfred stormed up the stairs with his podmen in close pursuit.

Eldred watched them go with a perplexed expression. He had just proven that he had the Bond, but Father was running off to lead the war himself like none of it mattered. He sighed and turned to Wallace. The old man was slowly bending over to gather up a few scattered candles. "Umm, well done, Wallace."

"Oh, thank you. It's strange. Not the usual."

"So you don't really have the Bond anymore?"

Wallace cleared his throat. "I wouldn't say that. I would say everything's harder when you've had a few years. Harder to run or swing the sword. The Bond's no different."

"How old are you?"

"Thirty-nine this summer."

Eldred pursed his lips. Thirty-nine was about as long as a Deiran could hope to live, while the Sun People—with their gift from the Mother—lived for hundreds of years. It would be even shorter for Eldred; Mercians only lived for thirty-five years at most. Time is fleeting. Time is precious.

After Wallace collected the last candle, they headed up the stairs.

"I've been wanting to ask, how did Lord Thom meet his end?" asked Wallace.

"Oh, he died well. He was standing in front of the dragon when it clawed him."

Wallace grinned. "That's the way to go. Fighting, buried with honor. I knew him back in the days when I served your grandfather, Berdic."

"He built the trap that caught the dragon."

Wallace gave a sharp nod. "He was the cleverest man."

EVENING

That evening, they had dinner in the Great Hall. It was a small affair. Outside of the family, it was only Alfred's podmen and two of the neighboring lords—Lord Trenth and Lord Hargraves—and their wives. Eldred was surprised not to see the lords from Bert. Perhaps Alfred considered them Harold's men.

Alfred took his spot at the head table with Ghyslaine and Eldred to his left. To Alfred's right sat Pounder and Stace—the oldest of Alfred's podmen, only slightly younger than Alfred.

As they brought out the boiled beef, Alfred was finishing his account of that afternoon. "Pounder couldn't hear either of them, nor could Bate or Mack. But I could hear each of them as clearly as a bell. Perhaps Mack heard a buzz around old Wallace, but none of them had a hint regarding Eldred."

Lord Trenth and Lord Hargraves nodded politely.

"I still don't hear Eldred," said Mack.

"Nor do I," said Bate.

Alfred smiled. "But I could, even at four arches removed. I'm thinking of bringing the trials here instead of the Academy. My wine cellar is perfect for it. If the squires pass, they can choose their own bottle of wine in celebration."

Mack laughed. "That would've suited me."

"That's the future. For now, it's the same old. Tomorrow, we find the right partner for Eldred. Then we run him over to the Academy and he works the arches. The same game. No wine for the boy."

"So he'll pass?" asked Lord Hargraves.

"I just said I ran him through the paces in my wine cellar." Alfred took a mouthful of beef.

"Then Eldred will be your heir again?" asked Lord Hargraves in a solicitous tone.

Eldred raised an eyebrow.

Alfred spat out the beef. "Let's not get ahead of ourselves. We're just having a quiet meal, not making royal pronouncements."

Lord Hargraves smiled. "Sorry, my liege. It just sounded like happy news."

Alfred nodded and pushed the chewed piece of beef aside, taking another mouthful.

Ghyslaine fixed her gaze on Alfred. "Why wouldn't Eldred resume his rightful position as your heir?"

"Yes. Why wouldn't I?" asked Eldred.

Alfred held up his left hand to quiet them while he finished chewing. "It's getting damned hard to eat. Things like this take some period of adjustment. It's a kingdom, not some spent farm."

Ghyslaine frowned. "I see. How long will this period of adjustment last?"

Alfred shook his head and took a long swig of wine. "More than tonight. Change the topic."

Conversation dried up after that. There was just the sound of chewing and slurping as everyone ate.

After a few minutes, Lord Trenth spoke up. "Excuse me, Eldred. I have a question."

Eldred pushed the bowl of meat away. He had loved it before the expedition, but it paled against the exquisite foods of Turicum. "How can I help you, Lord Trenth."

"It's about my son, Wybert. I heard from Morris that he did not survive. How did he die? Did he fight the dragon?"

Eldred sighed. "No, it was the wolves. He died fighting the wolves by our lodge."

Lord Trenth swallowed, his eyes a bit red. "He died fighting a wolf?"

"A pack of wolves. Not like the wolves down here. These were Hercynian wolves. According to the Sun People—the Wretcheds—they're the smartest wolves. They're certainly much larger. Lord Vance said Wybert killed one. He said Mance did as well."

Lord Trenth narrowed his eyes. "Where were you during the attack?"

"I was away. I'm sorry I was not there to help."

Alfred raised his fork. "You were there for the dragon, though. Weren't you, son?"

Eldred nodded.

Alfred's eyes gleamed. "The expedition was to battle the dragon. And—all things considered—it went quite well."

"Well, Father, it did kill Lord Vance, Lord Thom and Lord Osbert."

Alfred glanced at Ghyslaine. "That it did. Give the dragon its due. I sent five bonded warriors to battle the dragon. Some said that was too few. Forty Maldavians fought a smaller dragon and—what—only four of them walked away. Five—count Eldred, that's six—Deirans fight a larger, tougher dragon, and three of them survive. I was right. That tells the tale."

Mack slapped the table. "That's for sure!"

Alfred leaned forward. "There's a difference in strength. I'm not saying Maldavians can't defend themselves; Mercians too. But if I had sent forty Deirans, I expect not a one would have died. It would have just been a long ride through the Mother forsaken north."

Ghyslaine scowled. Bate and Mack snickered into their cups.

"Don't feel sad, Trenth. As Eldred said, these were tough wolves. Your boy was fourteen? Getting one of them was an achievement."

Lord Trenth nodded grimly. "Thank you, my liege."

"How did you kill the dragon, Eldred?" asked Lord Hargraves.

"Lord Vance slew it. He—"

Alfred slapped the table. "That's enough. We're Deirans, we fight as one. The man who blocks a blow gets the same credit as the man who stabs the enemy. There's honor for everyone, even Eldred. Raise your glasses. To victory!"

Eldred picked up his glass of water and joined the toast. Brave men had died.

Alfred wiped his mouth after his drink. "Now I must attend to matters of war. Hargraves, Trenth, come with me to my study. I have a new approach for dealing with the Corporians."

Ghyslaine waited with Eldred for the men to withdraw. "The expedition was very fortunate."

Eldred shrugged. "Some of us were."

Ghyslaine laid her hand on top of Eldred's right hand, his good one. "I am so very glad for that. But your father, he is too boastful."

Eldred lowered his voice. "Kings boast. Won't you want me to boast when I'm king? Shouldn't I tell the citizens how I helped kill the dragon, not some mangy wolf?"

Ghyslaine smiled. "I will never tire of your boasts."

A PARTNER

The hunt for a partner was scheduled to start right after lunch. The night before, Alfred had sent out messengers to all the nearby estates. The word was out that Eldred needed a partner for the trial and that the right partner would earn a reward of three gold aurum. Only those strongest with the Bond were urged to apply, since Eldred would be passing at four arches removed, a feat not matched in years. Fourteen warriors answered the call.

Ghyslaine and Eldred stood in a darkened corner of the cellar, watching as servants finished their work—placing candles, sweeping the floor and dragging clear the last few barrels.

Ghyslaine cleared her throat. "Harold passed at one arch removed. You must match or exceed him."

Eldred nodded. "I'm aware, Mother."

"I expect we will see him tomorrow. He went to Wetwood, aiming to harass Lord Digby for troops to use against the Corporians. I am certain that he jumped on his horse the moment he heard you were up for the trial."

"Father's new plans might be a bigger concern for him."

Ghyslaine shook her head. "No. Win or lose, Alfred is old. The next king does not have long to wait. Can you manage it? Can you pass at two arches removed?"

Eldred smiled. "I can't follow at all, but I can lead at four arches. It just happens."

Ghyslaine gripped his arm. "Don't settle for good enough. Test each warrior Morris brings until you pass with the most arches."

"Don't worry, Mother. I'll have my four arches."

Eldred squinted as Morris brought down the first prospect, Traden, followed by Pounder, Bate, Mack and Wallace—who were reprising their roles as auditors.

"Do you know him?" whispered Ghyslaine, looking over the slight fourteen-year-old warrior.

"I do. He passed the trial last fall with Noll. I expect he is more motivated by gold than any desire to help me."

Eldred set out to the center of the cellar and approached Traden with his hand extended. "Mother's blessings, Traden."

Traden took his hand and smiled out from under a wild mop of dark hair; a thin run of beard ran along his jawline. "Good to see you, Eldred. I was sorry to hear about the other squires. At least you made it."

"Thanks, the wolves were most fierce."

"I heard. And now you're looking to pass at four arches removed."

Eldred straightened his back. "That's right. I led four arches with my father in this cellar last night."

Traden glanced over at the alcoves. "Impressive. Shall we start in the center alcove?"

Eldred shook his head. "No point in that. We will start at one arch removed on the left. I'll lead. It works better that way."

Wallace held out a wooden sword to each of them. Eldred took his. Traden hesitated a moment before taking the remaining sword, the kid's sword. They moved to their positions—Pounder with Eldred in the leftmost alcove, Wallace with Traden in the adjoining alcove and Bate and Mack outside the alcoves to complete the bridge. Everything was as it had been the previous day.

After the first set, Pounder held up one finger and gave Eldred a worried look.

Eldred grimaced. "No matter. We'll try again."

After the second set, Pounder held up two fingers. Eldred walked over to the edge of the alcove to peer at Traden. "Is something wrong?"

Traden spread his hands. "I'm not hearing anything. Perhaps we should try in the same alcove."

Eldred gave a slight shake of his head. "No. One arch removed is the minimum for me."

Traden handed the sword back to Wallace. "Are you sure you changed, Eldred? You seem the same."

Eldred sniffed. "I've changed. Shame it won't be you getting the gold."

Traden shrugged. "Perhaps nobody will be counting those coins."

Eldred glared after Traden as he left the cellar, but as the day dragged on it seemed increasingly likely that Traden was correct. Eldred tried with each warrior, ranging in age from fourteen to twenty-five. Outside of a single set with a twenty-three-year-old warrior named Hewet, where they had six matches, Eldred never came close to passing. The result with Hewet could not be repeated.

Once the last prospect left, followed swiftly by Alfred's podmen, Eldred joined Ghyslaine in the corner and watched as Wallace stiffly gathered up the candles and went up the stairs, leaving them in darkness.

Ghyslaine drew her eyebrows together. "Are you certain this worked with your father?"

Eldred frowned. "Just him. Only him."

"Hmm. Perhaps it's better with him anyway. More official."

Eldred gestured towards the stairs. "You saw their faces. They all think I'm a fraud."

"They might be reluctant to say as much to your father. His strength will help us there."

Eldred took a deep breath. "Yes, I suppose it will."

Ghyslaine patted his arm. "Tonight at dinner, you need to act confident. You can't show any trace of concern."

"I can't. I'm spent. I practiced the trial all afternoon."

Ghyslaine looked him in the eye. "A number of lords answered your father's summons. More could arrive before dinner. They need to see you or they may start talking."

"I'll face them tomorrow. I need rest. I need peace."

Ghyslaine gently rested her hand on Eldred's shoulder. "Very well. Wilkey can bring your dinner up to your room. I'll have Morris raise the purse to a five aurum. That might inspire candidates of higher quality to show up."

"Fine. I just need a good night's rest."

CELEBRATION

Eldred dug through his bags to find the last container of lark's sauce, his favorite condiment of the Sun People. The last portion he had on hand, that is. The warriors of Buxton had captured his spare horse, the horse that had originally belonged to Yeowars when they set off on the expedition. The mount had a number of supplies—including more lark's sauce—unless the warriors had disposed of them or eaten them. Maybe he could get his supplies back. He'd have to ask Morris.

Eldred drizzled the sauce over the boiled chicken and turnips that Wilkey had brought. Not up to Turicum standards, but an improvement on the bland meal. As Eldred ate, he fished through his bags and pulled out the two packets of Balaur powder the Sun People had given him, safely enclosed in the sample bag. He chewed and studied the packets, occasionally rubbing the Deiran stone set between his left temple and ear.

He could hear the gathering in the Great Hall through the open windows. Loud voices and laughter drifted up, painting an image of carefree folk. Eldred frowned. Life would be easy if the Bond told you how to move, if the Bond made you into an invincible warrior. Whatever the Bond was doing for Eldred, it was not as useful as that.

Finally, he came to the last piece of chicken, which had just a dab of lark's sauce. Eldred slumped. It might be the last bit of lark's sauce he ever ate. He took a tiny bite, then another and another, and just like that, the sauce was gone. Eldred set down the stripped chicken bone and stuck the packets of Balaur powder back in his bag—at least he still had those.

As the noise from the celebration went on into the night, Eldred sat on the window sill of his darkened room, looking out over Boar's Tusk and up at the cloudy sky. He spotted a horned owl perched in a tree half a mile away. The owl enjoyed the night air, taking its time, scanning the ground below with its glittering eyes. When the time was right, the owl dived down and caught a rat. Eldred smiled as the owl feasted on its prey. It deserved the spoils.

Eventually, drunken guests started spilling out into the courtyard, getting their mounts from the stables—doubtlessly riding into town, where they had accommodations. As the din and noise dropped away, Eldred went to bed and pulled up the covers, frowning again at the wool blankets, so scratchy compared to the soft quilt on his bed in Turicum. One of the Sun People ought to have given him blankets for a parting gift. Avitus, that prancing prince of Turicum, could have afforded it. The Motherless bastard had everything.

He was lying in bed, thinking about the comforts of his home in Turicum, when he heard a fierce cry. Eldred propped himself up on an elbow and checked the door, which was closed and bolted. Eldred listened for a few seconds before he lay down on his back, alert. Corporian assassins? It didn't seem possible.

"He's up here!" shouted someone.

Eldred's heart started to accelerate.

A moment later, a loud thump on the door jolted him up into a crouching position on the bed. "Who's there?" shouted Eldred.

"I'll cut your eyes out!" shouted a voice on the other side of the door.

"Slit his throat!" bellowed someone else.

"He's in my head," said a third man.

The door shook under the hammering, but the heavy bolt locking the door held firm. Eldred leapt from the bed and grabbed his saber, pulling the blade free. "Get away! Get away from the door!"

The pounding grew louder, but he could still hear the men, each one speaking to how they would kill him.

Eldred went to the window. "Help! I'm under attack! Raise the guards!"

As he yelled, a panel near the top of the door splintered loose. Eldred stepped closer to peer through the gap and stared with wide eyes into Pounder's twisted face. "Pounder, what in Mother's name are you doing? Stop!"

Pounder gave him a sickening grin. "I'll rip you apart."

Eldred glanced past Pounder. Mack and Bate and a few dozen warriors filled the short hallway leading to the stairs. They were all raving. They were so close.

Eldred glanced around the room and seized the dresser, shoving it against the battered door. He tossed his sword on the bed and dragged the armoire over to pile on top of the dresser. Another panel of the door fell away. Eldred looked out to see Morris pushing his way through the men.

"Morris! It's the curse! Move them away from here!" shouted Eldred.

Morris came up behind Mack—who was staring at Eldred with a vacant expression—and grabbed his shoulder. Mack turned and drove a dagger into Morris's neck. Eldred yelled in surprise as Morris dropped to the floor with blood pouring out of him. The men paid Morris no mind. Those in the back shouted and raised their weapons. Those in the front continued to smash down the door.

Eldred grabbed the bed and heaved it up onto its side, jamming it behind the dresser and the armoire. Pounder reached through a gap and unbolted the door. The door was sliding open, inch by inch as Eldred's toes slid backwards across the flagstones. Pounder squeezed halfway through the entrance, dagger in hand.

Eldred let go of the bed and leapt up onto the window sill, gripping the window frame. Three stories down onto pavement stones. Pounder edged into the room with Mack right behind him. Eldred turned and stared at Pounder's bared teeth. "Stop, Pounder! You don't want to do this."

"Die, you Motherless shit!" shouted Pounder as he hurled the dagger, grazing Eldred's left shoulder. Eldred lost his balance and toppled backwards out of the window, screaming as he plummeted to the ground.

Eldred's right leg twitched, and he startled awake, grabbing for a figure sitting next to him. The person shrieked and shrank back. Eldred paused, looking groggily around the room. He had been lying on a bed. He was clutching his mother rather roughly. Wilkey stared at him with wide eyes and backed away.

Ghyslaine squeezed his shoulder. "That is enough, Eldred. Let me go."

Eldred released her and squinted at Wilkey across the narrow room. Harsh sunlight poured through two windows. The back of Eldred's head was throbbing. He reached up to feel a huge knot near the base of his skull. The right side of his body throbbed, a mass of bruises from ankle to shoulder. Eldred swallowed. His mouth tasted awful. "I need water."

Wilkey poured some water from a flagon into a cup.

Eldred reached out his hand. "Just give me the flagon."

He guzzled the water, feeling more focused as the liquid poured down his throat. After he finished, he wiped his chin and frowned. "I was attacked."

Ghyslaine nodded, her eyes full of concern. "Yes."

Eldred rubbed his temples. "It was Pounder—Pounder, Mack and Bate—the lot of them." He opened his eyes wide. "And they killed Morris."

"But not you," said Ghyslaine softly.

"He was trying to help me," said Eldred with a sigh. He glanced around the room. They appeared to be in a country cottage. "How did I get here?"

"The curse broke once you fell. That's what Bate said, anyway. When I arrived, you were on the ground. Pounder was standing over you, protecting you," said Ghyslaine.

Eldred scowled. "He's the one who made me fall."

"It was nothing he wished to do, or so he said. I had Wilkey and a few stewards load you on a cart. We brought you out here to my friend's house in the country. You slept all night. It is almost noon."

Eldred sat on the bed, leaning back on his arms, looking out the window. He sighed and looked Ghyslaine in the eye. "You should have sent him out to me like I told you."

Ghyslaine raised an eyebrow. "Wilkey, would you mind waiting outside? We need some privacy."

Wilkey bowed. "By your leave, ma'am." He went out the door, shutting it behind him.

"You shouldn't talk about that in front of others. It sounds like treason," said Ghyslaine.

"Whatever it sounds like, it would be my right. A son should get something from his father. I don't suppose I'll ever see him again now."

"Perhaps not. He returned as we were loading you on the wagon. He had gone to the town to visit one of his women. He wants you to leave."

Eldred glanced at the pale splotch of skin on the back of his left hand. "Fine. I'll go. I'll leave today. I just need Hobbie and my gear. I'm glad to leave."

"You should stay another night. You took a serious fall."

"Why give those murdering cutthroats another chance? I'll leave today."

"For Emon?"

Eldred crinkled up his face. "No. Not to your half-witted brother. I'll head for Tyrus. I told you, I have business there."

"So, you survived the fall just to get cut down by King Capuan? Do not be a fool."

"Have faith, Mother. Once I win, I'll have my own kingdom and my own named sword. I won't need anything from Father. But I need my horse and some supplies. And I need my gear. I must have my gear."

Ghyslaine folded her hands in her lap with a downcast expression. "I will send Wilkey to fetch your things, but I wish you would reconsider."

Eldred grunted and lay back on the bed, turning his head away from the light.

A Trap

When Wilky did not return in an hour, Ghyslaine sent another steward. An hour later, neither steward had returned from the castle.

Eldred rose from the bed and limped to the window. "What's taking them so long? How far are we from the castle?"

"It's a short walk. No more than half an hour," said Ghyslaine.

"They should be back. They're wasting my daylight."

"You should stay another day."

"No. I plan to get as far away from here as I can."

Some minutes later, Eldred saw them riding in the distance. Alfred was in the lead, followed by Pounder, Bate and Wallace. There was no sign of Wilkey or Hobbie.

Eldred slammed his fist against the window sill. "It's a trap! I should have left while I had the chance. Does anyone have a sword?"

Ghyslaine sprang up and joined Eldred at the window. "It cannot be. He just wanted you to leave."

Eldred gestured. "Then where's Hobbie?"

"Wait here." Ghyslaine turned and hurried from the room, calling for one of the stewards. Shortly, Eldred saw a steward sprinting towards the riders, waving his arms.

The steward met the men about a hundred yards away. Alfred shouted at the man and waved his fist. But the steward kept between Alfred and the farmhouse, all the time bowing and scraping. Finally, Alfred unbuckled his belt and passed over Capito to Pounder and the steward scampered out of the way. As Alfred advanced alone towards the farmhouse; his ruddy face bore a twisted scowl.

When Ghyslaine returned, Eldred glared at her. "So you asked him to hand over Capito."

Ghyslaine nodded.

"Was that for my benefit or his?"

Ghyslaine drew herself up to her full height. "For both of you. Let us meet your father in the dining room."

He took one last look out the window and limped after her.

Eldred stood in his bloodstained night clothes behind Ghyslaine's chair—leaning on it—as the single remaining steward opened the door for Alfred. Alfred gave a nod to Ghyslaine as he walked in, but he never took his eyes from Eldred.

Eldred tightened his grip on the chair. "Where are my things? Where's Hobbie?"

Alfred rubbed his hands together, before clasping them by his waist. "In the stables, I expect."

"I'm not leaving without him. I need my supplies too. I won't let you rob me."

Alfred raised his eyebrows. "Rob you? If you need Hobbie or your supplies, you need only ask."

"We did," said Eldred.

"What are you doing, Alfred?" asked Ghyslaine.

Alfred cleared his throat. "I think Eldred should stay."

Ghyslaine's eyes went wide. "What?"

"I have given it more thought. Eldred belongs here, with us."

Eldred narrowed his eyes. "I thought you wanted to be rid of me."

Alfred shrugged. "Rash words, son. I apologize. I was shocked to find Morris dead."

Eldred mouth fell open. "I didn't kill him! It was Mack. Your Motherless podman stuck his blade in Morris's neck. Your other stupid podman grazed me with his knife." Eldred pulled his shoulder free from his nightclothes to show the scabbed cut. "I fell three stories onto cobblestones."

Alfred tilted his head to the side. "We can spend all day fixing blame. It won't do any good. You should come back to the castle."

Eldred glanced at Ghyslaine and back to Alfred. "You want me to go back with you? Your men—the ones who actually murdered Morris—made a solid effort at killing me. They were lined up with their weapons drawn as they smashed down my door."

"I had them move your gear to another room. The stewards are reinforcing the door."

Eldred gave a mirthless laugh. "A strong door. That's nothing."

"Perhaps not much, but I will stay closer from now on. This—incident—happened when I left the castle for a short time." Alfred glanced at Ghyslaine. "I had some business in town."

Ghyslaine frowned.

"When I am with you, you aren't cursed. Isn't that right, son?" asked Alfred.

Eldred wrinkled his brow. "Seems not."

"What about when you next have business in the town?" asked Ghyslaine.

Alfred gestured towards Eldred. "We must all take care that the two of us stay close. I wouldn't want to lose another valuable servant."

Eldred took a half step forward. "What about me? I'm the one they wanted to kill."

Alfred sighed. "Well, where else would you go? Do you aim to take your rest in Emon, surrounded by a gaggle of Maldavians babbling on about how far they can see? Where is the honor in that?"

"Where is the honor in being stabbed in the neck?" asked Ghyslaine.

Eldred took a breath. "Actually, Father, I'm not headed to Emon. I have a plan—I intend to duel King Capuan."

Alfred placed his hands on the table and examined Eldred. "You think you would stand a chance?"

Eldred nodded. "I would. You could help me. You could lend me Capito. That would offset the advantage of his sword."

Alfred straightened up with an odd half smile. "Nobody has lasted three minutes with the man."

"I'm asking for your sword, not your opinion."

"Well, it's my opinion that's available. I'm sorry, Eldred. Once Capuan cut you down, I would lose my honor."

"Fine, just get me Hobbie and my gear, and I'll be on my way."

Alfred held up his hand. "You shouldn't be rushing off. We still have this business with the Corporians to finish. Why don't you see it through? We had our plan, right? Get you a partner for the trial. Your mother was keen to have you shed some Corporian blood as I recall."

"None of the partners worked, as I'm sure you heard," said Eldred.

Alfred smiled. "I'll be your partner. We'll have you passing at four arches removed. We know that works."

Ghyslaine leaned forward in her chair. "If he can pass at four arches removed, he should be your heir."

Alfred shook his head. "I'll leave it to Eldred to decide. Well, son, do you want to leave here with a named sword after we deal with the Corporians? Or do you want to stick around and be my heir? I'm not sure the latter makes sense, given your curse."

"You'll give me Captio?"

"No, another named sword."

Eldred pointed at Alfred. "A real sword? Not some rusted, broken thing? A real named sword I can use in a duel?"

Alfred looked Eldred in the eye. "Yes. I promise you. A worthy sword, one within my power to provide. A month—three months at the most— we'll defeat the Corporians and I'll escort you down to Finches Field myself—a royal sendoff."

Eldred looked at Ghyslaine. She shook her head. "This is all madness. You should rest here for the night and start making your way to Emon in the morning. You will find yourself beset the first instant that your father has some business. And he often does."

Alfred snorted. "You can't tell me that you don't want to pass the trial, son. And wherever you go, a named sword will give you status. It's your birthright. I'll get it for you, but we must deal with the Corporians first."

Eldred took a deep breath. "I'll stay, Father. But I'll make this house my quarters. Boar's Tusk is too crowded, too dangerous."

"No, son. We're leaving now to meet some people. I need you to change your clothes. I had Pounder grab some of your things." Alfred went to the door and waved to his men.

"Pounder tried to kill me."

Alfred shook his head. "Don't be silly, Eldred. Pounder's a loyal warrior. That was just your curse."

Eldred lurched across the room and stood behind Alfred, watching the riders approach. He kept checking the faces of the two podmen. They did not appear angry. As they drew near, Bate coolly looked Eldred up and down. Pounder shifted in his saddle and wouldn't meet Eldred's gaze.

Once the men dismounted, Alfred strode over to Wallace and grabbed him by both shoulders, staring at his forehead. After a few seconds, he grunted and turned to Pounder. "Give Eldred his clothes. We need to get back quickly."

Pounder pulled a sack out of his saddlebag and walked up to Eldred. Eldred felt his muscles grow rigid.

Pounder produced a weak smile. "I'm awfully sorry, Eldred. It was the curse. It had us all going. I—uh—I gave that dagger away. I don't want it anymore."

Eldred crossed his arms. "Couldn't you resist?"

Pounder looked down at the sack. "It wasn't something like that. Bate can tell you too." Pounder met Eldred's eye. "It was like you were stabbing us right here." Pounder pointed to the center of his forehead. "It filled me with an unnatural fury. But it stopped a minute or so after you hit the ground. I'm sorry."

Eldred took the bag and stared at Pounder—at a loss for words.

Alfred clapped his hands. "Well, hurry up, Eldred. We need to get back."

PROOF

Ghyslaine joined them for the ride back, paired with Eldred well behind the others.

"Are you up for this? Half of your body is a giant bruise," said Ghyslaine.

Eldred kept his eyes on the men. "I need that sword."

"Alfred's raising an army. You will be in the midst of hundreds of warriors, perhaps a thousand. What if your father is knocked unconscious? What if he is killed?"

"I'll be on Hobbie. Besides, it's the Corporians. They won't be able to stand against us." Eldred shrugged. "They probably wouldn't even stand a chance against the Mercians or the Maldavians."

Ghyslaine frowned. "So you will campaign and then you are off to Tyrus?"

"Yes."

"You have other options."

"Uncle Julian will put his children aside for my benefit?"

"You are seventh in line for the Maldavian throne. You will never be king, but you could live a life of honor. You could marry." Ghyslaine shook her head. "Besides, the kings of Mercia have short reigns. People considered it a marvel when King Marquart reigned for five years, winning duel after duel. Then he faced Capuan. The accounts made it out to be a brutal affair. Capuan cut off Marquart's hand and took Picus. He then used Picus to cut off Marquat's other hand and each of his feet. They said it took twenty minutes for Marquat to die; the spectators cheered the whole time. A Mercian king." Ghyslaine sniffed. "What sort of life would that be?"

Eldred pursed his lips. "I'm not blind, Mother. If I take power, it won't just be to cling to it, hoping to kill the next challenger who comes along. I'll change the world."

"How?"

"I'll show you once I get my chance."

"Hmph. And this new world of yours is so much better than life as a landed lord with a wife and children? Besides, the world does not change. I have lived long enough to see the truth of that."

"I'll explain everything when I receive you in Tyrus."

"You are as stubborn as your father."

Eldred harrumphed. "As if that could be true."

When they neared the castle, Alfred broke into a trot, evidently in some rush. Eldred took no chances and kicked his horse to match the pace. There were dozens of men on the wall. Eldred wiped the sweat from his forehead as he studied their faces. They appeared calm, but Eldred watched them carefully. They could hurl their veruta in an instant.

The gates swung open, and Alfred urged his horse into a gallop. What was his hurry? Eldred frowned down at his mount—a poor replacement for Hobbie—as it struggled to keep up under Eldred's weight. They charged into the courtyard then came to a stop. Eldred blew out his breath as he eyed the gate swing shut.

Alfred bounded down from his mount. "Get down to the cellar and prepare. I'll fetch our guests."

Eldred cleared his throat. "We should stay together."

Alfred gave a curt shake of his head. "Courage, Eldred." He strode towards the residence tower.

Eldred hopped down and stood next to his mount, holding the bridle as he watched Alfred depart.

Bate approached and gestured towards the Great Hall. "This way."

Wallace and Pounder were already walking towards the hall. Eldred took one last look at Alfred entering the tower and let go of the bridle. It was time to perform.

They could hear the raucous men before they got to the hall. The air rang with their loud voices, some arguing and a few singing a drinking song. When Wallace stepped into the hall, a swell of harsh laughter filled the air.

"The old boy's back!" shouted someone.

"Have you no shame at all?" called another.

As Eldred and Ghyslaine followed Bate and Pounder through the door, silence descended. The men at the nearby tables glowered at Eldred. Eldred paused in the doorway.

Ghyslaine tugged his arm. "These are Harold's men. Our men are up by the high table," she whispered.

As they walked together. Eldred picked out the familiar faces of some of Alfred's men up towards the high table, including Stace and Mack—the villain who had killed Morris just last night.

Eldred leaned towards Ghyslaine. "There are more of Harold's men."

Ghyslaine frowned. "And not just here."

Bate slapped Mack on the shoulder as he came up alongside him. "Come on. We're doing another round."

Mack turned and sneered at Wallace. "What? Again?"

"Get up," said Pounder.

Mack rolled his eyes as Stace pulled him to his feet. A number of men—including some of Harold's—started heading towards the kitchen, which held the entrance to the cellar.

As Eldred entered the kitchen, he caught sight of Wilkey and broke out of the procession streaming down the stairs. Ghyslaine followed him. He cornered the steward by a chopping block. "You were supposed to bring my things."

Wilkey held up his hands. "The king said he would go himself. He told me to get cooking."

Eldred glanced over the busy cooks. "So there is a feast tonight?"

"Harold arrived just before noon with his warriors. He brought many. The king's men have been arriving in small groups since this morning. We've been sending tray after tray of meat over to the tower. The king has the nobles gathered there."

"Which nobles are present?" asked Ghyslaine.

Wilkey shook his head. "I don't know. I've been here in the kitchen the whole time."

Ghyslaine narrowed her eyes. "Does he think a demonstration in the cellar is going to change anyone's mind?"

"It's been years since anyone passed the trial at four arches removed. It might make some people think," said Eldred.

Ghyslaine arched her eyebrow. "Did you see any great thinkers out in the hall?"

Eldred shrugged.

Over by the stairs there was a commotion, and the men started coming up rather than going down. Pounder appeared at the top of the stairs. "We have room for six more of Harold's men. That's it."

Eldred grimaced as he looked over the scene. "They're all younger."

"What?" asked Ghyslaine.

"All of Harold's men are younger. Father's men are all old farts."

Ghyslaine nodded. "Fewer in number and older. Not a recipe for success."

Eldred gestured. "Should we go down?"

"No, of course not. It's just the warriors down there. We should go down last, with your father."

The nobles started arriving after a few minutes. A few lords were accompanied by their wives. Those who were made a show of taking their wives' hands and helping them down the stairs.

Eldred grinned. "Will you be needing Father's help?"

Ghyslaine narrowed her eyes. "Don't be silly. The way you are lurching about, it may be me helping you."

Uncle Benedict spotted them and hurried over to catch Eldred in a hug. "Eldred! I'm so pleased to see you. What a great expedition. I knew you could do it."

Eldred took a half step back. "It's good to see you, Uncle."

Benedict gently took Ghyslaine's hand and bent to kiss her on the wrist. "Dear lady, I looked for you as soon as I arrived."

Ghyslaine smiled. "How kind of you."

It made Eldred uncomfortable to see her standing an inch taller than his uncle, but neither of them seemed to mind.

Benedict remained standing there for a moment, smiling at both of them, before he straightened up. "I should make sure we have our seats. I'm sitting on Alfred's side. I wish we were not doing this Alfred's side and Harold's side business, but it seems to be what they want. Oh, well." Benedict gave a quick nod and headed over to the cellar.

Benedict had scarcely started down the stairs when Harold entered the kitchen and directed a cold gaze at Eldred. Eldred folded his arms and stared back.

"I daresay Harold will be unhappy with the results of this demonstration," whispered Eldred.

"Let us hope so," said Ghyslaine.

"When he sees me—" Eldred paused, catching sight of a face behind Harold. Lord Ferris appeared gaunt—his goatee patchier than ever—but his eyes held strength as well as malice. "Oh, I thought he might have died."

Ghyslaine arched her eyebrow as Lord Ferris made his way down the stairs. "Not yet, unfortunately."

Alfred was the last to arrive. He stopped at the top of the stairs and extended his hand towards Ghyslaine. "Come, it's time."

THE CELLAR

Eldred descended the stairs with Alfred and Ghyslaine behind him, hand in hand. The cellar had undergone a considerable makeover. Racks of candles hung from the ceiling. Thick red carpets were spread across the floor. A double line of chairs filled with nobles faced the alcoves, half to the left of the stairs, half to the right. Benedict sat to the left—which was evidently Alfred's side—next to some empty chairs. Fewer nobles were seated on Alfred's side, but each side had the same number of warriors packed in the standing area behind the seats.

Once down the stairs, Ghyslaine went to join Benedict. Eldred followed Alfred out into the middle of the cellar. Alfred's men stood waiting by the alcoves. The old guard, Wallace, was covered in sweat and looked rattled.

Eldred sighed. He would not be the only one glad to get this over with.

Alfred gave Eldred a puzzled glance before turning to face his audience. "Does anyone here think I'm not the king?" Alfred looked over the room. "Well, is there anyone confused on this matter?" Alfred pulled Capito from its scabbard and held it up. "Does anyone think this is his sword?"

Eldred eyed Capito—gleaming in the candlelight—as Alfred glowered at the gathering.

Alfred lowered his sword. "Good. I'm glad that much is clear. Now, the Corporians invaded my lands. They built a Motherless city on my hills. And they killed the men I sent—a full silver pod—to the last man. Whatever insult this might be to other men, it's a greater insult to me, for I'm the king. I'm the one who's most aggrieved."

Alfred pointed Capito towards Harold, who was sitting next to Lord Ferris. "Whatever we have discussed before is moot. I'm the king; I lead the army. I'll build a perfect golden pod and wipe these Motherless Corporians from my lands."

Harold rubbed his temple and gave a small smile. "If only that were possible, Uncle."

Alfred stretched his arms wide. "Oh, but it is quite possible. I'll show you now. These alcoves are about the same as the arches, as everyone can see. I'll demonstrate my strength in the Bond by matching at four arches removed."

Harold crinkled up his face. "Excuse me, Uncle, but what will that prove? This is a children's game; it marks the passage to manhood, but the real warriors of Deira are all men already. We have no need for this demonstration. It has no bearing on how we plan for war."

Alfred returned to pointing Capito at Harold. "Hold your muddled thoughts, nephew. If you are still confused on the matter afterwards, I'll clear things up for you. Now, the demonstration."

Alfred turned and started towards the left-most alcove, where Stace was waiting. Eldred took a step after Alfred, but Alfred stopped. "Take your seat, son," hissed Alfred.

Eldred recoiled. "I thought I was—"

Alfred shook his head. "That's tomorrow. It doesn't matter for this. I'm using Wallace. Take your seat."

Eldred turned a shade red and headed over to sit next to Ghyslaine while Alfred strode purposefully across the cellar. Once Alfred was in position—facing Stace—he barked out, "Ready!" Pounder started sending the signals to Wallace, taking him through the motions. Eldred eyed the proceeding critically. Wallace was pretty sloppy, but Alfred matched him perfectly. When it was done, Pounder held up ten fingers. Eldred reached up and tugged his hair. He could have gotten a perfect set too.

Alfred bounded back into the center of the room as his half of the audience clapped uncertainly. "There you have it. I can match Wallace at four arches removed. He's an old warrior, and he never did better than matching in the center arch to boot. There can be no doubt that I have the greatest strength with Bond!"

Harold stood up, his face slightly flushed. "A few hours ago, you couldn't even match the old coot in the same alcove. Now you want us to believe that you are matching at four arches removed?"

Alfred squared his shoulders. "You just witnessed it."

Harold narrowed his eyes. "Who knows what we just witnessed?"

"If you have your doubts, run the trial yourself," said Alfred.

Harold scoffed. "What does this even matter? I gathered the men, and they'll follow me."

"You have some men. I'll use you for a reserve. But I'll lead the main force—a golden pod of my choosing, the force that'll decide this war."

Harold waved his hand dismissively towards the alcoves. "Based on this?"

"You try it, then. Take your best man and show us what you can do. You only ever passed at one arch removed. Care to try at four?" asked Alfred.

Harold scowled. "Perhaps I'll demonstrate just how easy it is to stick a sword through your old guard's chest."

Lord Ferris rose and put his hand on Harold's shoulder. "A disagreement, but let us not be disagreeable." He paused and considered Alfred for a moment. "You must see that this is an odd way to prove your strength in the Bond. It's just the trial we give the squires. It's no way to prove you still command the great power you held in your youth."

Alfred nodded. "Go on."

Lord Ferris smiled. "What about something more direct, a test closer in nature to actual battle? A mock duel between your pods, say, with wooden swords. We wouldn't want anyone getting too badly hurt."

Alfred chuckled. "I was looking to make things easy on my dear nephew, but if a beating is what he wants, how can I deny him?"

Ghyslaine shifted in her seat next to Eldred. "This is beneath your dignity, husband. A king need not brawl with his subjects."

Alfred held up his hand. "Quite true. A king need not do such a thing, but I choose to and a king can do whatever he wants. I have coddled my nephew long enough. I'll take care not to harm him more than necessary. Unless you choose to decline, nephew? Are you and your men too tired after your long ride? I would not wish to engage you in a mock battle if you are poorly rested."

Harold clasped his hands before him. "Not at all, dear Uncle. We are ready now. We can walk up these stairs and head to the courtyard this very minute. I see no need to delay."

Alfred raised his chin. "Nor do I." Alfred glanced around the room, his eyes settling on Wallace. "Wallace, find Wilkey and set him to fetching us ten wooden swords. Everyone else, get upstairs. Keep it orderly. This'll be a show to remember."

As the people streamed noisily up the stairs, Eldred and Ghyslaine went to Alfred. His pod was converging on him as well. To Eldred's eye, they appeared listless, lacking the fire that showed in Alfred's face.

Ghyslaine planted herself in front of Alfred. "You must not do this. You gain nothing that is not already yours, and you could lose everything."

Alfred frowned. "You still do not understand us even after all of these years. This is necessary, but it's also a gift." Alfred smiled. "You'll see. Lord Ferris is right for once. My subjects need to see me beat Harold. That's how I can get the men for my golden pod. Once the word is out, I can have my pick of anyone."

Ghyslaine narrowed her eyes. "You will not change your mind?"

Alfred glanced up into her eyes. "Impossible. Now take your leave with your doubts and uncertainties. I must prepare."

Eldred took his mother's arm and gently steered her towards the stairs.

"What is he doing?" whispered Ghyslaine.

"He has Pounder and Bate. Mack can clearly do some damage too—at least to stewards."

"Youth, the Bond—they both favor Harold."

"The Bond must be strong for Father if he can hear Wallace. That's what they say."

Ghyslaine sighed. "May the Mother make it so, but she has been gone now for so many years."

The Match

Eldred stood beside Ghyslaine and Benedict, watching the proceedings, part of the two hundred spectators lining the courtyard. The men faced each other in two lines. On one side, Harold full of confidence, flanked by his young podmen. On the other, Alfred with his pod: Pounder, Stace, Mack and Bate. The bright sun showed every line in their weathered faces. Pounder was the youngest, but he was more than eight years the senior of the oldest man standing with Harold.

"They should at least stand in the shade while they wait. Who can guess how long Wilkey and his stewards will take to find the swords? Do we even have ten of them? Only Morris knew where everything was," said Ghyslaine.

Benedict nodded. "At least they agreed to use wooden swords. Nobody will be too badly hurt, though this will make Alfred very angry."

Eldred glanced down at his uncle. "Why're you so certain Father will lose?"

"His men are not so old as Wallace, but time takes its toll," said Benedict.

"It's the strength in the Bond that matters, not the strength in your arm. That's what everyone says," said Eldred.

Benedict gestured towards Wallace, who was slouching against the wall on the far side of the courtyard. "He was once dangerous. It all goes, Eldred. The Bond, your strength. Only death in battle can prevent it."

Eldred examined Alfred's pod, some forty feet away. Alfred was animated, motioning to his men and speaking fervently. Sweat streaked down through Stace's gray hair. Bate glared sullenly at Harold's pod. Mack kept glancing over at Eldred. Only Pounder gave Alfred his rapt attention. Could it happen? Could they lose? How could Father and Pounder ever lose?

Two young stewards finally appeared at the door of the residence tower carrying wooden swords. They hurried across the courtyard to deliver the men their arms.

Benedict cleared his throat. "It is only till Alfred gets knocked down, then it will be over."

"A sharp blow to the head could keep him down," said Ghyslaine.

Benedict shrugged. "It's what he wanted."

Alfred raised his wooden sword, pointing at Harold. "Are you ready, nephew?"

Harold smiled. "Yes. Are you certain, Uncle?"

"I am!"

Each of the pods began to walk towards the center of the courtyard. The spectators were so quiet that Eldred could hear their footsteps. When the lines came within fifteen feet of each other, they halted.

"They are deep in the Bond," whispered Benedict.

In a flash, Harold and his men dashed towards Alfred's line with their wooden swords raised. They rained blows on Alfred's men in a flurry of movement, but no blow struck true; each was blocked or turned. Alfred's men did not strike back, apparently content to focus on defense. The fury of Harold's men ran on for one minute, then two. The clacking of the wooden swords sounded with rising intensity. Something would have to give.

Then—in an instant—all of Harold's men were on the ground, dazed. Silence filled the courtyard. Harold retreated as Alfred's pod glided past their dazed foes. As Harold neared the edge of the courtyard, he stopped and stood his ground, raising his sword defiantly.

Alfred's pod formed a half circle around Harold. Harold bared his teeth as he looked over the line of the old men. Finally, with a jerk of his hand, he tossed his sword to the ground and stood with his arms crossed.

Alfred studied Harold with a hard face and pointed to the ground. Harold shook his head. Alfred made his hand into a fist and stared at Harold, waiting. Harold looked over Alfred's men for a moment, then took a deep breath and went to one knee before Alfred. A light cheer erupted from the crowd.

Benedict smiled reluctantly, perhaps a trifle embarrassed for his son, Harold. "By the Mother, that was like looking back on the old days."

Alfred extended his hand, but Harold shot to his feet and stalked over to his men, who were beginning to stir. Alfred chuckled and went to each of his podmen, shaking their hands, slapping them on the back. Stace was dripping with sweat and Mack appeared out of breath, but none of Alfred's men appeared to have taken a hard blow.

Alfred turned and looked around the courtyard until he spotted Ghyslaine. He waved to her and strode over with his chest thrust out. He took her hands in his and kissed her roughly on the cheek. "There. What about that?"

Ghyslaine wrinkled her nose. "That was foolish."

"Well done, Father," said Eldred.

Benedict clapped Alfred on the shoulder. "That was amazing."

Alfred looked Benedict in the eye. "Did you feel it, brother? It was powerful. I had so much. I have always had the most. Now, I have more than ever before."

Benedict nodded. "I could sense it. Once you started walking, it truly set in."

Alfred gestured to the center of the courtyard, where Harold and Lord Ferris were helping the men to their feet. "They didn't touch us. They made a decent showing, but they didn't touch a single one of us. I chose to end the match, but I could have held them there all day, till they fell over from exhaustion."

"Should we go back down to the cellar for another demonstration with the two of us?" asked Eldred.

Alfred raised his eyebrows. "What? No. That's for tomorrow. I already told you."

Eldred froze, speechless.

Alfred turned away to Benedict. "But speaking on that matter, I want you to go to the Academy today. Speak with Headmaster Tibbot and have him prepare for Eldred's trial tomorrow at noon. Oh, and take Harold with you. I don't want him moping around here."

Benedict gave a slight bow. "I will see what I can do on both counts, Brother."

Alfred turned to watch Harold yell at his men. "Tell him he has nothing to be ashamed of. He was simply overmatched."

Alfred's supporters started to crowd in around him as Benedict made his way across the courtyard. Ghyslaine leaned in closer to Alfred. "A king should never fight such a match. It ended well enough today, but what if you were the one screaming at your men after defeat?"

Alfred released her hand and looked at her with steely eyes. "No true victory comes without risk."

Eldred and Ghyslaine stepped back as Alfred waded into the crowd of his supporters, thumping them on the shoulder and shaking their hands.

Harold had his podmen on their feet and headed for the stables with Benedict and Lord Ferris in tow. Many of Harold's nobles and warriors walked after them, but others made their way to the edges of Alfred's audience. The mock battle appeared to have changed their thinking.

"He should declare you his heir," said Ghyslaine softly.

Eldred shrugged. "To what end? My reign would be even shorter than that of the Mercian kings you were lecturing me about. I would only rule for the time it took for Pounder to close the distance."

"What if Harold acts against you? He has good reason to kill both you and your father."

Eldred rubbed his chin. "We are not like the Torvid, or your people, for that matter. If Harold wants either of us, he'll have to fight us in the open. You just saw how that would go."

"He should still declare you. It is the proper thing to do."

"I'll pass the trial tomorrow at four arches removed. That will say all that needs to be said."

SAFETY

Eldred yawned and plopped down on the bed, staring blankly at Wilkey and the other steward, Hawkin. "How does this work again, Wilkey?"

Wilkey stepped back and gestured at the upside down night table with a five foot high pile of stones stacked on it. "You just bolt the door and slide those rocks up against it. That's what Hawkin came up with."

Eldred exchanged a look with Ghyslaine, who stood at the foot of the bed. "That's no better than the armoire I pushed against the other door. It only took them a few minutes to hack that apart with their swords."

Hawkin smiled apologetically. "Well, if that situation arises again, this should slow them."

Wilkey nodded. "And you're on the second floor here. A jump down won't knock you out."

Ghyslaine frowned. "Alfred said the door had been reinforced."

"Reinforced with these stones. If you push them," said Hawkin.

Eldred sighed. "Fine. A few stones. I can leap down and run for it."

"We could go back to the cottage," said Ghyslaine.

"Too many of Father's men are camped around the castle. We'd need him to escort us, and who knows who would show up in the night," said Eldred.

Ghyslaine turned to Wilkey. "Can you give us a moment of privacy?"

Wilkey bowed low. "Of course, m'lady."

The two stewards shuffled around the stones and exited the room, shutting the door after them.

"Will you be able to rest here? The trial is tomorrow. You must be fresh."

Eldred leaned his head against the post at the foot of the bed. "I can sleep well enough. I'm ready to fall asleep this moment." Eldred gave a loud yawn. "The whole night he just went on and on. He described the mock battle in detail twenty times even though everyone had been there to witness the fight themselves."

"Yes. Today was his big day. Tomorrow belongs to you."

Eldred smiled. "I'll pass at four arches removed. Same as Father."

Ghyslaine walked over and kissed him on the forehead. "Just block the door after I leave. I will make sure Alfred stays in the castle."

"Thanks, Mother."

After she left and the door was secured, Eldred checked his bags, which were piled up on the dresser. All of his belongings were there, including the leather coat Sammanus had given him and the cloak from Lady Opimia. But it was the packets of Balaur powder that he looked for first and stood holding in his hand, encased in the transparent sample bag. This was the irreplaceable gift, the one which would give him the strength to win the Mercian throne. He could not be separated from it again.

Eldred settled down in the bed, tucking the sample bag under the pillow. His exhaustion washed over him, but as he was on the cusp of falling to sleep, he heard a noise from the hall. Not a loud noise. No pounding on the door. No shriek of anger. But it was something, and Eldred found himself listening, wondering. What if Father forgot and went into town? What if a mass of warriors was forming up on the other side of the door, preparing to attack?

After a few moments of furtive silence, the bruises down the right side of his body signaled their discomfort, and he rolled to his left, which felt unnatural. He lay there for a few moments before switching to lying on his back, but the dull ache of the bruises started up once more.

Eldred groaned and rubbed his temples. He had to be fresh tomorrow for the trial. They would all be there from the Academy—Headmaster Tibbot, Preceptor Garaint and Preceptor Grimes, and Harold too, along with Uncle Benedict. Would Father force Harold to conduct the trial? Eldred smiled tightly. Four arches removed, the best anyone had done in years. Even the Headmaster would have to admit that. Eldred yawned. He had to be fresh.

He shifted and turned many times while his mind raced through the possibilities of the next day. Finally, he settled on his back and drifted to sleep.

MORNING

Sunlight through the window stirred Eldred from his sleep. At first, he just nestled in the warm bed, not fully rested, though he was certain he would not fall back to sleep. As he lay there, feeling the chill air on his face, he glanced at the blue and gray leather coat with red and purple sewn lines piled on top of his other possessions. His lips twisted into a half smile. He didn't have much, but some of what he owned had quality, like the coat. It had saved his life. Perhaps nobody would care for it—perhaps they would find it garish or obscene—but that was what he would wear for the trial.

Eldred felt a surge of confidence once he dressed. He ran his right hand over the side of the coat—perfectly smooth—no sign of the packets tucked neatly in the inside pocket. The stewards had left his saber leaning against a chair in its scabbard. Eldred pulled it free and examined the blade, which remained sharp and true. If any Deirans did go mad, he would put the first one down, whoever it was.

A glance out the window showed a quiet courtyard, only a few stewards and women going about their morning duties. Eldred dragged the stones clear of the door and removed the bar. He pulled the door open, one hand on his sword, ready for whatever lay beyond. Fortunately, it was just an empty hall. He made his way down through the tower, tensing as he came to each turn, but he only encountered one of Wilkey's underlings, who shrank away.

All of the cooks turned to stare as Eldred entered the kitchen in the Great Hall from the side door. Wilkey gave Eldred a wry smile as he walked over to Eldred. "Why're you wearing that?"

Eldred shrugged. "I'm not going to make it easy for someone to stab me."

Wilkey chuckled. "Well, I suppose you know your business."

Eldred licked his lips as he eyed a great boar roasting on a spit over the fire.

"Ah, the young lord is hungry. Come take your seat in the hall." Wilkey pointed to the boar. "He is for this afternoon, after your trial. But I have fresh bread, boiled eggs and crisp bacon for your breakfast."

Eldred nodded and clasped Wilkey's shoulder. "As always, Wilkey, you're the best."

Wilkey smiled and leaned in. "Just be more than one arch removed—at least a little more than your insufferable cousin."

"I'll pass at four arches removed. It'll be the easiest thing."

Eldred looked over the fifty odd warriors eating in the hall as he took his seat at the head table. A few glanced up from their food, but nobody paid him much mind. He had only been sitting a few minutes when Wilkey brought out a large platter heaped with food.

Eldred plucked out a crisp piece of bacon and took a bite. "Excellent, Wilkey."

Wilkey gave a short bow. "I aim to please."

Wilkey was just stepping away when an older man plopped down in the seat next to Eldred. The man was tall for a Deiran, with gray streaked hair. He had a pleasant enough face, but his eyes held a trace of mockery as he reached over and grabbed a piece of Eldred's bacon.

Eldred slid his plate away from the man.

The man pointed at Eldred's meal. "Bring me the same, Wilkey."

"Of course, sir," said Wilkey.

Eldred frowned at the man. "Do I know you?"

The man finished the bacon and looked Eldred up and down. "I'm sure you've heard of me. My name is Dederick."

Eldred's eyes went wide. Dederick was one of the strongest with the Bond in all the kingdom. "I have. I was there when you led the golden pod against the Mercians at Finches Field."

Dederick wiped his chin with his sleeve. "That's right. I heard you were there, but I didn't see you afterwards."

"No. I had business in Hog's End."

Dederick rubbed his hairy neck. "Is that right?"

Eldred nodded.

"Well, you have more promising business today, I'll wager," said Dederick.

Eldred straightened in his seat. "Yes. I'm headed to take the trial at the Academy."

Dederick reached for one of Eldred's rolls. "Right, paired with Alfred."

Eldred wrinkled his forehead as Dederick bit a chunk out of the roll. "Yes."

"They say you're cursed, you know."

"I am," said Eldred.

"I hear Alfred's man, Pounder, chased after you with a knife."

Eldred glanced over the men eating their breakfast. "That's true. They were all mad. He was just at the head of the line."

"Then I guess you're really brave or really stupid."

Eldred snapped his head back. "What?"

Dederick gestured at the men. "These boys are just a minute away from cutting you open—ending your life. And yet, you're down here risking everything for a plate of food. A plate I'm sure Wilkey would have gladly carried up to your room."

Eldred scoffed. "I could hide, but I'm sick of that. Besides, they're bonded warriors. No door's going to hold them long."

Dederick looked Eldred in the eye, but broke off and nodded when Wilkey rounded the table carrying a platter. "Thanks, Wilkey. Looks good."

They ate with gusto, reducing the bread, eggs and bacon piled on their plates with a cacophony of chewing and gulping.

As Eldred was reaching for his last roll with his right hand, Dederick pointed at Eldred's bruised skin. "Is that from the fall?"

Eldred frowned. "Yes. It's all down my right side."

Dederick raised his eyebrows. "You're lucky just to have some bruises. I know that window."

Eldred shrugged.

Dederick suddenly raised his fist and smashed it down on one of his boiled eggs, splattering it on Eldred's sleeve. Men at the nearby tables glanced over in surprise. Dederick dusted the egg off his hands. "That would be most people if they took that fall, even Mercians."

Eldred felt his face growing red as he wiped his coat clean. "I'm not most people."

"No, of course not. Why, today, we're all riding to the Academy for your trial. It'll be the first trial I've ever seen for someone who already passed the age of ascension. And your partner—not some squire—but your father, the king himself. This after you couldn't match with any of the warriors they bribed to come and practice with you. I wonder, are we traveling all that way just to watch you fail?"

Eldred scowled. "No. I'll be passing at four arches removed."

Dederick narrowed his eyes. "Just like Wallace did yesterday?"

"If you like."

"It's not what I like. I'm asking a question. What's going on? Things are very strange since you returned."

"I'm simply taking the trial. Not much more to it than that."

Dederick shook his head. "Seems there's more. If there's anyone who shouldn't be headed to the Academy, it's you. We all heard the rumors about how you left."

"Can't believe everything you hear," said Alfred as he plopped down in the chair next to Dederick.

Dederick gripped the edge of the table and pivoted to face Alfred.

"Mother's blessings, son. I hope you slept well," said Alfred.

"Thank you, Father. Well enough. No visitors."

Alfred nodded and glanced at Dederick. "How many men did you bring?"

Dederick pursed his lips. "I have two pods here. Another three pods camped outside the walls."

Alfred thumped Dederick on the shoulder. "Good. With that, I think I'll have about one hundred fifty men for Eldred's trial. I expect that Harold will have a few more than that, but it should be enough to keep things in line."

"You think it'll come to that?" asked Dederick.

Alfred smiled. "Harold's no idiot. I'm sure he learned something from his lesson."

Dederick frowned. "Maybe. Maybe not. In any case, you'll need more than men to convince the Headmaster to sanction this."

Alfred chuckled. "I have some ideas on that. Besides, they owe Eldred a trial. He was there for thirteen years, for Mother's sake."

Eldred sighed and looked down at his empty plate. The Headmaster did have good reason to deny him.

"Oh, cheer up, son! It's your damned trial day. Let's see you smile," said Alfred.

Eldred crinkled up his face. "Sorry, Father."

Alfred rose to his feet. "Finish up, men! We ride on the hour. I have a few stops to make on the way.

THE ROAD

A force of eighty warriors set out from Boar's Tusk with Alfred, Ghyslaine and Eldred at the front. Before they had gone far, Alfred fell back and mixed with the men, joking with some of them. In particular, he spent considerable time riding next to Dederick, whom he engaged in an animated conversation. Eldred and Ghyslaine continued in the lead, with Pounder and Mack sticking right behind them.

Alfred returned to the front to call for a stop at the TInsley Bridge, the site of the first crossing they would make of the Clyde River. He spent several minutes astride his horse staring off into the woods, flanked by Stace and Bate.

Impatient to be moving, Eldred edged closer to Alfred. "Are we meeting someone, Father?"

Alfred shook his head. "It seems not."

Eldred peered down a track which branched off into the trees. "Perhaps they're late."

"Not this late," muttered Alfred, turning to look Eldred in the eye. "I was expecting thirty men."

"We don't need more men, though. Do we? It's just me taking the trial."

Alfred took a deep breath. "That's right. Move on!" He stepped his horse to the side of the trail and urged Eldred forward. He fell back in with Dederick towards the rear of the host.

Eldred turned to glance at the two old warriors.

"Is there a concern?" asked Ghyslaine, coming alongside Eldred.

"Father is missing some men."

Ghyslaine pursed her lips. "I would not be here if he anticipated danger."

Eldred nodded. "True enough. Father was speaking to Dederick earlier.

The riders are just here to discourage any fanciful action on the part of Harold's men."

Ghyslaine nodded. "Let us hope they behave with honor."

Thirty minutes on, they came upon two pods of men gathered by the road which led to the village of Lickford. Alfred charged up the line and rode ahead to meet the men, a sour expression on his face.

The men were mounting their horses while Alfred was shouting at them, when Eldred and Ghyslaine approached at the head of the host.

"And the rest?" called Alfred.

The leader of the men had his head bowed as he looked up at Alfred. "I don't know, my liege. When I spoke to Lord Barrington last night, I understood he would be coming."

"This is not something I will soon forget," said Alfred.

The man bowed his head lower. "We are here, my liege."

Alfred jerked his thumb towards the back of the line. "Fall in." He sat, tapping his chin with his knuckles as the two pods hurriedly made their way past.

Ghyslaine rode up to Alfred and Eldred followed. "Is everything well? Should we postpone the trial?"

Alfred huffed. "We can't postpone."

"Will we be gathering more men?" asked Ghyslaine in a soft tone.

Alfred shook his head. "No. If even Barrington won't show, then this little addition is all we can expect."

Eldred shifted in his saddle. "Do we have enough?"

Alfred narrowed his eyes. "You're asking if we have enough for your trial? Of course we do. You saw my demonstration. I defeated Harold, and my men didn't take so much as a single blow. I'll get you your precious trial. But this!" Alfred waved his arm. "This is disrespectful. There are some who will pay dearly for this insult." Alfred kicked his horse into motion and waved the men onwards.

THE TRIAL

The sight of the black arches and the Academy lying beyond them made Eldred uneasy. The Academy had been his home for almost all his life. Passing the trial had been his dream since he had been old enough to speak. It could all happen in just a few minutes. Well, if it would ever happen at all.

The headmaster stood in his spot as if it were a real trial day, attended by his senior preceptors, including Preceptor Grimes and Preceptor Garaint. However, there was no sign of the squires who lined up in attendance for normal trails. They must have confined them to their quarters, which made sense since to the left of the arches stood a mass of riders. Three hundred men? Four hundred? Far more than Alfred had brought. Eldred picked out Harold, Uncle Benedict and Lord Ferris mounted up in front of the troops. Harold and most of his men wore their battle armor.

Alfred continued on, leading his men towards the arches, giving Harold's army only the briefest glance. When he reached the spot where visitors usually watched the trial—where the road widened out—he dismounted and motioned for Eldred to follow.

Ghyslaine stared at Harold's band with a sour expression. "I do not care for this. They might come. I think they just might."

Eldred gave Harold another look. He was counting on his fingers, doubtlessly counting Alfred's men. Mother was right. Eldred took a deep breath. "I'd better go."

Ghyslaine laid her hand on his arm. "I will bring Hobbie to you if they charge. Look to me if you hear them coming."

"I will, Mother." Eldred gave Hobbie a scratch behind the ear and hopped down.

Dederick and four of his men also dismounted and followed after

Alfred, who was already at the center arch. Everyone else stayed on their mounts, ready for action.

The Headmaster stood with a wide stance and watched Alfred approach with an air of disinterest. Preceptor Grimes alternated between peering at Eldred and looking at the ground. Preceptor Garaint—who stood directly behind the headmaster—glared at Eldred with open hostility. Eldred blew out his breath. He could guess what they were thinking.

All eyes shot to the side at the sound of hoofbeats. Harold galloped towards them. Benedict and Lord Ferris followed at a trot. Harold pulled up his horse just as Alfred reached the preceptors with Eldred and Dederick's pod close behind.

Alfred nodded to Harold and the Headmaster. "Good day, gentlemen. A fine day for a trial."

Harold sneered as Benedict and Lord Ferris came abreast of him. "I don't agree."

Alfred put his hands on his hips and smiled. "You don't have to stay."

Harold pointed at Eldred. "He's not even a squire. Everyone knows he's past the age of ascension. And everyone knows he was kicked out of the Academy for cheating."

Eldred frowned and turned a shade red.

Alfred raised his left palm in a casual gesture. "You have no standing. You could bring ten times as many men. It would not lend a gnat's weight to your opinions. You don't even have the good manners to get down from your horse."

Benedict flinched at that.

Lord Ferris showed his teeth. "The headmaster has standing even if we do not."

The headmaster tilted his head, as if confirming there was truly a gap in the conversation wherein he could speak. "Good day, my liege. Good day, good sirs. Lord Benedict has given me some sense of why you have all come here today—and in such numbers. But still, given that this is a matter of some importance, perhaps we had best start at the beginning."

Alfred clapped his hands. "Very well. We are here for a simple task: the trial of my son, Eldred."

The headmaster looked Eldred up and down. "Ah, I fear these are not the usual circumstances. As you well know, we conduct trials here according to the rules and traditions going back a hundred years. All squires elevated and recognized as warriors of the Bond, blessed in the eyes of the Mother, do so here at these arches in trials conducted by the headmaster of the Academy, a position I am honored to hold at present. The substance of my concern lies in the fact that the young man, Eldred, is no longer a squire, having passed the age of ascension some months ago."

"As I said," interjected Harold.

The headmaster nodded.

Harold shifted in his saddle and gestured at Eldred. "You can take him and go home."

Eldred straightened his back and glowered back.

Alfred laughed. "I can do whatever I want. I can have Dederick conduct a trial for Eldred. You just have to stand here for a short spell, Headmaster Tibbot. And you should. Eldred deserves the chance to make up for the winter trial he missed due to the expedition."

"No!" shouted Harold.

The headmaster clasped his hands before him. "Of course, you can do as you wish, my liege. But it will not have any particular significance. The rules are quite specific. I am afraid you and your son have made a mistake in missing the deadline."

"Be fair, headmaster. Everyone makes an error here and there. You're taking a hard stance on this matter of greatest importance," said Alfred.

"I am sorry you see it that way." The headmaster glanced at Eldred. "Eldred was a fine student here at the Academy—good with the sword, fair with the staff. He showed some talent for reading that could help him in a role as a steward. All of us sincerely wish the best for him."

Eldred scowled at the suggestion of him being a steward.

Alfred raised his palms. "A hard stance from where I stand. But this is your area. You're the headmaster. However, there's also the king's justice. If someone were to make a mistake that denied a man his rights—especially a man of noble birth—why, that would be a matter for me to judge. I can be a hard man too."

The headmaster narrowed his eyes. "What are you talking about?"

"A botched trial," said Alfred.

"What trial?" asked the headmaster.

Alfred jerked his thumb back towards the arches. "Conducted right there, and you were present."

"For Eldred?" asked the headmaster.

Alfred nodded. "The same. You should know about it. I learned of it from your letter."

Headmaster Tibbot rolled his eyes. "I see. That was a practice session as you well know. I included that information in my note."

"Practice session, was it? I'm as familiar with our rules and traditions as anyone. There's no mention of practice sessions; just trials. Now, you were here for it and you're the headmaster, so that's covered. It happened where—the arches—where you just mentioned that all trials take place. It seems as if it was a trial from the sounds of it—if we want to strictly follow the rules," said Alfred.

Eldred cocked his head. Harold scoffed.

The headmaster raised his hands. "Fine, call it a trial then. He didn't pass. He and his partner matched five acts, but the auditors did not attest to the Bond. That is a fact."

Alfred grinned. "No, that's not quite right. My son matched five acts and the man conducting the trial forgot to ask the auditors whether they attested to the Bond."

"But they were just squires," protested Preceptor Grimes.

"They had the Bond. Isn't that right, Lord Ferris? Didn't Lord Vance say those squires manifested the Bond?" asked Alfred.

Lord Ferris shrugged. "He may have indicated as much at different times, but it has no bearing. Lord Vance is dead as are all of those squires."

Alfred clapped his hands. "That's right. Now they can't be questioned. It adds up to a botched trial—a blatant dereliction of duty by Preceptor Grimes!"

"Your son was cheating," said Headmaster Tibbot.

"Did you say anything at the time?" asked Alfred.

"We can ask him now. Well, Eldred, were you deceiving us? You and your friend, Dreven?" demanded the Headmaster.

Eldred's eyes grew wide. Of course he had been cheating, as they well knew. He'd been forced into it—at least to some extent. He looked at the Headmaster, then turned to look Preceptor Grimes in the eye. He stepped forward, opening his mouth, when Alfred stepped over and grabbed him by his jacket.

Alfred pointed at the headmaster. "It has no bearing. The question is whether Grimes made a mistake, just as we made a mistake. The question is whether we all want to take a hard line on things. Cause I can see my way to taking a very hard line—if that's the way we all want things done."

The headmaster sighed and shook his head.

Alfred squared his shoulders. "It doesn't have to be so. We can do this fair for everyone. My son has the Bond. Everyone would know it if the instructors here weren't so damned incompetent. We'll prove it right now to everyone's satisfaction. Nobody has to lose their head over it."

Headmaster Tibbot scowled at Eldred. Preceptor Grimes's face turned ashen as he looked down at the ground. Preceptor Garaint muttered something, but Eldred couldn't make it out.

"Rubbish!" shouted Harold. "Cheating on top of cheating. You'll do your trick with Eldred just like you did with that old, fat guard of yours."

"No tricks, nephew. And you'll be the proof of it. Get down from your horse and get your pod. It's time for you to conduct a trial for Eldred and myself."

Harold sat up straight in his saddle and laid his hand on the hilt of his sword. "No. I'll not play your games."

Alfred laid his hand on Capito. "Your king commands you. Do you defy me? Are you so quick to forget your lesson?"

Eldred widened his stance, ready to go after Harold.

Harold glanced over at Alfred's men with a furrowed brow. He turned to Benedict, who shook his head. He shared a longer look with Lord Ferris, who raised his eyebrows encouragingly. Harold scrunched up his face and opened his mouth. "I—"

"Get off your damned horse! I grow impatient," snarled Alfred.

Harold jerked back as if he had been struck. Then, as if all the fight had drained out of him, he clambered down listlessly as Lord Ferris winced.

Alfred pointed at the arches. "Go. And bring your Motherless pod."

Harold gave Eldred a sour look and walked towards the center arch. He gave a small wave in the direction of his host, and his four podmen dismounted.

Alfred watched him go. "Well, that's some measure of tradition for you, Headmaster. Harold did conduct the most recent trials."

The headmaster clasped his hands before him and frowned. Alfred headed to the arches, Dederick and his men close on his heels. Benedict and Lord Ferris dismounted as quietly as they could. Eldred took a last look at Preceptor Grimes before turning away. There had never been a man he held more dear.

Eldred peered through the center arch. Ghyslaine gazed at him with dark eyes full of hope. Dederick and his men were just a few paces behind the auditors. There would be no uncivil action, no matter how much Harold's expression suggested he desired one. Alfred beckoned, urging a faster pace. It was time to be done with it—five sets, starting in the center arch and ending at four arches removed. Five rounds to glory.

Harold grimaced as Eldred and Alfred stepped into the center arch and raised their swords. "Are you ready?"

"I stand ready!" called Eldred.

"Ready," said Alfred.

Harold started the set. As before, Eldred felt nothing in particular. He watched Harold's signals and went through the required motions. After the fourth act, Harold showed a hint of a smile. Eldred frowned. After the ninth act, Harold positively smirked. Then it was done and Harold raised seven fingers.

"What?" asked Eldred. He turned to Alfred. "Father, what happened?"

Alfred spread his arms, holding Capito off to the side. "We matched seven, son. Congratulations. You passed!"

Eldred gave the auditors a stunned look. "There must be some mistake. We were matching ten at four arches back in the cellar. Let's try one arch removed."

Alfred shook his head. "No, son. Not with seven. It isn't done."

Eldred held out his hand towards his father. "Well, did you feel it? You could always feel it before. What went wrong?"

"Nothing," said Alfred, taking his hand. Alfred turned to his host and raised Eldred's arm. "My son passed! Seven in the center arch!"

The riders let out a weak cheer. Ghyslaine clapped lightly as a tear streaked down her face. Alfred reached up to pat Eldred on the shoulder. "You did what was needed, son. Wait with your mother while I have a quick word, then we'll be on our way."

"You did this," sputtered Eldred. "You—we could have done four arches."

Alfred nodded. "Yes, son. I did this. I got you through the trial. I got you what we needed."

"What you needed!" snapped Eldred. "I should have had four arches removed, the same as you."

An angry glint showed in Alfred's eye. "Should you have, son? With who then? Who else but me hears even the merest whisper from you. Now go to your mother. Don't ruin your own ascension."

Dederick and his men trailed after Alfred towards the headmaster while Eldred walked unsteadily across the field back to Hobbie. As Eldred mounted up, Ghyslaine came alongside him.

"Why only seven?" asked Ghyslaine.

Eldred's eyes watered with anger. "That's all Father would allow me."

Ghyslaine frowned. "What?"

"He is playing some game. He doesn't even want a suggestion of me being the heir."

Ghyslaine's shoulders slumped. "Yes. That is right. We should go. Your future waits for you in Emon."

Eldred wiped his eyes. "No. Not without my named sword. He promised that. He gave his word."

Across the way, the headmaster and his preceptors bowed to Alfred and headed back to the Academy. Lord Ferris mounted up and rode back to Harold's host. Benedict rounded the arches and approached Eldred at a trot.

"Well done, Eldred! Seven in the center arch! You matched me!" shouted Benedict with a smile.

Eldred smiled weakly. "I guess I did."

Benedict laughed. "This was all worth it in the end. I didn't know what to expect. The whole thing seemed mad to me, but it worked out. You manifested the Bond. I'm so proud of you."

Benedict rode over and reached up to clasp Eldred's hand. Eldred looked past his grinning uncle to spot Alfred having a private word with Harold in the center arch. Those two didn't look friendly, but they appeared civil. Harold gave a low bow as they wrapped up their chat. Alfred slowly nodded once.

Stace led Alfred's horse over to him, followed by the rest of Alfred's podmen astride their mounts. Alfred mounted up and advanced towards his line of men. "Today I took care of some family business. That's all done now. Let's have a cheer for my son, who finally earned his sword." Alfred extended his arm towards Eldred as his men let out a throaty cry.

Alfred straightened his neck. "Tomorrow we turn to the work of the kingdom. I'll be picking warriors for my golden pod—the pod that will crush the Corporians and send them screaming out of their Motherless city. Each of you have earned consideration. I will not forget the loyalty of the men who rode here with me today!"

The men cried out—louder than before. To the left of the arches, Harold was leading his men away. The trial was over.

On the road back to Boar's Tusk, Eldred found a moment to approach Alfred when he was on his own, between his gabbing with the men up and down the line. "Will I be in your golden pod, Father?"

"No, son," said Alfred.

"But you need me close though, don't you?"

"I do. I'll have you back with a trusted pod while we do the fighting."

Eldred rubbed his chin. "It should be a pod I trust."

"Fine. I expect we can find a decent crew for you. I'll even share some of my spoils with them. They can pick from the field of battle the same as my men."

Eldred's face grew tight. "I want Lord Kenelm."

"What?" asked Alfred.

"I want Lord Kenelm with his pods."

"Oh, he's one of your men, then, is he?"

"He's an honorable man."

Alfred rocked his head side to side a few times before nodding. "Fine, but you work out his provisions. I won't be feeding him or his men during the siege."

"Very well," said Eldred.

Alfred wagged his finger. "Just stay close, son. I don't want anything to happen to you."

PREPARATIONS

Eldred watched the stable boys, farmers and stewards line up in the courtyard with the sun at their backs. In front of them was an assortment of stones, bricks and pieces of wood—their missiles. Their foes, a silver pod of twenty-five men, stood in lines of five, twenty feet away with swords and bucklers in hand. Wilky stood between the groups.

In a real battle, the riff-raff wouldn't have the time to grab their rocks before the warriors carved them to pieces, but this was practice. Pounder and Mack were in the pod this morning. Alfred always was. He was deciding who had what it took to be in his golden pod, who would be part of the greatest battle of the age.

"Let them fly!" bellowed Wilky, ducking back out of the way.

The men set into motion, grabbing up their rocks and hurling them at the warriors. Forty men threw junk at the pod but hit no one. The warriors looked almost bored as they turned the stones with their small shields or shifted to the side, out of harm's way. For five minutes it rained, then the men snatched up the last few projectiles, hurled them, and were done. Pathetic.

Next was the judging. Eldred sighed and sat down against a wall in the shade of the Great Hall. The judging took longer than the throwing. He had watched hours of it in the week that had passed since his trial.

The twenty-four warriors lined up, single file. Even Pounder and Mack lined up, though Eldred expected they were destined for selection in the end. Alfred stared at each man for half a minute. Those he deemed inferior were sent to join the group of two hundred prospects, anxious looking men who hungered for a chance to block the stones. Those deemed worthy joined Alfred's hundred twenty-five champions, at least until Alfred pulled them back out for another look.

Meanwhile, the stewards, stable boys and farmers gathered up their rocks and rubbish into fresh piles. It was their lot, just as it was Eldred's to sit and watch.

The next round was about to start when Dederick came out of the Great Hall with a mug in his hand and sat down on the ground next to Eldred.

"Morning, Eldred."

"Morning, Dederick."

The rocks were flying. Eldred tracked the more promising looking throws.

"How long do you suppose he will do this?" asked Eldred.

Dederick sipped his ale. "As long as it takes. He doesn't want a single bad egg in the mix."

Eldred glanced at the supposed champions. "Some of them look old and fat."

"Won't matter once the Bond comes up. You see them prancing out there. Oh, wait! That's one!"

A hunk of wood stuck one of the men in the shoulder, staggering him. A rock glanced off his helmet while he regained his footing.

Dederick laughed and slapped his leg. Eldred smiled at the break in the monotony. Their luck boosted the morale of the throwers, who threw more vigorously for the last half of the session.

The dust was settling as Alfred marched over to the unfortunate man. "You imbecile!"

The man removed his helmet. He was an older man, mostly bald with a few patches of gray hair. "I'm sorry. My foot got caught, my liege."

"You Motherless cur, you're a disgrace! You don't deserve the honor of being cut down by the Corporians. Leave now! Ride away and never return."

"But your majesty, I rode with your father, Berdic."

"He's dead now. Why don't you join him in that?"

The man slouched away, headed towards the horse lines extending from the stables. The warriors formed up for round's judgment. Dederick took another drink.

Eldred rubbed his chin. "That seemed a bit much."

"It's the ones like him that get others killed. The four he leaves have less magic, and so it goes. Another dead, less magic. Another dead, less magic. The next dies and the last one has no magic at all—just a regular Deiran getting slaughtered. Don't expect any tears from the others."

"Why was Father even considering him then? And come to think of it, why aren't you in there? Or are you already promised a spot?"

Dederick tapped his right temple with his finger. "I'm the other side of the coin. He can't use that man, since he's too weak. He can't use me, since I'm too strong."

"But he's making the perfect army."

Dederick grinned. "The perfect army of bonded warriors. Such an army has one voice, one mind that stands above the rest. Wouldn't be the case if he tried mixing me in. It would end up being my army."

Eldred narrowed his eyes. "Father passed at four arches removed. You passed at three."

"After your father did—I'm younger. It matters."

"You're the strongest?"

Dederick raised an eyebrow. "I would've said so—till you returned. Things seem different for Alfred since. Other than Alfred, it was just Lord Vance, your old traveling companion. He was worthy of his reputation."

"What about Lord Kenelm. He was the match of Lord Vance."

Dederick chuckled. "If he told you that, he was a liar."

"He was just as strong."

"Kenelm isn't nothing, but he's no Vance."

Eldred pointed upwards with his index finger. "He could resist my curse. Mostly, anyway."

Dederick shrugged. "I wouldn't measure strength in the Bond that way. That's just odd."

"Odd? They broke down my door and tried to kill me. Now I'm tethered to my father like some donkey."

Dederick took a sip from his mug. "Only since you lack the sense to leave."

Eldred rolled his eyes.

They sat in silence, watching Alfred make his judgments for a spell. When the last man was placed, Alfred started in immediately on the next round, picking twelve champions and twelve prospected to fill out a new silver pod for testing.

Eldred leaned over to Dederick. "Can he really kill all of the Corporians with just a single golden pod?"

Dederick shook his head. "No, of course not. Some would get away. That's where Harold and I come in—watching the wings. We'll each have far more men with us, but Alfred's made sure he gets all the glory. Best I can hope for is to spear a fleeing Corporian in the back." Dederick sniffed. "Still, it's better than nothing. I'll be looking for gold in their fair city—gold, silver, jewels."

Eldred frowned.

Dederick patted Eldred on the leg. "Oh, for Mother's sake. You'll get your share. I know you're in reserve, but once they break formation, we'll all be in it. I bet you kill a dozen."

Eldred narrowed his brows. "This is his war. I'm just here to get my sword."

NEWS

In the early evening, Eldred sat by the window, staring down into the courtyard. Riders from the town and nearby camps rode through the gate, arriving for dinner in the Great Hall. The gate stood open now throughout the day. Whether that was due to increased traffic or increased confidence, Eldred did not know. Likely it was both.

Eldred tapped his fingers and ignored his growling stomach. If Wilky had forgotten—and he had to allow the man was busy—Eldred could simply go down and take his meal with the others. His spot at the head table would be open. But instead he waited. He'd had enough of the warriors and their boasts for one day.

Finally, there was a knock at the door.

Eldred crossed the room. "Who's there?"

"It's me. It's Wilky. I have your supper."

Eldred flexed his hands then grabbed the upside down table loaded with stones. He slowly dragged it clear of the door—inch by inch—and slid back the bolt. He opened the door to find Wilkey holding a covered platter. The hall was empty.

Wilky stepped in. "It was still warm when I reached the landing." Wilky delivered the food to the table near the window. "It's the same as they are having but more of it. I gave you two portions of lamb stew as well as more turnips, more potatoes and an entire loaf of bread. Did you know your father has more than three hundred guests? I'm having to dig deep into the castle supplies."

"It smells good," said Eldred, still standing by the door.

Wilky hovered near the table. "If the king can't decide on his golden pod soon, we will exhaust my budget, and it's only spring."

"After the last session, I heard him tell Dederick that he'll complete the pod tomorrow. But he's in no hurry. The Corporians are hunkered down behind their wall."

Wilkey nodded. "Cowering like rats. I hope they do not keep you long, young master."

"Father will find a way. That much is certain."

Wilkey approached Eldred and gave a small bow. "Enjoy your meal. Good night."

Eldred smiled. "Good night, Wilkey."

Eldred slid the bolt and grunted as he shoved the stones back into place; it was harder to shove in than pull back. A woman started performing down in the hall as Eldred took his seat to eat. The song was faint to Eldred's ears but beautifully sung. The stew was well seasoned and full of tender meat. Once Eldred finished off the last of the meal, he stared up at the stars, content.

An hour later, someone knocked lightly at the door, breaking his reverie.

"Who is it now?" asked Eldred.

"Open the door. It's me," said Ghyslaine.

"What is it?"

"We need to talk."

"Can it wait?"

"No, I need to talk with you now."

Eldred groaned. "Very well." Once again, Eldred slowly dragged the piled stones clear of the door.

Ghyslaine entered the room with an envelope in her hand and watched as Eldred barricaded the door. "What is the point of that? I'll be leaving soon enough."

Eldred paused in his efforts. "If Father is down there drinking, how do I know that he won't be racing into town."

Ghyslaine frowned and took the seat by the window.

"Or he might be—going on a hunt. Who knows what he will do? I only know what they will do if he leaves. And there are many more now."

Ghyslaine pursed her lips. "This is not how you want people to think of you, son. You should be down in the hall beside your Father. It is his presence that guarantees your safety. Up here, hiding in your room, you appear weak."

Eldred gave the stones a last push with a grunt. "Almost like I'm cursed."

"There is the curse you have and the curse you make. Do not miss an opportunity due to a sour turn of mind."

"What did you need to discuss so urgently?"

"I have news from Julian. He replied to my letter."

"Did he acknowledge the count? You did include what I told you about the Sun People's count?"

Ghyslaine raised her chin. "I did, though he had no comment on the matter."

"Oh, what does he say then?"

"He was pleased to learn of your success. He congratulates you for your part in the victory over the dragon."

Eldred sat on the edge of the bed. "That's kind of him."

"And he found a pairing for you. Her name is Mateline. When her father passes, she will come into possession of a substantial tract of land, including rights over the town of Dinan. I have visited there. It is a pleasant town with skilled woodworkers and a brewery."

Eldred shifted on the bed. "That is likewise considerate. Did he include any description of her?"

Ghyslaine raised an eyebrow. "Are you wanting to know how tall she is, Eldred? Are you concerned she might be taller than a Deiran maiden?"

Eldred fluttered his hand. "Perhaps. It could be something to consider. You've seen what it's like here."

Ghyslaine narrowed her eyes. "But the one thing we know is that you will not be here. Your opportunity lies in Dinan. That is where you can have your children, live your life in peace and enjoy your own brewed ale."

Eldred raised his index finger. "And Tyrus. Don't forget my plans for Tyrus."

Ghyslaine glanced down at the letter. "How could I?"

"I'll need a wife. A king requires that. But I'm thinking that taking a Deiran wife might make the most sense. I almost have the Bond. I feel I'm very close. I passed the trial with Father. If I took a Deiran wife with me to Tyrus—one who came from a strong lineage, the right lineage—my son could have the Bond in a normal fashion, without this curse."

Ghyslaine looked Eldred in the eye. "If you aim to rule in Tyrus, you had best marry the tallest, hairiest Mercian maiden you can find. If your offspring are not giant, strapping, brainless fellows, I am quite certain they will be strangled by your rivals."

"Well, can we consider a Deiran bride?"

"You can consider any woman you like. But your uncle and I have found the right woman for you—the approved woman for you."

Eldred narrowed his eyes. "Approved? What does that even mean?"

"It means that I have provided you with an opportunity. Now is the time to be clear-eyed. There is no reason for you to accompany your father against the Corporians. You have no need for a named sword. We can leave tomorrow for Emon."

"Well, I gave Father my word. And I could use a named sword. It would have value in any circumstance. Or does Julian have a named sword he would pass to me?"

Ghyslaine sniffed. "I can inquire. But the value in being the landed lord of Dinan is that you may not need any sword at all. Would that not be the most pleasant way to live your life, son?"

Eldred shook his head. "No. I told you. I have plans—plans of great consequence." He made his hand into a fist. "And a sword—especially a named sword—will be essential."

Ghyslaine rose to her feet and paused. "Think on it tonight. With one decision, you can go from cursed to blessed. You can go from a man casting about for his path to a man settled on his own lands with a loyal wife."

Eldred grabbed the legs of the table and started sliding it back. "I'll consider your words, Mother. But don't forget—I gave my word."

DECISIONS

The prospects and champions alike milled about anxiously the next morning as Alfred selected the men for each round of his tests, twelve from each group. Each champion walked over to join Alfred reluctantly, their position in jeopardy. Each prospect hurried over, hoping for a chance to redeem himself.

After five rounds, Eldred counted thirteen men who had crossed the divide, one warrior having sunk down in the second match only to rejoin the champions after the fourth.

Alfred stood by Dederick, looking over his champions. "We've come to the final round. If you can get through this, you've made it!" Alfred turned to the prospects. "For you others, there remains opportunity under the command of Dederick. The trespassers have built a massive city on our soil—on the Mother's own blessed soil—full of Corporians of all ages and sizes. Young, old, strong and dumb—you will find all of these among the invaders."

"I'll engage their army, such as it is, with my command. I'll lead my pod to smash them, to crush them, to cut the life out of them. We will slaughter them on the field. Not a man will escape my wrath. As is my right, the spoils of that battle will belong to the men under my direct command."

"But, there's a city full of riches—a city brimming over with worthless Corporians. When we attack the city, all men—those under my command, those under Harold's command and those under Dederick's command—will have equal standing! None of you need go home empty handed. All of you with the taste for it will get your fill of blood."

Alfred smiled. "So no tears, no sad faces, if I don't pick you for this final test. Dederick's not that poor a leader."

Dederick scrunched up his face. "There'll be more treasure in the city than on the field in any case. I expect we'll see action. The Corporians will put up a fight once they see there is no escape." Dederick paused to grin. "And I bet somewhere in that city is their stone bearer! They'll find their courage when we come for her!"

The prospects cheered Dederick, but their eyes shifted quickly to Alfred as he started making his picks. As Alfred selected his champions for the final test, Eldred made his way over to where the stable boys and other unfit subjects had their rock piles.

One of the stewards had a collection of half-sized bricks stacked in front of him.

Eldred pointed at the pile. "May I join you?"

The steward bowed with flourish. "As you wish, sir."

Eldred knelt down and started setting the larger bricks to the side.

Alfred caught sight of Eldred and stopped, eyes growing wide. "What in Mother's name are you doing, Eldred? The throwers are not warriors in this exercise. Surely you can see that!"

Eldred dropped the brick in his hand with a clink and rose up to his full height. "I want to be in one of the rounds, Father, and this is the last. So, I aim to throw, unless—are you choosing me?"

Alfred sighed. "Fine. Throw if you must, son. You'll have your place. You'll be there beside my pod. Everyone knows."

Eldred nodded and resumed picking bricks out of the nearby piles.

Alfred chose the last champion for the round. The man walked forward with downcast eyes as the men behind him began to celebrate their assured good fortune. As Alfred turned to the prospects, they jumped up and down and waved their hands to get his attention.

"Give me one last try, my liege!" cried one.

"Pick me!" yelled another.

"I'm the one you need!" called a younger warrior.

Alfred made each selection without emotion—just jabbing his finger at the prospect. All twelve selections had been among the champions at one point or other. Those passed over wore long faces despite Alfred's earlier request. Everyone recognized the rare honor of serving in the golden pod that obliterated the Corporians.

In the center of the courtyard, the silver pod pulled on their helmets and readied their swords and bucklers. Wilky waited on Alfred's signal from the back row and called for the bombardment. "Throw, boys! Let them fly!"

Where before the stablehands had lobbed the heavier bricks and barely reached the front row of warriors, Eldred hurled missiles with startling velocity. At first, he threw sporadically, a bit uncomfortable at throwing stones at men standing so close. But as the warriors evaded and blocked, a deep frustration filled Eldred, and his motions grew faster. He threw separate rocks from each hand. The steward on his right and the stable boy on his left stopped throwing and started passing Eldred a steady supply of the largest rocks.

The warriors danced to the faster tune, preferring to dodge Eldred's onslaught while turning the smaller stones thrown by the others. The other hurlers started throwing in time with Eldred, picking the same targets. A man to the left of Eldred hit one of the warriors on the chest. Two men to the right of Eldred pelted another warrior on the leg,

In the chaos, Eldred hurled a brick right through the center of the pod. The first two rows dodged, but a warrior in the third row deflected the brick, which ricocheted to strike a glancing blow on Alfred's shoulder. Alfred screamed a loud curse but stayed on his feet.

Eldred froze in apprehension. His neighbors continued to hold out stones to him for a moment, before returning to throwing themselves. Soon, the missiles were spent and the round was complete.

Alfred threw down his buckler. He walked over and grabbed the man who had redirected the brick and pulled off his helmet. "You started thinking for yourself!" Alfred hit him in the face.

The man cried out and raised his hands.

Alfred struck him again on the nose. Blood poured out. "Cowed by a brick! You have no business being a warrior!" Alfred pushed him to the ground. "Crawl away and be gone! If I see you again—I'll kill you!"

The man rolled over in the dirt and slowly dragged himself away. Nobody met his eye as he pulled himself to the stables.

Alfred glowered after the man, then noticed the blood on his hand and paused to wipe it ineffectually on his padded leggings. He huffed and turned to Eldred, who stood stock still by himself, the men who had been standing beside him having melted away. Alfred narrowed his eyes and nodded. "Well done, son. I should have put you in sooner. You revealed these charlatans. I should have had you in every round."

Eldred raised his eyebrows and kept silent. He had wanted to be in every round, but not as a thrower.

Alfred waved dismissively towards the warriors. "Line up! It's time for my final judgment! I didn't like everything I just saw."

As Alfred made his final selections, Eldred walked over to Dederick. "What happened? I thought they were supposed to be invulnerable?"

Dederick raised his hand to cover his grin. "I told you he wouldn't have me near when he takes them into battle. And it's not just me; it's very noisy here. But it's good enough for a test if it's against a stableboy's arm. Not yours, though."

Eldred tilted his head. "That won't happen in battle though, right?"

Dederick slapped Eldred on the shoulder. "It's the Corporians, Eldred. Maybe in their own lands they would stand some chance. Here, it's just a race to see which of us harvests the most rings from their fingers."

FEASTING

Dederick left for Bert with his men after lunch. Alfred kept his golden pod behind for a banquet. Eldred joined the proceedings at Ghyslaine's insistence.

The warriors filled the Great Hall, feasting on roast boar, beef and fowl. Looking around the tables, Eldred noted how tall the men sat—for Deirans anyway. They were boisterous, but they did not spill their drinks. They used the supplied cutlery instead of eating the food with their hands. Alfred seemed changed as well. He limited his drinking to only three cups of wine and appeared to listen as much as he spoke.

Eldred leaned close to Ghyslaine. "What's happening? They all seem so proper."

Ghyslained arched her eyebrow. "They are realizing their greatness— their supposed perfection."

Eldred looked over the men, each one of them proud and smiling. "It can't last. Dederick says the siege will take months. And the food—they won't be eating like this the whole time. Wilkey and his cooks did a proper job of it tonight."

Ghyslaine nodded. "Yes, they cooked a great deal of meat."

Eldred cut a large chunk from his pork cutlet and chewed it slowly. As he finished, he cocked his head to the side. "Father is taking me on a provisions tour. He is stopping by several estates as he makes his way to Bert." Eldred paused and clasped his hands. "We leave tomorrow."

Ghyslaine gave a slight shrug of her shoulders. "If that is your choice."

Eldred shifted in his seat. "I have thought about what you said, about the Maldavian maiden."

"I presume you mean Mateline of Dinan."

"Yes—her. My thought is—my question, rather—how long exactly do

I have to think the matter over? I'm thinking that we are just off to campaign. It could take months. It could be as long as a year. They have high walls. Would it be just the same to her family if I gave an answer then as if I gave an answer now?"

Ghyslaine looked Eldred in the eye. "What do you think?"

"I don't see why it wouldn't. Besides—all of this seems rushed. I've never met her. I've never even seen a picture."

Ghyslaine glanced upwards. "She is the one for you—the one who was chosen. If you wish, I can request that she visit you in Bert. Julian might be able to persuade her family to agree. But they might just as well accept the supplications of her other suitors—sensible men for whom the lordship of a thriving town such as Dinan proves to be a greater inducement."

Eldred raised his right palm. "Dinan sounds fine."

"They have a brewery," interjected Ghyslaine.

"Which sounds pleasant enough—though I don't drink. But, Mother, my point is I'll be visiting several estates with Father. Some of the lords of these estates must have daughters. I could meet some of them. Perhaps one of them comes from a strong line."

"A strong line so your son can kill you in a fit of madness when he comes of age?"

Eldred grimaced. "Or not, since Father is not aiming to kill me."

Ghyslaine pressed her lips together and pushed her plate away. She had barely eaten any of her game hen. "You can live with our people, the Maldavians. You may also be able to live with the Mercians, if you can stand them. But you cannot live with the Deirans—not after that attack. Now is the time to act. If you cannot make up your mind, then brace yourself for when Mateline marries one of your cousins."

Eldred was just opening his mouth to speak when Alfred rose to his feet and raised his glass, eliciting a cheer from the men. "To brave warriors!" The men joined Alfred as he drank. Alfred set down his cup and looked over the men in the hall. "But it will take more than bravery. It will take patience." Alfred nodded. "Our foe has no little cunning as well as some strength. But Harold's there. Dederick's on the way. We will deny them supplies. We will force them out." Alfred paused and smiled. "When they come forth, it is us—the warriors in this hall—who will face them. We'll be the last people they ever see!" The men banged their cups.

Alfred nodded as the banging faded. "When we're done, I promise you more. We're unstoppable, invincible. I'll find new enemies—new foes of the Night Mother to slaughter."

"What about the Mercians?" called Mack from a nearby table.

"Why not?" They have the numbers to make it interesting," said Alfred.

Eldred crinkled up his face. That wasn't right.

From down the hall, a man yelled, "And the stinking Maldavians!"

Alfred glanced over at the man. "I've fought them before."

Eldred and Ghyslaine exchanged a look.

"It's our time. I'll have my due!" shouted Alfred. Then he set off to the tables, greeting the men and shaking their hands as they finished their meal.

Ghyslaine sat tight lipped, glaring at Alfred.

Eldred scratched his chin. "He was joking. He wouldn't attack Uncle Julian, would he?"

Ghyslaine sighed. "He did before. That is how I came to be here. You as well."

"I won't help him. I'll have gone to Tyrus."

Ghyslaine squeezed his hand where it lay on the table. "He needs you. You are imagining that you will have a say in the matter."

DEPARTURE

Alfred's men started off to Bert the next morning, heading out pod by pod in no particular hurry. Eldred watched them straggle out from the top of the residence tower, standing next to Ghyslaine. He wore the jacket Sammanus had gifted him with the packets of powder safely tucked inside. He always wore it now.

"What will you do while we're gone?" asked Eldred.

Ghyslaine smiled. "I will manage the stewards and run the castle."

Eldred cast a worried eye over the walls. "Is he leaving you with enough guards?"

"Alfred only took a few of the castle guards into his golden pod. A few others joined Dederick's forces, but most remain at their posts. And in any case, Benedict will be arriving later today with a few pods. He is tasked with defending Boar's Tusk."

"In case they get around us."

Ghyslaine nodded. "Yes, for that unlikely circumstance."

They spent a few minutes gazing out beyond the walls of the castle. Eldred pointed out a hawk that perched upon one of the taller buildings in the town. Ghyslaine spotted a small herd of deer crossing the River Clyde.

Looking far down the eastern high road, Eldred noticed a group of twenty men headed towards the castle. "Here comes Benedict now."

Ghyslaine squinted. "You cannot be certain that it is Benedict at that distance."

Eldred laughed. "No, I see him quite clearly."

Ghyslaine rested her hands lightly on the parapet, leaning forward slightly as she studied the oncoming riders. "Nobody can see that far."

"I told you. I've been strengthened by the Sun People. They treated me with their powder of Balaur when I was injured. I see more clearly, and it makes me stronger. I'm certain that's why I came to manifest the Bond, or at least have the noise."

Ghyslaine frowned. "Hmph. I wish it had worked as well for the Bond as it did for your vision."

Eldred arched his eyebrow. "According to Sir Aemilanus—one of their wise men—it did. He said my Deiran stone always worked. I probably manifested the Bond around the same time Harold did, but it didn't show. He showed me a demonstration with small bells. If you shook one of the bells next to one of the same size, it would vibrate. But if you shook a smaller bell next to a larger bell, nothing would happen."

Ghyslaine narrowed her eyes at him. "So you were too large?"

Eldred shrugged. "Perhaps. Now I'm too loud, like I'm screaming into their ears. It's only around Father that it works—works for him, that is. I'm certain my presence is the source of his renewed strength in the Bond."

"You have to stay close to him."

"I know. But what I'm saying is that just as I can see farther than you, I'm stronger than the other Mercians. That's why I'm confident I can defeat King Capuan. If I fight a duel, I won't be throwing my life away. I can win. Especially once Father gives me the sword."

Ghyslaine's face fell. "If you fight Capuan, one of you will die. If you win, there will be an endless stream of challengers to follow. And all for what? So you can be king of some foolish Mercians?"

Eldred took a breath. "Not just for that. The Maldavian maiden—"

"Mateline," said Ghyslaine.

"Yes, the maiden and the town, Dinan—they both sound very fine. A man could go there and pass his years quietly, pleasantly. But that's not what I aim to do."

Ghyslaine looked back at the riders, who were nearing the gate. "I will let Julian know."

Eldred grinned. "It will be good news of a sort—at least for one of my cousins."

Ghyslaine smiled mirthlessly. "Indeed."

An hour later—after an awkward hug that Benedict had insisted on—Eldred rode out of the gate atop Hobbie with Alfred and his pod. Benedict waved enthusiastically after them. Ghyslaine waved in a more reserved manner, though her eyes glistened.

THE BAND

Whereas Alfred's men had gone west—bearing slightly northward so as to take the great western highway to Bert—Alfred led his own pod in the opposite direction, following a route along a woodland trail.

Alfred had the lead, with Stace right behind, though he came up alongside Alfred whenever the trail was wide enough. Mack and Pounder stuck close to Eldred, almost penning him in at times. Bate always held to the rear.

The men were silent as they rode. Eldred studied their faces from time to time, recalling the role each played in the night of the attack. Pounder had been in front, the one who would have killed Eldred. But the others had not been far behind, and it was Mack who had killed Morris, stabbing the head steward in the neck. They showed none of that rage today with Alfred nearby, but if Alfred were to fall from his horse and smash his head, who knew what would happen?

When they turned off the trail onto a country road, Eldred pulled close to Pounder, oddly finding his would-be murderer the most approachable of the lot. "Whose estate are we headed to?"

Pounder gave an encouraging smile. "Lord Grimsley. It's maybe another six hours of riding to Stonor Hall. If we make good time, we should get there just around dusk."

"Does he have a daughter?" asked Eldred.

Mack laughed and came up on the other side of Eldred, sandwiching him between the two podmen. "We're going to get provisions to feed the army, not crumpet to feed your passions."

Eldred's face stiffened. "I don't mean that. I need a wife. Or—that is—

I'm seeking a wife. Someone to settle down with after we finish this business with the Corporians."

Mack and Pounder exchanged a look, and Mack started to laugh.

Pounder cleared his throat. "This—our visit today—it wouldn't be how you would see that done. That sort of thing is usually settled before anyone goes anywhere. And the women work it out. Doesn't your mother have someone lined up for you?"

Eldred frowned. "She has mentioned a Maldavian maiden, but I'd prefer a Deiran bride."

Mack nodded. "Who wouldn't? Show me a Maldavian woman who knows her place."

Eldred raised his eyebrow. "So does this Lord Grimsley have a daughter? And for that matter, is he strong in the Bond?"

Pounder tilted his head back and forth. "He has the Bond, but not in any heroic fashion. I've never heard of him leading a silver pod. He's decent. But I don't know if he has a daughter. I only know he has wheat."

Mack thrust his finger out at Eldred. "What you would need is to marry Dederick's girls if he had any."

Pounder shook his head. "Dederick just has sons—two sons. Only one of those ever passed the trial. That would be two years ago."

Eldred frowned. "I remember. He only passed in the center arch. Who else are we meeting?"

Pounder tilted his head. "Well, let's see. We are staying at Stonor Hall tonight with Grimsley. Tomorrow, we are on to Bushmead Manor to meet with Lord Louth. He might be more what you are looking for. He has led silver pods and he has daughters, though I'm not sure of their ages. Day after, we head to Harlington Hall and Lord Talbot. I've only ever been there once. Don't know about Talbot's offspring."

"Are you really marrying some girl before we even get to Bert?" asked Bate, who had come closer.

"No, but I'm not marrying the Maldavian maiden. I'm just hoping to meet someone," said Eldred.

"What about the curse?" asked Pounder.

Eldred took a breath. "I haven't forgotten."

Mack and Pounder looked off into the distance and edged their horses farther from Eldred.

Eldred frowned. "We've never really discussed it. Did you know what you were doing?"

Neither man replied. Eldred paused for a moment and continued on. "Well? Pounder, you smashed down my door. Mack, you stabbed Morris in the neck. What were you thinking?"

Pounder grimaced. "Like I told you before, it felt like you were stabbing me in the forehead. It made me so angry. I still knew who you were, but it didn't matter. I wouldn't want to hurt you, Eldred, but if Alfred goes missing, you had best get gone yourself. It would be all of us."

Eldred straightened up and met Pounder's eye. "I see."

Mack grunted. "WIth your face—that patch of dead skin—it might do to take another look at the Maldavian wench."

"Thanks for that," said Eldred.

Stonor Hall

The reception at Stonor Hall was not the grand one Eldred expected. The hall itself was little more than a large house with about six rooms and a roof that could use a touch of repair. They arrived as dusk was settling in and soon found themselves squeezed into a small dining room, eating a weak soup that consisted mostly of vegetables with Lord Grimsley and what Eldred supposed were the rest of his pod.

Alfred and Lord Grimsley argued back and forth regarding how much wheat would be supplied over what timeframe. Alfred wanted the wheat delivered over a period of months. Lord Grimsley kept coming back to the payment, for which all Alfred would say is that it depended on how much gold and silver was in the Corporians city. It seemed that Alfred would guarantee nothing but demanded a steady supply of grain.

Eldred hardly listened. He spent all of his attention on the pretty young woman who was waiting on the table. She seemed aristocratic, or at least reserved, or at the very least disinterested in her work. Her dark eyes flashed with mischievous energy. Her jet black hair hung down straight, fanning her shoulders. It did not hurt that she was of normal height.

While she was pouring mead into the cup of one of Lord Grimsley's men, the man suddenly pulled it away. She did not hesitate in slapping him on the back of the head and calling him a Motherless fool to the delight of the other diners. She packed quite a blow for such a small size.

After she worked her way around the table through Alfred's podmen, she got to Eldred and went to pour mead for him. He held up his hand. "Just water for me."

She paused, her arm outstretched. "Water? Where do you see water? If you want water, go fetch it yourself. I thought you Mercians liked your drink."

Eldred frowned as Pounder elbowed him in a jocular fashion. "I'm not Mercian. I'm the—"

The woman rolled her eyes. "We all know who you are. No need to apologize."

Eldred felt a hint of annoyance as he heard Alfred laugh along with the rest of them. But he was not upset with her. She had to be Lord Grimsley's daughter. Who else would feel so free in insulting the king's son?

After Eldred finished his bowl of soup, he took the opportunity to slink out to the kitchen, just across the hall. The young woman was sitting at a small table, taking her supper with an older woman.

A lively glint filled the woman's eyes. "What is it now? Have you come for your water?"

Eldred gave a short bow, holding the bowl in one hand. "My name is Eldred; what's yours?"

She arched her eyebrow. "What use does the great Eldred, son of the king and slayer of dragons, have with my name?"

"Just simple courtesy," said Eldred.

The woman nodded and rose to her feet to give a graceful curtsey. "My name is Elisant." She gestured towards the other diner. "This is my mother, Mabbot."

Mabbot regarded Eldred with thin, pressed lips as he effected another bow.

Eldred smiled. "So pleased to meet you. Are you by chance relatives of Lord Grimsley?"

"Should we be?" asked Elisant.

Mabbot sighed. "Oh, for Mother's sake, Elisant." She turned to Eldred. "I'm Lord Grimsley's cousin."

"Cousin?" asked Eldred.

"Yes, you know. Their parents were siblings," said Elisant.

Eldred sighed. "I know how that—works. But you live here?"

Mabbot gave Eldred a blank look. "I run his house for him since his wife died. My daughter helps me when we have an event, such as tonight."

Eldred nodded as he met Elisant's challenging stare. "I'm so pleased you do. Umm. I wonder if I might join the two of you for the rest of dinner. I don't really care to watch my father squeeze more bushels of wheat out from Lord Grimsley."

Elisant exchanged a look with her mother. "Why not?"

Mabbot spread her hands. "If you wish."

As she started to rise, Eldred waved his hand. "On, no. Please don't bother. I can get my own soup." He went to the pot on the counter and fished through it to find the few remaining pieces of meat.

Elisant was sitting quite straight when Eldred joined them at the table. "So, you were there when the dragon died?"

"I was there when we killed it," said Eldred, before taking a quick spoonful of soup.

"I heard Lord Vance killed it," said Elisant.

"He did, at the cost of his life."

Elisant gave him an expectant look. "What did you do?"

Mabbot rolled her eyes. "Don't pester him."

"I lured the dragon out of its lair into the trap that Lord Thom crafted. They had rocks balanced all around a canyon. I had to go in and search for it in the darkness," said Eldred.

"Using your Maldavian eyes," said Elisant.

"That's right. I found it in an open crater, bathing in a pool of green water. It was asleep. I had to throw rocks at it to stir it awake. Even then, it was not too interested in me."

Elisant raised her chin. "It did not want to eat you?"

"I don't think it did. But it didn't want to be pelted with rocks either. It chased me. I only barely beat it back to the canyon where they unleashed the trap. They hurled down rock after rock on the dragon, covering its hindquarters with a pile of dirt and stone twenty feet deep until it was still."

"And then you killed it?" asked Elisant.

Eldred smiled sadly. "No. Lord Osbert thought to, but he only stirred it to life. It grabbed him and pinned him to the ground. The dragon shredded Lord Thom and ate him."

Elisant frowned. "You just let it eat him?"

"I was helping Lord Kenelm. It had batted him through the air into a boulder. After that, we watched it worm its way out from the pile of rocks. It was just getting free when the lords charged it, vaulting Lord Vance into its maw."

"So he killed it from the inside?" asked Mabbot.

Eldred nodded. "That he did. He wedged his way into an opening of the creature. He choked it."

"What were you doing?" asked Elisant, narrowing her eyes.

"I ran forward—to support Lord Kenelm and Lord Ferris as they carried Lord Osbert to safety. But he was already dead."

"Hmm. But you did fight it?" asked Elisant.

"I struck its scales with my spear a number of times, but they were too tough. None of the others could harm it either."

"Mead! We need more mead!" It was Alfred calling from the other room.

"Can you go, dear?" asked Mabbot.

"Mother, why don't you go?" asked Elisant.

Mabbot gestured to the hall. "There is proper and there is improper—"

"Just go, Mother," said Elisant.

Mabbot hesitated, but as the calls for mead were joined, she rose to her feet and took a large jug from a shelf on her way back to the dining room.

Eldred smiled at Elisant and was pleased to see her smile back. For a moment, they said nothing, then Eldred broke the silence. "Tell me about your father."

Elisant crinkled up her nose. "My father?"

"Does he live here too?"

"No. He died last year."

"Oh, I'm sorry. Did he die in battle?"

Elisant looked down at the table. "No. He was a mason. He was working with a crew to build a chimney. It collapsed and killed him and another worker."

"So, he did not have the Bond?" whispered Eldred. He could see Mabbot crossing the hall.

"Do men with the Bond work as masons?" asked Elisant, her eyes darkening.

"I suppose not," allowed Eldred.

Mabbot dusted her hands together loudly. "What are we discussing?"

Elisant sniffed. "He was asking about how Father died."

Mabbot gave Eldred a hard look. "Why would that be any of your concern?"

"It's not. Most definitely not. I was just asking after him," said Eldred.

Mabbot leaned against the counter and her face drooped slightly. "He'll be dead a year ago next week. He died doing honest work. It will have been a whole year…"

Elisant rose and went to hug her mother, keeping her back to Eldred.

"I'm sorry to have disturbed you," said Eldred.

The women said nothing as Eldred left the room.

Alfred glanced up as Eldred sat down next to him. "Ah, there you are. Thought you got lost looking for soup."

Eldred gave a small shrug. "No."

Alfred gestured towards Lord Grimsley. "Your turn to bargain."

"Bargain for what?" asked Eldred.

Alfred raised a bushy eyebrow. "Won't your men need provisions? They won't be eating my food."

"My men?" asked Eldred.

"Lord Kenelm and his pods," said Alfred.

"Oh, yes," said Eldred.

Lord Grimsley cleared his throat. "The king did not leave much to bargain for. My current supplies are all committed between my promises to him and to Harold."

Eldred frowned. "Harold?"

"If you recall, the original war plans were for his men to lead the attack. I have committed shipments to provide for his men in the field," said Lord Grimsley.

"What's left?" asked Eldred.

Lord Grimsley looked upwards. "It's a few months until we start the summer harvest, but then I'll have potatoes, squash and carrots. In late summer, I'll have more wheat."

Eldred looked at Alfred. "Will we still be fighting?"

Alfred grimaced. "They have high walls, son. It wouldn't be prudent to plan for a short campaign."

The podmen were stirring, heading out to the porch. Alfred grabbed his cup and rose to join them. "Watch yourself, son."

When things settled, it was just Eldred sitting across from Lord Grimsley, who waved his hand impatiently. "How many men do you have?"

"I asked Lord Kenelm to bring three pods."

Lord Grimsley ran his right index finger over the fingers of his left hand. "It will be on the order of thirty bushels to provision your men for two months. Including transport, that will be two aurum, five denarii, providing you receive the goods in Bert, like your father plans to do."

Eldred's eyes got wide. "I don't have that."

Lord Grimsley smiled and made a circling gesture with his right index finger. "You can do the same as your father then. He is paying with loot from the Corporians."

"He is offering their gold and silver?" asked Eldred.

"Yes, but we must account for the element of risk. You might not win, after all. Or they might not have much in the way of precious metals. If I must wait until your successful return, I must charge you—five aurum."

Eldred stiffened in his seat. "Five gold aurum. That's robbery."

Lord Grimsely scowled. "My terms are quite reasonable. You are making war on a stone bearer in her own city—everyone says she could be there. And even if you are victorious, it could take a year or more."

Eldred placed his palms on the table. "The siege may take some time, but we will win. How can you doubt that? My father has built the perfect golden pod. We fight the Corporians on the Mother's own soil. Are you rooting for the invaders?"

"Of course not. Nobody doubts your father. He is an able man, but I am less certain of you. When the city falls, will you be quick, first to reach their gold? Or will you hang back, seeking safety? I don't know. I doubt anyone is certain what you will do."

Eldred sighed. Seeking safety? All he had ever done was travel to the north and fight the greatest dragon that ever lived. "Fine."

Lord Grimsley smiled. "I'll have the documents for you to mark in the morning before you leave."

As Lord Grimsley started to rise, Eldred gripped his arm. "One last thing. I was curious about Elisant. Umm, her father had no trace of the Bond. Is that right?"

Lord Grimsley gave Eldred a searching look. "Broddi? No, none at all. He was a bricklayer."

Eldred glanced down at the table, before looking back up into Lord Grimsley's eyes. "I see. And do you have a daughter?"

Lord Grimsley carefully removed Eldred's hand from his arm. "No. If I did, I would have her run my house, not Mabbot."

Eldred nodded.

Lord Grimsley gazed down at Eldred with a somber expression. "It's not done this way. Your mother—she is the one who must find you a match. There are low-born men who scour the land looking for their own brides, but you should not aim to join them. And if you were to succeed that way, it most assuredly would not lead to marriage with a noblewoman."

Eldred frowned. "My mother found me a Maldavian bride."

Lord Grimsley tilted his head. "Well, look at you. It might make sense. Best you follow your mother's lead." He took his cup, leaving Eldred alone in the room.

Eldred and Alfred's podmen were housed in the barn while Alfred slept in guest quarters inside the house. When Eldred came in for breakfast in the morning, Lord Grimsley had the papers ready. He looked quite pleased as Eldred glanced through the document and signed. Five aurum—a fortune—and Eldred would not even have any provisions to show for it until summer.

Platters of boiled eggs, fresh brown bread and rashers of bacon were set on the dining room table. When the bacon was gone, Mack called for more—he was eating as much as Eldred. Eldred looked up expectantly, but it was only Mabbot.

Lord Grimsley had taken a seat across from Eldred a few minutes earlier. When Eldred looked away from Mabbot, he found Lord Grimsley smiling at him.

"She's gone," said Lord Grimsley.

Alfred lowered his half-eaten egg. "Who is?"

"Elisant—my cousin's daughter—I had her sent away last night, before you and your men settled for the night."

Alfred frowned. "What business is this?"

Lord Grimsley gestured at Eldred. "Your son showed an interest in her, but it was not prudent."

Alfred sat back and grinned. "Is that right? About time."

Mack slapped the table. "Eldred's on the hunt. It was all he talked about on the ride yesterday."

Eldred flushed slightly and raised his hand. "No, no. I'm looking for a bride."

Alfred chuckled and pointed at Lord Grimsley. "And you think his cousin's daughter is the right one for you?"

Eldred glanced apologetically at Mabbot, who had come back in from the hall and was standing by the door frame. "Sadly, no."

"Whyever not? I remember her from last night. She was feisty, Don't move your drink!" said Alfred, which set his men to laughter.

Eldred rolled his eyes. "It was just a thought, Father. Just a thought."

Alfred dug in his ear with a finger. "A foolish one. You must have heard. Your uncle sent your mother the name of your approved bride."

"A Maldavian," said Eldred curtly.

Alfred looked him in the eye. "That's the one."

"I want to marry a Deiran."

Alfred shrugged. "I can understand that better than anyone. Nonetheless, your mother told you the name of your bride. Now—if you are looking to have fun—Bushmead Manor, where we are headed tomorrow, is not far from Upper Swell—a decent sized town. I'm all for fun. We don't need a name from Julian to have some fun."

Eldred sighed as Mabbot fled out of the hall in her embarrassment. "Let's just get the provisions, Father. It is time we pressed on to Bert."

As they continued their journey, Alfred made contracts for more provisions from the other lords, but there was never much left for Eldred—who was only able to sign for some bushels of winter wheat from Lord Louth along with some potatoes. Lord Louth did have daughters, including one of appropriate age, but Lord Louth hid her away.

Alfred smiled. "Your bride is already known to you. Don't confuse the matter."

Eldred took a small measure of revenge when he refused to accompany the other men on their questionable visit to Upper Swell. Alfred and Eldred were locked together now, a bond within the Bond. Alfred could leave, of course, but if someone happened along and killed Eldred, that would be the end of his grand plans.

BERT

Five days later, they wound their way along the high road down a small hill, making their approach to Bert in the early afternoon. A fifteen foot high wall of coarse brown stone circled the town, which was good sized, perhaps one sixth the footprint of Boar's Tusk. A tower near the center of the city showed over the walls, as did a few peaked roofs of some large buildings. Strangely, the main gate stood open, with only a few men on guard.

"Shouldn't that gate be shut?" asked Eldred.

Alfred frowned back, still annoyed about Upper Swell. "If that's what it takes to lure the Corporians down here, I'll pull the gate down myself."

Mack laughed just off to Eldred's left. Pounder was silent on the right. The two always penned him in when the road was wide enough to permit it.

"Gates should be shut or at least properly guarded when you are at war," said Eldred.

Mack's eyes twinkled. "It's your mouth that should be shut."

Eldred pushed his hand out. "Give me space. You'll be wanting to give me space."

Mack and Pounder eased out a bit, but they were still within arms reach. Eldred rode with tight shoulders for the final miles into Bert.

The five guards at the gate saluted Alfred crisply as the party rode past and continued towards the tower in the center of the town. Along the way, they passed a handsome inn two stories high. The houses looked tidy, but the yards were overrun with tethered cows and goats as well as scattered flocks of chickens.

Eldred wrinkled his nose as they passed a pile of dung eight feet high. "Ugh. Why this mess?"

"It seems the townsfolk are not very charitable. They've pulled in all their livestock from the commons," said Pounder.

The odor fell away as they entered the commons in the center of the town. The tower Eldred had seen over the wall stood in a grassy field, attached to a good-sized estate. The heroes, the champions of Alfred's golden pod, lounged on blankets beside dozens of white linen tents spread across the field, most of which were set on the other side of a stone lined creek that split the commons. Alfred beamed and headed towards a narrow bridge that crossed the creek—rushing to be reunited with his troops. As his horse stepped onto the bridge, he pulled up and looked back at Eldred. "Don't wander off. Stick with your men."

Eldred glanced over the tents.

Alfred shook his head and pointed to three isolated tents with a few tethered horses on the nearside of the creek. "Over there. You stay where you can see me." Alfred frowned. "No, closer than that. Stay where I can see you."

Alfred trotted across the bridge—his podmen in tow—and headed towards a clear area in the center of the tents. The men at the tents were grabbing their gear and heading out to meet him. They formed a long line and waved their swords as they cheered for their king.

Eldred took a deep breath, relieved to be able to look left and right and not find Mack or Pounder. But they were still glancing at him from across the way, checking on him every minute—not that they would ever catch him if he turned Hobbie around and galloped out of the gate. But what would be the point of that? He needed the sword.

Eldred nudged Hobbie towards the tents. As Eldred approached the first tent, a smartly dressed young man stepped out of the entrance. Eldred's eyes went wide. It was Dreven!

DREVEN

Dreven looked up at Eldred with an impish smile, a mop of hair covering his slightly oversized forehead. "About time you got here."

Eldred grinned. "What do you mean? And what're you doing here?" The boy had grown an inch or two. Had he turned fifteen?

"I'm Lord Kenelm's personal steward. Three weeks ago to the day, I was out plowing the south fields near the River Stour, and I was doing all the work—mind you, the ox was hardly making an effort. Brun—one of Lord Kenelm's men—came up on his horse. He rides up very matter of fact and he looks down at me—cause he is towering up on his horse like you are now—and he says, 'Are you Dreven?' And I go, 'Who's asking?' And he says, 'Lord Kenelm sent me to fetch you. You're his new steward.' And just like that, I'm a steward."

Eldred hopped down from Hobbie to shake Dreven's hand. "Well done. Well done."

Dreven's face fell as he caught sight of Eldred's right cheek. "Oh."

Eldred paused. "Ah. Yes." He reached up his right hand to tap his cheek, then stuck out his left hand, which had a dead looking patch of skin as well. "Spoils of the expedition, I suppose."

Dreven nodded. "Lord Kenelm talks about the expedition every night. But while he told me about the other squires, he never spoke of your injuries. I'm sorry."

Eldred shrugged. "I came back—that's good fortune enough."

"Well, and you have the Bond; you passed the trial."

"That's right," said Eldred with a sour face. "In the center arch."

"Who cares what arch? You did it!"

Eldred smiled. "Yes. You're right. We each got some of what we wanted."

Dreven punched Eldred lightly in the stomach. "Thanks to you. I don't suppose it was just happenstance that Brun found me in that field."

Eldred gave Dreven's shoulder a push. "Don't be messing with a warrior who has the Bond."

"As a former squire, I'm more than the match of you," said Dreven. "And so I command you to come with me to see the king's quartermaster. We've been here three days, and he won't issue my lord any supplies. That's why he's out hunting with his podmen."

Eldred gave a sheepish smile. "I'm afraid that is not going to change. Lord Kenelm's men and you—I suppose—are counted as my men by my father. So I have to provide for you."

Dreven took a step back. "What do you have?"

"Nothing at the moment, but in two months we will have quite a store of potatoes."

"Two months?" asked Dreven.

"After that we should mostly have food. It's all scheduled."

Dreven clasped his hands. "Hmm. The lord's men enjoy hunting well enough, but they have not been finding much. The whole area has been picked clean."

Eldred pursed his lips. "We'll find something. If we have to, we can buy livestock from the commoners with the promise of Corporian gold."

"You think they're that dumb?"

"It's how I've paid for everything so far." Eldred grinned. "The good news is that if I die, I don't have to pay anything."

Dreven cocked an eyebrow. "Nice to have a backup plan."

LORD KENELM

Lord Kenelm and his men didn't return until after dusk. Lord Kenelm was off his horse and walking into his tent when Eldred stepped out in front of him.

"Greetings, Lord Kenelm," said Eldred, thrusting his hand out.

Lord Kenelm stepped back and raised his left hand to his temple. "Oh, you startled me, Eldred. I didn't expect you."

Eldred dropped his hand to his side and gave a short bow. "It's good to see you again."

Lord Kenelm nodded slowly and looked back at his men, who were crowding around the fire, putting their rabbits and fowl on the spit for a late dinner. "Yes, I'm glad you're here. I have some questions."

"Oh, of course," said Eldred.

"Let's move off by the creek," said Lord Kenelm.

They paced fifty feet down the river in silence. A smattering of laughter carried over from the tents across the creek where Alfred's golden pod was camped. As Eldred swept his eyes over their campfires, he spotted men singing and drinking. It appeared an entirely different world from the three quiet tents behind them where exhausted men waited for their paltry supper. From Lord Kenelm's expression, it was clear that the same thought had occurred to him.

Lord Kenelm glanced back towards his men.

"You have some concerns, Lord Kenelm?" asked Eldred.

"Yes, I do. Let me start with the noise. Where has it gone? I don't feel anything."

"It's still there, but so long as my father is near enough, it won't affect you."

Lord Kenelm tilted his head. "I suffered for weeks as we came south. You mean to say your father can will it away?"

Eldred shrugged. "I don't know. It's just that way. It pleases the Mother that it be so. But if my father should ride away, the noise is stronger now, much stronger than when it taxed you. If he should ride away, I think you might try to kill me—both you and your men."

Lord Kenelm frowned deeply. "Is that true?"

"It happened with his men. I have hopes, because of how you were before, that you could be different."

Lord Kenelm clasped his hands in front him. "We are going to war. Who can say for sure where Alfred will lead his golden pod? The enemy could separate us."

"We must stay close. This is not some vanity on my part. It serves my father. When I'm close, he has all the power in the Bond he ever did and more. He leads the golden pod as the kings of old did in their day."

Lord Kenelm looked towards the camp across the river. "I heard some part of this tale from Dederick before he joined forces with Harold at their city. But I must ask why we depend upon this strange occurrence when we could simply have Harold or Dederick lead the men in standard fashion."

Eldred rubbed his chin. "Why do we depend upon it?"

"Yes, why not take more men to battle under the command of younger leaders, men sound enough in the Bond without any strange contrivances?"

Eldred blinked. "Because Father does not wish it so. He wants to lead."

Lord Kenelm twisted his lips. "That I understand. He is reckless and vain. But why are you here, and it follows, why am I here with my men?"

Eldred turned away. "Well, I support my father. He is the king."

"Do you? When I got your message and came forth with my pods— three pods per your request—I was happy for you. You were going to battle. I assumed you were once again the heir. But when I arrived here, I found you were not. I learned you passed the trial but only in the center arch. I discovered that my men were not accounted for in any battle plans. We are expected to hang back and avoid contact if possible. Our only function is to escort you."

"This is a vital role," spluttered Eldred. "And valued. My father said you and your men can plunder the battlefield. The others, Harold's and Dederick's men, are limited to looting the city."

Lord Kenelm sighed. "I know you mean well. But you have not thought this through. Of course my men will not loot the bodies of enemies that Alfred and his pod kill. It's not a matter of permission but a matter of honor."

Eldred shrugged. "Well, we shall have the city then."

Lord Kenelm took a breath and shifted his shoulders. "And honor raises another concern as well. It pains me to say this, Eldred, but as a lord of my people, they would accept my declaration if I were to pledge myself and them to support the heir to the throne. There's honor in such a pledge. But I seem to have pledged myself to a warrior who merely passed the trial in the center arch. I myself passed at two arches removed."

Eldred rubbed his hands together. "I hadn't thought of that."

Lord Kenelm frowned. "No, I'm sure you hadn't."

"You can withdraw, of course. I would understand."

Lord Kenelm shook his head. "No, that would bring even more dishonor. I'm here. My men are here." Lord Kenelm put his hand on Eldred's shoulder. "But moving forward, you must consult me before making any commitments that involve us."

Eldred grimaced. "I'm sorry. I'm truly sorry."

Lord Kenelm smiled and squeezed Eldred's shoulder. "It's as I said when we parted at Hobart Gap—you need never apologize to me. We live now on borrowed time."

"That's true," said Eldred hesitantly.

Lord Kenelm threw up his hands. "And we might have good fortune. Perhaps some Corporians will notice us and engage. We can hope."

Eldred gave a weak grin. "I'm sure some will find their way around the golden pod."

INTRODUCTIONS

Lord Kenelm's men were still waiting on their meal—which Dreven was preparing—when Lord Kenelm introduced Eldred around. Despite Eldred's thirteen years at the Academy, he was not familiar with most of the men. Many had trained in the North and only came to the Academy for the day of their trial. Others were older men who had ascended before Eldred had paid attention to such things.

Such was the case for Brun, Lord Kenelm's second in command who led the second pod. His lined face showed his years—Eldred thought him to be in his late twenties—but his thick arms and broad chest made him out to be the strongest of the men. He peered out at Eldred from underneath a mop of long unruly black hair as they shook hands.

"Well met," said Eldred with enthusiasm.

Brun gave a quick nod with an expression that started as a faint smile before fading to something less encouraging.

"Eldred is our charge. We must protect him above all else," announced Lord Kenelm to the men in general.

"I've heard you can run," said Brun.

"What?" asked Eldred.

"Up with the dragon. I heard you can run fast. That's what you do," said Brun.

"I did do that," said Eldred. "I can run. I can fight too."

"So you have the Bond?" asked Brun.

"I passed the trial in the center arch just a few weeks ago," said Eldred.

Brun scratched his neck. "Well, that will be something to see if we fight. A Mercian with the Bond. You should be dangerous?" He ended his statement with a tone that changed the meaning to a question.

"Right, but we'll be hanging back," said Eldred.

"I've heard," said Brun.

Lord Kenelm motioned towards the oldest man present, if appearances were to be believed. "This is Frewin. He served with my father."

Probably your grandfather too, thought Eldred as he reached his hand out to the grizzled gray haired man. "Pleased to meet you, Frewin."

Frewin wiped his hand on his tunic before taking Eldred's hand. "Thank you, m'lord. That is, if you are a lord. Are you a lord?"

Eldred frowned. "I just passed the trial in the last few weeks. Such things are still being worked out."

Frewin looked Eldred up and down. "But you are the son of the king? That much is true?"

"Yes," said Eldred sharply. He had tired of this topic a long time ago.

"Frewin," said Lord Kenelm with a warning tone, before moving on to the tallest man in his troop. "This is Colle, leader of my third pod."

Eldred marveled at the man's height, only a few inches short of Eldred, a regular giant for a Deiran. "A pleasure."

"Mine's the pleasure," said Colle. "My lord here told us about what you all did up North. Seems quite brave to lure a dragon."

"It was," said Lord Kenelm.

"Thank you," said Eldred.

Of the other men, it was the younger ones that stood out to Eldred: Dogory—a bubbly young man who had just ascended the previous year at the age of fifteen—and Hallet, who had advanced seven years before but had actually spent time at the Academy as a student unlike the others.

CHOPPING

Lord Kenelm and his men were off early the next morning, heading towards Bert's southern gate to try a new, more distant hunting ground. Dreven started the day by tidying up the camp. Eldred watched for a while before joining in. They stacked blankets, dug a fresh latrine and picked up leftover bones from the previous night's supper.

When it came time to split some wood, Dreven took a break and watched Eldred work an ax on a nearby oak tree. The shaft felt good in Eldred's hands as he lopped off branches and cut them to size. Swinging an ax brought almost as much pleasure to Eldred as swinging a sword.

Dreven sat on his rear in the grass—leaning back on his elbows—and considered Eldred's wood pile. "I reckon that's enough."

Eldred glanced over at Alfred's men across the river. They were riding in twenty man horse formations that passed through each other at speed. "A bit more won't hurt. Better to get more now and let it dry out."

Dreven shrugged. "If you like."

Eldred set to work hacking down a gnarled branch.

Dreven motioned towards the creek. "They say that it runs all the way to the Southern Sea."

Eldred paused and wiped some sweat from his forehead. "You should follow it down and visit me sometime."

Dreven sat up. "What do you mean?"

Eldred waved his hand towards his father's warriors. "After this, I'm headed to Tyrus."

"To be with Mercians?" asked Dreven.

"To rule them. If I can defeat King Capuan in a duel, I will win his crown."

Dreven stared at Eldred for a moment. "Are you serious?"

Eldred furrowed his brows. "Of course I am. Why do you doubt it?"

Dreven pursed his lips. "I don't know. I suppose he's won many duels."

"I've won duels too. I fought six duels against the Sun People and won each one."

Dreven blinked. "The Sun People?"

Eldred gestured impatiently. "The Wretcheds."

The corners of Dreven's lips turned almost imperceptibly upwards. "I see."

Eldred shook his head. "They're much tougher than you think. They'd easily be the match of any Deiran except for the Bond."

Dreven's smile leaked out. "Except for that, then. But still, would one of those Wretcheds be the match of the Mercian king? He has a named sword and he's strong, stronger even than you."

"He's not. At least, I don't think he is. The Wretcheds made me stronger. They gave me their medicine when I was close to dying. I still have some of it. And for the sword, my father will give me a named sword once we deal with the Corporians."

"His sword?"

Eldred frowned. "No. But—he says—it will be a suitable named sword that he can get hold of."

"So, you will have two named swords when you win."

"Yes, I suppose I will."

Dreven grinned. "You should give Capuan's sword, Picus, to me, then."

"What does a steward need with a named sword?"

"I wouldn't be a steward if I had one. I would be a warrior."

Eldred grinned. "I suppose you would be." He hefted the ax and cleaved a gnarled branch from the tree.

Dreven idly pulled up some grass as Eldred cut more branches from the tree. After a few moments, a burst of boisterous voices carried over from across the creek.

Dreven got to his feet. "What is it?"

Eldred shielded his eyes from the noon sun. "It's Dederick. He's come down to meet with Father."

REPORT

Alfred received Dederick in the shade of three tall birch trees just south of the tower that stood over the Bert commons. All the men of the golden pod and more besides stood in a half circle before them. Eldred could easily see the two great men clearly from the back of the crowd, but Dreven shifted from side to side on his toes, trying to get a look.

Dederick raised a cup of wine in salute to Alfred. "The Corporians show themselves."

"On their walls?" asked Alfred.

Dederick smiled. "Outside their walls."

Alfred rubbed his hands together. "Are they trying to break through?"

Dederick tilted his cup towards Alfred and smiled. "No, they just line up—thousands of them, two thousand at least. Harold and I had our forces up on the plateau yesterday. I could tell he was thinking about it."

"He must show restraint!"

Dederick rubbed his neck. "So far, he does. But by the Mother, the thought comes natural enough. If I hadn't come down today, I would be up there considering it myself."

"What does this army of theirs do? Does it truly just stand there?"

"Mostly. Two days ago a smaller contingent came out to scatter red stones everywhere around the gate. This could be a means to get us off our horses. Hard to say at a distance. I still think we could charge them. They have straight lines with tight spacing. They would be tough to split, but a determined enough attack would roll them up into corpses."

Alfred knuckled his chin. "What is your opinion of their gate?"

Dederick grinned. "They leave the gate open—more hospitable than you might think."

Alfred chuckled. "Open is it?"

Dederick nodded. "They have sixty-foot walls, but they offer us everything. Oh, we've seen archers. I've no doubt a mass of archers is hunkered down on top. But we could be in their formation so quickly I expect they would shoot more of their own warriors than ours."

"What are these warriors like? Do they have quality?" asked Alfred.

"We caught a few riding west for Corporia—smaller and weaker than a Mercian." Dederick shrugged. "I don't think much of them. I don't see why you should."

Eldred frowned as the nearby warriors glanced at him.

Alfred took a breath. "Were they out again this morning?"

"I didn't wait to see. I left at sunrise and rode hard to get here. I ordered my men not to engage, but if Harold goes, you can count on some of my men charging too. If you want the action, you need to get up there."

"By the Mother, you're right," said Alfred. He gestured to the crowd. "Pack your gear, men. We leave in fifteen minutes. Tomorrow we will wash in their blood."

Suddenly, everyone was jogging in all directions.

Dreven turned to Eldred. "What about Lord Kenelm? He won't be back until tonight."

"He won't wait. You heard him." Eldred frowned. "You stay here and let them know."

Dreven shook his head. "I'm going with you. I daresay Lord Kenelm can puzzle it out. And I won't have you standing alone by yourself out there."

"Not likely," said Eldred, as he watched Bate and Mack approach on horseback.

Mack pulled up his horse right in front of Eldred, an unpleasant grin across his heavyset face. "Time to ride, princeling."

Dreven stepped next to Eldred. "I'm coming too."

"That would be right useful," said Bate. "We might need to try a bumpkin charge."

Mack snorted. "It's the pair, don't you know. This is the squire that Eldred was planning to cheat with."

Bate's eyes went wide with surprise. "Is it really? What're you doing here?"

Eldred frowned. "He's Lord Kenelm's steward."

Dreven straightened his back. "That's right."

Bate shrugged. "Fine. Pack his gear, then, steward. We leave now."

CAMP

Dusk caught Alfred's army on the march. One by one, the pods stopped off the side of the road and made camp, stretching out in disorganized fashion over a mile. Eldred and Dreven settled forty feet from Alfred's tent, herded into the spot by Mack and Bate. Fortunately, the two podmen left and joined Alfred. But Eldred did not go unwatched. One of Alfred's podmen always kept an eye in his direction.

Dreven sat on his blanket, enjoying a meal of bread and dried meat, his first sample of Alfred's provisions. "You should try some, Eldred. It's not half bad."

Eldred wandered to the edge of the road and looked back the way they had come.

"They'll just be getting back to Bert," said Dreven.

Eldred grunted. "I know. I can't help but look. It will be odd out there tomorrow without them."

"Hmph. You mean just out there with me—a steward?"

Eldred waved off Dreven's comment. "No, that's fine. But if tomorrow is the battle, they'll miss sacking the city." Eldred shook his head. "I'll have embarrassed him for nothing."

Dreven leaned forward. "What do you mean?"

"He told me last night. He only came because he thought I was the heir. But instead he's here as the guardian of a nobody."

Dreven wiped a few crumbs from the corner of his mouth. "I don't know about that. He seemed excited when the messenger came with your request. And before that he was recounting some part or other of your famed expedition every night. And always very respectful about you. Not a single sour word."

Eldred paused and glanced at Alfred's camp. Alfred and Dederick were scratching in the dirt with sticks as their podmen looked over their shoulders. "That was before I dragged him down here."

Dreven arched an eyebrow. "I suppose. But still, it seems you have some credit with Lord Kenelm. Besides, I think it will look more dramatic with just the two of us out there. When the Corporians look out, they're going to see your hulking self on your giant horse—standing back and watching the fighting. They're going to think you're the king."

Eldred looked thoughtful. "You know I wanted to be king."

Dreven wagged his finger. "You ought to act the part too. You ought to yell out whatever the men are doing. They'll think you're shouting orders."

"Hmm, that would be the giveaway if they knew anything. Deirans fight in silence. They only need the Bond."

"Other Deirans still need to speak. Other Deirans have things worth saying too."

Eldred smiled. "Meaning yourself?"

Dreven nodded. "But if the Corporians get confused and come for you, then I will go from being a steward to being a warrior. What other name applies to a man who kills an enemy in battle."

"The greatest battle of the age—"

"Squire, peasant, steward, warrior. I think it may happen."

"Wouldn't you go back to being a steward after?"

Dreven took a breath. "Never." He looked abruptly out into the darkness of the road. "It's not bad, mind you. Lord Kenelm is a good sort even if he goes on about your expedition more than is interesting. But I would be a warrior, and you can't just lay down your sword and be a steward after that."

Eldred approached and sat on the ground next to Dreven. "You know, when my father went with me to the Academy—when I took the trial—he told Headmaster Tibbot that we—you and I—had passed the trial that day when we practiced before him at the arches. He said that's why I deserved another crack at it. Well, if I passed, then so did you."

Dreven scoffed. "That's the sort of argument that only makes sense when your father is the king."

"Right, well—you're not even eighteen. We will be out there tomorrow while a golden pod fights a huge army. As weak as the Corporians are, that will still have to take some time. There could be transference. You could still take the trial—even though, well, you know."

"Even though I was expelled for cheating."

"If you passed now, it would be proof you hadn't cheated before."

Dreven idly rubbed his hands together. "I guess it might. Or at least might be taken for such. Still, I'll mainly be hoping a few Corporians make it around your father."

"Me too." Eldred frowned at the dirt. "Well, I guess we had best turn in. We still have a two-hour ride in the morning to reach the city."

Dreven raised his chin. "Tomorrow will be our day."

⟡

BATTLE DAY

Dawn arrived with a cloudless sky. By the time sunlight touched the tops of the trees, men were forming up and riding out, urged on by the promise of a warm breakfast up the road at Dederick's camp.

Eldred and Dreven stood side by side, horse bridles in hand, waiting for Alfred to come out of his tent. They shivered each time the pine scented wind came up, slicing through their cloaks.

"Is he ever going to get up? Pounder left half an hour ago. It's time we were going," whispered Dreven.

Eldred nodded. "Oh, he will. He cares about this far more than we do. I expect he's been thinking about this day ever since he decided he would lead the battle himself."

"Then why won't he get off his ass?"

Eldred shrugged. "I don't know. Perhaps he's worried they won't come out. If they would just come out, we wouldn't have to pay anything for the provisions. The whole thing could be settled before a single denarius comes due."

"You're worried about money?"

"I've never owed anyone before. It's unsettling."

Alfred emerged from the tent with a smile on his face, a small loaf of barley bread in hand. As he stood and stretched his back next to Dederick, his podmen collapsed the tent and started to pack it up.

Alfred turned towards Eldred and grunted softly. After a moment's hesitation, he handed the rest of his loaf to Dederick and walked over to Eldred with his arms out, catching Eldred's cold hands in his own. "A fine morning, a beautiful morning, to do the Mother's business."

Eldred nodded. "Did you sleep well?"

"Damn well. I've been too long sleeping in beds." Alfred gulped in a deep breath of the cold air. "This is what life is. The smell of the cook fire, the trees." Alfred glanced at Dreven. "Who's this?"

"That's Dreven," said Eldred.

Dreven gave a short bow.

"Are you one of Kenelm's men?" asked Alfred.

"Yes," said Dreven.

Alfred looked him over. "You don't look long out of the Academy."

"No, I'm not. I was there just six months ago," said Dreven.

"So, you know Eldred," said Alfred.

"I do," said Dreven.

Alfred rubbed his chin. "I don't recall you ascending in the last few trials."

"I—uhh—I didn't pass the trial," said Dreven.

Alfred narrowed his eyes. "Then how did you end up with Kenelm?"

Dreven raised his palms. "I'm his steward. I was expelled from the Academy. I heard—well, some said—that you demanded it."

Alfred jerked his head. "What? You're the farmhand! Why, what in Mother's name are you doing here?" He turned to Eldred and pointed at Dreven. "What is this about? Why are you mixing with this sort again?"

Eldred rose to his full height. "He's my escort. He's the only one here to accompany me since you left Lord Kenelm behind in Bert. All because of a few provisions."

Alfred waved his hand dismissively. "Enough! That's quite enough." He glared Eldred in the eye. "You stay back where you are supposed to. No more of your nonsense. This is no game. Men's lives hang in the balance." Alfred paused for a last disapproving look at Dreven before marching back to his horse, which Mack held by the reins.

Dreven's eyes were open wide. "By the Mother, he doesn't seem to care for me."

"He doesn't care for anyone," said Eldred, placing his hand on Dreven's shoulder. "Don't worry. We have a simple task—hang back and watch them fight. Everything will be fine."

Mack and Bate maneuvered their horses to settle behind Eldred and Dreven. As he passed, Mack spit on the ground, not two inches from Eldred's boot.

Mack grinned as Eldred stepped back. "Time to get on your nags, cheaters. I don't want you holding up my breakfast."

"Watch yourself!" said Eldred.

"I'll be watching you instead, princeling," said Mack.

Eldred and Dreven mounted up and made their way to the road with Mack and Bate tight behind. Shortly after, Alfred and Dederick appeared on their mounts and led the way. Eldred was back in a box of Alfred's podmen, ahead and behind.

Eldred sighed. If only the Corporians had the poor sense to show themselves, then all this unpleasantness could end and he wouldn't owe anything to the stupid provisioners. It could happen. If they came out yesterday, then why not today?

DEDERICK'S CAMP

They had been riding for hours, winding their way up hills and through woods, when Eldred caught a whiff of roasting meat. He turned to Dreven. "Smells like bacon."

Dreven sniffed. "I don't smell anything."

Eldred scanned ahead, looking for Dederick's men through the trees that lined both sides of the road. "It can't be far now."

Dreven sat up higher in the saddle. "I hope they left something for us."

A few minutes later, Alfred and Dederick turned off the road, following a well worn track into the woods. As the party followed after, they came to the periphery of Dederick's camp. Horse lines with dozens of mounts appeared to the sides of the track. Tents and rumpled blankets were scattered in small clearings, but only a few of Dederick's men were visible.

After a turn through a dense patch of trees, the track came to a wide glade bustling with people. From atop Hobbie, Eldred could see everyone. Hundreds of warriors sat in clusters on the flattened grass eating breakfast. Three enormous roasted pigs lay on boards in the middle of the clearing, where stewards hurried to cut everyone a generous portion of pork. Eldred felt his mouth watering.

Eldred hopped down and handed the reins to Dreven. "Watch him. I'll get breakfast."

"Just remember, some of it's for me!" called Dreven, but Eldred was already hurrying away.

Eldred returned to the edge of the glade bearing two platters, one with a measured allotment of meat and rolls and the other heaped with the same.

Dreven eyed the heavier platter in disbelief. "Are you really going to eat all that?"

Eldred motioned towards Alfred, who was seated on a log some ways off with all of his senior warriors crowding around him. "I have to go where he goes. He could be sitting on his horse all day, waiting for the Corporians to show, or he could be all day in their city hunting down their stone bearer. I'll eat while I have the chance."

Dreven shrugged and took his platter. They sat down on the grass and began their feast.

After a few bites, Dreven stopped to wipe the grease from his chin. "You were right about the bacon. You have a good nose for food."

Eldred paused, a roll halfway to his mouth. "I suppose I do." As he chewed, Eldred studied the men around him. Alfred's men had ridden for two hours up a steep mountain road, but they seemed fresher and more boisterous than Dederick's men, who appeared a tad sullen at the arrival of their guests.

Eldred nodded slightly as he gulped down some hot, oily pork. Dederick's men—and Harold's, for that matter—had watched the Corporians parade themselves outside their gate for the last two days. For that was the word—the Corporians had come out the previous day. Either force could have ridden them down and taken the city. But they had followed orders and kept their swords in their sheaths. Today it would be Eldred's turn to follow orders while the golden pod sucked up all the honor. He glanced down and frowned at his plate. He was eating the same food as Father and his golden pod, but they were enjoying a victory feast. Eldred would just watch from the back.

Eldred's mood soured even more as he spotted Harold walking over to Alfred and Dederick with his podmen and Lord Ferris trailing behind.

Dreven followed Eldred's gaze. "Oh, your cousin."

Eldred sniffed. "The heir."

Dreven smiled weakly. "Well, you'll be closer to the action. And, like we said—who knows, perhaps we'll get to fight someone."

Eldred grunted. Across the meadow, Harold didn't bother bowing to Alfred before he set in arguing about some matter.

Dreven stood up to get a better look. "What do you suppose he wants?"

"It could be anything. He has to have everything. Perhaps he wants to lead the charge with his men."

"It might just be something about provisions."

Eldred shook his head. "Nobody cares about provisions anymore. This will be over this afternoon if those Motherless idiots show their faces. Everyone's fighting for their share of honor and loot, trying to wrest a tiny bit from Father and his men. Harold probably wants permission to enter the city first, giving his men first crack at the citizens."

"Hmph. We have to collect enough for three pods. We should go first. You have to ask your father."

Eldred raised an eyebrow. "Just the two of us? The Corporians would kill us."

Dreven pushed Eldred's words to the side with his hand. "Only if they put up a fight. If they cower in their houses, it's only a matter of who gets to the finest houses first. And don't tell me you wouldn't be the best at kicking down doors."

"Well, I might be a good door kicker, but I have to follow Father closely. If we get too far apart, it'll be these men who'll be looting my corpse." Eldred gave the nearby men a calculating look.

"That's unfortunate," said Dreven. "We need treasure enough for three pods."

"Perhaps we can just loot the people who come out to fight. I don't fancy the idea of breaking into people's houses to kill them," said Eldred.

"If you put it that way, it sounds uncivilized. Still, they're invading our lands, and it's going to happen in any case."

Eldred frowned. "I know." After he finished the last of his rolls, he pushed himself onto his feet. "Do you want anything more?"

Dreven made a face. "No, I ate too much."

As Eldred turned towards the makeshift kitchen, Pounder broke through the trees into the glade, riding fast. He waved his right arm as he scattered the seated warriors from his path. "They're coming out! They're coming out!"

Everyone was on their feet as Pounder approached.

"How many?" called Harold.

"All of them! By the Mother, they're pouring out. It's already a thousand, if it's a single one!" cried Pounder.

Alfred narrowed his eyes. "Only a thousand?"

Pounder gestured back in the direction he had come. "They're still coming. The gate's still open."

"Are they keeping to the wall?" asked Dederick.

"Tucked in there like a litter of piglets," said Pounder.

Alfred clapped his hands together. "Then it's time for the slaughter! Men, line up. It's time to ride. Get moving!"

"Find your mounts!" shouted Dederick. "We're going too!"

The men surged into motion; Alfred's men formed up in the center of the glade while Dederick's men clumped together in groups on the edge of the woods. Eldred and Dreven found their way to the rear of Alfred's formation, followed by their shadows, Mack and Bate.

Eldred smiled into Mack's glare. "So you are out of the fighting, too?"

"Shut up, princeling," said Mack.

At the front, flanked by Pounder and Stace, Alfred raised Capito in a salute. "We are the purest, the ones favored by the Mother—her last and greatest creation. These men lining up by their walls may as well be dung rats." The men laughed. "That's right. I expect an army of rats would have more spirit than these dull-witted fools. We'll kill them all and not lose a single man. That's my plan! That's what I can do!"

A cheer rose from the men in the glade. "Kill them all! Kill them all!"

Alfred smiled fiercely. "When I became king and had my first blood match with the Maldavians, my advisors said I couldn't fight four hundred men with only fifty warriors. It couldn't be done, they said. They said it wouldn't work. I won't do that, I told them. So you'll withdraw, they asked. No, I said, I'll fight. But how, they asked. I told them that I would fight only fifty Maldavians. But they have three hundred more than that, my advisors said, their knees shaking. They were scared. I said the other Madavians will just have to wait their turn to die!"

"Kill them all! Kill them all!" shouted the men.

Alfred opened his mouth wide. "We have even more work ahead of us today, thousands of enemies in the field, a mass of archers hunkered over atop the wall thinking we don't see them, and only a hundred of us. Mother have mercy." Alfred raised his hands to his face in a pantomime of fear as his man laughed. "Mercy on those cowards, that is. Some might have to wait an hour for their death. There'll be no mercy from us. I won't let these Motherless worms pollute our land for even one extra minute. First, we kill those outside. Then we butcher those cowering within. It may take all day, but we will kill the lot of them."

"Now—" Alfred pointed at his troops standing in front of him—"you're the killers. You'll kill the most. But you—"Alfred waved to Dederick's men, who were looking on with stony faces— "you get to kill your share too—and enjoy your share of the bounty. First, hold position! You must wait for us. Once we have the gate, then you come riding quickly. Once in the city, everyone's sword is free."

Dederick raised his fist. "For the king!"

"For the king!" echoed the men.

Alfred nodded, then looked to Pounder, who pointed at Eldred. Alfred peered over at Eldred. "We're good! Follow me, men. It's time."

To Battle

Alfred led the procession out through the eastern edge of the glade with his men lined up in pairs. After them came Eldred and Dreven, right behind Mack and Bate. Dederick and his two hundred brought up the rear. The track started off flat with scattered trees and bushes to either side and continued that way for about a mile. Eldred heard the river before he saw it. He came out of the trees and saw a windswept hill of waving grass rising steeply from the far bank.

Alfred's men stepped their horses down the muddy bank into the river at its widest point, perhaps a hundred feet across. As Eldred urged Hobbie into the water after them, Harold's forces emerged from another path. Harold led them out—charging forward—cutting off Dederick, who resignedly pulled up his horse and brought his men to a halt.

Harold chased after Eldred and Dreven as their horses waded through the stream. Dreven's mare was practically swimming, but Hobbie strode forward comfortably, the water barely coming up to Eldred's ankles.

"Come out to watch men fight, Eldred?" called Harold.

Eldred looked back. "Same as you."

Harold offered a thin smile. "Not the same as me. I'm leading more than five hundred warriors." He gestured at Dreven. "You just have him."

Dreven jerked his head around. "I'll kill as many today as anyone."

Harold shook his head. "I know who you are. I know what you are—just another peasant boy in over his depth."

"Only till we get out of the river," said Dreven.

Eldred smiled. "We'll be up by the fighting anyway. We might actually get some honor if someone slips through." He pointed at Harold. "You have to hang back until they take the gate. How it's changed. Before I came back, all of this was going to be yours. This was to be your victory, your triumph. Now, you're just a bystander."

Harold glared.

"What were you arguing about with the king, anyway?" asked Dreven.

Harold stiffened. "What? Are you speaking to me?"

"Back at Dederick's camp, you were arguing with the king," continued Dreven.

Harold scoffed. "Nothing of your concern, boy."

"I bet you wanted to lead the charge. Isn't that right, cousin?" asked Eldred.

"No. That's not it. I told him that he didn't have enough men. We counted them yesterday—more than three thousand warriors. Even if they're Corporian with two left feet, that is too many for a golden pod, even a 'perfect' golden pod."

"Three thousand?" said Dreven.

"Yes. I heard him telling the old story about his first blood match as I left the camp. He doesn't seem to understand the math is different this time," said Harold.

Eldred looked Harold in the eye as Hobbie stepped up out of the water. "Bonded warriors are the greatest creation of the Night Mother."

Harold slid his eyes away to glance at Dreven as he rode up onto the bank after Eldred. "But Deiran stewards are just glorified servants. Best you turn and flee when the king and his warriors get swallowed up. But don't come riding towards me. You'll find that Corporian scum have just as much respect for you as I do."

Dreven flushed and started to turn back towards Harold, but Eldred pointed to Mack and Bate who had ridden ahead. "Pay him no mind. Look, we fell behind."

Dreven gave Harold a hard look but trotted after Eldred on the track that led up the hill. Harold watched them go, a big grin on his face, sitting on the bank while his men swelled up around him.

The track rose through a series of grueling switchbacks as it climbed the hill. With no trees, the sun beat down, quickly drying Eldred's clothes. The men in the golden pod were well mounted on strong horses and—of course—Hobbie made the climb seem effortless, but Dreven's mare struggled on the ascent, and the two men fell further back. Down below, Harold's men had finished crossing the river and started up the track. Dederick's men took their turn in the water.

Eldred and Dreven were three quarters of the way up the hill when the last of Alfred's men disappeared over the rise. Eldred eyed Dreven's horse with concern; it was foaming at the mouth.

"Is she alright?" asked Eldred.

Dreven slowed his mount as he gently stroked her neck. "She'll be fine. It's been two long days in the saddle and now this endless hill."

Eldred glanced back towards Harold, who was closing the distance rapidly. He would certainly pass Dreven's hapless horse shortly. A flush of embarrassment filled Eldred. "I don't want to get too far away from Father. He should've stopped at the crest. You know—umm—you know what will happen if he gets too far away."

Dreven hopped down to walk beside his tottering mount. "Well, don't wait for me. I'll find you up there."

Eldred glanced back at Harold, now only a hundred feet behind. "We won't start the attack until everyone is up top."

Dreven nodded. "Right."

"Very well," said Eldred. He patted Hobbie lightly on the neck, and the horse bounded forward.

When Eldred turned at the next switchback, he muttered a curse. Harold had come abreast of Dreven and was keeping pace with him. It looked as if they were arguing. Eldred was of mind to turn back, but he still couldn't see Alfred over the crest of the hill. He pressed on.

THE PLATEAU

After passing the last switchback, the track leveled out and entered a vast grass covered plateau. Alfred's men formed up in a single line facing the immense Corporian city which sat square in the middle of the flat a mile away. Eldred gazed at the city as he made his way towards Alfred, who was out in front of his men alongside Pounder talking to some of Dederick's scouts.

The massive stone walls of the city had a reddish hue, which lent them an alien presence. Only a few squat towers showed over the fortifications. A giant mass of men milled around outside, lining the length of the forward wall, split to either side of a wide gate set in the center. Men still trickled out to add to the formation. Thousands. It had to be thousands. They looked well equipped too, with gray shields and long spears.

Atop the walls stretched a thin line of archers, a smattering of women in their company. Unlike the warriors below, they wore no helmets. Their tanned faces and bright green eyes matched the descriptions of Corporians that Eldred recalled from the old stories, though the variety in their hair color was something of a surprise. A few had normal black hair, but others showed red, brown and blonde hair, as if their stone bearer couldn't make up her mind.

"Eldred, get over here!" shouted Alfred.

Eldred pulled his attention away from the city. Alfred and Pounder were facing him with expectant faces. Eldred placed his hand on Hobbie's neck and approached.

As Eldred reached them, Alfred grimaced. "About time. I thought you were supposed to have the fastest horse."

"I do. I was with Dreven," said Eldred.

Alfred scanned the surroundings. "And where is he?"

"He is still coming up the hill. His horse was—having difficulties."

Alfred waved his hand dismissively. "Well, we won't be waiting on him."

Eldred glanced over to where Harold was just entering the plateau. "He should be just behind Harold."

"I have reports that they are standing on some red stones," said Alfred. "Make use of those eyes of yours and tell me what you see."

Eldred squinted. "I—I can't really see much of the ground. There's too many men."

Alfred turned to Pounder. "I told you so. He can't see the stones if they are standing on them."

Pounder nodded. "Yes, but I think we should know more. It's all footmen. These rocks could be there to trip up our horses."

Eldred gestured towards the wall. "I see archers too."

"We know, Eldred. I was just asking you about the stones," said Alfred.

At that moment, Dreven crested the plateau on foot, leading his mare.

Alfred blew out his breath. "Oh, there he is. That's inspiring. Can he manage a little ride towards the city? He'd better. Because if there is a single mention of his name in the stories of this day, I'll make you sorry—and it will be far worse for him."

Eldred's face grew tight. "Yes, Father."

The last of Harold's men rode past Dreven as Eldred approached. Dreven flashed a smile. "I think she's doing better, and it looks level from here."

Eldred waved at Dederick, who was leading his men up onto the plateau, before turning his attention back to Dreven. "Good. We don't have long. Father won't give the Corporians a chance to change their minds."

Dreven patted the mare's neck. She was breathing easier. "She's definitely better."

The sounds of hoofbeats filled the air. Eldred turned to see Alfred's men trotting forward. "Good, because they're off. He's not even waiting for Dederick to get in position."

Dreven gingerly put his foot in the stirrup and carefully mounted his horse. He sat and stared at Alfred's advancing pod and the huge host that awaited them. He cast a quick eye back towards Harold's line, five hundred strong. "Perhaps your cousin is right. Your father should take everyone. They've a lot of warriors over there."

Eldred raised his eyebrows. "So now you agree with Harold?"

"Only on this point."

Eldred tapped Hobbie. "Let's go."

BATTLE

Alfred and Pounder led the golden pod forward at a measured trot with Eldred and Dreven trailing behind. Eldred kept glancing over the Corporian host, a hard knot settling in his stomach. Hobbie was the fastest, but was there some way down off the plateau that was not packed with Deirans or Corporians? If he became separated from Alfred, both armies would be a danger.

When the line of riders came within a hundred yards from the wall, the arrows started flying. The battle was on. The pod split into two galloping wings, one with Alfred, the other with Pounder. They streaked to the left and the right, men low in the saddle, wielding their bucklers to block arrows with precise movements—they had all passed the rock throwing trials at Boar's Tusk. A few archers appeared to target Eldred and Dreven, who were hanging back, but none of their arrows had the reach.

As the Deirans closed on the Corporian line, they unleashed their veruta, hurling them into the ranks. Most bounced harmlessly from raised shields, but a number found their mark. Alfred got two, Pounder at least one. Dozens of Corporians slouched over, injured or dead—Eldred couldn't tell which with the masses of men pressed around them. The wings swept by each other as they made a long pass of the Corporian line, slowing as they approached the end. The Corporians stayed put, uninterested in pursuit.

After a brief pause, Alfred started another pass, and Pounder followed suit. But it was an empty gesture as most of the Deirans had already thrown all their veruta. Only a handful of Corporians fell. Again, the golden pod slowed as they broke away, but the Corporians kept their feet planted on the ground. Alfred steered his men away from the walls as the Corporian archers continued their attack. Eldred scanned over the men. Nobody had any serious injuries.

Dreven gestured at the enemy ranks. "They didn't give chase. Seems they're brighter than Mercians."

Eldred shot Dreven a look. "Look at their numbers. Maybe they should charge."

Dreven smiled weakly. "Sorry. Just—you know—once they move, that would be the death of them."

Eldred shook his head and looked up at the archers on the wall, trying to discern if they had likewise run low on missiles. As he looked through their ranks, he spotted someone—a noble woman whose handsome face framed with blond tresses appeared at most a few years older than Eldred's, dressed in a flowing white gown better suited to a party than a battle. Her arms glittered with silver and gold bracelets, but it was her eyes that entranced Eldred, deep green eyes. They radiated a mischievous charm as she smiled down on Alfred's retreating force. She leaned over the wall and spread her arms wide. As if on cue, the Corporians began to wave their arms and chant, "She can, she can." They kept repeating it over and over.

Eldred mulled over the meaning as Alfred and Pounder brought the wings of the golden pod back together. He turned to Dreven. "She can do what?"

"What?" asked Dreven.

Eldred pointed at the Corporian line. "'She can'—what they're saying."

Dreven's lips twisted in a reluctant grin. "They're saying 'chicken'. Look, see they're moving their arms—like a chicken."

Realization dawned on Eldred as he looked again—they were flapping their arms. The woman above was laughing now, sharing her mirth with two handmaidens who stood close behind her. "Oh, the accent. But—but it's only them who have died. We haven't taken any casualties."

Dreven squinted. "It seems to me as if they have just as many as they started with for all practical purposes."

Eldred gave a small nod. It was true.

Alfred looked fit to burst. Whether from the taunting or because he had been obliged to retreat, Eldred couldn't tell.

Pounder approached Alfred hesitantly. "We could use the veruta from Harold and Dederick's men. If we make a few more passes, we might loosen them up."

Alfred rolled his eyes. "Do you think so? You think they will just stand there while we kill them fifty at a time? Do you think they will wait while you go down in the woods and whittle up a thousand veruta? Use your brain!

They can just walk back through their bloody gate whenever they like."

Pounder flinched. "Sorry."

Alfred turned towards Harold's formation and raised his fist. Then he opened and closed his hand ten times. There was a stirring in Harold's line as some of his men started forward.

On the wall, the lady—was she their stone bearer?—leaned forward, a pleased expression on her face, no sign of concern at all.

"Reinforcements?" asked Stace, who had come up behind Pounder.

Alfred's face turned red. "Don't be stupid. They'll be holding our horses. We're going in on foot."

The nearby warriors turned to look at the Corporians, who were nearly dancing as they shouted their taunts.

Pounder glanced at Stace and then turned back to Alfred. "They have numbers. We can even things out a lot if we take Harold and Dederick. We go from one hundred to eight hundred."

Alfred pressed his lips tight. "You think I don't know that? Dismount!"

There was a momentary hesitation.

Alfred barked, "Get off your Motherless horses! It's time to do warriors' work. What did you all think my golden pod was meant for? Did you think we were headed to a tea party?"

The men stepped down. Ten pods of Harold's men came up to meet them. Eldred noticed Lord Ferris among the riders. The man's dark eyes focused on Eldred momentarily as he approached. Eldred met his stare with a steely look.

Harold's men looked disappointed as they came to understand the situation. They had ridden forward to do battle, but now sat with reins of Alfred's mounts in hand. Eldred looked back to give Lord Ferris an amused smile, but only the merest flicker stirred in Lord Ferris's dead eyes.

Alfred faced his men. "You said you wanted to kill them all. Well, here's your chance. They have some pretty gray shields and some spears, but behind those they're just Corporian bastards waiting for their turn to die. I don't think we'll win. I know we will. Who are the real warriors? Show me now! Fall in!" With that, Alfred started marching towards the city walls.

The men came up around him without comment, silent in the Deiran way, forming a crescent two men deep in front of Alfred. Ahead of them, the cries of the Corporians became jubilant. Eldred watched nervously as the arrows started to fall again on the golden pod. They looked so few. A glance at Dreven's face confirmed he felt the same.

The Corporians held their position, waiting for the Deirans to advance through the hail of missiles, but they had the decency to stop their taunts. The golden pod moved forward unhurriedly, casually blocking the aimed missiles without a care. Eldred felt an odd sensation as they made contact with the Corporian line. The ringing of swords filled the air.

Eldred could see everything from atop Hobbie. As he watched, a smile started to spread across his face. His hands felt warm, and he felt light in a strange way, almost giddy.

"Oh," said Dreven, standing up in his stirrups to see better.

The Deirans were a blur of motion against a sea of gray shields, laying one flat after another. Finally set to motion, the Corporians looked to swallow the small crescent of warriors by flooding in from the sides, but to no avail. The golden pod defended itself fiercely, showing the same adroit defense that Alfred had used against Harold in their scrimmage. Stab where the enemy would, the offending spear was blocked or dodged. The bonded warriors, meanwhile, drew blood everywhere—twice as fast, twice as strong and above all, fearless.

The golden pod pressed slowly for the gate, surrounded on all sides by a convulsing mass of Corporian soldiers. Eldred could only make out the falling waves of the taller Corporians. Eldred glanced to the wall where the graceful woman still stood. She was looking out past the carnage, calmly studying the disposition of Harold and Dederick's men in the back. When she briefly rested her eyes on the area near Eldred, he waved to her. She blinked in surprise. Eldred made a clumsy half bow in his saddle, which earned him a confused smile before she turned her attention back to the battle below.

"Well met," came a voice behind Eldred.

He turned to see Lord Kenelm riding past Lord Ferris, followed by his men. Brun looked sour but ready for battle. Hallet looked surprisingly fresh. The others, including young Dogory and old Frewin, looked ready for bed. Dreven cheered and clapped his hands.

"You made it!" shouted Eldred.

Lord Kenelm smiled tiredly, shading his red eyes. "We rode all night. We didn't even stop for food." He gestured towards the walls. "What's happening?"

"We're killing them. They can't touch us," said Dreven.

Lord Kenelm leaned on the pommel of his saddle. "Good. I'm happy to leave it to Alfred today." He motioned his men into a line with Eldred and Dreven at the center.

"Don't relax too much. Once Father takes the gate, everyone will come up. Then it's on to the city. Just a few minutes more," said Eldred.

Lord Kenelm covered a yawn. "It's a large city. I expect it'll take hours to kill everyone."

"Hours to loot everyone, anyway," said Dreven.

"I hope they have pretty coins. I don't want a pocket full of old maids," said Hallet.

"Gold and silver in any form suits me. You can melt it down," said Brun.

"I bet their temples have gold," said Hallet excitedly.

Brun nodded. "We'll find the most riches wherever their stone bearer is hiding."

Eldred nodded slowly. "That's true." He looked up again at the noble woman, who appeared transfixed as she studied Alfred's rampaging warriors below. Would she escape? He was surprised to find himself hoping she would. He didn't want her coins.

In the battle, the golden pod cut through the center of the Corporian lines, drawing close to the still open gate. Perhaps five hundred dead enemy warriors lay scattered before the walls, lying on the suspect red stones that had worried Alfred moments before. Eldred spotted three broken Deirans amidst the corpses and wondered if Alfred had chosen them by mistake. Nevertheless, those bonded warriors who remained appeared more than the match of the cowardly Corporians, fairly called so now as their lines began to break. A mass of them streamed back inside the city.

"Who're the chickens now?" crowed Dreven, but nobody laughed.

The expression of the Corporian noblewoman turned grave. As Eldred watched, she raised her fist above her head. Behind her, the handmaidens lifted red banners and began waving them frantically. Eldred looked around expectantly. Would a fresh host burst out through the gate? Had she summoned some tamed dragon?

Instead, Eldred's eyes went wide as a powerful wave of nausea swept through him, leaving his hands clammy and wet. A sensation of white hot heat started at his feet and slowly rose through his body—through his calf, through his legs, past his groin, up through his stomach—while Eldred screamed with all of the strength of his lungs.

Lord Kenelm stepped his horse closer, grabbing at Eldred. "What's wrong?"

When the wave reached Eldred's head, it was as if a thousand hammers were pounding his mind into oblivion. He was gone.

ESCAPE

Eldred stirred and found himself lying on the ground. His eyes were open, or he thought they were, but he couldn't see anything; he couldn't move. There were voices. Lord Kenelm was saying something Eldred couldn't make out. Brun kept repeating that it was time to go. Dreven's voice was close, like he was right beside Eldred.

"Pull him up!' shouted Dreven.

It occurred to Eldred that Dreven was talking about him. Slowly the mottled darkness began to lift. He became aware of a foul taste on his tongue. He blinked and noticed Dreven was straining to push him up from under his right shoulder, Dreven's face trembling with effort. A sickening turn of his head showed Lord Kenelm wrestling with his other arm. He felt multiple hands grabbing at his sides and legs. They were lifting him towards Hobbie, trying to place him in the saddle as the horse knelt.

"No time! No time!" shouted Brun—panic clear in his voice—but the men kept to their task and set Eldred in place.

Eldred reached out and weakly grabbed Hobbie's neck, his legs dangling uselessly below him.

"I've got him," said Dreven, perching on the back of the saddle.

Eldred felt Dreven's arms around him as Hobbie stood up—steady as a table—and he gasped at what he saw. The Corporians were coming. Running forward in packs. Coming by the hundreds, by the thousands. Eldred saw them for just a moment, still choking on the vile taste in his mouth before Hobbie carefully turned and trotted away from the city.

Looking into the sun felt like a dagger probing Eldred's brain. The shouts of the Corporians boomed behind him. Eldred couldn't make out their new cry, but he hardly cared. Before him, the Deirans swept away in full retreat.

Tears came to his eyes—seven hundred Deirans fleeing from a rabble army scattered across an open field. How could it be?

Dreven pulled Eldred back as he started to slide off. "I have you."

Eldred glanced to his right. Lord Kenelm was hunched in his saddle, his face pale. Eldred spat, trying to clear his mouth. "What's happening? Why do we run?"

Lord Kenelm shook his head listlessly. "We don't have it."

"Have what?"

"The Bond. We don't have the Bond."

Eldred fought down the bile rising in this throat. "How?"

A grating voice snapped at Eldred from behind him. "You fell." It was Brun.

Eldred tried to turn but couldn't. "What?"

"What did you do? You were screaming and fell and then it was like something hit me in the nethers and the Bond was gone," said Brun.

Eldred shut his eyes. The light was too bright. "I didn't do anything."

"I heard you drove the warriors at Boar's Tusk mad!" shouted Brun.

"That's enough," said Lord Kenelm.

A verutum crashed to the ground a few feet ahead of Hobbie. Eldred opened his eyes at the sound and then snapped them shut, trying to block the light. The Corporians were throwing veruta, throwing the Deiran's own weapons at them. A thought bubbled up in Eldred's head. "Where's Father? I can't be away from him."

"He fell. They all fell when you did," said Lord Kenelm.

"That's what I said. It all happened when you fell!" barked Brun.

Eldred tried and failed to push himself upright. "I have to get back."

Dreven patted his arm. "It's alright. Nobody has the Bond. You're safe."

"This is all that bastard's fault!" shouted Brun, getting louder.

"Shut it," hissed Lord Kenelm. "We can settle this back at camp."

Eldred closed his eyes again as Brun mumbled something incoherent. They were dead then: Father, Pounder, the others—their blood likely still oozing out onto the red stones. Did they even wake to know it? It hadn't been him. It couldn't have been. It was the noble woman. It had to be. She had not cut Father's throat, but she had brought them all down. He felt tired and empty. Father was gone, and the world seemed different.

The last of the other Deirans were disappearing over the lip of the plateau, perhaps two hundred yards ahead. No more veruta fell. They were clear. As they came to the track down the hill, they formed a single line with

Lord Kenelm in front. Eldred and Dreven were right behind on Hobbie.

Eldred covered his eyes with his hands and peeked out through the gaps between his fingers. The tail end of Harold's forces were crossing the river below. "I can't go to the camp. There'll be someone there, some warrior. I can't be down there without Father."

"We have to get down from here," said Dreven.

Lord Kenelm glanced back, a worried look in his eye. "There will be warriors most places."

"Let's just get off this Motherless hill!" called Brun.

Lord Kenelm nodded. "We'll start with that."

"Fine," muttered Eldred, one hand plastered over his right eye while the other gripped Hobbie's mane.

They were three quarters the way down when Dreven called out, "They're waiting for us!"

Eldred spread his fingers slightly and peered through to see Lord Ferris sitting on his horse with three pods arrayed around him. "No! They're waiting for me."

"What?" grunted Lord Kenelm.

Eldred shut his eyes. "It's Ferris. He has three pods."

Lord Kenelm blew out his breath. "Three. That's the match of us. That bastard. I'll kill him."

"Or he'll kill you," said Eldred softly. "I can't go down there anyway. You have to get me away from here."

Lord Kenelm said nothing and continued down the hill.

"What are you doing?" asked Eldred.

Lord Kenelm shrugged. "It's too steep. This path is the only way we're getting you down the hill in your saddle. And Lord Ferris—as you know better than most—he acts dangerous, but he's a coward. We'll get off this hill, then we'll find somewhere to go."

"Let him fight," said Dreven.

When they reached the base of the hill, Lord Ferris's men formed a line and started forward. It was a moment before Lord Kenelm said anything. He was probably used to just thinking of what he needed his men to do. "Match their line. Eldred, Dreven hang back."

Eldred frowned as he looked over Lord Kenelm's men. They looked half dead already, and now they didn't have the Bond. The only reassuring aspect was that Lord Ferris's podmen appeared only slightly fresher.

Lord Ferris approached to a distance of fifty feet and halted.

"What do you want, Ferris?" croaked Lord Kenelm.

Lord Ferris pointed at Eldred. "I'm taking him."

"No. You're not. He's the king's son," said Lord Kenelm.

Lord Ferris gave a faint smile. "As of this day, he is the king's cousin, and he's coming with me."

"Move aside," said Lord Kenelm, drawing his sword.

Lord Ferris stayed put, leaning back in his saddle and crossing his arms. "I think you ought to give this some consideration, Kenelm. This time it's you who needs to adapt to changed circumstances."

Lord Kenelm paused for only a moment. "Draw swords!" His men drew their blades.

"By the Mother, he's going to do it," said Lord Ferris with a laugh. "The man has no sense. Swords free! You can kill any man, except for Eldred. King Harold wants him alive."

Both sides held up their swords, but neither moved. It was different without the Bond, and they all looked pasty and sweaty, like the kick to the nethers that Brun had mentioned earlier had just been delivered.

Loed Ferris waved his arm. "Go on! Do it! They're right there!"

The men on Lord Ferris's left edged forward, but those on his right stayed put. Lord Kenelm stepped his horse forward and the scrimmage was joined.

Eldred peeked through his fingers as the men exchanged weak sword thrusts. The first man to fall—one of Lord Kenelm's—was knocked out of his saddle and struck the ground where he sluggishly dodged the horse's hooves.

This opened a gap in Lord Kenelm's line which Lord Ferris and two of his men took advantage of, riding straight at Eldred, swords raised. Eldred tried to take his hands from Hobbie's neck but couldn't keep his balance without holding on. Hobbie backed away.

"Hold on!" said Dreven, who snatched a verutum hanging from the side of Hobbie's saddle and hopped down. Of all of them, he was the only one untouched by the Corporians' spell.

Dreven sprinted towards the man in front and stabbed up at him, catching him in the gut. The man screamed and dropped down behind his horse. Lord Ferris tried to run Dreven down, but Dreven dodged aside and jumped up to club Lord Ferris on the back with his short spear. Lord Ferris let out a cry and dropped his sword.

"To me! To me!" screamed Lord Ferris, turning to flee for the second time that day as Dreven chased in pursuit, but the other man continued towards Eldred, raising his sword with a shaking arm.

"Dreven!" cried Eldred, but it was too late.

The warrior closed the distance on Eldred and thrusted out to stab Hobbie in the neck.

"No!' shouted Eldred as the great horse toppled out from underneath him, dropping him hard to the ground.

Eldred lay dazed, watching Hobbie kick and scream. The warrior stepped his horse to the side, clear of Hobbie's hooves and stared at Eldred with clouded eyes. He could have easily dismounted and killed Eldred, except for Lord Ferris's orders. Suddenly, Hobbie seized up, clenching his legs tight, and moved no more.

Tears of rage squeezed out through Eldred's eyes. He turned to the lurking warrior. "You Motherless bastard!"

The man shifted in his saddle, pointing his sword at Eldred. But before he could make a move, Dreven appeared behind him and hurled the verutum into the man's back. The man crumpled forward and slid off his horse.

Dreven rushed up, kneeling beside Eldred. "Are you hit?"

Eldred gave him a weak push. "It's Hobbie."

Dreven glanced blankly at the still horse. The blood was still flowing from his neck wound. "He's gone."

"Kill them!" snarled Eldred, trembling with rage. "Kill them all."

Dreven glanced back to the melee. Lord Kenelm had been unhorsed but was still fighting back against two mounted men, weaving about on unsteady feet. Hallet lay on the ground, eyes open and empty. Brun was in retreat with two of Lord Ferris's men chasing after him. Lord Ferris hung back while his men pressed their advantage.

Dreven took a breath. "I will!" He dashed to the corpse of the warrior he had just struck and jerked the verutum out of his back. He sprinted to the aid of Lord Kenelm, skewering one of his assailants in the leg. When that man turned and fled, his leg wet with blood, Dreven stabbed the second in the groin, dropping the screaming man to the ground where Lord Kenelm finished him before dropping to his knees, exhausted. The tide was turning.

Dreven ranged through the melee, the sole combatant with any energy, stabbing any opponent who held their ground. In a few minutes, it was over. Lord Ferris rode towards the ford with eight shaky men in tow, several bearing deep wounds. Dreven leaned on his spear, watching them go. He had pursued them twenty yards down the road.

Lord Kenelm still knelt beside the body of the man he had killed, breathing hard. Dogory, the youngest of Lord Kenelm's men, was still in his saddle. Colle, the leader of the third pod, was wrapping bandages around the arm of Frewin, the most grizzled of Lord Kenelm's men. Edwy lay gasping on his back; he looked to have multiple wounds. The rest all lay still, quiet, except for two of Lord Ferris's men who lay on the ground, but still had strength enough to groan.

Brun returned to the battle site and dismounted next to Lord Kenelm, helping him to his feet. He gestured at Lord Ferris's men. "What about those two?"

Lord Kenelm grimaced, his face pale except for a bright red cut above his right eye. "Leave them. Collect all the mounts you can. Get everyone up who can ride. We leave now."

Brun's eyes narrowed. "What? You're going to leave our men for the crows?"

Lord Kenelm licked his lips. "It's a ten-minute ride to the camp. We have no time."

Brun turned to glare at Eldred, who had dragged himself over to Hobbie's body, pulling himself up to where he could gently stroke Hobbie's neck. "He'll get us all killed."

Lord Kenelm frowned. "We're here to protect him. That's why we came. Now get moving! Colle, give him Mouse. You and Brun help Dreven get Eldred up. And somebody look after Edwy. I'm not leaving him."

Dreven peeled Eldred's arms free of Hobbie's neck. "It's time to go," he said softly.

The tears ran freely down Eldred's face. "He was a champion. The greatest horse in Turicum. The greatest horse."

Colle got one arm while Dreven struggled with the other. Brun sighed and grabbed Eldred around the waist. Mouse, Colle's enormous Shire horse, stared blankly down at Eldred. The large man's horse was the only suitable choice.

"Can you get him to kneel?" asked Dreven.

Colle shook his head. "We need to get him up."

"Pull yourself up or we'll leave you," said Brun.

"No," said Dreven.

"Shut up, steward!" snapped Brun.

"Not anymore! I drove them off and saved your sorry life," said Dreven.

"Calm down; you're spooking Mouse," said Colle.

The horse had taken two steps to the side.

"Come here, sweet boy," said Colle, steadying his horse.

Eldred reached out and grabbed the saddle.

"That's it," said Dreven.

It took another few minutes, but they shoved Eldred up into the saddle, and Dreven climbed on behind him. By that time, the others were assembled.

Lord Kenelm started north along the river, slouched over on his saddle. Seven riders followed after: Brun, turning to look out for pursuit; Dogory, whose youthful face was blank with exhaustion; Colle, the giant Deiran who had passed his horse to Eldred; Frewin, the old campaigner with a sour disposition; and Edwy, wrapped in red spotted bandages and clinging to his horse. Eldred and Dreven made up the balance on Mouse, who was proving to be a suitable riding horse.

Eldred took one last tearful glance at Hobbie as they rode away, lying beautiful in death as he had been in life. "We chose each other," he whispered.

FLIGHT

They had not been riding long before Brun started up. "What're we doing?"

Lord Kenelm glanced back, his face haggard with exhaustion. "We're getting some distance."

Brun threw up his hands. "Barely. They'll catch us within the hour if they mean to."

Lord Kenelm took a ragged breath. "We're on the Corporian side of the river. They may think twice while they lack the Bond."

Brun raised his chin. "Maybe we should too."

Lord Kenelm made a dismissive gesture. "It's my decision."

Brun turned to glare at Eldred, who was one horse back behind Dogory. "You heard Lord Ferris. Harold's the new king, and he wants him."

Lord Kenelm nodded. "I heard."

Brun turned rigid. "Well, are you supporting him? Are you supporting Eldred's claim? Because it must seem to everyone that you are."

Lord Kenelm rode on without answering.

Brun pointed back at Eldred. "We'd be the only ones supporting that claim. Harold's men up front, they saw what happened. They saw what he did. And even besides that, who's going to stand for him?"

Lord Kenelm shook his head slowly from side to side. "This is not about that. This is not about Harold as king or Eldred as king. We're here to keep him safe. Back there, that was our dealings with Lord Ferris."

"We killed five men!" snapped Brun.

"You didn't," said Dreven.

Brun snapped around at Dreven. "What's gotten into you, boy?"

Dreven straightened himself in the saddle. "I drove them off while you fled."

Brun's face flared red. "I'll shut your mouth."

"You want to try?" asked Dreven.

Eldred cleared his throat. "I'll make no claim. Harold is king."

Everyone turned to look at him.

Eldred's chin trembled for just a moment. "I didn't do anything up there by the city. I just fell. That's all. So stop saying that I did. But for the crown, Harold is who Father wanted. If he's dead up there"—Eldred mashed his lips together—"if he's dead, well, then Harold's the rightful king."

Dreven placed his hand on Eldred's shoulder.

Brun gestured back the way they had come. "Then why are we running?"

"I can't go back there. Someone will kill me," said Eldred.

Lord Kenelm grunted. "We'll figure this out. These dealings are best done across a high wall. We'll get to Evenwood and work things out. Back there, that was just me and Ferris. Everyone knows how it is with us. Just because he says he's on a mission from the king doesn't mean I can't fight him."

Brun narrowed his eyes at Eldred. "We have warriors in Evenwood too."

Eldred sighed. "I know."

CAMP

As evening came on, Eldred looked around the campfire, listening to the burbling river nearby. Lord Kenelm and his men lay sprawled on the ground; not one had been awake even two minutes after they had settled down. Only Dreven had any life in him, and he was out hunting for food in the trees and low bushes that marked the area. Evening is a good time for a hunt, especially if you have no food.

As Eldred settled his back against a tree trunk, he stole a worried look at his legs. They were as limp as noodles and had no feeling. Reluctantly, he poked his thigh—nothing. He pinched his knee—also nothing. But he could feel his butt planted firmly on the ground. He had strength up through his back. And his manhood—that worked; he could feel that. He shuddered in relief.

His left hand stole up to his fatum lapides, running behind his left temple, while his right hand gripped a tree root, keeping him balanced. "How long?" he muttered. Even one fatum lapis was known to cure serious injuries, and he had three.

They'd said he'd fallen. Hobbie was tall—he squeezed his lips tight at the thought of his dear horse. But a fall like that, it would never hurt a Mercian. A Mercian could get up from anything. He continued tracing his fingers over his head. There was a roundish lump on the right side of his head above the ear. It didn't hurt. Could that have done the damage? A blow to the head, it might do anything; it could make you go lame. A little cut at the base of his skull on the back of the neck—how did that happen? It had already crusted over. There was no stinging; the skin felt fine all around it.

Eldred sniffed and reached inside the jacket, the fine blue and gray leather jacket that Sammanus had gifted him. The packets were there, still intact. Why wouldn't they be? He swallowed and looked at Brun's face as he lay sleeping. The man still looked angry; even his snoring had a nasty ripping sound.

It would be good to be able to walk now. The powder—that was the key to defeating Capuan, to laying the Mercian king to rest in a duel. But to die with two full packets of Balaur powder, that would be the stupidest mistake he could make. Eldred glanced through the trees. It was dark enough now that his night vision was starting to work. Why wouldn't his legs move? What if they came when he was like this, just sitting—a lame man leaning up against a tree. He'd die.

He spotted Dreven off in the distance. He had something in hand, some reward for his effort. As he got closer, Eldred made out one rabbit and a skinny pheasant. A wide smile came immediately to Eldred's face. It had been a day for Dreven. On a day when everything else had gone wrong, the lad had come through—the man had come through. He'd gotten Eldred off that disastrous plateau, driven off Lord Ferris and his men, and now this—a successful hunt to top off the day.

Dreven paused at the edge of the camp by the horses, eyeing the sleeping men. "Just you and me for dinner then. Do you want the bird or the rabbit?"

"I'll take the bird," said Eldred.

"Very well," said Dreven. He settled by the fire and started to pluck the bird's wings, making quick snapping movements with his wrist as he pulled the feathers free. "How do you feel?"

"Worried."

Dreven continued on the bird for a moment. "Are you sure about giving it up?"

"The crown?" asked Eldred.

"Yes."

Eldred shrugged. "It seemed it already gave itself up. I couldn't even go to the camp to argue with Harold. Someone would go crazy—some warrior. There must have been one that stayed back. So—it's gone. I'm set for Tyrus like I told you back in Bert."

Dreven nodded. "Right."

Eldred glanced away.

"I'm sorry about Hobbie. He seemed like a great horse," said Dreven.

Eldred rubbed his eyes. "He was. He was that." He gave a strange little laugh. "You know, I was up there to get a sword—a weapon for my duel with King Capuan. I was just up there for a sword. Now"—he made a sweeping gesture—"I can't walk and Hobbie is gone."

"You'll walk," answered Dreven immediately. "That's the Mercian side of you."

Eldred nodded his head vigorously. "I'm sure. That's definitely for certain. But how long will it take? If someone came now—I would be like this. That's why I need hot water."

Dreven looked up. "For cleaning?"

"No. I'm going to use something the Wretcheds gave me. A powder that can cure anything."

Dreven tilted his head. "The Wretcheds have something like that?"

"Yes, and they gave it to me."

"That was generous of them."

Eldred looked down at the ground. "Well, I—suppose it was."

The pheasant was sizzling in a pan on the fire when Dreven handed Eldred the tin cup a quarter full of hot water.

Eldred handed him one of the woven packets of Balaur powder. "Just nick it on the corner. I don't want to use it all."

Dreven pinched the packet and made a small incision with his knife.

Eldred shook a small dusting of powder into the cup. "You know, I've carried this everywhere. This is the first time I've used it."

Dreven raised his eyebrows. "You're going to drink it?"

"No. It doesn't work that way." Eldred tugged clumsily at his pants. "Help me."

Dreven grabbed the hem of the pants and pulled them free.

Eldred dabbed a cloth into the cup and started spreading the thin liquid over his legs.

Dreven returned to the fire to rotate the rabbit spit. "So that will help you walk?"

Eldred continued the careful application of the mixture. "Yes, by morning."

"Good."

It was another twenty minutes for the food to cook. Dreven was just moving it out of the fire when Brun's snoring caught in his throat.

Suddenly, he sat up, looking around. "Oh, that's more like it, boy. Now you're doing it." He nudged Lord Kenelm. "Your steward finally did something right."

Lord Kenelm opened his eyes listlessly. But after he smelled the food, he pushed himself up.

The meal, paltry enough for two, was even less for eight. As it worked out, the rabbit and bird were passed around the circle, with each man taking a bite before passing it on to the right. Each taste seemed vanishingly small compared to the mouthful of the previous man. The rabbit went three times around, the bird four. The last rounds of each offered only the merest hint of flesh to be scraped from the bone. The silent feast ended as the men lay on their sides and returned to sleep. Nobody even asked Eldred what he was doing with his pants off.

The Screaming

The pain started in his feet, a white hot burning sensation that could not be escaped. The fire spread, running up his body, burning his skin as he writhed and screamed and grabbed and pulled. He fought without knowing who he fought. He bit and ripped and yelled and threw a thousand damning curses into the darkness. He pounded his fists, punch after punch after violent punch. Then, finally, after ages, it was over. Eldred took a breath and lay still.

Someone—not him—was groaning. Eldred cracked open his eyes; it was Colle. The big man lay on the ground grabbing his head. Eldred blinked and looked over the scene. Brun was sprawled on the ground, laying still. Lord Kenelm was getting to his feet, blood running from his nose. Dreven stood nearby, dusting the dirt off his clothes. Dogory peered out from behind a tree some twenty feet away, eyes wide. Frewin glowered at Eldred from near the remnants of the fire. Edwy still slept.

Eldred tried to rise, but his legs remained useless. He frowned. The potion hadn't worked yet. It was almost morning; the sun was just on the edge of dawn. He was about forty feet from where he had bedded down for the night. Lord Kenelm and Dreven converged on Brun, rolling the unconscious man onto his back. There were traces of blood around the man's mouth.

"What happened? Were we attacked?" asked Eldred.

Lord Kenelm kneeled next to Brun, shaking Brun's shoulder. "In a manner of speaking."

"Who did it?" asked Eldred.

Frewin pointed at Eldred. "You did."

"What? No. I was just having a nightmare," said Eldred.

Dreven left Brun's side and sat next to Eldred. "That's how it started."

He lay his hand gently on Eldred's shoulder. "You were yelling, screaming at the top of your lungs."

"I never heard anyone yell that loud," said Dogory from behind the tree.

Eldred narrowed his eyes. "What happened?"

"Well, we tried to wake you. This being the Corporian's territory and all, it didn't seem wise to have you sounding off," said Dreven.

"You tried to kill everyone!" snapped Frewin.

"No, he didn't," said Lord Kenelm. "He was just yelling. He wouldn't have hurt anyone if we had left him alone."

Frewin frowned. "Yes, if we had let him give our position away."

Eldred rubbed his forehead, brushing off traces of dirt as he did. "I'm sorry. I just had a bad dream."

Dreven raised an eyebrow.

"What?" asked Eldred.

Dreven reached over and tapped the outside of Eldred's coat, right over the spot where he kept the Balaur powder.

Eldred frowned. "That's nothing to do with it," he muttered.

Dreven shook his head. "No more," he said softly, so only Eldred could hear. "We can't have more of this."

Eldred sighed. "Fine."

Twenty minutes later, the camp was packed up and Dreven had even found a number of nearly ripe goose plums, enough that everyone had one. Lord Kenelm, Dreven and Colle struggled to get Eldred up into Mouse's saddle. Brun, who was back on his feet, had declined to help.

Edwy, however, still lay unconscious with one of the plumper goose plums set next to his head. Lord Kenelm knelt next to the man, watching his breath.

"What are you going to do about him?" asked Brun.

Lord Kenelm looked south down the river. "We can't stay here."

Brun gestured in the same direction. "If they were coming, we would have had a real fight last night."

"Seemed real enough," said Dreven, pointing to a bruise on his arm. He was perched behind Eldred on Mouse's saddle.

Brun shot Dreven a dismissive glance. "I'll stay with him. If he perks up, we'll be along in no time. Otherwise, well, I'll take care of it."

Lord Kenelm stood up. "What will you do if they come?"

Brun jerked his thumb towards Eldred. "If he's not here, I don't see why they'd bother us."

Lord Kenelm nodded slowly. "Don't count on that if it's Ferris."

"You'll see me tonight, one way or the other," said Brun.

Thus it was that six men rode away from the camp: Lord Kenelm, Dogory, Colle, Frewin, Eldred and Dreven.

WOODED TRAILS

Eldred looked over the troop as they made their way along the river. Lord Kenelm seemed stronger, more like himself, Colle and even grizzled old Frewin also appeared fresher, just a bit of food and a poor night's sleep having had great effect. "So I hit Brun in the face?" he asked softly.

Dreven continued his study of the bushes, verutum in hand. "You did. More of a glancing blow with the back of your hand. That's why he's not dead."

Eldred snorted. "Not dead? He was barely injured."

"He was injured enough. No more of that powder, thank you. If you had caught one of us"—Dreven shook his head—"that would have been it."

Eldred frowned. "Then why not leave me alone?"

"That's what it became soon enough. But even dragging yourself around, you were quick. That's how you got Brun. I guess it's a good thing the powder didn't work."

"Didn't work yet," interjected Eldred.

"And won't work. I expect the worst thing any ill person can do is to rub some filthy powder they took from some Wretched all over their body."

Eldred grimaced. "They're the Sun People, not the Wretcheds. And they know more than we do. They lived with the Mother for hundreds of years. They built wonders and art and many things. I have seen them."

Dreven narrowed his eyes. "But it didn't work."

Eldred sighed. "No."

"You should be patient. Trust your fatum lapides. Those are truly from the Mother, not from those treacherous Wretcheds. They're the gift you should be counting on."

"Perhaps," said Eldred.

After a short noon break when they ate some nuts, there was some excitement when Lord Kenelm's men chased after a small mob of deer and Dogory came back with a small fawn draped over the back of his horse.

"We'll eat good tonight," said the young man with a smile on his face.

Eldred eyed the deer hungrily. His appetite was still strong even if his legs weren't. He suggested they stop and cook it immediately, but Lord Kenelm led them onward.

In the late afternoon, they were still plodding along when suddenly Lord Kenelm whipped around in dramatic fashion and stared at Colle, who had been riding behind him. Eldred gripped the pommel of the saddle and pushed himself up to watch. Lord Kenelm slowed his horse to a stop and stared in Frewin's eyes as he came up alongside. Finally, Lord Kenelm studied Dogory. All four men were silent.

"What's happening?" asked Eldred. Mouse had stopped some ten feet short from where Lord Kenelm was clustered with his men.

"It's back," said Lord Kenelm.

Eldred sucked on his teeth. He knew what Lord Kenelm meant. "And the noise?"

Lord Kenelm blew out his breath. "Not yet. The Bond is weak, at least weak compared to what it usually is. Still, I expect the four of us could do the Corporians some harm if they showed up."

"Or you could kill Eldred," observed Dreven.

Lord Kenelm glanced at his men. "Yes, we could." He put his hand out towards Eldred. "I wouldn't want to."

Eldred nodded. "I know. It had been the same with Pounder. I guess he's dead now." He considered the names of men who had died outside the city by his father's side. Mack and Bate—he wasn't sad about them.

"Well?" asked Dreven.

"We'll go ahead. If we are far enough apart, we shouldn't have too extreme a reaction," said Lord Kenelm. "And tonight, separate camps, just in shouting distance."

Eldred looked distractedly at the river. "Right, of course." A grim foreboding crept over him. He could see them coming in his mind's eye. He could see the four men hacking him to pieces. It could be them.

Eldred and Dreven sat on Mouse as the four riders galloped away.

"We can't go with them. Evenwood cannot be your sanctuary," said Dreven.

Eldred sighed. "I know, but I need more than your help to get in the saddle."

"Actually, there are many people who don't have the Bond. We aren't that rare."

"But who would help me? Harold will get the word out quick enough. There will be a price on my head."

Dreven's eyes twinkled. "This must be a tributary to the River Stour. When they meet up, we shouldn't be too far away from my town, Mamble. I've cousins who raise pigs. I'm sure they could push you up on Mouse's back."

"There will be risk. I'd have to get out of the kingdom, all the way to Maldavia. Only my Uncle Julian can keep me safe."

"I'm sure he would justly reward the men that brought you to him."

"I hope so," said Eldred.

TWO CAMPS

The camp Eldred shared with Dreven was up off the river in the midst of a thicket. The low hanging branches blocked out the late afternoon sun and gave Eldred the vague sense that he was underground rather than in the woods. Dreven had gotten a good fire going before heading out to forage, leaving Eldred on his own.

As he sat, dragging himself from one perch to another around the fire, unable to get comfortable, one thought filled his mind—the fawn. He couldn't stop thinking about the coming meal, a tasty grilled piece of venison. He knew he should be thinking about his predicament, how to get to Emon and the protection of Uncle Julian, but all he could do was salivate in anticipation of dinner.

Eldred was about to change spots again when he caught sight of Lord Kenelm approaching, carrying slabs of meat skewered on two daggers. He was caught between worry at the realization of Lord Kenelm bearing arms and his overwhelming desire to eat.

Lord Kenelm paused two hundred feet away, half hidden behind a bush. "Send Dreven!" he called.

"He's not here. Come closer. Bring the food!" called Eldred.

Lord Kenelm hung back. "Is that wise?"

Eldred glanced around and saw no sign of Dreven. "Just bring it!"

"Dreven! Dreven!" called Lord Kenelm, searching from side to side.

"It's fine. You would already know if it wasn't, or at least I would," said Eldred, eyeing the slabs of meat.

Lord Kenelm took one last look and hurried over. Eldred wasted no time spearing one of the hunks of meat with his own knife and pulling it off Lord Kenelm's blade. The venison was too hot to eat without discomfort, but that didn't slow him down.

Lord Kenelm shoved off the remainder of the meat onto a clean rock next to the fire and took a smaller piece for himself. "I've been thinking—I don't think you can join me in Evenwood. It's too dangerous."

"I know. I must make my way to Emon. Dreven says he has cousins who can help if we make it to Mamble. How far do you think that is?"

Lord Kenelm tapped his chin. "You can get there before noon tomorrow with an early start. But even closer is the hamlet of Crudwell."

"Dreven didn't mention that."

"I know a man there, a vintner by the name of Ceolwin. I believe he might be persuaded to take you in his wagon."

Eldred took another bite. "I would trust Dreven's cousins more."

"As would I," agreed Lord Kenelm. "However, at the speed at which you are going, it would take you a week or more of riding to reach the border. And"—he gestured at Mouse—"you're a very noticeable figure. An injured Mercian-ish looking man sharing a horse with a young Deiran. You'll attract too much attention. In Ceolwin's wagon, you could be hidden from sight among the barrels. He could also go much faster. I think he might be able to deposit you across the border in only a few days. Lutetia would be the nearest city."

Eldred jabbed his dagger in Lord Kenelm's direction. "That's only if we go right through the heartland on the old road. We're sure to meet a warrior somewhere along there. If the noise comes back…" He shuddered.

They looked up a minute later at the sound of Dreven tromping back through the dry leaves. He had his verutum in one hand and a few walnuts in the other. "Oh, it's ready," he said with a smile.

Both men beckoned him over.

"Eat your fill. I reckon we'll get twenty pounds off that fawn," said Lord Kenelm.

Dreven dropped his spear and the nuts, and stabbed a good sized piece of venison with his knife.

"Lord Kenelm was just telling me about Ceolwin," said Eldred.

Dreven narrowed his eyes. "Ceolwin the vintner?"

"Yes, he might help us," said Eldred.

Dreven frowned. "He's not known hereabouts as a helpful sort."

"He owes me a favor," said Lord Kenelm. "I rescued his wife from some kidnappers a few years back when he was delivering his wares near Evenwood."

"Isn't she dead?" asked Dreven.

"Yes, for a few years now. But I helped him then. He can't forget such a debt," said Lord Kenelm.

Dreven made a sour face. "I don't know. Gold might motivate him more. Do we have any?"

"I only have a few coins with me," said Lord Kenelm.

"I can promise him Uncle Julian's gold," said Eldred.

"Harold's gold will be closer at hand," said Dreven.

They ate in silence for a minute. Eldred helped himself to a second hunk of venison.

"What if we took a hostage?" asked Eldred.

Dreven shook his head. "There's nobody he cares about—not more than gold anyway."

"I'll promise him five blessed aurum then, likely more gold than he has ever had," said Eldred.

Both Lord Kenelm and Dreven raised their eyebrows.

"You think your uncle will pay that much?" asked Dreven.

Eldred shrugged. "He'll have to deliver me to prove me false."

"There is that," said Lord Kenelm.

"But the road," said Eldred with a frown. "If we go through the heart of the kingdom, the noise might trigger any number of warriors who pass us."

"You can head north, as we did for the expedition. If you take the old road to Regillium, there is a passable road heading south from there straight to Emon," said Lord Kenelm.

"That's longer," said Eldred.

Dreven winced. "He won't agree to that. None of the folk around here would. We don't like that place."

"Then you must take your chance with the noise," said Lord Kenelm.

"No, no"—Eldred shook his head—"that I cannot do. If the Bond's come back for you, the noise will come back for me. I cannot be sitting in some old wagon when a score of warriors goes berserk."

They ate in silence for a moment until Dreven spoke. "I could ride ahead to Emon and have your uncle send men back to meet you and Ceolwin at Hobart Gap on the northern route. The old vintner might go that far for a decent enough payment."

"He'd want more than five aurum?" asked Eldred.

Dreven spread his hands. "Who knows? We can ask. Lord Kenelm can ask. But the question is, will your uncle send men? Make no mistake, Ceolwin will dump you out there. He won't go a wagon's length further."

"Uncle Julian should," said Eldred, but there was a question in his voice.

PARTING

The pain went deep, burning into Eldred's flesh. Starting from his feet and creeping up through every limb, every joint, he could only open his mouth and howl his anguish. He thrashed and fought and screamed for the blood of his enemies until he suddenly woke and found himself lying face down and bloodied in a bush, with small cuts and scrapes on his hands and face. He licked his lips and swallowed, finding a terrible taste in his mouth. He pushed himself up and away from the scratchy plant to find himself in an unfamiliar place, somewhere out in the woods.

He was about to start dragging himself away when Dreven called to him from a nearby tree. "Are you yourself again?"

Eldred squinted up at Dreven, who was nearly thirty feet up the tree. "What are you doing up there?"

Dreven started climbing down. "Keeping away from you!"

Eldred sighed and looked at his scratched-up hands. "Again?"

Dreven dropped down from a low branch. "Yes, just for the last hour of the night, it seems. Only tonight I did as you said and kept away."

"I didn't use any powder. You saw that," said Eldred.

Dreven nodded. "I know. You are—you're just not well. Stay here. I'll go get Lord Kenelm and Colle."

Eldred started to raise his hand.

Dreven waved it away. "I know, I know. I'll make sure they leave their weapons."

Eldred felt his face and head as Dreven trudged away—more bruises and cuts. A deep worry settled in his stomach. Two nights of this now—two nights of going berserk. What did it mean? The powder had helped before. It had been such a powerful cure. Had the Wretcheds tricked him? Or was he just losing his mind?

The men returned presently with Dreven leading Mouse. First Lord Kenelm approached Eldred with Dreven just behind him. When that was carried off without incident, Dreven waved Colle to come forward as well. Everyone was feeling stronger, so while Eldred's legs still hung limp, they were able to help him drag himself up in the saddle in short order.

Since the noise was still absent, Lord Kenelm and Colle walked beside Mouse as they went to the main camp. Eldred pulled Mouse up when they were a hundred feet from the fire ring. Brun was there, sitting by the fire with a hunk of venison, but Eldred couldn't spot Edwy.

"Is Edwy down by the river?" asked Eldred.

"No," said Colle.

Lord Kenelm shook his head. "Brun came by himself. He got in late last night."

"So…" said Eldred.

"Brun said he died a few hours after we left. It took all day to cover the body with rocks. He had no shovel."

"Oh," said Eldred. He noticed Brun was glowering at him.

Lord Kenelm stayed back as Colle went forward to get them some breakfast.

"I'll ride ahead with you. I'll double back to meet them once we deal with Ceolwin. We should be a day ahead of any pursuit. I doubt they left their camp until the Bond restored itself yesterday," said Lord Kenelm.

"How do we even know he's there?" asked Eldred.

"We don't," said Lord Kenelm. "In that case, it will just be Dreven's cousins and a slow ride on Mouse."

Colle returned, leading Lord Kenelm's horse. He crossed over to scratch Mouse behind the ears as Lord Kenelm mounted up. "You bring this horse back to me. Do you hear, steward?"

Dreven frowned. "I fought in battle. I drove our enemies from the field. I'm not a steward anymore."

Colle shrugged. "Steward or warrior, it doesn't matter to me. Just bring Mouse back."

Eldred glanced down at the big Deiran who had hoisted him into the saddle many times. Was this lanky horse as dear to him as Hobbie had been to Eldred? The expression on Colle's face said it might be so. "He'll do it. Won't you, Dreven?"

Dreven grunted. "Fine."

Then they were off.

CEOLWIN

It took an hour's ride to reach the River Stour, which roared past with impressive force. At more than two hundred feet to the far side, Eldred was not sure he could have crossed safely. Fortunately, their way lay across the shallow mouth of the tributary they had been following as they headed downriver to the east. They followed a trail that ran along the base of wooded hills that bordered the River Stour to the south. After a few miles, the land flattened out and the path left the trees as a widening road that crossed through fields of wheat. They passed a few houses, mostly set on the side nearer the river, but nobody was out and about in the early morning.

Lord Kenelm turned off the road when they reached a small, rutted track that led south towards a stand of trees. "This leads to the vineyard. It's another half mile on the road to Crudwell proper."

"And another ten miles to Mamble," Dreven added.

When they came out on the other side of the trees, they could see the wide expanse of Ceolwin's vineyard stretching out across the dry hillside, a maze of twisted vines with patches of freshly sprouted green leaves. The track continued on to a huddle of two smaller buildings next to a large storage shed. Two fierce looking dogs came bounding off the porch of the nearest building, barking as they came.

Lord Kenelm edged ahead, shielding Mouse from the charging hounds. "Calm, calm yourselves. We've just come to visit your master," he scolded the dogs.

The dogs retreated before Lord Kenelm while Eldred and Dreven followed behind.

Presently three men came out of the building onto the porch. The man in the middle—a thickset older man wearing an unpleasant expression— whistled for the dogs, who reluctantly returned to his side. To his left stood a tall lanky man who projected a bored attitude. To the right stood a young man, maybe only thirteen years of age.

Lord Kenelm waved as he continued forward. "Greetings, Ceowlin."

Ceolwin, who appeared to be the older man, patted one of the dogs on the head. "What are you doing down this way, Kenelm? Don't tell me you suddenly developed a taste for fine wine."

Lord Kenelm shook his head. "No, I've come to ask for your help."

Ceolwin gestured towards Eldred, who was clinging to Mouse's neck. "Like I couldn't guess that."

"He's—" started Lord Kenelm.

"I know who he is. Everyone does," interrupted Ceolwin. "He's the king's own little Mercian. The question is, why did you drag him here?"

Eldred felt his face get hot. "I'm nobody's Mercian."

Ceolwin looked Eldred over. "Is it you who has the taste for wine then?"

"No," said Eldred flatly.

Lord Kenelm came to a stop before the porch. "We need you to transport Eldred to Hobart Gap. This is a matter of great urgency."

Ceolwin turned to the man on his left. "Did you hear, Orm? It seems our visitors have mistaken us for coachmen." He frowned. "And Hobart Gap? That's in the middle of nowhere."

Lord Kenelm blew out his breath as Mouse came up alongside him. "This is a serious matter, Ceolwin. What news has reached you here regarding the battle with the Corporians?"

Ceolwin rubbed his left eyelid. "None."

Lord Kenelm sat up straighter. "King Alfred fell in battle. Harold has set himself on the throne, to which"—he turned to eye Eldred—"we have no disagreement. However, other lords have elected to act in a dishonorable manner. We must get Eldred to Maldavia now, before anything untoward happens."

Ceolwin frowned at Dreven before returning his gaze to Eldred. "Well, that's sad news indeed, a shame. However, it does not sound like a situation where a simple vintner like myself, who has no concern about such matters, should involve himself. Besides, the prince appears to be well horsed and even has a distinguished citizen of Mamble to aid him. Why don't you just ride on to Hobart Gap on your own?"

"I have gold," said Eldred.

Ceolwin clapped his hands. "Hmm, did you hear, Orm? The young man has a store of gold. Would this be for a purchase of wine, good prince?"

Eldred took a breath. "Yes, a wagon load of your finest wine. Fill every inch of your wagon with your barrels, just leave a spot for me."

Ceolwin smiled. "That's sensible, a rush order of fine wine to Hobart Gap, perhaps for a rustic celebration to mark the occasion of your cousin's ascension. Though sensible, such things come at great cost."

"How much?" asked Eldred.

Ceolwin scratched the gray stubble on his chin. "Oh, I should say twelve aurum."

"Twelve golden aurum?" said Dreven incredulously. "It should not cost that much if you stacked all of your wine barrels on the cart, not even if you had five times the wine stored as you do."

Ceolwin ignored Dreven and continued to face Eldred. "Do you have the coins, prince?"

Eldred pushed himself up on Mouse's neck. "My Uncle Julian, the king of Maldavia, he will make good on the debt."

Ceolwin turned back to Orm. "I don't know, Orm. I wonder if the good Maldavian king knows the promises his nephew is making. It would be a shame to travel all that way to find the prince misjudged the desires of his uncle."

Eldred felt his shoulders grow tight. He took a breath and remembered the nauseating haggling with Lord Grimsley in Stonor Hall. "For your risk, I'll make it twenty aurum."

Ceolwin's face lit with a glow of satisfaction. "That is well considered. For the promised sum of twenty aurum, I can see making a rush delivery. I take it, Lord Kenelm, that you will be good for any amount the Maldavian king is short?"

Lord Kenelm shot him a steely glance and nodded curtly. "I hope I don't have to say that you should make sure of Eldred's safe delivery. There should be no accidents or mistakes—not when we are paying such sums."

Ceolwin laughed. "Accidents? I will do my best, but the world cannot be made wholly safe simply by the promise of future payments. Surely, your lordship and the prince are well aware of this sad fact of life?" Ceolwin paused, but continued when Lord Kenelm stayed silent. "Very well. Orm, take Roger and start packing the wagon. Perhaps his lordship and our young resident of Mamble will join in, if they truly are in such a rush to see this done."

Lord Kenelm glanced at Dreven and dismounted.

They left Eldred leaning against a flat stone next to the steps up to the porch and followed after Orm and the young boy. One of the dogs approached Eldred, very friendly now that a contract had been worked out with his master. Eldred smiled as he half-heartly fended off the dog's efforts to lick his face.

Ceolwin brought out a platter with a sliced loaf of wheat bread and a block of butter and sat on the stairs, holding it out to Eldred. "Are you injured? Can you suffer the bumps and jostling of the wagon?"

Eldred took a slice of bread and eagerly spread a thick coating of butter. "Oh, yes. I'll be fine."

"Good. For safety, we must travel at the greatest possible speed," said Ceolwin. He gently pushed the dog away from Eldred so he could eat.

Eldred took a bite and closed his eyes at how wonderful the bread tasted. It must have been baked that morning. But then his eyes shot open. "There's one thing."

"And what is that?" asked Ceolwin, scratching the dog behind the ear.

Eldred clenched his chin. "I—I sort of go mad in the morning, just before people would wake."

Ceolwin raised an eyebrow. "What do you mean?"

Eldred's eyes grew soft. "I scream and yell. I thrash around. If you came near, I might harm you. But if you stay back, then it should all be fine."

Ceolwin tilted his head and blinked. "Of course. This can happen with a rushed delivery."

THE WAGON

It was an hour before the men finished packing the wagon. The bed of the wagon ran for five barrels along its length and three barrels across its width. The wagon was packed to capacity except for two absent middle barrels directly behind the driver's bench at the front. This was to be Eldred's lair, covered on top with a patched beige tarp.

Ceolwin sent Orm and the boy into the house to fetch supplies while he presented Eldred with a bill for twenty aurum which he insisted Eldred sign. Then everyone helped Eldred up over the bench into his hiding spot. Eldred settled back on a blanket against a heavy barrel, noting that he had two bottles in reach, one for water and one for relieving himself.

Lord Kenelm reached down and patted Eldred on the shoulder as Orm started fastening the tarp. "I must head back. My men and I also have ground to cover."

Eldred reached up and clasped his hand. "Thank you so much, Lord Kenelm. You have taken such risks—I hope they come to nothing. That is my dearest hope."

Lord Kenelm smiled weakly. "It's just more of the same with Ferris. Don't give it a thought. You're nearly there for your part. Four days bouncing around back here until you reach Hobart Gap, then perhaps a day or two of waiting if young Dreven rides slowly."

Dreven rolled his eyes and crouched down next to Eldred. "I'll go as swiftly as Mouse allows. I'll be there too. I'll go with the Maldavians to meet you at Hobart Gap, even if I have to ride all night."

Eldred took Dreven's hand and shook it. "Just be safe."

Dreven smiled. "A quick jaunt over to Lutetia. What could be easier?"

They stepped out as Orm pulled the tarp over.

"Farewell!" called Eldred.

A few minutes later, the horses were attached and the wagon jerked forward, causing the barrels to slide an inch or so. Orm drove the wagon with Ceolwin perched on the bench beside him. The boy, Roger, was left behind to watch the vineyard.

As they had left, Orm had stuck a number of supplies back in Eldred's den. Eldred dug through and found a bag of hard apples, helping himself to the one that looked the juiciest. He smiled as he ate the wooden fruit. He was alone now—or with strangers, in any case—but that made him relaxed. He might go berserk or bring down a band of crazed warriors upon him, but Lord Kenelm and Dreven were safely away. He doubted that Ceolwin or Orm would put themselves in any danger on his account. He trusted them not to.

And the noise, was it even there anymore? Perhaps it had been broken just like his legs, which lay uselessly before him. If that were true, if the two were somehow related, it might be a worthwhile trade. Not that he didn't want to walk—of course, he very much did want that. But the noise—that could be so deadly. Just one warrior would be the end of him. At least now, if it did happen, it wouldn't be Lord Kenelm driving the blade into his heart. That would have been unfortunate.

After half an hour, Orm made some comment about leaving Crudwell behind, to which Ceolwin grunted in return, but that was all that passed for conversation up front. Eldred was tempted to curl up in the blanket and try to sleep, but he feared having one of the fits. So instead, he clambered forward and peered out the front of the wagon from under the flap of the tarp.

A few minutes later, Ceolwin swatted the tarp in front of Eldred's face. "You should stay back. There's no point in all our effort if you're going to stick your nose out."

Eldred glared at Ceolwin's butt, being unable to see his face. "I will see anyone long before they see me."

Ceolwin sniffed. "That's true, until it's not. If you see a hint of anyone, you get away from there."

"I will. I'm not an idiot," answered Eldred.

They clattered down the road for an hour before they came across anyone, a farmer with a cart full of hay.

Eldred spotted him well in the distance and ducked back into his hiding spot. "Tell me when he's past."

Ceolwin grunted.

After that, there were a few other passersby: a merchant with a heavily laden wagon of his own and a single hunter who sported a bevy of dead pheasants over the neck of his horse. Ceolwin appeared to know the merchant and called out a greeting, but the hunter passed in silence.

Then came the riders. Eldred saw them first, cresting a saddle between two hills in the far distance as they came along the road. He could only make out their number, which appeared to be ten to twelve men. "Men coming; should we get off the road?"

Ceolwin made a dismissive gesture. "To go where? It's all clear hereabouts. Best we keep on. We're just delivering wine."

Eldred frowned to himself behind the flap. Presently, the men disappeared from sight behind some trees that lay up the road. Eldred tensed as he waited for them to come out from the trees. When they finally did, he felt his stomach drop. Lord Ferris rode at the head of their formation. They were only half a mile away.

"Oh! Oh, no. It's Lord Ferris," said Eldred.

Ceolwin shushed him. "Just get back there and stay quiet."

"He's the one hunting me," said Eldred, his voice rising.

"I said be quiet!" snapped Ceolwin.

Eldred felt his heart speed up. "If they go crazy, just get away from the wagon. Let them have me."

"What are you talking about?" demanded Ceolwin.

Eldred tightened his grip on the wagon where he was holding himself up. Lord Ferris was smiling and talking to a man with an ugly scar on his left cheek who rode alongside him. "They might sense me—I have a noise," mumbled Eldred. "If they do, they'll kill me right here. They'll go mad as they do, but just move out of their way. They might spare you."

Ceolwin cursed under his breath. "Just one more thing—is it? Is this the last? Now get back away from the flap."

Eldred went silent but continued peering out from under the flap, watching the face of Lord Ferris as he came on, waiting to see if his jovial expression turned dark. At a hundred yards, Lord Ferris continued to gab on at his attentive companion. Eldred marked the narrow eyes and smattering of pockmarks on the face of Lord Ferris's friend.

"You heard what he said, Orm," muttered Ceolwin. "If there is trouble, jump down and get under the wagon."

Orm shifted on the bench but kept silent.

Eldred held his breath as they came within fifty yards. He could catch some of what Lord Ferris was saying. Something about a magnificent throw. Wulsin? Wulsin had the magnificent throw. That seemed to be the name of the man riding beside Lord Ferris. But then Lord Ferris turned his focus on the wagon and stopped in the middle of the road. His men lined up alongside him, blocking the way—ten men, two pods. His expression was different now—expectant, but not angry, not like it would be from the noise.

Orm slowed the wagon and came to a stop twenty feet before the line of men.

Lord Ferris smiled and made a short bow in his saddle. "Good day, merchant, or I should say wonderful day, a day for celebration."

"So is each day," answered Ceolwin, his voice steady and relaxed. "But if you will excuse us, we are rushing to make a delivery and must be on our way."

Lord Ferris raised his palm. "Ah, but you see, I have need of your wares. I see you carry a load of barrels. What's inside?"

"I carry a load of wine, already bought and paid for," said Ceolwin.

Lord Ferris slapped his thigh. "Excellent! Perfect. I'll take one barrel for my men."

"If only I had an extra barrel, I would gladly give it to you. But as I said, this delivery is already bought and paid for," said Ceolwin.

Lord Ferris raised his chin and narrowed his eyes. "Nobody is asking you to give anything to anyone. I will pay for a barrel. I will give you a reasonable price. What is it that your patron has promised you for one? I'll double it."

Ceolwin took a slight breath. "Well, that is quite noble of you, good sir. I wish that my man here had possessed the good sense to load an extra barrel, but I fear he did not."

Lord Ferris issued a grainy laugh. "Perhaps the day is not as great as I thought. I had thought us fortunate in coming across a merchant on this road, but I had hoped for beer, not wine. And now I learn that I am to get nothing, not even a Motherless cup of your pissy wine for Wulsin, my best man here." His men stayed where they were.

Inside the wagon, Eldred peered out from under the flap and gripped the hilt of his sword.

After a pause, Ceolwin spoke. "I do not wish to ruin your celebration, good sir, or to in any way disappoint you or your friends. While I cannot sell you a barrel, I can freely fill your waterskins for no charge at all. Just hand your bags to my man, and he will fill them. I'll take it out of his pay, since he lacked the sense to load an extra barrel."

Ceolwin reached over and swatted Orm on the shoulder. Orm let out a small yelp and climbed down from the wagon. There was bustling then as Lord Ferris's men crowded forward on their horses, handing down their skins.

"That's more like it!" proclaimed Lord Ferris.

In a few minutes, Orm had filled their sacks from one of the barrels in the back of the wagon.

Lord Ferris raised his waterskin above his head. "Let us toast our new king, King Harold! Did you know of this, merchant? Have you heard word of this change?"

"No," said Ceolwin.

"It is a welcome change," continued Lord Ferris. "Long past due. To King Harold! May he reign for twenty years!"

Eldred frowned. Twenty days would be too long.

The men sucked on their waterskins. Lord Ferris appeared satisfied with the taste of the wine. "And to Wulsin, of the steady arm and accurate aim!"

The men gave a brief but enthusiastic cheer and drank again as Wulsin bowed from his saddle.

Ceolwin lightly clapped his hands. "I'm so pleased to see you smiling, m'lord. But I fear I must move on. Deliveries to be made, as you know."

Lord Ferris nodded. "Of course, you must not keep your patron waiting. But first, let me pay you. Your oafish man, his stupidity embarrassed you today, but I think he may not be able to afford this largess."

"No, sir. It is not necessary," protested Ceolwin.

Lord Ferris dug in his pocket. "I insist." He tossed two silver denarii to Ceolwin, who snatched them out of the air.

"You are too kind, good sir," said Ceolwin.

Lord Ferris maneuvered his horse to the side of the road, leading his men in clearing the road. "Good travels, merchant."

Orm urged the horses onward, and the wagon jolted into motion. Eldred sank down to the floor of the wagon, drained of energy. After a space of a few minutes, Eldred whispered, "Are we away from them?"

"Yes, now stay back there and be silent," muttered Ceolwin.

Eldred obliged, taking the blanket and leaning back against a shaking barrel. Against his better sense, he slowly let himself be rocked towards sleep. He was almost nodding off when Orm applied the brake, and the wagon jerked to a halt.

"By the Mother!" said Orm.

TEARS

Tears ran down Eldred's face, dripping onto the wagon bench where he rested his elbows. Ceolwin and Orm were both down off the wagon. Ceolwin was bossing Orm about as Orm worked to untie the rope, the rope which ran up over the tree branch to where Dreven's corpse hung, choked about the neck and swaying in the breeze. Mouse lay in the grass, a bloody wound coating the side of the horse with red gore. Eldred's face shook with rage—the lucky throw of that Motherless bastard, Wulsin. Eldred clenched his fists. Luck could go both ways.

"Why would they do this?" asked Orm. "He was just a boy from Mamble. Those were bonded warriors. They should leave simple folk like us alone."

Eldred furiously wiped away his tears with the palm of his hand. "He wasn't. He was a warrior. He chased them from the field."

The men glanced at Eldred for a moment before returning to work on the knot.

"Just cut it! Just cut the damned rope. We have to get him down!" yelled Eldred.

"We'll get him down," said Ceolwin calmly.

A moment later, they did resort to Orm's knife. Orm gripped the rope and walked up the base of the tree as Dreven's corpse slid down into Ceolwin's arms. Ceolwin lowered Dreven to the ground and used his blade to free the noose from around Dreven's bruised neck.

"We have to go back! He must be buried in Mamble with his family," said Eldred.

Ceolwin brushed Dreven's hair from his face. "We will. I will, but we need to get you away from here first."

Eldred gave a hard laugh. "There'll be nobody waiting for us at Hobart Gap. The plan's done."

Ceolwin squinted up at Eldred. "We will do what Dreven meant to do. We'll take the southern road past Boar's Tusk to Lutetia."

"We won't make it," sputtered Eldred. "There'll be a hundred warriors crawling on that road. When the noise returns, it will just take one to kill us all."

Ceolwin gestured back along the way they had come. "We made it past them. They were just a few feet away from you without issue. Maybe your noise—or whatever it is—has been cured."

"He has to be buried within seven days by the Mother decree," said Eldred.

Ceolwin nodded. "Two, perhaps three, days to Lutetia. Then a faster ride back with an empty wagon. I'll get him there in time."

Eldred wiped his eyes. "You just want your gold."

Ceolwin sighed. "Gold has its value. So does my word. If the new king, your cousin, has his men out looking for you, then we had best be quick about our business. He need only order the roads blocked and we would be undone."

Eldred glanced at Dreven's body. "Then where—"

"We'll make room," said Orm.

Eldred stayed where he was, elbows on the driver's bench with his legs hanging down into the hiding space, while Ceolwin and Orm unloaded a barrel off the back of the wagon. Dreven's face was pale, bloodless, but it still showed the sense of him. His mouth was open, but there was a slight rise at the corner of his lip, as if he were about to tell one of his jokes. His eyes were closed—Ceolwin had shut them—but they looked like they could just open.

Off the side, Eldred could see Orm rolling the barrel far out into the field where he stopped to drain it into the soil and cover it up. Meanwhile, Ceolwin took one of the beige tarps over to Dreven's corpse and rolled him up in it. He was fixing the last rope around Dreven when Orm returned to carry the body around the back of the wagon. Eldred pulled himself around, now sitting backwards on the driver's bench. They had shifted the barrels around, leaving only two barrels in the middle row of the wagon—two empty spaces for Eldred's hideaway, then a barrel, then an empty spot for Dreven, then the last barrel.

As Ceolwin and Orm hurried at fastening the tarps over the wagon, Eldred glanced at Mouse where he lay in the grass. They'd never have caught Dreven if he had been on Hobbie, but it wasn't Mouse's fault. Eldred blew out his breath and wondered when word would make it back to Colle. And when—Eldred's face grew hard—would vengeance make its way back to Ferris and his lapdog, Wulsin.

The rest of the journey passed as if in a fog. His legs refused to heal. The morning fits continued—the screaming, the pain and the fear were a sorry start to each passing day. He spent two days of monotonous travel leaning against the front of the wagon, looking back into his hiding space at the barrel between him and Dreven's corpse. With his dark vision, he could look through the narrow gaps between the barrels to see Dreven's tarp-wrapped leg on one side and tarp-wrapped rear on the other. They had settled him to rest sitting up.

It would have been best—Eldred was sure—just to have been a farmer in Mamble. Dreven had always said how he hated the idea of it, but surely any life, even one with hard work, was better than being chased down and hung by the worst people. And if—not that it happened that way—they had not tried cheating at the Academy, then would not have the Headmaster chosen Dreven for the expedition? Would he have died with the other squires? Was it better to be ripped apart by wolves than to be hung? Eldred did not want to think about it, but it was all he could do. The best thing for Dreven would have been that he never met Eldred.

Eldred did not notice when they entered Lutetia on the morning of the third day. If Ceolwin or Orm had made any mention of it, Eldred did not hear them. He was startled when the men pulled back the tarp, blinding him with the sunlight. Maldavians—he recognized them by their slightly taller stature and since one of them had the vision—climbed up into the wagon to help Orm get Eldred down. Their wrinkled noses showed their disgust as they took hold of Eldred. The wagon hold had become fragrant from more than one source.

Once they had Eldred down, he watched as they helped Orm unload the barrels. Nobody would touch a drop of the wine—Eldred was quite certain of that. Presently the mayor appeared, a distant relative of Eldred, or so he was told. Eldred grunted in return to his greeting. That was when Ceolwin approached, bill in hand. Eldred watched the exchange with detachment. Twice the mayor asked Eldred if he should pay and twice Eldred nodded.

Eldred was surprised when Ceolwin settled for three aurum and ten denarri in coins and a promissory note for the balance. The old merchant did not seem to have his usual fight in him.

Before they left, Ceolwin and Orm approached Eldred.

"We'll get him there. I promise," said Ceolwin.

"Plenty of time," added Orm.

"Thank you. He should be with his family," said Eldred.

Ceolwin extended his hand. "And you with yours. Best of luck to you, young prince."

Eldred took his hand. "Thank you, Ceolwin. And you, Orm. You have done more—risked more—than I had any right to ask."

"Sometimes people help," said Orm.

Ceolwin nodded. "I'm sorry about Dreven."

Eldred took a deep breath and turned away, his lips squeezed tight. "I'll see them pay. Ferris, Wulsin, I'll hang the both of them. Or I'll just kill them." He reached up and brushed the fatum lapides that were set behind his left temple. When he looked back, he saw their expressions—they had not believed him, the threats of a crippled prince having little weight.

They hurriedly gathered a few supplies from the Maldavians and were on their way with Dreven, hidden from sight. Eldred waved and watched them go. Days of hard travel, but both men looked relieved to be back on the road. They were leaving their greatest burden behind.

The Maldavians wasted little time. Once Ceolwin was out of sight, they started draining the wine into the gutter. Eldred scratched his chin. Filth by association, but which was worse, Eldred or his dead friend?

The mayor was even more efficient than Ceolwin at getting rid of his problems. Eldred was carried to a stable where a tub was hastily filled with hot water. The stewards wanted to burn Eldred's possessions, including his leather coat and his sample pouch with its attendant packets of Balaur powder, but Eldred mustered enough energy to hold them off. They reluctantly settled for cleaning the items, though they could not conceal their displeasure with the task.

Meanwhile, a carriage had been made ready along with a detail of ten soldiers. When they brought Eldred out of the stables, still damp, the mayor was on hand to wish him well. If only there was time, the mayor lamented, he so wished to enjoy a meal with Eldred. Alas, there was not. They shoved Eldred into the carriage where he sat across from two burly stewards. His lunch was in a basket.

EMON

Two days later, the carriage entered the outskirts of Emon, passing small farms and clusters of houses in the approach to the city proper. Eldred watched with rising apprehension from the back seat. He was close to his goal, but now what? He had last visited Emon four years before on the occasion of his trials, which had gone well. In all his life, it seemed that the vision trials had been his greatest success, maybe his only real success. He crinkled up his face and considered the expedition—they had killed the dragon, but so many died. And now he was here, back with his Maldavian relatives.

Eldred frowned. Uncle Julian had never much liked him—he had shrugged indifferently when Eldred had passed the far vision trial. But Julian was like the warmth of the sun itself compared to his wife, Sibylle. Eldred had visited Emon for five weeks, and in all that time, Sibylle had said no more than a dozen words to him.

Their sons were not much more pleasant. Cyran, the heir, and Oudin were years older than Eldred, but he had towered over them even back when he was fourteen years old. They had not let Eldred forget it—Mercian this and Mercian that. And Cyran didn't even have dark vision, only far vision. In a fight, Eldred could kill them both. He glanced down at his legs. Well, not now, but before.

Roscille, the daughter, was closer to Eldred in age, probably the same age, he thought. After he had passed the dark vision trial, she had made him a berry pastry. It hadn't been that tasty, but it was a kind thought. She was nice and even a bit pretty and not too tall, Eldred reflected. Or she hadn't been, but she might have grown. Eldred frowned at the possibility.

They were coming to the city walls, which were useless. They had stone gates, which were functional, but the walls themselves were earth barriers that had lost their form and were now essentially mounds of grass covered dirt. Skilled warriors on horseback could ride right over them if they so wished. At least they demarcated the city proper.

Eldred rubbed his chin as they passed through the eastern gate with their contingent of soldiers behind and headed up the Avenue of Kings towards the palace, passing regal estates on both sides. If only Mother were here, she could talk to Julian. She would know what to say, and Julian liked her well enough, as had always been evident. But she wasn't; he was on his own.

Eldred bit his lip. It was about sanctuary—he would be asking for sanctuary. He was a cripple begging for food and shelter. Father would be ashamed. And Eldred had already spent a small fortune of Julian's money on a delivery of wine that had been poured in the gutter. Did Julian know? Some of the soldiers had ridden ahead. Was that the information they had carried? Eldred frowned. Julian must already know. Should Eldred make mention of it?

They came upon the palace, which was more like a manor house as Eldred saw it—a two story building with tall windows set along the ground floor. Not very defensible; raiders could enter any room they wished with only the effort of cracking the glass. The castle at Boar's Tusk was immeasurably more sensible.

The carriage glided to a halt outside the main entrance to the palace before a short stone stair that led up to the entry hall. A number of finely dressed stewards stood on the steps. The nearest walked over and said something to the coachman. The carriage jerked forward, leaving the soldiers behind on their horses.

Eldred shifted, looking back at the palace. "What's happening? Where are you taking me?"

The two stewards sitting across from him looked at each other. The one on the left stood up and thrust his head out the window. After a moment, he ducked back in. "We are headed to the royal stables."

Eldred pointed back towards the palace. "You need to drop me off first."

The steward raised his eyebrows and smiled weakly. "No?" He made it sound like a question.

"Yes," said Eldred, slamming his fist onto the bench where he sat.

The steward's eyes grew wide, and he shuffled a half step back, which was all the room the carriage allowed.

The other steward leaned forward. "We can work it out once we get there. It is only a little more than a hundred yards from here."

"Fine!" snapped Eldred, settling back in the seat.

The steward who had been standing sat down, perching lightly on the seat and watching Eldred carefully.

Eldred directed his attention out the window at the royal gardens through which they were passing. Early spring blooms showed on many trees and bushes. He noticed a yellow warbler singing its song in a nearby tree and felt the tension in his shoulders lessen. He could go back and beg for sanctuary after his short visit to the stables.

Presently, a ramshackle building appeared on the right, made of dark wood that looked almost black with age. Horses were tied outside the building, and a cart half filled with wooden chairs was backed up to the entrance. Somebody was shouting, "He is here! He is here." A dozen people came out of the building, two with the vision. It took a second for Eldred to recognize them, but at the front was Roscille, followed by Oudin. She hadn't grown.

"What's this?" called Eldred as Roscille approached the wagon.

Roscille gave a friendly smile. "I am setting this up for you, cousin."

Oudin wagged his finger at her. "Do not forget my help."

The stewards who had ridden with Eldred opened the door, making ready to get Eldred down. A few men behind Roscille and Oudin came over to help.

Eldred gestured at the stables. "But why here? Is this about the payment? I can explain."

Roscille raised her eyebrows. "No, there is no issue with any payment. Is that not right, Oudin?"

Oudin gave a sly smile. "There is no charge to stay in our stable, cousin."

Roscille boxed her brother lightly on the arm. "Of course not. I am sorry, Eldred. I thought someone would have explained. Mother chose to put you here because of your condition—your morning fits. We had word of them from the riders. She—thought this was best."

Oudin rubbed his hands. "Only because she is lazy and sleeps late. I thought it would be a welcome change to hear your screams echoing through our halls."

Eldred raised his arms to the stewards, who were pressing around to lift him out. "So there is no issue with your father?"

Oudin gave a small laugh. "I would not say that is entirely the case. There is some back and forth with the new Deiran king, your other cousin. Apparently, he thinks you betrayed his army to the Corporians."

Roscille looked Eldred in the eye. "But that simply cannot be the case. It is nonsense. Is it not, Eldred?"

Eldred nodded as they took him out through the door. "Yes. I just fell from my horse. It was the Corporians—they did something, some spell. It just affected me first."

Oudin looked Eldred over as the stewards hoisted him up by his arms and legs. "Makes perfect sense to me." He beckoned the stewards. "Bring him this way."

They carried him past the cart and through the entrance of the stables. Eldred had never been in these stables, but their layout was similar to those at Boar's Tusk. The inside was empty of horses, a few stalls had cots set up in them. They carried Eldred to a large room in the back with open windows looking out over the gardens which extended into the distance. A fancy looking bed was set up in one corner. Two wide couches were set in the middle of the room, facing each other. The stewards grunted as they dropped Eldred on one couch. Roscille and Oudin took a seat on the opposite couch.

"There is no smell," said Roscille. "We have not used it as a stable for years."

"You have your own larder, and I made sure you have beer and wine. Do you care for a drink?" asked Oudin.

Eldred shook his head.

"Hope you do not mind if I do," said Oudin. "Oh, and this is Elisiard." He pointed at the oldest of the stewards, a frail looking man with a lined face. "It is past noon, so a beer is called for with all the work I have been doing."

Elisiard smiled easily, and his clear eyes twinkled. "Of course, Master Oudin."

Roscille clasped her hands. "You are in fine hands with Elisiard. He practically raised the three of us."

Oudin leaned back on the couch. "At least that part of your welcome is of true royal quality."

Roscille lifted her hand towards the tallest of the young stewards. "Guyon will also be here with you for most of your stay. Other stewards will be in and out."

Guyon gave a quick bow.

"And once she arrives, Mateline will have her own complement of help," added Roscille.

"Who?" asked Eldred.

Oudin laughed. "Your fiancée. Did you not know her name?"

"Oh," said Eldred, feeling his face flush. "Mother made some mention of some arrangement, some prospect. I didn't know—is this what has come to pass? Will she be staying here?" He looked around the stable.

"No," said Oudin, his face alive with mirth. "She will stay in proper rooms. She is neither accused of treason, nor does she have screaming fits as she greets the day."

Roscille biffed Oudin on the shoulder once more. "You must excuse him, Eldred. He is useless, as befits someone who will never be king."

"Ouch," said Oudin, reaching up to take a mug of beer from a small tray Elisiard carried. "But fair, as you always are, my dear sister."

Elisiard offered goblets of water to Roscille and Eldred.

Eldred sipped from his. "I suppose this proposal will all be on hold while matters get worked out."

Roscille raised her hand towards Oudin, blocking the comment that was already forming on his lips. "Wait, dear brother. This is no joking matter, not to decent people, in any case." She turned to Eldred. "I should let you know, Eldred, that your marriage to Mateline is of the utmost importance to Father. Mother and I are making ready plans for your wedding within the week. Mateline herself should arrive from Dinan sometime tomorrow."

"Oh," said Eldred with a frown. "What about the treason?"

Oudin grinned. "Now you own up to it, then?"

Roscille rolled her eyes. "Father sent an envoy to Boar's Tusk yesterday. He will set this matter to rest. We also look to him to return your mother, Lady Ghyslaine, to us. Though nothing definite has been stated, it seems that her movements are restricted while the Deirans wait for satisfaction."

Eldred leaned forward, a dark scowl across his face. "If that Motherless bastard, Harold, harms her in any way, I'll wring his scrawny neck."

Roscille pursed her lips. "We have word that she is treated well."

Eldred glanced at the floor. "Yes, Benedict would make sure of that. He wouldn't let anything…"

After a tense minute, Oudin gestured to Eldred. "You will like Mateline. I know her well through my hunting companion, Domard, her cousin. We often roam the woods near Dinan. She is warm and kind and also strong, like yourself."

Eldred narrowed his brows. "What do you mean, strong like me?"

Oudin shrugged. "Just what I said. Anyway, what about the battle? You were there?"

Eldred winced and looked down at his cup. "Yes. I was."

Roscille gave Oudin a sideways look. "Perhaps our cousin requires some rest. Eldred, are you tired?"

Eldred nodded. "I might like a break."

Roscille rose, and Oudin followed a second later. "We will be back to join you for dinner, just the two of us. If you have no objection, I will send Lady Genevote out to examine you. She is the royal physician."

"Yes, please," said Eldred.

Oudin clapped his hands together. "I hope to hear everything at dinner, Eldred. The battle, the dragon—you have all the most interesting news."

Roscille sighed. "I am afraid that you will find everyone wanting to hear your tales, Eldred. Even Father expressed interest in your famous expedition. But for now, get some rest." She took Oudin's arm and left.

After a moment, Elisiard approached. Only he and Guyon were left. "Would you care for anything to eat, sir?"

"I'm getting married," mumbled Eldred.

"A roast beef sandwich, sir?"

Eldred looked out the window into the garden, another yellow warbler was taking to song. "With horseradish."

EXAMINATION

L ady Genovote sat still and tall on the couch opposite Eldred, wearing a light gray cloak tied at the waist by a gold-colored rope. Her thin face looked old, but strong, dominated by her inquiring eyes. She had the vision, as did her male assistant, Perreux. He wore a dark cloak and twisted his small frame to look at his mistress.

The physician tapped her finger on the arm of the couch. "So, you say you have been this way for a bit more than a week."

Eldred nodded. "Ever since the fall."

"At which time you hit your head," said Lady Genevote.

"That's correct," said Eldred.

Lady Genevote gave Perreux a meaningful glance. "However, you say you possess three fatum lapides."

Eldred brushed the hair away from his left temple. "I do. These are they."

Lady Genevote leaned slightly closer, examining the stones from six feet away. "I should have expected them to have some effect by now."

"Yes. That's right. By the will of the Mother, they should heal me. I should be healing, but I'm not. I'm just the same. I can't walk. And in the morning, I have those fits I told you about—every damned morning," said Eldred.

"How distressing," said Perreux softly.

Eldred glanced at Elisiard, who was standing off to the side. "Yes, quite so. They're keeping me in the stables due to them. What can you do to help?"

Lady Genevote clasped her hands at her waist. "These are all very troublesome afflictions. However, my visit today is not about these matters."

Eldred narrowed his brows. "It's not?"

"No. Forgive my indelicacy. My question, my focus, for the moment is rather more on your personal nature. Are you functioning as you should?"

"What do you mean?"

"She means your private parts," said Perreux.

Eldred turned a shade red. "Functioning? Yes, I function. It's my legs that have issues."

Perreux gave an apologetic smile. "She does not mean simply purging oneself. She refers to other functions, specifically the functions related to reproduction."

"Oh," said Eldred.

"Well, are you serviceable?" asked Lady Genevote.

Eldred scowled at the two of them. "What does it matter to you?"

Perreux raised his eyebrows. "It is quite important for your upcoming marriage."

"Fine, then. It's—all good," said Eldred, still flushed.

Perreux nodded slowly. "You are certain?"

"Yes. I'm certain."

"How so?" asked Perreux.

Elderd sighed. "In the morning, after I have my fits, it is—serviceable."

"Good," said Lady Genevote. "I am pleased we could confirm this point. We shall take our leave."

Eldred pushed himself up as she and her assistant started to rise. "Wait. What about my legs, the fits?"

"Be patient. Time is the great healer, and you are but a young man," said Lady Genevote.

"But don't you have some treatment? Isn't there anything you can do?" protested Eldred.

Perreux shook his head.

"In Turicum, they have physicians who can treat people. I was nearly dead, and they brought me back to life," said Eldred.

Lady Genevote raised her eyebrow. "You mean the Wretcheds who disfigured your face and left your hand scarred?"

Eldred's eyes burned. "When I was nearly dead."

The corners of Lady Genevote's mouth curved slightly upwards. "If we come across a Wretched who practices medicine, we shall be sure to send him on to you. In the meantime, we must be going."

Eldred glared after them as they left.

When they were gone, he turned to Elisiard. "Is that normal? Are these the questions people consider here before a marriage?"

Elisiard pondered for a moment. "Not normally, sir. Perhaps it is the nature of your injury that raises these questions."

"Well, I don't like it."

"I understand, sir."

"This entire engagement is mad. The Corporians are invading the Motherland. Harold holds my mother captive. And here in Emon, the big concern is my newly announced wedding and whether or not I am serviceable. It makes no sense."

Elisiard nodded. "We must keep on. Whatever else is happening in the world, we each have our duty."

QUIET NIGHT

Roscille and Oudin returned for dinner as promised. Uncle Julian and his wife, Sibylle, skipped the event, as did their oldest son, Cyran. Eldred did not miss them but took their absence as a sign of trouble. Eldred ate heartily, unlike his companions, who barely touched their food, though Oudin consumed a great deal of beer for such a small man. Elisiard kept everyone's cup full and said little. Nonetheless, his warm smile and calm presence filled the drafty stables as he looked after Eldred as well as the two charges he had raised.

Eldred found himself grinning along with Oudin as he told the story of the battle with the dragon for the third time. Both of his cousins loved the tale, though they had no interest in his descriptions of the Wretched.

Afterwards, Eldred gave in to Oudin's protests and related the events of the battle with the Corporians and the treacherous encounter with Lord Ferris in the aftermath. Eldred grew teary-eyed as he described the death of Hobbie.

"Your horse?" asked Oudin, clarifying who or what had died.

"Yes," said Eldred, his chin trembling.

Oudin set his beer down on a low table. "But surely it is the death of your father that upsets you more."

Eldred rubbed his forehead with his fingers. "I couldn't even see him. Even before the Corporians did their spell—it was the lady above the gate who signaled for it, I'm sure—I couldn't see him in the mass of Corporian warriors. When the spell hit me—I don't know why it hit me first, but it was not from me—I screamed and fell from Hobbie's back. When they dragged me back to the saddle, it was already over. We were winning the battle one moment, killing those Motherless bastards so easily, and the next we were in full retreat, running for our lives." Eldred shook his head.

"You should have taken us," said Oudin.

"What?" asked Eldred.

"Oh, come now, brother," said Roscille.

Oudin waved her off. "No, it is true. I agree, Eldred, this spell—not any treachery of yours—robbed the Deirans of their precious Bond. Now, the Bond is quite fine; I would not wish to fight any bonded warriors. But once you lose it, you lose everything—nothing you can do but run. For us, the Maldavian marksmen, what can they take from us? Nothing! We kill them before and after, if they do this spell."

"What if they took your far sight?" asked Eldred.

"How could they do that?" asked Oudin.

Eldred rubbed the back of his neck. "They had a stone bearer. Perhaps she would find a way."

"Well, we must find our way home," said Roscille as she rose to her feet. "Thank you for your fascinating accounts, dear cousin. Mother and Father surely missed a most entertaining evening, but we should leave you to your rest. Mateline should arrive in the early afternoon tomorrow, and you must be rested."

"And presentable. Get your hair trimmed," said Oudin as he gathered himself up.

Eldred blinked. "Fine. I'll do my best."

Oudin chuckled. "Do not worry. She is very kind. You will like her."

"Of course he will," said Roscille.

They left, taking much of the good cheer with them. Eldred sat, looking over his shoulder at the bed, feeling tired down to his bones.

"If you are ready to sleep, I can have Guyon run and get some more stewards to move you over to the bed," said Elisiard.

"I don't want to sleep. I'll wreck all of this," said Eldred, gesturing about the room.

"That is why you are here, in these quarters. And besides, we had some word of your difficulties. Let me show you," said Elisiard. He crossed the room and pulled out a steel gauntlet attached to a chain that ran under the bed. "The frame was crafted from ancient oak. Not even your strength can break it."

Eldred glanced at his left wrist, already scarred and pale.

Elisiard smiled. "I will wrap your arms in fine linen."

Eldred nodded. "Send Guyon then. This place is better than I realized when I arrived."

"I aim to get you moved to the palace soon. Everything just takes time here. Nothing can be hurried," said Elisiard.

"Nothing but weddings," said Eldred.

✣

MATELINE

ateline stood taller than either Uncle Julian or Oudin, who flanked her on either side. Her long dark hair showed more curls than you would ever see on a pure Maldavian maiden, and her chin was too square. Her arms, which were bare from just below the shoulder, looked powerful. She was strong—just like Eldred, part Mercian—just like Eldred. But her eyes, steely as they were, had the vision—both far and dark if reports were accurate. In any case, they were not happy as they looked down at him, though he was thoroughly cleaned and freshly coiffed. She kept focusing on his right cheek—the one with the dead looking patch of skin. Eldred fought the urge to cover it with his hand.

Uncle Julian had just finished saying something, and there was silence.

Eldred jerked himself straighter on the couch and forced a smile. "A pleasure to meet you."

Mateline glanced over at Oudin, then back at Eldred. "I am honored to meet you, Lord Eldred."

Uncle Julian gestured to the couch opposite Eldred. "Let us sit and speak for a few minutes."

Julian sat in a chair that Elisiard brought forth. Roscille, Mateline and Oudin sat on the couch, with Mateline in the middle, towering over the other two. Elisiard and Guyon stood back, as did two new stewards, who appeared to belong with Mateline.

Julian surveyed the gathering with a somber eye. He did not look much changed over the four years since Eldred had last seen him. He still had a full head of hair with just a touch of gray in his neatly trimmed beard. His eyes were cold but showed the vision as clearly as Mateline's. They matched his face, which seemed blank except for a slight trace of disdain, which seemed appropriate for a king.

The king waved his hand. "Tea, please, Elisiard."

Elisiard had anticipated the request and poured five cups of steaming tea, which he brought out on a tray. Eldred set his cup on a low table while the others sipped from theirs.

"This is pleasant," said Roscille.

Oudin smirked. "Yes, very pleasant."

Eldred racked his brain for something to say. "I heard Dinan is nice."

Mateline tilted her head as she looked him in the eye. "Did you?"

"Yes, I heard you have a brewery in your town," continued Eldred.

"We do. The family that runs the brewery calls their ale by the name 'Dinan Stout'. Have you tried it?" asked Mateline.

Eldred shook his head. "No. I don't drink."

"Oh," said Mateline.

Julian stirred, looking at Eldred with a hard face. "I sent my envoy to settle matters with King Harold."

Eldred grimaced at the mention of his cousin's title. "I see."

"They had sent a claim of your treason as a justification for holding my sister. Is there anything to that?" asked Julian.

Eldred clenched his jaw. "No, nothing at all. I just fell. Whatever happened, it was the Corporians's doing. It was their dark spell."

Julian looked Eldred over. "Oudin said as much, but I wished to hear it from you. In any case, I am sure we can settle the matter, but such tales—be they true or false—carry the reek of dishonor."

"I'm sorry for that, Uncle," said Eldred.

Julian frowned. "It is Mateline you should apologize to. She will have to defend your actions for times beyond counting."

Roscille rolled her eyes. "Really, Father."

Eldred turned to find Mateline staring at him like a bird of prey might. He swallowed and bowed his head. "I'm sorry."

Madeline nodded. "I am sure it is a misunderstanding on King Harold's part."

Eldred frowned. Now she was saying it too.

Julian set down his cup. "Well, I must get back to meet with my council. We have a pugnacious new Deiran king on our border and a host of Corporians behind him. I will leave you young people to your fun."

There was a pause as Julian rose and left the stables, then Roscille invited Matelin to knit with her. One of the stewards brought forth needles and yarn, and they started on their crafting. Eldred couldn't help but note that

Mateline's fingers appeared a good deal slower and clumsier than Roscille.

Oudin set down his tea cup and called for a beer. He took a long swig and smiled at Eldred. "Tell me again about the Corporian warriors."

COURTING DAYS

Three more days passed with pleasant visits, more pleasant perhaps since Uncle Julian did not come again. In that time, Roscille knitted a fine blanket emblazoned with a dragon. Mateline knitted a formless black cap that Eldred could wear securely provided he did not abruptly turn his head. Eldred thanked each of them for their gifts.

In other developments, Mateline's cousin, Domard, arrived for the impending wedding and came to lunch at the stables with Eldred's usual visitors. He brought a restless presence to the group, constantly shifting in his chair. Unlike Oudin, he had no interest in Eldred's tales.

Eldred mulled over the news Oudin had brought while he ate a roasted chicken that Elisiard had thoughtfully cut into pieces. Everything had been worked out with Harold. Eldred shook his head as he glanced out the windows at the surrounding garden, which looked quite lovely in the afternoon sun. Per Oudin's report, Harold had dropped the charges of treason against Eldred and promised to release Ghyslaine in one month. It seemed too reasonable.

Eldred shook his chicken leg at Oudin. "What did your father give Harold to move him on these matters? I know Harold well, and it's not like him to surrender anything without getting something in return."

Oudin shrugged and paused his discussion with Domard about their last hunt. "It was my father's envoy, Bourguin, who settled the matter. I do not know that he did anything but speak reason with King Harold."

Eldred frowned. "He did not offer up a town or some land in order to change his mind?"

Domard's mouth twisted into a grin. "You think Julian surrendered the city of Bath to the Deirans just for you?"

Oudin smiled. "No. I would definitely hear if we gave up anything of that sort."

"Gold, then, perhaps?" asked Eldred.

"Your weight in gold would beggar the kingdom," said Domard with a laugh.

Oudin picked up his mug of beer. "Nothing like that. It was just reasoning with him, I believe. He did not wish to interfere with your upcoming nuptials."

Mateline looked up from her knitting for a moment before resuming her work. Domard gave Eldred a dark look and turned to face the gardens.

Eldred set down the chicken leg. "He's more considerate now that he is king." He glanced at Roscille. "I suppose the wedding is on."

Roscille continued her work on her new creation, which appeared to be the start of a sweater. "Of course it is. Mother sent for Mateline's parents just before we came. We will set the date for three or four days from now."

Eldred stiffened. "So soon."

"So long, you mean," said Domard.

"Yes, that's right," said Eldred.

Mateline continued her work on her project—Eldred could not tell what it was—without comment.

"We should have a hunt. Bag a fine trophy for the wedding feast. It is the least I can do for my dear cousin," said Domard.

Oudin raised his cup. "A splendid idea. With a few hours' ride, we could reach some excellent hunting grounds. Mateline, what about you? You should come. It's for your feast."

Mateline raised her head. "I am making Eldred a scarf."

Oudin tilted his head. "What about it, Eldred? Can you spare your bride-to-be for one afternoon? You have the whole rest of your life to sit with her—I mean, stay with her." Oudin reddened slightly.

"Oh," said Eldred quietly. "No, of course, please, do go, Mateline. It looks like the perfect day for a hunt."

"We could use your bow, cousin," said Domard.

"I do not know," said Mateline, pushing her hair out of her face.

Roscille wrinkled her forehead. "I think it would be fine if you went. I will keep Eldred company."

When Mateline set down her knitting and departed with the men, she was the happiest that Eldred had ever seen her.

After Elisiard had cleared away the lunch plates, Eldred sipped a glass of water and watched Roscille as she deftly attended to her work. "Why is any of this happening?"

Roscille did not look up. "You mean the wedding? This is how it is done."

"I don't think I'm right for her. And I don't think she is right for me, though I suppose if I need a nursemaid, she is the only one here that could pick me up on her own."

Roscille rolled her eyes. "You have royal blood in you. You are seventh in line for the throne. This is a good pairing for her house. And for you, her parents can make a fine dowry. Between that and some land Father means to grant you, you should be quite comfortable."

"So it is pure chance that she is half Mercian?"

Roscille frowned. "She is less Mercian than you are, as anyone can see."

Eldred recoiled.

Roscille sighed. "I am sorry. I did not mean that. But she is only an eighth Mercian, through her father's line."

"I understand. I just never thought to marry any sort of Mercian. I never wanted to be one myself. People think I'm pure Mercian with my appearance. I always wanted to be like my father, a proper Deiran, a bonded warrior." Eldred paused and clasped his hands. That is all Father had ever wanted, too. "I wanted that for my son. Now, instead, it seems I'll raise a Mercian child in Dinan. Judging by your brothers, how they treated me when I visited before, it won't be an easy life."

"Do not make any assumptions based on those two. And in any case, it is somewhat unsettling for anyone to see a person of Mercian appearance who has the vision. You and Mateline are both exceedingly rare. Besides, Oudin likes you well enough now."

"I suppose I like him too." Eldred drank from his cup. "You can go if you want. I know you'll be busy planning the wedding. I'm comfortable here. I have Elisiard and Guyon to look after me."

Roscille paused and flexed her fingers. "I should like your wedding to be well executed."

Eldred smiled. "I have full confidence in you."

A VISITOR

Roscille sent her apologies about missing dinner and—as far as Eldred could tell—the three hunters had not yet returned, so Eldred made an early night of it. After the crew of stewards made an appearance to help Eldred over to the bed, Elisiard secured the manacles to Eldred's linen wrapped wrists. The two stewards withdrew to their bunks, and Eldred lay in the dark, looking out on the trees shaking in the wind.

Normally, in past days, Eldred would toss and turn. That had always been his manner of sleeping. But he made a point to stay still, for any shift in position surfaced the limits of the chains. He knew that once he felt that restraint, it would fill his mind. Nonetheless, he was grateful for the manacles. He could sleep without fear of attacking anyone, even if he did walk the bed halfway across the room in the depths of his fits.

It was still early when Eldred heard a faint gurgling sound from the stall where Guyon was sleeping. Eldred lifted his head to look more closely, but everything was still, and the noise did not repeat. Eldred lay his head on the pillow and turned his attention back to the window.

Ten minutes later, there was a brief rustling from Elisiard's stall.

Eldred pushed up on his right elbow, half lifting himself from the bed. "Is that you, Elisiard? Are you both up?" Eldred waited for a reply, but none came. In a louder voice, one that would wake anyone, Eldred continued. "Elisiard! Elisiard! What's happening? Are you well?"

After a pause, he heard a voice. "How strange." It was neither Elisiard or Guyon.

"Who is that? What are you doing here?" demanded Eldred.

A small bearded man whose eyes glimmered with the vision came out from around the side of the stalls bearing a knife. Eldred could see blood on the blade.

"Who are you?" yelled Eldred. "Help! Help! We are under attack! Help!"

The man stood by patiently as Eldred screamed into the night. When Eldred finally petered out, the man gave a small bow. "I am an assassin, the finest of my trade."

"What do you want with me?"

"Is it not obvious?" The man chuckled. "This is all so odd. I never speak to my charges. Some are fast enough to grunt something, but they die before anything more. But this"—he gestured at the manacles—"really removes the need for any skill at all. A lame Mercian in an isolated stable chained to a bed; my true crime will be in keeping all of my pay."

Eldred wet his lips. "Who paid you? I'll pay more."

The assassin furrowed his brow. "That is what you all think—that the Torvid have no honor." He wagged his finger at Eldred. "But you are all wrong. We were the Mother's true first creation—you cannot count those ghastly First Born, pale barbarians she trapped in a cave for her son's amusement."

Eldred looked again at the man and caught the difference. His eyes shone like a Maldavian's with the vision, but they were shaded red. The man truly was a Torvid. A deep fear filled Eldred's heart—there was no deed too depraved for his kind. "So you have honor," squeaked out Eldred.

The man showed a toothy grin. "I just told you—you dumb ox."

Eldred cast his mind for something to say. "I—well—I'm to be married."

"I doubt it." The assassin moved to the foot of the bed and pulled back the blankets.

Eldred curled himself up off the bed as much as he could to watch him. "Don't come near me. Stay away."

He laughed and pricked Eldred's left foot with his dagger.

"Stop it!" shouted Eldred.

His eyes flashed with excitement. "My patron spoke of this. He wondered if you were faking this injury. I must investigate. Thus will I deserve my full reward." He stabbed Eldred's still foot, releasing a spurt of blood.

"Stop it! You Motherless piece of garbage. Stop it! Leave me alone!"

He stared at the blood leaking out of Eldred. "You must be lame. Nobody could sit through that. Still, I may as well check." He reached over and drove his knife deep into Eldred's calf.

Eldred felt no pain—no pain at all—but the horror of the moment echoed through his brain. His upper body writhed, and he screamed to the heavens, but his legs lay dead still.

A horrible smile spread over the man's face. "I bet I could just cut your leg off. That would be all the proof he could want."

"No! No!" shouted Eldred.

Then they rushed in, Oudin and Domard. Oudin bore a dagger in his hand, Domard a sword. They set on the Torvid—who had been caught unawares and retreated across the room. At the edge of the stalls, Eldred spotted Mateline nocking an arrow on her bow.

Eldred jerked on the chains, rocking the bed, but he could not pull free. The wet pool of blood spread across the mattress. As he fought the bed, he heard a cry and turned to see Domard fall to the ground, clutching his throat with bloody fingers.

Eldred paused to watch the man turn on Oudin, moving with terrific speed. The murderous assassin drove his blade into Oudin's gut then danced back out of reach from Oudin's faltering counter attack. Oudin caught hold of the back of a chair to stay on his feet and Mateline let fly her arrow, but the Torvid ducked safely away and smirked.

Eldred looked upon the assassin's face with a frightening realization. The man could not have been more relaxed or mirthful; he was just making sport with them, just playing with them. "Run, Mateline! Run for your life!"

Mateline notched the next arrow, paying Eldred no mind.

Oudin, perhaps realizing he was overmatched, staggered back as the assassin walked purposefully forward in pursuit. Mateline's next arrow just missed the little man's head, which he bobbed in apparent excitement. The Torvid snatched Oudin's knife from his hand and giggled as Oudin came up against the wall. Oudin was gasping for air and lifted his arm as if to keep the assassin at bay.

Mateline's next arrow made the little man jump. But the next moment, he stepped under Oudin's outstretched arm and drove Oudin's own dagger into his shoulder. In an odd courtesy, he lowered Oudin gently to the floor. As he stepped away from Oudin, he dodged another arrow. Mateline gained all of his attention.

"Run, Mateline! Run from here!" shouted Eldred.

She nocked another arrow as the assassin began to walk slowly in her direction, offering the full width of his chest to her aim.

"You can't hit him!" screamed Eldred.

He flashed a delighted smile. "So true."

"Die now," snarled Mateline, letting her arrow fly.

The arrow flew true, but the man gave the smallest half turn, and the arrow passed him by less than an inch away. He strode forward as Mateline threw down her bow and rushed to meet him with her bare hands. Eldred shouted and pulled the chains for all he was worth, but to no avail.

Eldred felt his heart drop as the assassin's blade cut into her side. She screamed and struck out at the Torvid, but he tumbled backwards and rolled across the floor coming up in a theatrical bow. Mateline stood holding her side.

He winked at Eldred. "It always takes a while to kill a Mercian."

"Leave her. You weren't paid for her," said Eldred.

The assassin pursed his lips. "True, but it will be better this way." He dashed towards her, catching her arm and driving his dagger into her shoulder.

Mateline staggered back. She raised her hand that had clutched her side and caught the little man around the neck. His eyes flew wide in surprise. As he stabbed her again in the side, she shook her other arm free and got both hands around his neck. In a fury, he stabbed her five times in quick succession and then there was a terrible crack from his neck and he went limp in her hands. She hurled him against a wall, and he dropped to the ground in a tumbled heap.

Eldred pulled on the chains. "Unlock my chains. I can go for help."

Unheeding, Mateline crossed the room to her cousin on unsteady feet, dripping blood behind her. When she turned him over, the neck wound was clearly seen. Domard was dead. Mateline stifled a sob.

"Unlock me!" shouted Eldred.

"I cannot," mumbled Mateline. She crossed to where Oudin lay, dropping to her knees by his body. There was a trace of movement, Oudin still lived.

Eldred felt momentarily dizzy and stopped pulling on the chains. He looked down, the mattress was matted with his blood and his heart was beating faster. "I'm not well," muttered Eldred.

Mateline keeled over next to Oudin, laying beside him.

Eldred felt his strength go and fell back onto the bed. His mouth felt dry. "Help. Help us!" he called. But his cry was weak. He cried out a few more times before he sank down into stillness.

HENREIT

Eldred became aware of someone shaking him by the shoulders. He took a tired breath and opened his eyes to find Roscille leaning over him. She gave a faint smile as Eldred blinked in the bright sunlight. As he went to move his arms, he was caught up, still chained.

"He is awake," said Roscille.

Uncle Julian came into view on the other side of the table, looking down. "Finally."

A brief shudder passed through Eldred's torso. He licked his dry lips, and looked back and forth between the two. "Mateline? Is she?"

Roscille pressed her palms together in front of her chest. "She was badly injured. Lady Genevote is tending to her and to Oudin at the palace."

Julian grimaced. "He lies on the edge of death."

"Elisiard?" asked Eldred.

Roscille shook her head. "No. He perished. Domard and Guyon, too."

Eldred swallowed. "He stabbed Mateline many times, but she finished him. He was here to kill me. That's what he said." He abruptly pulled on the chains. "Can you get these off of me?"

Julian turned to a genial looking Maldavian with a thin mustache and a heavy-set build standing by the foot of the bed—where the assassin had stood; nobody else was present. "Henreit, go look for the key. It must be with Elisiard." Julian returned his gaze to Eldred. "What else did this man say?"

Eldred blew out his breath as he peered down at his leg. The blood-soaked mattress had been covered by a blanket and his wounds were neatly wrapped. From the corner of his eye, he noticed a naked body on the ground—the assassin himself.

Julian stepped closer to Eldred. "What did he say?"

"Well, not much. He was a confident bastard and very fast. I was just lying here, getting ready to sleep, while he killed Guyon and then Elisiard. I barely heard anything. Then he came out and did that." Eldred nodded towards his foot. "He wanted to see if I was truly lame. He wanted to find out to make his patron happy. That's pretty much all he said before Oudin and Domard charged him. He killed Domard. Then he took down Oudin. Mateline was very brave."

Julian frowned. "All Torvid are confident and fast."

Eldred sighed. "It shouldn't be. It should never be, but I think Harold was his patron. No true Deiran would choose such dishonor, but the man is a fool and a coward. He doesn't deserve my father's crown."

"You had best leave these matters to me," said Julian.

"I have. Look around—this is not my doing!" snapped Eldred.

Roscille stepped back from the bed, but Julian stood where he was, unmoved. Henreit appeared from around the side of the stalls bearing a key and paused, taking in the scene.

Julian leaned in closer. "You are a young man, nephew. I forgive you for your ill-considered words. You are going away now, with Henreit. You will stay with him, causing neither him nor myself any trouble, until such time as I send for you."

Eldred glanced at Henreit, who came forward to try the key in his right manacle. "Who is he?"

Henreit smiled. "I am your cousin. Surely, you remember. I was there at the feast after your far sight trial."

"Oh, of course" said Eldred. He had no recollection of the man, who— as Eldred observed—did not have the vision. Eldred looked up at Julian and gestured at the corpse with his newly freed hand. "How can he protect me from assassins like him?"

Henreit moved around the bed, reaching for the remaining manacle. "It will not just be me. I have thrown together a trusty band consisting of my townspeople. I am the mayor of Branath."

"Branath?" asked Eldred.

Henreit released the remaining manacle. "A small town an hour to the east from here. I have been in charge of it for the last two years, thanks to Uncle Julian."

Eldred lay back and peeled the linen wraps from his wrists. "Why is it safer in Branath?"

Henreit gestured excitedly at Eldred. "We will not be in Branath. We will be out in the woods at a secret place, safe as houses."

Julian nodded. "They will not be looking for you in these parts. The word will be that you are traveling south to Belum. By the time they realize their mistake, I will have settled this matter completely."

Eldred pushed himself up on his elbow. "But—"

Julian held up his hand. "Let me finish. I am headed back now to be with my son, whom I hope will be alive at the end of the day. I agree that this is not a perfect plan, nor one free of danger despite the earnest efforts of Henreit. So I give you this as a parting gift—my own set of throwing knives."

Julian produced a leather wrapped bundle and set it on the bed next to Eldred. "With your Mercian brutishness and your Deiran tendencies, I am certain that you would rather fight your foes up close, but your circumstances have changed." He pointed at the bundle. "This is how you must learn to fight if you wish to survive. Mateline may not be there to save you next time. Now, farewell, dear nephew, son of my beloved half-sister. I am certain we shall meet again."

Julian took his leave. Eldred sat up on the edge of the bed to take some bread and water that Roscille brought him.

"Can I see Mateline and Oudin before I go?" asked Eldred.

Roscille shook her head. "No, there is no time. But trust them to survive. Mateline will heal, and even my dear brother is stronger than people know."

"I'll miss them," said Eldred, surprised at the depth of his feeling.

"In any case, our means of transport approaches," said Henreit.

Eldred looked out the window. "You mean that hay wagon coming through the gardens?"

Henreit grinned. "You are fooled, cousin. It appears to be a hay wagon with a single driver, but it has been hollowed out. Hidden travelers ride within."

"I'm familiar with that trick, or at least a trick of that sort," said Eldred somberly. "It is not a happy memory. But tell me, who is inside?"

"Who else, but yourself?" chuckled Henreit. "Oh, and a famous healer, the true gem of our expedition."

The wagon came to a stop beside the stables, and a tall man, a Mercian by his appearance, popped up from within the hay bales and climbed up over the front onto the driver's bench. A pale young woman with white hair climbed out after him, a First Born, unmistakable though he had never seen one before.

Henreit grew excited as the three travelers approached. "Eldred, meet Eldred, your doppelganger."

Eldred looked the Mercian over. He appeared to be a least six years older than himself, as well as four inches taller and fifty pounds heavier. He lacked the vision. He also lacked an odd patch of dead-looking skin on his face. Eldred raised his eyebrows. "I can tell the difference."

Roscille clasped hands before her. "Of course you can. But he will mostly be in a carriage and you are not so famous that everyone will immediately see through him."

The big man thrust out his hand. "Good to meet you, Prince Eldred. My name's Blasio."

Eldred took his hand and smiled back. "Good to meet you, Blasio. You're taking some risk."

Blaisio glanced down at the assassin's corpse. "Oh, that kind's no trouble. I heard the housemaid killed him."

"Not the housemaid. My fiancée," said Eldred.

Blasio shrugged. "Well, a woman, anyway. I've no worries. It's the easiest three denarii I could ever hope for. I just go on a carriage ride to Belum. Always wanted to go there anyway."

"I hope it's that simple," said Eldred.

Henreit slapped his hand down on the shoulder of the driver of the wagon. "This is Balian. He has far sight, noble vision like yourself, though he is a farmer, a skilled farmer, perhaps the best in Branath."

Eldred shook hands. The man did have the vision. "Good to meet you, Balian."

Balian nodded. "And you, prince."

"And this"—Henreit gestured grandly towards the First Born—"is Weltrude, the finest healer hereabouts. It was amazing luck that she was in Branath this morning when the message arrived from Uncle Julian."

The young woman whose pale face was set with deep blue eyes stepped forward and brushed Eldred's hair away from his left temple. "Three fatum lapides; are you the only one to have such?"

Eldred cocked his head. "I don't know; perhaps."

She pointed at his legs. "You are having trouble with these?"

"Yes, since I fell from my horse. Can you treat injuries of that sort?" asked Eldred.

A gleam appeared in her eye as she bowed her head. "Mother willing, anything is possible when one has the right knowledge."

"That is so," agreed Eldred. "So, Balian is my bodyguard?"

"He will be your main bodyguard, but I have a number of formidable men who will meet us on the road. This is rather like your famous expedition to the north, is it not?" asked Henreit.

"I suppose," said Eldred.

Henreit wrapped his arm over Eldred's shoulder. "But now you go with your own true people, your family, people who care for you."

Roscille raised her eyebrow. "Let us not be too familiar, Henreit. Remember, Eldred is in line for the throne."

Henreit raised his hands in mock surrender. "Of course, of course. I only meant to say what an honor it is for me to lead this expedition."

"Do not be confused, Henreit. Eldred is in command. And you will see him returned in the finest health, or you will deal with me," said Roscille firmly.

Henreit put out his hand towards Weltrude. "I will, and in even better health than he now possesses."

Roscille gazed at him cooly.

"Well, we must make ready then. Blasio, one last duty before your trip?" asked Henreit.

The big man clapped his hands. "Why not?"

Roscille stayed with Eldred as the others unloaded hay bales off the back of the wagon. She pointed to the assassin's corpse. "Whoever paid for him can cheaply have another. Torvid need few inducements to commit murder."

Eldred narrowed his brows. "If there is another like that, I'll be dead."

Roscille tapped the bundle on the bed beside Eldred. "You need to learn new skills. Change, the ability to adjust to circumstances, is the truest sign of greatness. While you cannot walk, while you are so afflicted, you must fight the Maldavian way—from a distance. If you had these knives beside you last night, you could have slain that Torvid dog before he stabbed my brother or killed sweet Domard."

Eldred crinkled up his face, thinking about how easily the Torvid had dodged Mateline's attacks. "I could have tried."

Roscille placed her hand on top of Eldred's. "You must do more than try, dear cousin. So many doubt you. So many think ill of you. You must prove them wrong. I see the champion inside you."

"You do?" asked Eldred.

"My brother and Mateline—they fought for you and now suffer greatly for their effort. Though the assassin has died, our true enemies remain untouched, without punishment." She pressed the bundle into his hand. "You must ready yourself for vengeance."

Eldred glanced down at the bundle of knives. "I will. I'll seek vengeance for both of us."

✤

THE ROAD

The journey started with a flurry of questions from Weltrude regarding Eldred's injuries as she examined his bandages, but Henreit popped up over the hay and shushed her. "Not until we are out of the city. Our enemies could be anywhere."

So, they sat in silence, lightly bouncing with the wagon as it rolled down the road. Elderd was propped up between two hay bales, one arm stretched out on each. Weltrude sat near Eldred's feet, watching with interest whenever his legs shifted with the wagon's motion. In half an hour, they left the city headed north. The road changed from cobblestones to something smoother. Eldred blinked his eyes and shifted his torso as he fought to stay awake in the warmth of the sun.

After a few hours, Henreit poked his head up over the hay. "We've done the hard part—escaped from Emon. Not many people live out here, though we might meet some hunters on the road."

Eldred frowned. "Are we camping then?" He had liked the open air of the stables, but remembered all too well how easily the Torvid had ambled inside.

"No, of course not, not with such fine people on the expedition as ourselves. We have only a few nights under the stars for the trip. You will be impressed with the estate where we are staying, much finer than those old stables," said Henreit.

"Your family estate?" asked Eldred.

Henreit chuckled. "It could become such, but that is for later. Tonight you meet the rest of the men, the proper start of the expedition."

Eldred grunted. A true expedition had a point, some challenge to be overcome. Hiding in the woods was something different.

In the early evening, they reached the rendezvous spot. The wagon rocked violently as Balian maneuvered off the road under the trees. As they came to a stop, a small cheer went up. In short order, men appeared and cleared a path through the hay, and Balian helped Weltrude down.

Eldred weighed his distaste for being manhandled against his desire to get out of the wagon and allowed Balian and five other men to pick him up. They settled him against a log near the fire, where a tall thin man tended a large cookpot.

A thin cook, thought Eldred, the perfect fit for this mismatched band. Eldred glanced at Balian, who was talking with Weltrude—the only man with vision other than himself. The rest didn't look exactly soft—they had strong hands and arms—but they were the hands of farmers, not warriors. A Torvid assassin could likely kill them all before anyone drew a weapon.

"A toast! A toast to the expedition!" called Henreit as he walked back from a nearby wagon—there were three others besides the one that had carried Eldred, each piled high with all manner of things: chairs, mattresses, even potted plants. Henreit carried a tray with four crystal goblets in one hand while he poured wine with the other into the men's outstretched cups as he passed. He set the tray down on the log next to Eldred and filled each goblet to the brim with dark red wine.

The men lined up, shifting impatiently as they waited. Henreit passed the first goblet to Weltrude. "To beauty and wisdom in one."

She blushed bright red.

He passed the second goblet to Balian. "To duty and honor."

Balian took the goblet and nodded gravely.

Henreit passed the third goblet to Eldred. "To nobility and greatness."

Eldred took the drink, careful not to spill it. "Thanks."

Henriet held up the last cup. "It is no easy thing to pass out so much fine wine without taking a drink myself." He grinned as the men chuckled. "We go now on an excellent expedition to serve and protect my cousin, Eldred, whose noble eyes see through both darkness and distance. To Eldred!"

Henreit drained his cup with a dramatic gesture. The line of men followed suit. Weltrude took a long sip and drained half her goblet.

Eldred watched the others then took a small peck of wine from his cup.

Henreit gave a slight head shake. "Is something wrong, cousin? I brought only good wine and this is the best of it."

Eldred smiled apologetically. "I don't drink."

"But what about your Mercian side? They love their drink," said Henreit.

Eldred set down his cup. "I'm not Mercian, and I don't drink wine—a habit from my long years at the Academy."

"Oh, yes. I remember now," said Henreit, eyeing Eldred's nearly full goblet. He clapped his hands. "Well, the good news is that I brought two cases should you change your mind. But now, you are due a round of introductions. I present to you the champions of this expedition."

Henriet gestured to the first man in the line, a short but stout looking young man with a dark beard and friendly eyes. Along with Balian, he had taken the greater share of Eldred's weight when they had taken him down from the wagon. "I present to you Gervese of Branath, the best neighbor a man could hope to have. There to help through any contingency."

Gervese gave a deep bow. "Always glad to be of service."

Henreit nodded to the second man, a wrinkled man with a gray beard and mustache. "Madalulf of Branath is our oldest citizen."

Madalulf glared at Henreit. "I am here to do as much as anyone."

Henreit smiled and turned to the next man, a spindly youth with a long neck. "Pernet here balances us out in the age department."

Pernet gave Eldred a weak grin.

"Rollon will keep us well fed. Best cook in Branath," said Henreit.

The suspiciously thin cook held up his cup and smiled at Eldred.

"Guillotin is your man if your livestock have trouble," said Henreit.

Guillotin, a fat man with a wispy beard, gave Eldred a blank look and slowly nodded.

"Raduard is as hard a worker as any man is," said Henreit, addressing the last man in the line.

Raduard, a fit looking man except for his heavy cheeks, gave a short bow. "I do my best."

Henreit gave an exaggerated bow. "Your champions, Eldred."

Eldred looked over the line of scruffy men. "Well met."

When nobody else spoke, Eldred cleared his throat and continued. "I think, I hope, we have a most successful trip or expedition. We'll face danger, perhaps." Eldred looked down and frowned. "But I hope not."

Henreit clapped lightly and the others joined in, except for Weltrude and Balian. "Well said. For those who are curious, the danger is quite real. I saw the corpse of the Torvid assassin at the palace. I was there with my Uncle Julian and cousin, Roscille."

Madalulf's face turned more sour. "Nobody told me it was a Torvid."

Pernet shrugged. "What difference does it make?"

"There is a difference," said Balian quietly.

At the mention of the assassin, Eldred picked up his bundle of knives and unrolled it on the ground. Nine blades were tucked within—three short knives with gleaming green handles, three medium sized blades with pale white handles and three long knives with dark blue handles.

Pernet, Gervese and Guillotin crowded around to look at the handsome weapons.

"I was there when Uncle Julian gave him those. Those are the king's own knives," said Henreit.

"Waouh," said Pernet.

"They are no better than any other blade so long as it is sharp," said Madalulf.

"We should put them to the test. I saw a Serpent board somewhere," said Pernet.

Gervese nodded. "I packed it under the mattresses—at the bottom."

The two went in search of the missing board.

When they returned, Henreit perched on the log in the space Weltrude had vacated. "Did you play Serpent when you visited last?"

Eldred shook his head as he watched Pernet and Gervese hang the board on a tree some fifteen feet from where he sat. Two painted serpents—one red, one green—stretched across the board, broken up into triangle shaped segments, starting from the tail on the left and ending with the fanged heads of the creatures on the right.

Henreit mimed throwing a knife. "Two players take turns. First, you throw at the tail. Whoever hits a tail first sets his color. Then you walk up the serpent with your knives until you hit the head. But if you are on the head of your snake and hit your opponent's snake anywhere, then you lose. So be careful on that last one."

"Sounds simple enough," said Eldred.

Henriet grinned. "Do not bet with anyone—especially Balian. This is a—well, it is not a game nobles should expect to win. Our illustrious cousins prefer their bows. This is for the common folk."

"We'll see," said Eldred.

Pernet challenged Eldred as soon as he retrieved his own knives—three worn looking blades. He paused before his first throw. "We often wager a blade. The winner takes their pick from the loser."

Eldred glanced at Henreit, who gave a slight shake of his head.

"Not today, Pernet. It is the prince's first game," said Balian.

Pernet smiled wide. "Sometimes we do it."

Balian raised his eyebrows. "But today, we do not."

Pernet's first throw bounced off the tree, earning him a laugh from the observers.

"Are you showing the prince how not to throw?" asked Rollon as he stirred his pot.

Pernet's next two throws were more accurate and stuck in the board, but missed both serpents.

Eldred looked over his collection. "Which size would you recommend, Henreit?"

Balian leaned in across Henreit. "Smallest is always best for Serpent."

Eldred took one of the small green handled knives and eyed the target. After lining up his throw a few times, he released it, only to watch it fly wide of the tree and disappear out into the forest.

Henreit got to his feet. "Oh, no. Not so hard, cousin. You don't want to lose these."

Eldred pulled back on his next throw, barely reaching the tree. His third throw bounced off the tree trunk a foot below the board.

"Nobody becomes a Serpent master on their first day," said Henreit.

"No," agreed Balian.

Everyone but Rollon, who still tended his pots, and Weltrude, who was off somewhere, joined in the hunt for Eldred's missing blade which they found after a few minutes.

After two more rounds, which improved for Eldred in that he did not throw his knives as far, Pernet hit the red serpent's tail.

"We finally have a color," observed Madalulf.

Six rounds later, Pernet was halfway up the snake and Eldred had only stuck one knife in the board. Rollon started dishing up the stew, and Weltrude returned from the woods. As much as Eldred wanted to stop for dinner, he played on for eight more rounds until Pernet finally found the serpent's head. Eldred was still looking for the tail.

"Not bad," said Henreit.

Balian nodded.

As Eldred ate the bitter stew—he had been right about Rollon's cooking—he watched the others play and saw beyond doubt that Pernet was by far the worst player aside from himself. On the other extreme, Balian was the winner of every match he played, always with the green serpent. He never failed to find the snake's tail in the first round.

Eventually, the warmth of the fire made Eldred drowsy and he called Henreit over—Weltrude and Balian came as well. "I'll sleep soon, but it's best I'm a ways apart from the rest of you for my morning fits—to limit the damage."

Henreit gestured at the fire. "Do you wish to stay here? I can shift the others."

Eldred waved off the suggestion. "No. I just need a few blankets. The night is warm enough."

"You need not move," said Weltrude.

Eldred pushed himself back, higher against the log. "Well, I have hurt people. I didn't mean to, but I did."

Weltrude held out a bulbous brown root. "I mean, I found a cor root. I went looking after dinner. The juice squeezed from mashed cor root brings the deepest sleep when mixed with the right herbs."

Henriet smiled at Weltrude. "The wisest healer, just like I promised you, cousin. You should try this concoction. You might even find it to your taste."

Weltrude wrinkled her nose. "No," she said slowly. "Alas, that is a serious drawback with cor root. I suggest we mix the preparation with warm wine. That is the best way to mask the taste."

Eldred eyed the proffered root. "Are you certain it will help? I'm slower now, but if I get hold of someone, I could snap their neck."

Weltrude frowned. "My people have the greatest healing arts of all the Mother's children."

"Don't be insulting, cousin. Just take it," said Henreit. "Do not make a fuss over a cup of wine."

Eldred glanced over the impatient faces of Weltrude, Balain and Henreit and glumly nodded his assent. When the final mixture was presented to him half an hour later, he almost gagged at the odor. He looked up at Weltrude, who was standing over him. "All of it?"

Weltrude nodded firmly. "Yes. Best one quick quaff to get it all down."

Eldred let out a sigh and shuddered as he poured the foul concoction down his throat. Afterwards, he groaned several times while Henriet patted him on the back. "That was the worst thing I've ever had!"

"I once ate a fly," offered Henreit.

"I'd crunch a hundred flies before I'd take another cup," muttered Eldred.

Weltrude laid her hand on Eldred's shoulder. "You will sleep with the blessing of the Mother."

Eldred opened his mouth to complain but paused. A deep warmth radiated up from his stomach through his torso, relaxing every muscle as it passed. He felt his mind sinking down, descending into sleep. He heard them talking beside him but paid them no mind. He smiled. "Oh, that's nice."

RESTED

Eldred woke to the gentle rocking of the wagon, blinking at the sun high in the sky. Tall moss-covered trees framed his view in all directions. He groaned contentedly; his back and shoulders felt easy and relaxed.

"At last," said Weltrude. She was sitting down by Eldred's feet. Behind her, the hay wall stood—rebuilt. "It is almost noon."

Eldred smiled. "A full night's sleep. I haven't had that in weeks. And the fits? No fits?"

"Nothing dangerous. You did mumble quite a bit. You stirred at times but not enough to wake."

"Did I thrash around?"

Weltrude shook her head. "No."

"Oh, I can't say enough thanks—a peaceful night. Your terrible brew proved its worth." Eldred pushed himself up into a sitting position. "Anything to eat?"

Weltrude handed over a plate that had been beside her. "Old bread and two cold fried eggs. No fresh bread until Rollon is set up in the kitchen at the mansion."

Eldred took the offered food and started eating. "A mansion?"

Weltrude shrugged. "That is how Henreit described it."

Eldred noticed the bandages were off his legs, which were painted with a reddish clay. "Oh, is that your work?"

Weltrude nodded. "Yes. The royal physicians treated you to the best of their ability but left it entirely to your nature to address your injuries. This mixture will speed your healing. Some of those wounds were deep."

"Yes, the assassin just stood there, stabbing my foot. He wanted to see if I was faking the injury." Eldred swallowed a dry chunk of bread. "Do you have enough ingredients for more of that potion for sleep? Is there anything you can do to make it taste better?"

A smile rose to Weltrude's lips. "I shall have to harvest more cor root, for its potency fades quickly once harvested. But in woods like these, if you know the art, you can find them."

Eldred set the empty plate to the side and considered his legs. "What about my legs? What can you do about them?"

Weltrude's eyes gleamed. "Let me show you." She went to a small chest standing near the back of the wagon and pulled out a small children's hammer with a rounded orange stone for the head.

"That's your equipment in there?" asked Eldred.

Weltrude returned to Eldred's side and kneeled. "Some of it. Watch carefully." She set down the tiny hammer and took Eldred's right leg in both hands, laying it across her knees. Then she gripped the ball of his foot in one hand while she took the hammer in the other and tapped Eldred's ankle. Eldred's foot jumped.

Eldred's eyes went wide. "How did you do that?"

Weltrude set Eldred's leg back on the floor. "Did you feel anything?"

"No."

Weltrude narrowed her brows. "Hmph. In answer to your question, the First Born—my people—have the greatest knowledge of pain. It was our purpose to serve the Son, to provide him the training he needed to know his power, to find his strength, to drive the Wretcheds from the land. We were the closest to him."

Eldred raised his eyebrows. The First Born were but barbarians claimed by no stone bearer whom the Mother had captured. The Son had hunted them in the Caves of Carcerem for his amusement, though Eldred supposed that could be considered training of a sort.

Weltrude continued. "Our wise ones learned the ways of healing, to fix the crushed bones and twisted joints that the Son brought upon us as he reached for his perfection. They learned of the lines of power that run through a person's body, the lines that animate us."

"This sounds useful," allowed Eldred.

Weltrude bowed her head. "I just tested your lines of power."

Eldred gestured at his foot. "You mean the jerk just now?"

"Yes, that shows your flow of energy to your leg is not interrupted as can happen from an injury."

"You mean my fall from Hobbie at the battle?"

"You have my meaning," said Weltrude.

Eldred drew his brows together. "Are you saying I'm not injured?"

"That is right—not in any normal way."

Eldred looked down at his legs. "So what can you do?"

"There is nothing to do. You are well."

Eldred swallowed. "But I can't walk."

Weltrude gestured at his legs. "But you are well. The energy flows through you. Your muscles are strong and toned. You may have a lesser imbalance, but your fatum lapides will straighten that out in time."

Eldred paused. "One of the citizens of Turicum, when I visited there, told me that my fatum lapides could act against each other. He said they may each have separate minds and thus might cancel effects that the other would normally show."

Weltrude narrowed her eyes. "You mean a Wretched?"

Eldred nodded. "Yes, but he was wise. He also understood medicine and the healing arts."

Weltrude clasped her hands tightly across her lap. "What of it?"

Eldred took a breath. "Well, I guess I take his meaning to be that we can't just wait on my fatum lapides to sort things out. We should try something. What else can we try?"

"I would not give any thought to the words of a Wretched. Even if he were wise, which I doubt, he would only lie to you."

"He did know quite a bit. He healed me when I was near death, and even now I possess some of his medicine, a powder he made from the brains of dragons. I didn't have much luck using it, but perhaps with your knowledge you could get it to work."

Weltrude made a face. "I would not recommend that. If you use such a foul treatment, you will only do yourself harm."

"But I can't stay like this. I have to do something."

"You are well, prince. You merely have a minor imbalance. I am certain that if you show patience, you will regain your ability to walk."

Eldred rubbed his hands together and frowned. She had seemed to know her business. The potion had given him the first good sleep since the battle, and she had made his leg twitch, but it felt like a horrible mistake to do nothing. After a pause, he spoke. "I'm sure you're right."

They settled into an uneasy silence for the remainder of the day's ride.

STYLISH TRAVEL

The troop stopped to set up camp in the late afternoon in a glade off the road. Henreit immediately set the crew to unpacking the three wagons piled high with furnishings. Eldred leaned against the tree where they had placed him and watched as the men set up a dining table ringed with eleven high backed chairs and four wide beds topped with thick mattresses, each accompanied by a chest of drawers. There was also a delicate writing desk that appeared to be Henreit's. Rollon got out his pots and started a fire with help from Gervese. And, of course, there was the Serpent board. Madalulf challenged Guillotin to the first match; they were the two most closely matched in skill.

Henriet squatted down next to Eldred. "You look much fresher today."

Eldred smiled. "My first full night's sleep in weeks—thanks to Weltrude. She even worked on my feet. Look, I have my bandages off."

Henriet nodded. "She is a wonder. But everything is going well." He gestured at the dining set, which looked odd in the woodland setting. "This is a most successful expedition. Do you not agree?"

"For comfort, I suppose."

Henriet pointed at the largest bed set on a frame of dark red wood. "That is for you. Think of how well you will sleep tonight."

"Yes," said Eldred, grimacing slightly. It would take more of that nasty brew.

There was a brief stirring as Madalulf hit the tail of the red snake.

"Do you want to challenge the winner?" asked Henriet.

"Not today. I'll give it a rest."

After a few minutes, Balian and Weltrude went off into the woods.

Henriet chuckled. "Those two."

"Are they together?" inquired Eldred.

"Not yet. Maybe never. Balian lost his wife in childbirth less than a year ago."

Eldred turned to look at Henriet. "Was it Weltrude who helped?"

Henreit shuddered. "Yes. Lost both Biette and the child. Sometimes the Mother makes a harsh judgment. That is where it is difficult being the mayor. You wish to help everyone, but what can one do?"

"Yes," said Eldred. He took a breath. "So, she is not always right."

"What?" asked Henreit.

"Weltrude. Her skill, her knowledge, has limits."

Henriet raised his eyebrows. "But of course. She is the most excellent healer though. Are you not wanting the potion tonight? She has gone off to look for another root."

"No. I want the potion. I just mean she doesn't know everything. That's all," said Eldred.

"Nobody knows everything. Perhaps the Mother does, or the Son, but none of us." Henriet glanced back to the Serpent game. "Looks like Madalulf will take it. Just as well; he complains too much if he loses."

Balian and Weltrude returned before dinner. Weltrude showed Eldred a dark, twisted root she had found under a decaying log. Balian presented Eldred with the hare and pheasant he had speared with his verutum.

Eldred stroked the fur of the rabbit where it was not bloodied. "You have good aim with both the knives and the spear. You would make a good warrior."

Balian laughed lightly. "I will stick to farming and the occasional hunt."

Eldred looked up. "You do not want the honor, the glory?"

"Those are fine things for some. But I would not wish to kill another man," said Balian.

"Unless it's an assassin?" asked Eldred.

"Yes. If it were possible," said Balian.

Dinner was a jovial affair. They set Eldred at the head of the table and did not make fun of him when he took water instead of wine. Henreit led them in toasts to Uncle Julian, the Mother and the Son. Each time the men downed the entire contents of their cups. The pheasant came out after the salt beef that Rollon had prepared. Eldred felt a warm glow of appreciation when Balian, and the others insisted that he have the greater share of it.

After dinner, everyone played Serpent save for Eldred, Henreit and Weltrude. The other players were affected by their drink, but not Balian, who remained true to form. He won a match against Madalulf where

Madalulf did not even find the red serpent's tail. Afterwards, Madalulf's curses rang through the woods.

When the time came for Eldred's potion, he gulped the whole cup in one quick motion. He had to fight briefly to keep it down, but then they bore him away to his bed under the sky. As he watched the multihued stars from under heavy lids, it occurred to him that it was not just his body that relaxed—it was his mind as well. He could think of the battle and his lost father, of noble Hobbie, of strong Mateline and brave Dreven without feeling the rage, the pain. He was at peace.

THE MANOR

A light spring rain started falling as the wagon exited the trees and started rolling over gravel.

"We are here," announced Henreit loudly. "The place looks better than ever."

Eldred shifted between two bales of hay, glancing up at the ivy draped walls of the four-story estate. As the rain fell harder, the troop hurriedly pulled down the hay at the back of the wagon and rushed Eldred up the main steps to the second floor; the first story was set halfway into the ground. The breadth of the place was astounding, not much short of the palace at Emon, though with its broken windows and half collapsed stables, it had seen better days.

Past the entryway stood a remarkable room that was open three full stories to the roof. Twin stairways with landings between the floors circled up past the third floor to the fourth, drawing a wide oval aperture that focused Eldred's attention on the majestic composite painting that dominated the room from far above.

The men set Eldred in the dust on the second step as they rushed out to bring the furnishing in out of the rain. He gripped the banister and examined the room—the furniture had fallen into heaps of debris but the walls were richly adorned with art, though no piece could match the grandeur of the painting on the ceiling: a noble lion ranged across a sandy desert, a unicorn ambled through a forest accompanied by a nude female companion, a white stallion ran with abandon across a meadow—not the same face or proportions as Hobbie, but it was a Nonus horse. The last frame in the composite was even more compelling; Eldred could not pull his eyes away.

He was staring when Weltrude and Henreit approached, carrying a chest between them.

Henreit glanced upwards. "Is it accurate?"

Eldred crinkled up his face. "Mostly. The colors are right—body black as night, eyes like dark sapphires, teeth brilliant white. But, fine as it is, this is only a painting and, compared to the real thing, it's small. It was the presence of the dragon that made it so frightening, so exciting. It could reach out and grab you. So quick."

Henreit grinned. "That is why I thought of this place when I received Uncle Julian's message. It seemed the perfect place for you."

Eldred swept his eyes over the piles of rubbish.

Henriet laughed. "No, no no. Do not think of this place that way. It is beautiful, and we will freshen it up. I did not bring all these men to sit in idleness. Each wing is a maze of luxurious rooms just waiting for some tender care. Downstairs is a huge kitchen—you will have to see it. You could throw a loaf of bread through the air and not hit the other side. And for guests who are not so well behaved, a tiny dungeon. So do mind your manners. And on the roof, a garden. Not so fine now, perhaps, but these men of Branath know how to tend plants. We shall seed the garden and clean out the glasshouses."

Eldred blinked. "A glasshouse on the roof?"

"More than one; two," said Henriet.

"In good repair?" asked Eldred.

Henriet nodded. "When I was last here, two years ago, they were."

A smile flashed across Eldred's face. "Then that's where I'll sleep."

Henriet looked at Weltrude and back at Eldred. "Are you serious? I do not know if we can get your bedframe up the final stairway. Also, it could be wet."

"Just have someone check it. It won't bother me if it's a bit damp as long as the rain doesn't hit me in the face."

"It is what he wants. It might be good for him," said Weltrude.

Henriet shrugged. "I will have Gervese go up and check once they finish unloading the wagons."

"Thank you," said Eldred.

Henreit started up the stairs, side by side with Weltrude. "We are headed to the third floor. That is where I stayed last time. When you are tired of the cold, you can join us there."

Eldred grunted and watched them climb. Fresh air, the stars—the choice was made.

THE ROOF

They paused, gasping, before the last flight of stairs up to the roof, setting Eldred down against the railing around the center room. The narrow wooden stairs rose steeply, climbing up twenty feet to a landing at the roof level. Moisture had warped the wooden floorboards into an uneven mess.

Henreit gingerly placed his foot on the lowest stair, eliciting a loud creaking noise. "I am not sure this is advisable. You can see yourself—this is unsound."

Eldred shrugged. "It's just a few steps up."

Henreit glanced at Weltrude and Balian. "What do we think?"

"I'm a man, not some whale," said Eldred. "I could carry all of you up there in one go if my legs worked. Can't all of you together manage just one man?"

Madalulf crossed his arms. "Mother's piss. I say we drop this one down the stairs. I am tired of lugging him up."

Eldred glared at the old man. "What did you say?"

Balian sighed. "He is merely tired, prince." He waved Gervese over. "It is time to resume."

The men crowded in and hoisted Eldred up on their shoulders with his face towards the ceiling, then Balian and Gervese squeezed together and started up the stairs. One step brought them a foot higher than Madalulf and Pernet, who were following just behind. The next step made the height difference two feet. Almost all the weight rested on the shoulders of Balian and Gervese as the other four men struggled up the stairs after them.

They were halfway up when Madalulf slipped and fell, pulling Eldred after him, sending everyone tumbling down in a mass of flying elbows and kicking legs. As they poured out the bottom, Eldred and Pernet rolled across the landing and crashed into the railing, which buckled under the impact.

Pernet screamed as his head and shoulders hung out over the forty-foot drop, but he stayed where he was, pinned by Eldred's hip against what was left of the railing. Balian was there in an instant, pulling Pernet back onto the landing. Eldred scrambled to push himself back to a safe distance.

Madalulf lay on the floor, gently probing his bruised face. "It was not my fault. The cripple weighs a ton."

Henreit frowned. He stepped behind Weltrude, who was examining the battered young Pernet as he leaned against Balian. "We just need to work together."

"What we? I didn't see you carting this ox up the stairs," said Madalulf. Henreit frowned. "We all take our turn."

"Oh, we do, do we? When is it your turn? Next week?" asked Madalulf.

Balian settled Pernet against the wall and stood up. "That is enough, Madalulf. Go get Guillotin. You can take a break."

Henreit stepped forward. "Leave Guillotin to his work. I will do my share, as I said. Well, that is, if Eldred still wishes to reside on the roof."

Everyone turned to look at Eldred.

Eldred gazed at them defiantly and slid himself over to the stairs backwards on his rear. "I'm going up—on my own." He reached back and put his hands on the stairs and hefted himself up one stair. Then he repeated the motion and sat on the second stair, his legs hanging down listlessly.

Henreit gestured at Eldred and smiled, like a man showing off a pet dog doing a trick. "How about this?"

As Eldred kept going, Balian waved over Gervese and the two men followed Eldred up.

The cool night air felt good against Eldred's face as did his heart, beating faster in his chest. Getting up the stairs had been the best exercise he had enjoyed in some time. But now the men grabbed up Eldred and hurried past rows of raised beds topped with green leaves through the double doors of the eastern glasshouse, where they deposited him on his bed. They had managed the bedframe after all.

As the men stepped away, rubbing their arms, Eldred lay back and smiled, feeling better than he had in some time. The greenhouse pleased him. It had an earthy scent, but the air was fresh enough, thanks to a few missing panes. They had swept it out well enough, leaving the room empty except for Eldred's bed, which was matched with a dresser and a small side table where Eldred's throwing daggers were laid out on display.

Dinner was acceptable—some sausage served with some boiled greens. Rollon was definitely a cook rather than a celebrated chef, like Julian's palace had boasted. But that also felt right. For the first time since Turicum, Eldred felt like he had a place of his own. The best part was that Gervese had left after dropping off dinner, leaving him to himself.

Eldred lay back on the bed for an hour, studying the night sky through the curved glass and listening to the breeze. He was starting to get sleepy when he yawned and pushed himself up into a sitting position. Nobody was there. "Gervese. Gervese, where are you?"

Eldred waited, but there was no response. After a minute he yelled again.

This time Gervese scurried through the door, clutching a lamp and a bundle of blankets. The burly man gave a low bow. "Apologies, prince. I was just fetching bedding from downstairs."

Eldred glanced at the bed. "I already have enough to keep me warm."

Gervese lifted the blankets slightly. "These are for me. I am to keep you company."

"Are you sleeping in here?"

"I could, or"—Gervese shrugged—"I could set up in the shed just to the side."

"Are you sure it's not too wet?"

"Either is fine by me," said Gervese.

"Why not the shed, then, if you truly don't mind," said Eldred.

Gervese nodded. "Very good. Was there something you required?"

"Yes. I need the potion from Weltrude. Otherwise, I can't sleep up here."

Gervese bowed. "I will ask." He shut the doors and dashed away through the falling rain.

Eldred lay back and waited for Gervese to return. First came five minutes; the estate was large, but not that large. Then ten minutes passed. Eldred sat up and called for Gervese, getting no response. Finally, after what seemed to be well more than twenty minutes, he saw a bobbing lamp approaching, and Gervese opened the door.

Eldred fixed Gervese with a hard gaze, though Gervese might not have been able to tell in the dim light. "Where have you been?"

Gervese made a short half bow. "Sorry, prince. They needed help moving Henreit's bed up to the third floor."

"And the potion?" asked Eldred in a clipped voice.

"I asked. Balian said she is still out looking for a root. He said she will bring up a potion as soon as she can. Do you want me to go back down?"

"No, that's fine. Just keep an ear out in case I call for you."

Gervese nodded. "Very well. Goodnight, prince."

Eldred watched through the glass as Gervese made his way to the shed just to the side of the glasshouse. He set down the lamp and spent a few minutes dragging out boxes and pots. Finally he went inside and extinguished the lamp.

Eldred waited, fighting off sleep. He was almost nodding off when the right door of the glasshouse silently slid open to reveal Weltrude. She did not have the vision, not that Eldred could see, but she moved confidently in darkness. Eldred beckoned her inside, and she shut the door behind her.

"You have chosen your quarters well, prince," said Weltrude.

"There is another glasshouse if you fancy one for yourself."

Weltrude smiled. "I have pleasant quarters with the others."

Eldred gestured at the cup she bore in her hand. "You found a root?"

She nodded. "It took some searching, but I found a number under the ruins of the stables."

Eldred took the cup and sniffed the contents. "This smells stronger than it did before."

"Each cor root has its own nature, just as people do. It will serve."

Eldred made a face and downed the bitter drink, coughing afterwards.

Weltrude retrieved the cup from his slack grip. "Sleep well, prince. No dreams."

Eldred lay back as the numbing feeling spread from his center. "Thank you." He yawned. "It's working."

BREAKFAST

Eldred blinked awake with the late morning sun shining down in his face. The rain had passed. He lay still for a moment, feeling a deep relaxation through his neck and shoulders. It felt good to lie on his back. It felt even better to have gone through a night without attacking anyone or being tied up. If hunger had not stirred in him, he could have lain there all day. As it was, he pushed himself up into a sitting position. The doors were shut. Eldred noticed how dirty the windows were in the light of the day; something for someone to attend to.

After a long yawn, he yelled for Gervese, but no answer came. He waited a few minutes and called again with the same result. It was twenty minutes before anyone came.

Henreit waved from outside on the glass, holding a tray in one hand.

"Come in," said Eldred.

Henreit entered and set the tray down next to Eldred's throwing knives—eggs, bacon and toast. "Ah, it is warm in here."

"Comfortable, not too hot." Eldred raised an eyebrow. "I must have called Gervese a dozen times."

Henreit gave a small smile. "Balian has him hauling out the old carpet. You can already see the difference downstairs."

Eldred took a piece of toast. "Yes, I'm sure that's helpful, but I need someone up here—someone who can hear me call."

"Of course, of course. There is much to do up here as well. The garden is quite overgrown, and these windows could use a polish."

Eldred paused, the toast halfway to his mouth. "The windows, yes, but the garden? What are you doing? We are just staying here a few days, maybe a week or two. Why are you bothering with the garden or any of this other nonsense?"

Henreit grinned. "I know, but this place is no ordinary place. You have seen only a small part of it. I have Raduard and Guillotin cleaning out the baths. Madalulf and Pernet are helping Rollon tidy up the kitchen. Weltrude is sweeping. There is so much to do."

"Where are the baths?" asked Eldred.

"Down on the first floor. The marble is perfect once you remove the grime."

"Are you moving here?"

"Perhaps yes, perhaps no. But someone should inhabit the place. Perhaps you will make this your residence."

Eldred shook his head. "I don't think so."

Henreit smiled. "Oh, that is right. You would live in Dinan with Lady Mateline. It is a nice place during the summer months. I have attended the harvest festival there several times; very friendly, very busy. But does it suit you? I am not sure. You strike me as a man of solitude."

Eldred crunched through a piece of bacon. "Well, I suppose fixing the place up is something to do. Gervese can clean these window panes, but first I need to get set up out there."

THE GARDEN

Eldred sat in a wide wooden chair in the leafy shade of a trellis set in the center of the garden watching as Pernet worked his way through the raised beds that ran in long lines across the roof of the estate. They were all farmers—or so Eldred supposed—so any of them could have done the work. Even Eldred could have weeded the beds if someone had told him which plants were desirable and which were not. But they had chosen Pernet, perhaps because he appeared to be one of the weaker men on the expedition. The slight young man, whose face still bore the bruises from the tumble down the stairs, methodically made his way through the raised beds, pulling out more than he left and placing the refuse in a burlap sack that he occasionally dumped over the side of the roof.

Eldred was watching the man work when Weltrude came up after lunch. Eldred waved her into one of the chairs near his. "Where have you been? I told Henreit I wanted to see you an hour ago."

Weltrude took the most shaded chair. It was bright sunlight now, and she wore her bonnet pulled down low over her face, but Eldred could see her face harden. "I was gathering herbs."

"Oh. Good. Well, I wanted to speak with you. We need to sort this out."

"On what matter, prince?"

Eldred sighed and looked out over the forest that stretched away in front of them. "You have done well with your potions, but I still can't walk. I need your help, your focus, to cure me."

Weltrude pursed her lips. "I showed you the other day; the lines of power lie true in you—running down your back, through your midsection, down to your legs to your feet. There is nothing my arts can address. With time and your fatum lapides—all three of them—you will have a full recovery, if you have not already recovered."

Eldred frowned. "What do you mean?"

Weltrude raised her thin eyebrows. "I mean you should be able to walk now. I have seen leg injuries. I have seen those whose limbs have withered. But that is not your situation. I can see at this very moment that your leg muscles are toned, strong. You need only stand up."

Eldred slammed his fist into the arm of the chair, cracking it. "That's nonsense. If I could walk, I would get up right now. You think I want people dragging me around, carrying me about like some dead pig?"

She pressed her lips together. "I would not presume to know your mind, prince, but I do know the strength of the Mother. What she has blessed has the power to heal. Any one of your stones should have healed you by now—if they are real."

Eldred pointed towards his left temple, where the three stones were set. "They're real enough. Do you doubt it? Do you wish to test them? You just don't understand the diabolical power of the Corporians. They stole the Bond from a field full of warriors and did something even worse to me. You just don't know what they can do."

Weltrude gave a thin smile. "The strength of the Mother is absolute."

Eldred scoffed. "The Mother? She died a hundred years ago. The Sun People showed me."

"The Mother lives on. We only live through her blessings. Who are these people who deceived you?"

"The Wretched—that's how you know them. You call them the Wretched, but they know more than we do."

Weltrude took a breath. "They are a filthy people who would not speak the truth even if they knew it."

"No. You're wrong about that, too."

Weltrude shrugged. "You are a prince. Who am I to debate you?"

Eldred sighed. "I do not mean to debate anyone, but I cannot walk."

Weltrude rose to her feet. "I shall bring the potion tonight, if you wish. Is there anything else?"

Eldred blew out his breath. "No. Nothing."

Eldred watched her walk back to the stairs, headed down into the cool bowels of the building below. She walked slowly and steadily with her back straight. At least she would make the sleeping potion.

Eldred gave a little shudder and looked over at Pernet. The man focused determinedly on the task on hand, not so much as glancing in Eldred's direction. He had definitely watched the whole scene. He was making good progress with the weeding, uncovering tomatoes, peppers and beans among the plants Eldred recognized. The garden seemed to be in surprisingly good shape for having been left unattended for a hundred years or so.

Eldred sat, half in the sun and half in the shade, gazing out over the forest. After a spell, he reached into the sample bag tied around his waist and plucked out one of the two woven packets. "By your bones, Sir Aemilanus, this had better work," he muttered. He cleared his throat. "Pernet, I need a kettle of hot water, a bowl and some washcloths."

TREASURES

Henreit came to dinner in the early evening, joining Eldred under the trellis. While Gervese went below to fetch the meal, he set two black cloth bags on the table between them. He turned to study the rows of raised beds. "It is beginning to look quite civilized up here. I trust you are comfortable?"

Eldred shifted forward and back on his chair. "It's fine. It's good." He ran his hand through his hair and looked distractedly at the bags. "What's this? What did you find?"

Henreit leaned closer. "Are you well? You seem unsettled."

Eldred reached up and tugged at his hair. "Just stir crazy. I've been sitting here all day."

"Ah," said Henreit. "That is most unfortunate. Perhaps, despite the fine view up here, you might find more to engage you down below. We are discovering many treasures, such as these." He opened the first bag and removed a silver goblet decorated with interlocking flowers. He gently set it in front of Eldred.

Eldred picked up the goblet, looked at it for a second, and set it down. "Pretty."

Henreit gestured at the cup. "A rare find, completely unblemished. And the workmanship—you cannot find such a thing nowadays."

Eldred pushed the goblet back across the table. "That would depend on where you looked."

"Hmph. Well, perhaps such a delicate item is not to your taste, but this might capture your attention." Henreit pulled a silver dagger out of the other bag. A series of red and green stones ran the length of the handle.

Eldred took it out of Hereit's hand and stared at it before making a face. "It's a girl's knife."

Henreit's chin tightened. "Whether for a boy or a girl, it will fetch a handsome sum."

Eldred nodded distractedly and handed it back. "I suppose it might."

Henreit turned the dagger over in his hands, wiping the blade in a few places with his index finger. "I am certain we will find more valuables such as these. Others have come before, but none have made so systematic a search. We are truly restoring this palace to the grandeur it so richly deserves. These treasures can help provide the funds to furnish and repair every single room."

Eldred drummed his fingers on the arm of his chair.

"Are you certain you are well? You seem very out of sorts."

Eldred straightened abruptly. It was the jitters from the powder—felt more powerfully now than back in Turicum since he could not walk it off. "I'm just hungry."

"You should have Weltrude look at you; she—"

"No! That—that will not help," said Eldred.

Gervese appeared at the top of the stairs, carrying a heavily laden wooden platter.

Henreit smiled. "Well, if it is just your appetite, the food has arrived. I hope it settles you. Rollon made a fine chicken stew and finally baked a few loaves of bread. I selected the perfect red wine to accompany our meal." Henreit picked up a bottle off the platter as Gervese set it down. "Would you care for some?"

Eldred waved away the offered bottle. "No, thank you. I will have wine enough with my potion tonight."

Henreit poured a glass and inspected the dark red wine. "A shame to drink it that way. It is meant for enjoyment, not for choking down medicine."

Eldred sniffed the air and made a face. "That's the best use of it for me," he muttered. He sniffed again while looking around the rooftop. There was something there, something new, something unnatural.

"Do you object to the food?" asked Henreit.

"No. There is an odor on the breeze—a foul odor."

Henreit sniffed. "I do not smell anything—only the stew, which is delicious."

Eldred beckoned over Gervese, who was sitting on the edge of one of the raised beds twenty feet away. "Did you clean out the other glasshouse?"

Gervese hesitantly rose to his feet. "Balian had me working downstairs today. Did you need it cleaned?"

"No, but I need to check it. Go below and get Balian and two others—not Pernet or Madalulf. I need to go over there."

Gervese glanced at Henreit. "They were just settling down to dinner when I came up."

Eldred crinkled up his face, pausing an instant to consider. He could not say why, but he felt a sense of menace. "Get them now. It will only take a moment."

Gervese looked at Henreit one last time, as if hoping to hear some other suggestion. But when Henreit merely sipped his wine, Gervese headed towards the stairs.

Henreit continued his meal, scooping up a chunk of chicken and potato. "Do you need it as an office? A spare room?"

Eldred shook his head. "No. I just need to inspect it."

The men arrived shortly, with Balian at the front. He crossed to the trellis, wearing a pinched expression. "I checked that glasshouse yesterday, prince. There is nothing there. You are quite safe."

"I'm not frightened. I want to see what's inside. I'm smelling something," said Eldred.

Balian glanced around the roof, which was growing dark as evening shifted into night. "There is a breeze. You might be smelling something from a mile away if your sense of smell is so keen."

Eldred frowned. "I did not ask Gervese to get you so we could discuss the weather. I need to see in the glasshouse. Carry me there. I'm sure we all want to get back to our food."

Balian's shoulders stiffened as he slowly nodded his head. "Of course." He motioned Gervese forward.

Eldred laid his arms over their shoulders while Guillotin and Raduard grabbed Eldred's legs. Balian turned back to Henreit, who was dipping his bread in the stew, and grunted. "Get the door."

Henreit got up, still nibbling on his bread and led the way through the raised beds to the glasshouse on the other side of the roof. When he reached the door, he dusted off his hands and pulled it open. The men carried Eldred right up to the entrance. An unpleasant odor wafted out of the room.

"Was this the smell then?" asked Balian.

Eldred sat, suspended in the arms of the shuddering men, looking through the room. There was a pile of old mildewed blankets—that was part of it. A few pots sat off to the side, filled with murky greenish water. Tall grasses grew out of cracks in the floor, and a few bushes were pushing their way into the room through missing glass panes.

"No. Not exactly, but it was similar," said Eldred.

"Are you done?" asked Balian.

"Yes, that's enough for now. Shut the doors, Henreit. We can go through the glasshouse more carefully tomorrow. No need to interrupt anyone's dinner any further," said Eldred.

Balian pressed his lips together. "Very thoughtful, prince."

WAITING

Eldred propped himself up on the edge of the bed, lightly patting the mattress with one hand as he waited. He considered sending Gervese back down to find out what was keeping Weltrude, but he took a breath and restrained himself. The burly man had already entered the shed to sleep. Perhaps Weltrude just had to make him wait. It might be a game to her.

It was another half an hour before the door opened silently and Weltrude stepped purposefully into the room with a cup in one hand.

Eldred sighed. "At last. I was ready to sleep an hour ago."

Weltrude folded her arms across her chest. "I was speaking to Pernet. He told me what you did this afternoon."

"I cleaned myself up."

"He showed me the bowl. I could see the residue—of your Wretched powder, the one you mentioned before."

Eldred nodded. "I used it. I've no intention of staying a cripple."

"Well, whatever your desire, you cannot carelessly mix medicines. If you are painting yourself all over with this noxious powder, then you should not be taking my potions."

Eldred paused for a moment, staring at the floor, before turning to look into her eyes. "I need the potion. I can't sleep on the roof without it."

Weltrude shook her head. "I have taken vows: vows for healing, vows to the Mother. The medicines I craft, the treatments I conduct—I do everything according to my vows. They may mean nothing to you, but they mean everything to me. And if my treatment should harm you, or—Mother help us—if you perish, the king will surely put me to death."

Eldred raised his palm. "Stop your fretting. Nobody is going to die. Just hand me the potion."

Weltrude scowled. "A First Born woman, Affra—a healer like myself—lost a baby and the mother in a delivery for a noble family in Emon. Or they died—I should not say she lost them, for she was very capable like myself. The husband grabbed her by the neck and choked her. She fought him to get free. She barely escaped from the city."

Eldred tilted his head. "Nobody's likely to care that much about me. And besides, everyone knows that I asked you for the potion. I sent Gervese down for it more than once. Henreit is not going to hurt you. Nobody here would."

"Not everyone who cares for you is present."

Eldred clenched his jaw. "Be reasonable. I'm using the powder since there is nothing else to try. If you have some alternative, I would love to hear it. And don't say that my legs are fine and I need only stand up. By the blasted Mother, I can't bloody well stand up."

Weltrude glared at Eldred.

Eldred put out his hand. "The potion, please."

Weltrude stood, unmoving.

Eldred took a deep breath. "As you said, I'm the prince. The potion."

Weltrude's face grew tight, but she handed over the cup. "I will tell Henreit and Balian you insisted."

Eldred nodded. "By all means."

She frowned. "You have been warned."

"Thank you, Weltrude. Just remember, I need this every night."

Weltrude turned and left without comment.

Eldred made a face and gulped down the contents of the cup. Now to sleep. Settling into bed was a chore, but Eldred had a system. He threw back the covers, dragged himself up from the bottom of the bed and then lay himself down, pulling the blankets over. His legs rested at the wrong angles, which made Eldred sigh. If only Weltrude would spy on him like this, she would see how ridiculous her thinking was. No man who could walk would do the exasperating things he was forced to do.

As he lay there, feeling the warm soothing sensation from the potion spread from his belly up through his body, he heard a tinny voice in the distance, growing louder and clearer as he drifted closer to sleep. Oh, it was her. She had said she was just down below him a floor or two where they all were. She seemed to be whispering softly, but he could hear her quite clearly. Eldred frowned. There must be some passage in the stones that carried the sound. He didn't want to listen in. He only wanted to sleep.

"Are you certain?" asked a voice, another voice, a man's voice.

"I am," said Weltrude.

"Why would he do that?" asked the man.

"Perhaps he is frightened. He is too cowardly to fight his cousin, so he fakes this injury," said Weltrude.

"Hmm. It could be a way to seem important. He likes it when he orders us to carry him around, like tonight at dinner. He just had to look in the other glasshouse," said the man. It was Balian. She was talking to Balian.

"I told him this afternoon that I know he is faking. He knows that I know," said Weltrude.

There was a pause before Balian spoke. "That is a worry. If he wants this kept secret, you may be in danger."

Weltrude sniffed. "Gervese is by his door."

Balian scoffed. "You could kick Gervese in the ass without waking him. If the prince can walk, he could come down here tonight."

"I said that he can walk," said Weltrude with a note of irritation.

"Then he can walk. I do not doubt you. And the darkness favors him. He has the dark vision. If he comes down, he might do you harm," said Balian.

"He is a brute. He threatens all kinds of harm to everyone if he does not get the potion," said Weltrude.

Eldred made a face.

"So long as he does not get you. I will not allow it," said Balian.

"Do you mean it?" asked Weltrude.

"You know I do. You must know by now," said Balian.

"I—I wondered. You were always so proper, always such a gentleman. For all the world, it seems like you are the real prince. Not that oaf," said Weltrude.

"They are all like that, all the nobles. Though I guess this one is too lazy to even stand on his own feet," said Balian.

"He is frightened, scared," said Weltrude.

Eldred scowled.

"He might be, but you are not. You face the toughest situations, and I have never seen you cry," said Balian.

"I shed tears some nights for those I have lost," said Weltrude.

"Not tonight. I do not wish you to cry tonight. Come to my room and be with me. I will watch over you," said Balian.

"And if he comes down?" asked Weltrude.

Balian chuckled. "I will stab him in the gut. Not even you will be able to put him right afterwards."

Eldred drifted deeper into sleep as he heard a door open and shut.

He woke in the morning with a vague memory of a dream wherein a cloaked figure walked outside the estate during the night. The building had looked quite lovely when viewed with dark vision. The figure paced around the side of the manor to a giant pile of refuse. They had frozen then, baring their teeth at the piles of old furniture and decaying rags.

AN ODOR

The next day got off to a poor start when smoke wafted over the side of the roof, filling the air with a noxious odor like burning hair. Eldred made a face and sat up in his chair under the trellis. He glanced over at Madalulf, who was puttering around, dragging rubbish out of the other glasshouse. "What's this? What's happening?"

Madalulf carried a bundle of dried vines over to the railing and tossed it over. "They are burning the pile, all the junk from the house."

Eldred shook his head. "In Mother's name, why are they doing that? Don't they remember I'm up here?"

Madalulf smiled but not with any trace of sympathy. "I doubt they forgot. It was full of rats. They had to burn it."

Eldred frowned. "Idiots. They could at least burn it when the wind is blowing away from the estate."

Madalulf shrugged and started walking back to the greenhouse.

"No! No!" called Eldred. "Go get him. I want to speak to Henreit. And bring up Gervese and Balian as well."

"Now?" asked Madalulf.

"Yes, now. Right now," said Eldred.

Madalulf ambled to the stairs at the center of the rooftop.

Within a few minutes, Heneit came up the stairs with Balian, Gervese, Weltrude and Madalulf in tow. Henreit sniffed the air. "Oh, this is very bad. I am most apologetic, Eldred. I did not know this would happen."

Eldred glared with reddened eyes. "You didn't know fire causes smoke?"

Henreit pulled out a handkerchief from his pocket and covered his mouth. "We can put you back in the glasshouse."

"There's no point to that with all the missing panes. I need to go downstairs."

"That is very hard," said Henreit.

Eldred gave him a level look. "I got myself up the stairs. I can get myself down. Just get me over there."

Henreit sneezed and wiped his nose. "What do you think, Balian?"

Balian cocked his eyebrow. "If he tumbles down, well—the railings are shot."

Eldred fanned the air in front of his face. "Let's go. This is insufferable."

It was a slow process to get down the stairs. On each step, Eldred pushed up onto his hands and lowered himself to the next stair down, sliding his legs out before him. Balian and Gervese kept close watch, retreating backwards before him. Soon enough though, Eldred was down.

On the fourth floor, Henreit and Madalulf had placed a chair for Eldred next to the central opening near a section of railing in good repair. Henreit leaned against the rail as the others went to the third floor to join in the cleaning.

Henreit pointed down at the men. "They are clearing out the eastern wing of the third floor. The western wing is in good shape. That is where we are all staying for the moment."

"I know. I heard you," said Eldred.

"What? Up on the roof?" asked Henreit.

"Your voices. I heard some of your voices last night."

"That is strange. The walls are stone. I do not hear anything in my room," said Henreit.

Eldred rubbed his chin. "Maybe there's some conduit in the walls. I heard the voices as if they were right next to me."

"Who was it?"

Eldred sighed. "I couldn't tell. It was all—it was muttering."

"Hmph. Well, you should know that the men like to joke around."

"What?" asked Eldred.

Henreit raised his eyebrows. "Well, they make jokes. You should not consider what they say too seriously."

Eldred narrowed his eyes. "What do they say?"

"As I said, they make jokes." Henreit made a sweeping gesture with his hand. "But now, they are busy, working hard. I believe they will start on this floor the day after tomorrow. These upper floors are tidier. The worst is the basement floor. There we have only just cleared out the last bit of the kitchen. But do not worry; it is very clean."

Down below, Madalulf and Pernet were tossing strips of carpet over the railing, which trailed plumes of dust as they dropped onto the stone floor below. Balian and Gervese carried dilapidated furniture down the stairs with some of the other men. Even Weltrude was busy sweeping.

"They're busy. How much are you paying them? I've never seen people make such an effort," said Eldred.

Henreit smiled. "They are common people, not like the nobles and warriors with whom you have associated. Nobody does anything for them. If they have something, it is because they have earned it. They wake up each morning ready to earn their keep."

Eldred watched Gervese jog back up the stairs after carrying a load down to the first floor. "Warriors train. That takes effort."

Henreit motioned with his hands, palms down. "It is not the same. That is made up work. Down there, they are doing real work."

"Training is real work," said Eldred.

"Not like this. We will fix this estate, get it into the grandest condition, perfect. And nearby, there is a small town. Unfortunately, a bit more of a ruin. But there is some stone there, and we are surrounded by woods, great for building."

"To what end?"

Henreit looked Eldred in the eye. "For us. We are the same, you and I."

Eldred frowned. "How so?"

"Well, to be blunt, neither of us is quite right. I lack the vision. And you, well, your bloodline was already a question, and now you cannot even walk."

Eldred's eyes darkened. "I will walk again. And I'm set to be married to Mateline and inherit Dinan."

Henreit smiled and bowed his head. "Her bloodline is also off. Oh, no!" He held up his hands in an appeasing gesture as Eldred started to bristle. "Please do not take offense. I am just being straight with you. In any case, you will not find such a fine estate as this in Dinan. That is a simple village."

Eldred glared. "Don't speak ill of her. She saved me. She and Oudin took on the Torvid and killed him. She snapped the bastard's neck as he stabbed her." He shook his head. "Anyway, what do you need me for in any of this? You don't need me to clean things or build a settlement."

Henreit traced his thin mustache with his finger. "Perhaps not, but I lack the proper eyes. People will not settle here unless the leader has vision. Even if you are a man with questionable blood, you possess both far sight and dark vision. It means a great deal to our people."

Eldred looked around the cavernous interior of the estate, taking in the painting of the blue-eyed dragon above. "So, we would live here? That's your plan?"

"Why not? You would prefer Boar's Tusk?"

Eldred shook his head. "No."

"Or Emon, where they kept you in the stables?"

Eldred sighed. "They were royal stables."

Henreit swept his arm in a grand gesture. "This is a special place. They think we are hiding like obedient mice, but we are building a future."

"We'll see. At least for now, we hide."

⚜

A SIGHTING

Later that afternoon, Eldred was back up on the roof dozing in his chair under the trellis. He woke to a light breeze blowing over his face, free now from the smoke which had choked the air earlier. He opened his eyes and scanned the trees spreading far off over the hills into the distance towards the mountains in the west.

He reached for his goblet on the table next to his chair and took a sip of water, glancing over at Pernet as he did. The man was puttering about the raised bed. He had finished the weeding and was now planting cuttings he had taken from the plants. Eldred sniffed. Pernet was being useful, though not in any important way. What was the use of tending the garden anyway—or of all the cleaning they were working on so feverishly below?

He clapped his goblet back on the table. The clouds were unusual, towering plumes of white that rose up towards the heavens in odd shapes as they sailed across the sky. One looked like a bear, or had the head of a bear anyway, with a wide open mouth ready to eat some foe. Another bore the shape of a sword, though the sword was bent, a huge misshapen sword. A sword of that size could kill a thousand enemies.

Eldred cast his eyes to a nearby cloud, one almost directly overhead. This cloud lacked any distinctive shape, being more or less a flattened disc broken up into segments by the wind. As he watched the fragmented cloud glide past, he caught sight of a golden shape flit from one section of the cloud to another.

Gripping the arms of his chair, he pushed himself up straighter. He focused his eyes, staring intently. In the lower layer of mist, he could just make out the shape circling, a huge golden bird, an eagle.

Eldred jabbed his finger upwards. "Pernet, do you see that? Do you see that up there?"

Pernet looked over with a confused expression. "See what?"

"Up there, in that cloud. There's a huge eagle, a huge eagle with golden feathers."

Pernet shaded his eyes with his hand as he took a brief glance. "No. I cannot say as I do."

"Well, it's there."

Pernet shrugged and went back to his planting.

"Go get Hernreit. No—go get Balian. I want him to see this."

Pernet paused, a small planting dangling from his hand. "You want me to get him now?"

"Of course, now. The eagle could fly away. It could fly away at any moment."

Pernet made a face, but set his planting down; it looked like a small tomato plant. "Alright, if you say so."

"I do!"

It was several minutes before Pernet returned with Henreit and Balian in tow.

Eldred pointed. "Up there. That cloud." It had drifted from being overhead, but Eldred could still make out the faint shape that navigated its interior.

Henreit and Pernet studied Balian's face as he made his examination.

"Well, do you see it?" asked Eldred.

Balian lowered his head and turned to Eldred. "I just see a cloud."

"There is an eagle there, just inside. It keeps circling around. I can't see it the whole time, but I see it most of the time."

Balian nodded and rubbed his hands together.

Henreit scratched his chin. "Do you think it is a danger? Is that why you needed us to come up?"

Eldred wrinkled up his face. "No. I don't think it's a danger. I'm not frightened of it. I'm not frightened of anything, despite what some people are saying. I think it's unusual. It's huge, a huge eagle. I don't believe I have ever seen such a large bird. And it's acting strangely. It's hiding in that cloud."

Henreit glanced up. "Very odd, but I do not see there is anything for us to do regarding the matter."

"I just wanted Balian to see it. He's supposed to have far sight."

Balian smiled stiffly. "My vision is not as noble as yours, prince. If there is nothing more, I will get back to my work."

"Are you saying it's not there?" asked Eldred.

"No, no. He did not say that. He just cannot see it," said Henreit.

"He can speak for himself," said Eldred.

Balian paused. He had halfway turned to head back to the stairs. "The bird is only there for you to see."

"Not a bird, an eagle," said Eldred.

Balian raised his eyebrow. "Is there anything more?"

Eldred pursed his lips. "No, not for you. Pernet, go down and get me some hot water. Bring it back quickly, and I need towels too."

Henreit walked over and sat by Eldred as the two men made their way to the stairs. Eldred locked his eyes on the cloud.

"An interesting development," said Henreit.

"I thought so," said Eldred.

Henreit glanced down at Eldred's legs. "So, is this water for the treatment that Weltrude was telling me about—the treatment with the powder from the Wretcheds?"

"Yes," said Eldred, still looking up at the sky.

"Is that altogether wise? Weltrude was telling me—and she is a fine healer, the finest I have ever met—that taking an unknown treatment from untrustworthy people could be dangerous."

Eldred scoffed. "Dangerous? What's dangerous is being weak, being crippled, sitting here waiting for some assassin to show up and finish the job."

"Nobody will come here. I have chosen this place most carefully," said Henreit.

"They do. You said yourself last night that people come hunting for treasures."

"Very few. There are rumors that scare the fainthearted away." Henreit raised his index finger. "But do not worry; they are merely stories shared among commoners. I have visited here quite pleasantly twice before."

Eldred waved his hand dismissively. "Fine. Even if we are well hidden, some trouble is going to come bubbling up, and I need to be ready. Now, Weltrude's healing is good; I need the potions. Those are helpful. But she's not aiming to cure me. She just advises me to stand up—as if I don't have the wit to think of that myself."

Henreit shifted in his chair. "Well, I would not wish to promise she can cure you. She has spoken of some concerns. But what if she is right about the Wretcheds's powder? I mean, you are already in a delicate position as regards your legs. What if this powder makes things worse? What if you cannot move your arms?"

"That won't happen. This powder—it's the powder of Balaur, the powder of dragons—is the most potent ingredient the Sun People have for healing. I should know. They used it on me. They brought me back from near death."

"Ah, well, and you used it yesterday?"

"I did."

Henreit gestured softly towards Eldred's legs. "And did it work?"

Eldred frowned. "No. Not yet. Any cure is going to take some time. The Corporians did something terrible, not just to me. They knocked the Bond right out of an entire army. That's never happened before. And what has happened to me has never happened before. That's why Weltrude is so confused on the matter."

"I see. So you intend to keep on taking these treatments?"

"I do. I was looking to save the powder for a duel with the Mercian king. But now, well, I have no choice."

Henreit smiled encouragingly. "I hope it works."

Eldred looked back up to the cloud. "As do I. As do I."

A Friendly Game

A few hours later, after his treatment, Eldred sat shaking with the nervous energy that came from the powder. The bird and cloud were long gone, leaving Eldred to shift in his chair this way and that with an ever rising level of frustration.

Gervese frowned as he watched Eldred from amongst the raised beds where he was picking tomatoes. "Are you well, prince?"

Eldred laughed. "Well? No, I'm not well. But you know that. I'm sitting here bored out of my mind."

Gervese raised his half-full basket. "Would you like to help harvest?"

"I can't harvest. I can't walk up and down the beds."

Gervese bent over and reached for a ripe tomato. "You might consider doing something, just to pass the day."

Eldred shook his head. "There's not much I can do. And of that which I can do, there is even less I will do. I'm not going to scrub the floors while Henreit stands over me."

"Well, you are a prince."

Eldred sighed. "I'm a prince who can't walk, who can't fight. I'm hiding, and I even need help for that."

"What about a game of Serpent?" asked Gervese.

Eldred gripped the arm of his chair and took a deep breath. "Alright, that's something. I suppose I should practice with the knives."

Gervese smiled. "Good. I will get Pernet and the board. Best you start with him."

Eldred scowled. "Because he's the worst."

A few minutes later, the game was set. Gervese hung Pernet's Serpent board on a post in one of the garden beds some twenty feet from Eldred's chair. All nine of Eldred's knives—three small, three medium and three large—were laid out on a table next to him. Pernet stood nearby with his three old battered blades in hand.

Pernet glanced over Eldred's gleaming collection. "Shall we play for knives today?"

"Not today," said Eldred.

The game got off to a slow start. Only a quarter of Eldred's throws even stuck in the board. Pernet didn't do much better, but finally one of his throws found the tail of the red snake. Eldred tapped the arm of his chair as Gervese and Pernet collected the scattered blades. On his next set of throws, Eldred switched from the small blades to his medium sized blades. The change did not improve his game.

As Pernet slowly made his way along the red snake, Eldred continued his efforts to hit the tail of the green snake. He came close a few times but never hit.

"A tough game; more difficult than it looks," ventured Gervese as he returned Eldred's blades after Pernet advanced to the red snake's head, the final target.

Eldred favored him with a frosty glare.

"Shall we bet now? I could always hit your snake and lose," said Pernet with a hopeful smile.

Eldred declined and switched to his heavy knives, hurling them with great force as he bounced them off the board.

Pernet threw up his hands after he narrowly missed the red snake's head. "Oh, so close!" He held up his last knife for the round. "I am feeling lucky. I am a lucky ducky."

Gervese motioned caution to Pernet as Eldred's face grew tight, but Pernet took no notice. He didn't make the throw, though.

On Eldred's next round, he took one of his heavy blades with the dark blue handles and threw it with all the strength he could muster. It sailed over the board and carried on, spinning end over end.

Gervese ran over to the far edge of the roof, looking down. "I do not see it. It must have gone into the trees."

Pernet giggled. "You have the arm, just no aim."

"Shall I go down and look?" asked Gervese.

Eldred frowned. "No, the game's over. That's Pernet's knife if he can find it. I'm done with it."

Pernet's eyes grew wide. "Is that right?"

Eldred gestured. "Just go."

DREAMS

Eldred did not have to wait on Weltrude that night. She sent the potion up with Gervese, not bothering to make an appearance. Her judgmental attitude was not missed. Eldred forced it down and made his preparations for bed as Gervese settled down outside.

As the warm relaxation filled his body, spreading out through his chest, arms and neck, Eldred heard faint mutterings from the floor below. Whether it was Henreit, Weltrude, Balian or one of the workers, Eldred could not say. Nothing in their feeble words caught his attention as he drifted off to sleep.

In the depths of the night, he saw a cloaked figure descending a darkened stairway, stepping down each step quietly, purposefully. When it reached the bottom of the stairs, it continued on into a short corridor that led to a large open door. Inside, someone was moving around, gathering things by flickering candlelight.

The figure moved to a small alcove and waited and then waited some more. Meanwhile, the fat man in the room picked out more items to stuff in his sack, stroking his wispy beard as he considered his options. The shadowed face of the figure twisted in irritation as it watched the man collect his goods. Finally, the man had gathered all he could fit in the bag and he came out, stopping to latch the door behind him before shuffling down the corridor, passing by the alcove without taking notice.

But after the man passed by, he stopped and sniffed the air. He stood there for a moment, testing the air, then he turned and held out the candle. "Is someone there?"

His question was met with silence. He took a hesitant step forward, back towards the latched door. "I can explain," said the man as he waved the light back and forth in front of him. He moved forward, his fat face creased with worry. "It is my share, really."

As he came even with the alcove, he paused, staring at the floor as he lifted his eyes, his mouth opened in horror. A scream, a shout, was bubbling up through him about to erupt. But before the sound was born, an arm shot out of the alcove and covered his mouth while another drove a dagger deep into the man's heart. As the man collapsed, the figure grabbed him and lowered him silently to the floor.

The man lay on his back on top of his bloodstained brown cloak, moving his arms weakly, aimlessly. The figure picked up the bag and walked halfway down the corridor toward the door where they stopped and faced a wooden carving on the wall. The figure pressed some part of the carving with their index finger. A click sounded, and the figure pushed the center of the carving back, which opened like a small door. The figure paused, looking back at the fallen man, and waited. Then, as the man's breathing wound down and stopped, the figure stepped up through the door and disappeared, shutting the entrance behind him. A thin line of blood snaked its way from the man's torso to the wall as the dream faded away.

ALARM

The predawn light shone red through the glasshouse panes when Henreit burst in upon Eldred with Balian and Weltrude just behind him. Henreit grabbed Eldred and shook him, waking him as Eldred feebly tried to push him off. Eventually, Eldred opened his eyes halfway and grumbled. "What're you doing? Get out."

Henreit plopped down on the bed next to Eldred. "Guillotin was killed in the night."

Eldred wet his lips and swallowed. He could still feel last night's potion heavy in his head. "Oh, him?"

Henreit gestured dramatically. "A good man of Branath. And the tragedy—he won't be going home now."

Eldred pushed himself up to sitting, coming slightly more awake. "Was it a Torvid? Have they found us? You said they couldn't."

Balian shook his head. "I think not. It seems Guillotin surprised one or more intruders in the kitchen last night. Most likely simple thieves; we found quite a few supplies missing."

Eldred rubbed his neck. "Yes. A Torvid would have killed us all, wouldn't he?"

Henreit bent over, resting his arms on his knees. "We are still not safe. Thieves or Torvid, they killed Guillotin just the same. They could do the same to us. We must pack up the wagons and leave as soon as we can."

Eldred groaned and lowered himself back onto the bed. "I don't know."

Weltrude's eyes glittered. "Is there at last something that the prince does not know?"

Eldred sighed. "Well, if there is some band of bandits to fight, it would be better for us to do it here. We have stone walls, and the doors are still sound. Better here than out on the road, especially at night for all of you."

"What if it was a Torvid?" asked Henreit.

"Then it's still better here. They're quick bastards, but they can't knock down walls," said Eldred.

Weltrude turned to Balian. "What do you think?"

Balian nodded. "The prince makes a point. Facing a Torvid on the road in the dark would be a nightmare."

Henreit frowned. "Just two nights, then we could make it back to Emon."

Eldred scoffed. "I thought you loved it here. I thought you were going to clean this place up and make it your palace."

"Not if it means we die," said Henreit.

"In any case, Uncle Julian does not want me back in Emon. So we would be camping until he changed his mind."

Henreit bent over further, his face growing pale.

Balian grunted. "Well, they had their best chance last night and chose not to use it. Perhaps our foe is weak."

Eldred pulled the blankets back up over his shoulders. "Yes, very true. Instead of cleaning today, you just need to bar the doors and windows on the first two floors. Did they take the horses?"

Balian shook his head. "No."

Eldred laughed. "Then they aren't even good thieves. Set a guard on the stable in case they get their nerve back up. Where did they even go? Did someone look for them?"

"I could not find their tracks," said Balian.

Eldred raised his eyebrow. "Really? Well, until we know more, I'm going back to sleep."

Henriet blinked. "A man died."

Eldred turned away on his side, thinking of his father, of Hobbie, of Dreven. "It happens every day, and so does sleep. Come back in two hours with breakfast. Maybe you'll find some tracks by then."

✵

AN AFTERNOON
REFRESHMENT

Eldred sat out on the roof under the trellis. His upper body was in the shade, but his feet were getting red in the sun. They didn't hurt. Eldred wished they would. A burn ought to cause pain. He frowned. There was a different mood to the place since the man had met his unfortunate end. The change up on the roof was the presence of Gervese.

Gervese normally did watch Eldred, especially in the evening and always at night. But in the middle of the day's work on the palace, he was usually down below carrying out more trash than anyone. And even if he had been assigned to watch Eldred, he would have worked on the garden or tidied up the extra glasshouse. Now, instead, he stood ten feet away from Eldred, clutching the hilt of his sword with worried eyes.

Gervese was certainly strong for a Maldavian; not as strong as a Mercian, but probably stronger than many—even most—Deiran warriors. Nevertheless, he was a farmer by trade, and it showed in the way he stood, the way he strapped on his scabbard and in the clumsy way he gripped the sword so tightly. Eldred could not imagine the enemy who could not simply walk up to Gervese and stab the man in the neck.

Still, Eldred understood the intent and appreciated it at that level. Even though Gervese was likely no more protection than Pernet or Madalulf, the others clearly believed he was. So in this regard, they honored Eldred. It was likely Henreit's idea, given that he was the only one who even made a pretense of caring for him.

So Eldred sat, watching the tree-covered hills and cursing Guillotin for getting himself killed. It just made the whole business of hiding that much more of a nuisance. As Eldred looked out into the woods, idly tapping his lips with his index finger, he noticed a rock on a ridgeline in the distance, perhaps two miles away. Eldred paused his finger; the rock had an eye.

Eldred stared intently, willing his eyes to focus tighter on the odd rock. He could just make it out. The eagle was back, staring at him through a small gap in the rocks. Only its enormous eye showed.

Eldred slapped his hand on the arm of his chair. "Go get Balian now! It's back. The eagle is back over on that hill."

Gervese stepped forward, pulling his sword halfway out of its sheath. "What?"

Eldred jabbed his finger in the air. "It's back."

Gervese paused and slid his sword back into its sheath. "The eagle?"

Eldred nodded. "Yes. Now hurry!"

Gervese frowned. "Very well." He turned and jogged to the stairs.

Eldred resumed watching the bird. It didn't move. It must have seen him, but it stayed where it was.

Five minutes later, Gervese returned with Henreit.

Eldred gestured. "Where's Balian?"

Henreit raised his eyebrows. "He cannot come. He is managing our defense preparations downstairs."

"What? This will just take a moment. I want him to look at this."

Henreit gave a short nod. "Normally, he would. But they are doing what you requested. They are covering the windows. It is very time consuming. And everyone, I do mean everyone, is on edge."

Eldred shook his head and muttered, "Not even sure he has far sight."

Henreit's eyes went wide. "Oh. Well, that is—"

Eldred waved his hand. "I didn't mean it. I just mean he doesn't seem to see things. That's all I'm saying."

"Well," said Henreit.

"That's fine. He would just say he sees the hill. We need something else."

Henreit nodded. "Right."

Eldred waved his index finger back and forth as he considered. "We need—we need some bait."

"What?" asked Henreit.

"Nobody can see him over there but me. We need him closer. We need to draw him in. How about the rabbits? I heard Balian caught two hares last evening."

Henreit pursed his lips. "Well, uh, the rabbits? I believe Rollon is planning to use those in a stew."

Eldred shrugged. "He can make something else. The rabbits are perfect for this. Gervese, go fetch those rabbits."

Gervese looked to Henreit, who gave a pained expression but said nothing.

"Oh, and some wine," said Eldred.

"For the bird?" asked Gervese.

"No, for me. I've gotten a taste for it from taking the potions. Two bottles should do."

"I thought you found the potions disgusting," said Henreit.

Eldred shuddered. "Oh, yes. But I can sometimes make out the taste of the wine separately."

"Very well. I will join you. I could use a drink myself," said Henreit, taking a seat as Gervese trotted off.

Eldred chuckled. "If only the eagle were as easy to wrangle as you." He stopped laughing as he noticed Henreit's somber expression. "Oh, are you still upset about your man?"

Henreit sighed. "I have known Guillotin for years. I talked him into coming on this expedition. He did not wish to come. He said it was impractical, and now he is dead—stabbed through the heart."

Eldred narrowed his eyes. "You say he was stabbed in the heart?"

Henreit nodded and put his hand on his chest. "Yes, just once, right there. That is all it takes. We are but fragile mortals, unwound from the coil of life in an instant."

"Was he wearing a brown cloak?" asked Eldred.

Henreit tapped his chin. "I cannot say. Does it matter?"

"Oh. Ah, there's Gervese," said Eldred.

They uncorked the first bottle while Gervese hung the two rabbits high on the post they had used for the Serpent game the previous day.

"You think the eagle will come for them?" asked Henreit.

"Why not? Eagles scavenge readily enough. And this place clearly has its attention."

Henreit sniffed. "If it doesn't come, perhaps Rollon can still use them."

Eldred made a face and took a swig of wine. "I don't think so. Balian will just have to go hunt for more."

Henreit eyed Eldred's empty glass. "You should probably slow down a bit."

Eldred laughed. "Why?"

"You could get sick drinking on an empty stomach."

Eldred raised his hand with his index finger just a quarter inch from his thumb. "It's but a thimble full for me. I'm twice your size. Twice anyone's size, even counting the worthy farmer, Gervese." Eldred motioned towards the man, who had gone back to gripping his sword.

"You are not used to drinking," persisted Henreit.

"I have Mercian blood; we can drink the most of anyone." Eldred's lips twisted. "And heal faster than anyone." Eldred frowned and poured himself another cup as Henreit studied the half empty bottle with concern.

A Visitor

Eldred woke up and shielded his eyes from the sunlight. Keeping his eyes cast downwards, he noted that Henreit had left and that someone had draped a blanket over his feet. He wanted to kick it off violently, but of course, he couldn't. He turned his head quickly to look for Gervese and felt a sudden dizziness that sank down into his stomach. Gervese wasn't there. So much for duty.

As Eldred went to survey the roof garden, looking for whoever was supposed to be watching him, he saw it standing there just twenty feet away. Ten feet tall, heavier than Eldred, the eagle clutched a rabbit in its claw.

Eldred felt he would be sick, but he gripped the arm of his chair and steadied himself. The bird posed motionless, pushing out his chest, lush with plumage. A soft breeze blew across its feathers, which rippled golden in the sun. Its eyes held intelligence, looking almost human.

As Eldred wet his lips, he felt a growing sense of menace. It stood so close that its power seemed to radiate in the air. The talons which gripped the rabbit could just as easily grab Eldred. Its beak—wet with blood?—was long and sharp enough to rip the arm of a man, even a Mercian's. The hairs on his arm started to stand up.

Eldred cleared his throat and pointed at the rabbit. "I told them—I had them—put that out for you."

The eagle's gaze did not waver. Eldred slowly pushed himself up in his chair and cursed himself for leaving his knives in the glasshouse. He could reach the bottle on the table. It had more heft than his cup, but neither would bother his guest. "Gervese," hissed Eldred. Then he yelled. "Gervese!"

But nobody came. The eagle stretched taller, and Eldred stopped yelling. For a moment, the eagle simply stood there, looking Eldred over from his head to his splayed feet. Then it turned its head slightly towards the stairs. In a second, it spread its wings and stepped silently up into the air, gliding from its perch and disappearing over the edge of the roof.

Gervese stepped from around the stairs.

Eldred waved frantically. "Come quick! It was here. It's just over the edge."

Gervese spun around and blinked.

"No!" shouted Eldred. "Get over here. It just went down there."

Gervese ran over, jogging past Eldred stopping at the railing and looking out into the hills.

"Below you!" called Eldred.

Gervese glanced in all directions before turning back to Eldred. "The bird?"

Eldred gazed off towards the hills. "The eagle. It was just here. It took the rabbits."

Gervese wrinkled his brow as he studied the post. "Oh."

"It was huge. There is no larger bird in all the world."

"Do you want me to get Henreit?" asked Gervese.

Eldred leaned back in his seat. "No. That's fine. Where did you go anyway? You were supposed to be guarding me."

Gervese looked away. "Well, they needed me. I helped them move furniture to block the back staircase. It only took a few minutes."

"Hmph. Very well. Just get me some hot water and towels," said Eldred.

"I am not sure I can," said Gervese.

Eldred narrowed his eyes. "What?"

Gervese took a breath. "I will get Henreit. He can explain."

"I don't see that there is anything to explain. Just get me what I asked for."

An anguished look crossed Gervese's face. "I will be back with Henreit."

CHOICES

Henreit sat across from Eldred with his hands folded on his lap. "I am afraid she insists."

Eldred scowled. "Who is she to dictate to me?"

"She is the healer. We—when she heals people in Branath—we do as she advises. We do not put aside her suggestions."

"Not even when she doesn't know what she's talking about?"

"But is that so, truly? Just using the Wretcheds's powder seems unwise to me. Now you mix in her medicine, which is powerful—I have seen the way it puts you to sleep—and you add a few bottles of wine; it does cause concern."

Eldred knocked his wine cup from the table, sending it rolling across the roof. "I need the potion." He smiled menacingly, showing his teeth. "You've never seen me sleep without the potion. If you had, you would not join her in playing this stupid game."

Henreit raised his palms in a calming motion. "She can make the potion. You can take the potion. But she wishes you to skip one day of your other treatment. Is that such an onerous request? You can resume tomorrow if only you take your drink in moderation."

Eldred scoffed. "Moderation? You're lecturing me on moderation?"

"I watched you fall asleep in your chair."

Eldred shook his head vigorously. "That has nothing to do with the potion. And if you fear a few bandits, you will not want to encounter me tonight. All of you together, I could hurl you from this roof."

Henreit clasped his hands and sighed.

"Well?" demanded Eldred.

Henreit spoke softly. "I do not wish to argue, dear cousin. Do we not have enough to occupy ourselves?"

Eldred scratched his chest. "Fine. Fine. We will both be ruled by her. She can measure out my drink. She can choose how I address my injuries. Oh, but I forgot—I'm not even injured. I'm just frightened, just faking." Eldred slammed his fist on the table.

Henreit scooted his chair backwards. "There is no need—"

"You're wrong! There's great need. Bandits lurk in the woods. My family conspires to kill me. My cousin holds my mother hostage. My fiancée fights off death. Our dear uncle weighs my value against my cost. And the longer I sit here—a cripple—the worse it all gets. You're playing games, fixing up this palace, pretending you're leading some great expedition. I tell you: my time grows short. A missed treatment from the Sun People could cost me a great deal; it could cost me everything."

Henreit slowly rose from his chair. "I cannot compel her—you know that. If you ask Gervese for hot water and your Wretched powders, he will bring them, but that is all you will get."

As Henreit walked away, Eldred threw the table to its side.

QUESTIONS

Eldred woke the next day after a dreamless sleep. That—at least—was an improvement. He watched the sun climb over the hills in a groggy stupor for some hours before hunger came. When he called for Gervese, it was old man Madalulf who shuffled in carrying a platter of bread and cheese.

Eldred pushed himself up into a sitting position and took the offered plate. "Where's Gervese?"

Madalulf eyed Eldred dourly. "He went with the others to bury Guillotin."

Eldred stuffed a chunk of bread and cheese in his mouth. "Doesn't that leave us a bit thin here?"

"We have men by the doors. Besides, nobody has seen any more of the bandits."

Eldred gave a small laugh. "Did anyone ever see them?"

Madalulf frowned. "Guillotin did."

Eldred paused before his next bite. "Did he, though?"

"What do you mean?"

"These bandits don't make much sense. They come in here, which could be dangerous, just for a bit of food?"

Madalulf shrugged. "Spoken like someone who has never been hungry."

"Oh, I have. I crossed the mountains to Turicum. That was no easy journey. Now, these supposed bandits, they killed your friend easily enough, but did they take more food, more wine? No. They just ran off and left the horses. Real bandits wouldn't do that."

Madalulf crossed his arms. "So Guillotin was killed by fake bandits? Or are you saying he wasn't even killed and now they are burying him alive?"

Eldred crinkled up his face. "Get some men up here. I want to see where this happened."

Madalulf laughed. "No, prince. All the others are occupied. It is just me, and I will not be ferrying you down there. Not when you could just walk down there yourself."

Eldred's mouth grew tight. "She doesn't know what she's talking about."

"She is the finest healer in these parts—well, in Branath, anyway."

"Yes, in Branath, where you're as brilliant as anyone."

Madalulf glared. "At least I keep myself clean, cripple. But thanks for saving me time. No need to bring you lunch today."

Eldred clenched his fist. "I'll be telling Henreit—"

Madalulf reached over and knocked the plate out of Eldred's hand. "I'm certain you will, prince." With that, Madalulf turned and left the glasshouse.

Eldred sat for a moment, mouth slack with shock, but then a red heat started pouring through him. "I should've grabbed him," Eldred muttered. "Broken his neck." Eldred looked to the side of his bed—the bread and cheese were scattered across the floor. Eldred rubbed his forehead and sighed. "No. No."

Slowly, he gathered his clothes and dressed himself in a loose fashion. Then he scooted to the edge of the bed and twisted over onto his stomach to slide gracelessly to the floor. He collected himself and started dragging himself backwards in a seated position, moving fairly quickly.

The stairs from the roof to the fourth floor, it was a long way down the warped steps. Eldred sat a minute eyeing them, making up his mind. Finally, he started down. "Just can't tumble." He didn't, not as carefully as he went. He was past the fourth floor and down to the landing halfway to the third before Weltrude saw him and ran up to meet him.

She wrinkled her brow. "What do you think you are doing? Where is Madalulf?"

Eldred leaned against the wall, forehead with a slight sheen. "Just out for my morning crawl, part of my act."

She leaned over the railing. "Madalulf? Pernet?"

Eldred chuckled. "What are those two going to do? They couldn't lift my arm."

"You are supposed to stay up there. That is what you wanted."

Eldred pushed away from the wall, headed to the next flight of stairs.

"I'll go back once I'm ready. On my own—I won't have them touch me again."

Down on the second floor, Madalulf, Pernet and Rollon trotted out. Madalulf and Pernet wore swords on their hips; Rollon carried a hatchet.

Madalulf made a rude gesture. "Shit."

Eldred took no help, so the squad followed him down the stairs, bickering as they went.

CRIME SCENE

Eldred sat on the stair second from the bottom looking down the hall towards the kitchen door. Light from the kitchen windows illuminated the scene. Pernet stood halfway down the corridor, pointing at the floor. The others lined up behind Eldred on the stairs.

Eldred gestured impatiently. "That's where it happened? I thought he died in the kitchen."

Rollon stepped past Eldred to the foot of the stairs. "It would be bad luck if he had died in there. You cannot bake good bread where a man has died."

Eldred raised an eyebrow. "Perhaps, though I don't see why. Who found him?"

"Balian found him. He always checks the building first thing in the morning," said Weltrude.

"Hmph. And I suppose he is part of the burial detail," said Eldred.

Weltrude nodded. "There is a small graveyard over by the abandoned settlement."

Eldred narrowed his eyes and pointed towards the wall next to Pernet. "That's dried blood. Is it Guillotin's?"

Madalulf shrugged. "You can clean it yourself, if you find it so objectionable, prince."

Eldred frowned. "Come closer and repeat yourself."

Madalulf stuck out his chin. "So you can kill me too?"

Eldred shook his head and turned to Rollon. "And you were missing items? What did the thieves take?"

Rollon scratched the back of his balding scalp. "Not much: a few bottles of wine, a few tins of fish."

"And that was it?" asked Eldred.

"Well, that day, yes."

"What do you mean 'that day'?" asked Eldred.

"I mean yesterday morning, after Balian found him, I noticed some missing bottles."

"Have bottles gone missing other days?"

Rollon shrugged. "Seems like every morning a few more are gone. I expect we will run out shortly."

Eldred craned his neck to survey those standing behind him. "Persistent bandits. Did anyone have a dispute with Guillotin? Did he steal someone's livestock? Sleep with anyone's wife?"

Everyone was silent.

"Surely he annoyed someone," said Eldred.

Madalulf smirked. "Not everyone has your talent, prince."

Eldred made a dismissive gesture and looked over the scene. Faded blood trails led past Pernet's feet to the wall. A few feet further on, a small alcove. Eldred tilted his head. Up by the kitchen door, a wooden carving was set into the wall. "Oh," said Eldred.

"Oh, what?" asked Pernet.

Eldred licked his lips. "I may have seen this in a dream. I sometimes have dreams that are true."

"What do you mean?" asked Weltrude.

Eldred slid down from the stairs and turned to scoot down the corridor past Pernet, who watched with his hands on his hips.

Rollon followed behind Eldred. "Where are you going?"

"I'm checking something," said Eldred. He stopped alongside the carving, studying it. It showed the moon rising high over a crest of mountains with stars set behind. Eldred stretched up towards the carving and started prodding it.

Pernet came up behind Eldred as the others drifted over. "What are you doing?"

Eldred pointed at the carved moon positioned a few inches out of his reach. "Press that."

Pernet made a face but stepped around Eldred and pressed. A sharp click sounded. Eldred pressed and the center of the carving swung open.

"What? How did you know about that?" demanded Madalulf.

Weltrude gasped and retreated to the stairs.

Eldred glanced after Weltrude before turning to Madalulf. "I had a vision in my dream. The killer, whoever it was, went in there. He took the items but Guillotin had already collected them. In that sense, the killer was no thief."

Pernet cautiously eased his face into the opening. "I see a ladder going down."

Eldred smiled. "Good. Someone needs to go down and investigate."

Madalulf drew his sword. "No need, prince. I found the killer."

Eldred glared. "Don't be stupid."

Madalulf pointed his sword at Eldred's legs as the others scattered back out of the way. "You just could not help yourself. All you had to do was sit up there on your ass instead of sliding all the way down here on it."

Eldred backed against the wall, bracing himself with one hand while raising the other one in front of himself. "You can't kill me! I'm the king's nephew."

Madalulf grinned. "You are right. Even a vile murderous prince has more worth than a common man to a noble's eye; the king's eye is no different. But I do not aim to kill you—I just want to make you dance. Stand up!"

Eldred thrust out his arm. "Put down your sword and fight me on equal terms, you coward."

Madalulf darted forward and stabbed Eldred in the leg. "On your feet, prince. My blade insists."

Eldred grabbed for the sword but came away with a gaping cut on his hand as Madalulf pulled the blade free.

Madalulf stepped back out of reach. "Come get me, prince."

Eldred stared at his bleeding hand. "Stop him! Why are you letting him do this?"

Madalulf came in again, stabbing Eldred with deep thrusts in each leg as Eldred tried to bat away his sword with his injured hand. Blood ran freely, pooling around Eldred's calves.

"Have you all gone insane?" cried Eldred.

Madalulf stepped back and lowered his sword. "You can walk." He turned to Weltrude. "He can walk. You said he could. Gervese said he could. He got the rabbits down."

"No! That was the eagle!" shouted Eldred.

Madalulf scoffed. "The bird only you can see?"

Weltrude covered her mouth, looking at Madalulf with wide eyes. "Whatever else is true, you must stop."

Rollon stepped forward and tried to pull Madalulf back. The two grappled, rocking back and forth.

"Do not fall for his act. We finish him now, or he will kill us all!" said Madalulf, spitting with rage.

Rollon lost his footing on the blood slicked stones, and they crashed into Eldred, with Rollon's bony ass cracking Eldred's skull against the wall. Everyone was yelling as Eldred slumped down. The sound died away as his vision faded to blackness.

A Sincere Apology

Eldred woke with a burst of restlessness. He moved his arms and curled up his spine, looking to move off his back, but a deep weakness radiated throughout his body and he lay back limply.

"Oh, good," said Henreit.

Eldred opened his eyes and found himself lying on a bed in an unfamiliar room with high stone walls and large windows looking out into the night. Henriet sat close at hand holding a goblet. His face was shadowed by the candlelight behind him, but Eldred could make out a faint smile on his face.

"I am glad to see you with your eyes open. Weltrude—as always—stitched you up masterfully. Still, we were all quite worried for you," said Henreit.

Eldred held up his right hand. The bandage wrapped around it was dry, but his sliced palm pulsed with nauseating pain. "Is that so?"

Henreit widened his smile. "Very much so."

Eldred peeled back the covers. His legs were wrapped in a maze of bandages. A few pinkish spots showed through. Eldred sighed; his voice weakened. "Even Madalulf?"

Henreit's eyes went dark. "That man is mad. He was already difficult before, but now he has gone well past the sphere of acceptable behavior. I am so sorry I left you here in his care. I have known him for seven years, but I never dreamt he could behave in such a monstrous fashion."

Eldred cautiously poked at the bandages on his legs with his left hand. No pain. Nothing.

Henreit watched as Eldred probed his wounds. "You need not fear. We have locked him away. He resides in the cell I told you of down on the first floor. Balian is there watching him."

Eldred lay back, leaving his legs be. "Balian? He's the one who found the body."

"Yes, what of it?"

Eldred made a face as he itched his side. "Madalulf is a Motherless fool, but he is not the murderer. We must keep him confined, but we must not rest."

Henreit leaned back in his chair. "How could you think Balian had something to do with it? He is no murderer either. Besides, it is impossible. He is always with Weltrude."

Eldred frowned. "That does not mean anything. Balian could be the one, or not. There is a killer among us. We were not beset by strange bandits who wandered in out of nowhere."

Henreit furrowed his brow. "What do you want me to do?"

"The opening—the murderer went down there. There might be some clues to tell us who it is."

Henreit gave a quick nod. "Pernet already climbed down. The ladder leads to a small windowless cell. He found a few empty bottles of the missing wine. Otherwise, there is only a small table, a chair and a few books— nothing of value."

Eldred jabbed with his left index finger. "That proves my vision. The bottles; the killer did climb down."

Henreit set down his cup. "Perhaps. Though I do not understand the value of this knowledge. Should the killer climb down into this room or should he not; what is the difference? And these visions of yours—we only learn of them now with Guillotin's death. This is not ideal. There are some who harbor doubts."

Eldred sighed. "I had visions some time ago when I was with the Sun People, when they healed me. It must be the powder."

"You must stop using their foul medicine."

Eldred gestured towards his legs. "No. I need it to clear up this mess. Weltrude did her best—or I hope she did—but I'm barely held together. I need my powder now, along with hot water and towels."

Henreit tilted his head. "She will not approve."

"I don't care. After this horrible attack by your man, a citizen of Branath, I need to heal. I need to walk. I won't allow her or anyone to get in the way of that."

Henreit made a sour face. "Fine. I will see you get your powder. I will have them bring your things. You can keep my room. But I hope you see this was all a misunderstanding."

"I hope it's the last one." Eldred gestured towards the door. "And the books. Have Pernet bring all of them here. I need to see them."

Henreit rose to his feet. "Very well."

"And the potion; I'll be up for a few hours, but have her make it now. I don't want any last minute games."

Henreit frowned. "I will see what I can do."

STUDIES

An edgy euphoria that Eldred had come to associate with the application of the powder coursed through him, but now there was something else in addition to it: an amazing transformation. The bandages were off—both on his legs and his right hand. The wounds had been deep and looked ugly, even with Weltrude's neat stitching. That changed after the application of the powder solution. First the color of the wounds softened from dark red to a soft pink. Then the wounds themselves disappeared over the course of thirty minutes, fading back into normal healthy skin decorated with unnecessary thread. Eldred's right hand was healed, fully healed. He moved it without pain. His legs remained inert though, even though the wounds were gone.

Eldred gave his legs a worried look. What would it take? Mercian resilience, three fatum lapides and the most powerful healing ingredient of the Sun People had all failed so far. Would he ever walk again?

His possessions, such as they were, sat on a night stand near the bed. His daggers were neatly rolled up in their fine leather case and his packets of powder—one half spent and one whole—stacked next to them in a transparent sample bag.

The bed was strewn with a dozen dusty books that Pernet had grudgingly dropped off. Most were thick tomes detailing the family trees of Maldavian nobility. They had been hard to follow at first since they were of olden days, detailing family relations from more than a hundred years in the past. The great families were listed there, including Uncle Julian's line, though not with the prominence they now held.

Two books of a different sort stood out. One was a small pocketbook with a supple black leather cover. It held few pages, and only the first twenty of those had any writing, which was all the same sort—counting in sets of fives, each with four vertical dashes struck through by a line. Eldred made out the total count as seven hundred sixty-seven. Seven hundred sixty-seven what?

The other unusual book was the most worn, with torn pages and others that were on the verge of falling out. What was there was barely legible, written in a tight scrawl that ran characters together. A personal account of some sort, Eldred slouched against the headboard and started to read.

JOURNAL PART 1

T*his is my story, my account of the ill-fated expedition into Pergamon. I cannot reasonably expect anyone shall find it, but write I will, if only to pass the time.*

Affairs were set in motion when Zlatan, a citizen of Pergamon, arrived in Belum leading a merchant caravan. Though caravans from Pergamon were common in former times, none had arrived in twenty five years, not since the Mother disappeared and Bonitus marshaled his host to go in search of her.

This situation confused some commanders who should have known better, and Zlatan was initially permitted to display his wares in the central Belum marketplace. It made quite a sight with fine china and Pergamon crystal not seen in a generation. The caravan crew itself was remarkable. Many people had never seen Pergamonese men with their curly blond hair and many hued eyes: sapphire, green, rose and black, among others. And nobody had ever seen such beasts as bore their goods or even heard tales of them. The strange humpbacked creatures—camels they named them—towered over the men, stinking hulks smellier and uglier than any horse.

When I, Duke Philippot of Belum, first approached their stall, I was of two minds. The people loved their goods and formed a snaking line of customers ready to gratefully hand over their coins for the wonders on display. And the Pergamonese were charming in their fashion; Zlatan in particular stood forth and engaged with the people, smiling and shaking their hands while he took their money. But I could not forget my duty. Bonitus, the Son, had attacked Pergomon and they were our enemies.

I have always been—and given the current situation, always will be—a man of duty first. I impounded the goods and had the city guard round up Zlatan and his men. I allowed those who had made purchases to keep their goods, but I denied the others their demands to seize the remaining items. A just man may not steal, not even from his most despicable foe. Thus did Zlatan's company enter my jail and his goods enter my storerooms.

While I had easily managed the situation, this was not merely a city affair. The involvement of the Pergamonese made this a matter of state. I sent word to the king in Emon. Two weeks later, Prince Gaufroi arrived leading a mounted force of one hundred men, elite fighters each blessed by the Mother.

Of the prince, what should I say? Of course he was twice blessed by the Mother as I am myself. My initial impression was mixed. I respected his aura of command and strength. He was only fifth in line to the throne, but every conversation regarding the successor to King Acelin included Prince Gaufroi more than his standing warranted. But to my mind, his treatment of the prisoners— including torture and murder—greatly exceeded what the circumstances required. They were simple merchants looking for profits in the wrong place. They were not selling crystal goblets as part of some devious plot to invade Gauraci.

So it was that I dealt with Prince Gaufroi with formal politeness delivered in a distant manner. I did not care for his methods, but I acknowledged he could be king one day. I provided him and his men room and board, and averted my eyes from the borderline excesses they subjected upon my citizens when they were not busy tormenting the Pergamonese. I was counting down the days until he dispatched the merchants and returned to Emon with their goods.

On the evening of the fifth day after he arrived, he surprised me by requesting a late night audience. A number of aspects of the request were unexpected. First, the hour was late for a matter which could surely wait until morning. Second, the request was quite pleasant, not the blunt commanding manner I had seen in earlier messages from Prince Gaufroi. And lastly, he was requesting to see me rather than demanding I appear before him, an option which his rank allowed.

I left my dinner guests with honest words of regret. The stewards were just serving the dessert course, a sweet cake covered in blackberries. I bid them to save me a piece and made my way to my audience chamber where I found the prince waiting. This worried me for an instant since making him wait, even if I were punctual, could be seen as an insult. But the prince bowed low and joined me at my council table with a warm smile on his lips.

At first, I did not understand why we were meeting. He recounted the confessions he had extracted from the prisoners. They had a device that allowed them to traverse sandstorms, which the prince explained was merely a great deal of dust blown up into the sky by wind. They had traveled from Chalcis, which the prince described at length as a fabulously wealthy city defended by only a motley collection of Pergamonese oafs. The ruler of that city—a woman—supposedly had a ruby larger than a plum set in her crown.

I smiled and nodded. It was a great courtesy of the prince to keep me informed of his investigation, but I had guests and a warm cake waiting for me. Finally, I interrupted the prince as he was going on about the immense amount of gold leaf used in decorating their temple to Korinna, stonebearer to the people of Pergamon.

This is all well and good, I told Prince Gaufroi, but what is it you wish of me?

The charming smile returned to his face, warmth radiating from his twice blessed eyes. You must come with me, he said. You must join me in the greatest conquest in the history of Gauraci: the sacking of Chalcis.

I choked on the wine I was drinking and swallowed with difficulty. Surely you must approach the king, I said. If you aim to match the strength and power of Pergamon—protected by the mighty Korinna whose power was second only to the Mother—you will need all of our strength plus the armies of the Deirans and Mercians as well. Did not the great Bonitus—most beloved son of the Mother herself—set upon Pergamon with the greatest host ever assembled only to disappear without a trace?

The prince laughed softly. Such is the thinking of fat old men who are just sleeping their final days until death, he stated. Besides, I have it from our captives that Korinna has also been absent for these last decades as has her capital, Megara, which is lost to the storms.

I frowned, for I did not like the insult in his words. I was quite fit—though perhaps heavy then if compared to my current state. But the disappearance of Korinna—that was news to me, news to everyone. Her presence had been a source of worry for many years as we all wondered how she might choose to apply her power. Encouraged, I asked him what it would cost me.

He clasped my shoulder. I look to you to join me with one hundred of your finest guards. We will return with such riches that you can build a truly fabulous palace, one worthy of such a great duke as yourself.

I held my arm stiffly. My palace was from the ancient days, as fine as any building in Emon. But then I saw that his expression bore no trace of mockery. His face and voice radiated confidence. I saw then that he was certain he could sack this plump city. Would he not know? He had the readily compelled knowledge of the merchants at hand. If the people of Chalcis had any wits about them, would they have sent this sad caravan of fools to alert us to their weakness?

A wiser man might have taken leave to get council, might have considered the many risks implicit in such a bold endeavor. But for the cost of only one hundred men and the supplies to outfit the expedition, I could gain half the riches of Chalcis. I hurriedly agreed to his conditions. I feared he need only send word to Bath or Emon to find a replacement for me if I did not quickly close the matter.

A Lesson

Weltrude rapped on the door and entered the room with her chin raised high. Balian trailed after her, only a step behind.

Eldred set the journal down next to him on the bed. "Oh, do you have the potion?" He turned his eyes to Balian. "Or is this about the murder?"

Weltrude lifted a cup. "I am delivering that which Henreit demanded I deliver. After all, I should not want you to become violent, as you always hint you might."

Eldred gestured to a table next to the bed. "There is good. I'll take it after a bit. I'm delving into the books that Pernet brought up. I find them quite interesting."

Balian narrowed his brows. "They are all old, are they not, prince?"

Eldred picked up the pocketbook with the sums and handed it to Balian. "Except for this one. It seems to have been updated recently."

Balian raised his eyebrows. "How do you know that?"

Eldred pointed at four small flowers set on the edge of the table. "Those were tucked in the spine. If you look, you'll see one is fresh. There are more like it up on the rooftop."

Balian grunted and paged through the book. "It is full of scratches."

"It's a count. The total across all the pages is seven hundred sixty-seven," said Eldred.

Balian handed the pocketbook to Weltrude, who was looking over his shoulder.

Eldred tugged back the blankets covering his legs. "You might find this more interesting, Weltrude."

Balian stepped back as Weltrude leaned forward, dropping the pocketbook on the table next to the potion. She ran her hands over the area above the knee where Madalulf had inflicted his deepest cut. Instead of the angry red wound that had been there before, she found smooth pink skin. She quickly checked the other wounds and found them the same. Only her tight regular stitching gave any clue that there had been any injury at all. She straightened up, shaking her head.

Eldred pointed to his legs. "It's the powder. It cured these wounds. I told you it has great potency."

Weltrude stared at Eldred's legs. "The powder did this?"

Balian cleared his throat. "Does this mean you can walk, prince? Has the powder cured your legs completely?"

Eldred grimaced. "No, just the wounds. I still can't walk."

Balian nodded at Weltrude. "You are fortunate that Weltrude treated you, or you may not have lived long enough to take your treatment."

Eldred nodded hesitantly. "That's true. Of course, Madalulf only stabbed me because he thought I could walk, because he heard that from— someone."

Balian took Weltrude's hand as she began to grow red in the face. "Is there anything else, prince? If not, Weltrude and I should be going."

"Well, you found the body," said Eldred.

"You mean Guillotin?" asked Balian.

"Yes. Anything odd to report about it? Anything you found at the scene?" asked Eldred.

Balian's face held a blank expression. "No, prince."

Eldred pushed himself up higher against the headboard. "Don't you find it odd that the killer climbed down the ladder into that tiny room?"

"That may have been what happened. We are still trying to make out the facts," said Balian.

Eldred gestured at Weltrude, who still looked red in the face. "I told everyone about my vision. And Pernet found the empty bottles."

"Of course, prince. We will leave you to your studies," said Balian evenly.

Eldred frowned as he watched them leave.

It took half an hour for Eldred to find Prince Gaufroi's family tree in the books. He was born three years after the Mother disappeared, the nephew of King Acelin. He had a younger brother named Magner. According to the text, neither was married or had children. Did their line end or had their families sprouted after the book was written? Eldred had to search through several books before he found Duke Philippot's family tree. He, likewise, lacked heirs.

Nonetheless, the journal referred to real people who lived during the period described. Eldred mulled over what it meant as he drank the potion and prepared for bed.

DREAMS

As Eldred drifted off to sleep, he heard the voices.

At first, it was Balian's. "Are you well? What is the matter?"

There was a long pause before Weltrude replied. "He is unnatural."

Balian sighed. "You mean the wounds? He explained that. It was the Wretcheds's powder."

"No powder—no medicine—could heal wounds such as those so quickly. This force comes from within him," said Weltrude.

"You mean his fatum lapides? He is thrice blessed."

"Even that should take time. I know a healer who worked with a patient who had a fatum lapis. The patient never regrew skin over the course of a few hours," said Weltrude.

"It may be good that he did. Perhaps he will show clemency for Madalulf," said Balian.

"It is not good," said Weltrude.

"Why not?" asked Balian.

"What will it take to kill him—before he kills us?" asked Weltrude.

Eldred felt their words floating away from him as he slid deeper into sleep. He was dreamless for a time until a scene slowly crystalized out of the darkness. A hooded shape sat on some stool or a kind of bench beside a table. It faced the wall and was carving into it with a knife, scratching out a single vertical line four inches high. It required a few passes of the blade. When the groove was deep enough, satisfying the man—it did seem as if it were a man—he set the knife on the table. Oddly, there was another hand there resting beside the knife, an extra hand that was not attached to anyone.

Eldred focused on the hand, freshly severed by the blood that oozed from it, and puzzled for a moment. Then his vision drew back, going wider.

Bones were strewn all across the floor: arms, ribs, skulls, legs—human bones spread across a dank chamber. At the table, the man picked up the hand by the thumb, gripping it between his own thumb and finger, and sniffed it.

275

BREAKFAST

The next morning Eldred woke to find breakfast already beside him on the table: eggs, sausage and a hunk of bread. He didn't know who had brought it; the door was shut—probably Gervese. He lay there for a few minutes, smelling the cooked meat and staring out the window. In this room, Henreit's room, he did not have the same wide field of vision that he had become accustomed to on the roof, but it was warmer and cozier.

Eldred was sitting up, eating, when Henreit knocked and entered.

Henreit's eyes were bloodshot. "Good morning."

"Did you sleep well?" inquired Eldred.

Henreit shook his head. "No. How about yourself?"

Eldred took a bite of sausage and shrugged. "I always sleep well if I take Weltrude's potion, though I did have another vision—I think."

"Oh, what was it?"

"I saw a figure sitting in a room full of human remains," said Eldred.

"The same person you saw kill Guillotin?" asked Henreit.

Eldred picked up the bread. "It may have been. I couldn't see his face; I think it was a man."

Henreit rubbed his chin. "A killer who stabs the victim is most likely a man. It is not a feminine act. A woman would find some other means."

Eldred nodded. "I think you're right."

Eldred was scooping up the eggs with the bread when shouting erupted in the hallway. Henreit jumped to his feet as Gervese burst through the door.

Gervese waved his hands in the air. "It is Madalulf. Balian just found him down in the prison. Someone stabbed him to death."

Eldred tossed his bread on the floor. "I have to get down there and see what's happened."

Gervese shook his head. "They are coming to see you. Balian found one of your knives."

Eldred's eyes went wide. "What?"

Balian arrived a minute later, carrying a long blade with a dark blue handle on a white towel that was stained red. The rest of the troop lined up behind him, some with swords in hand. They stood behind Balian as he held up the knife for Eldred to inspect. "Is this yours?"

Eldred felt his chest tighten. "Yes, but that doesn't mean anything."

Pernet raised his sword. "I think it does."

Eldred shook his head vigorously. "You think I killed him and left my knife behind? Why would I do that?"

"Perhaps you were under the influence of your powder?" asked Weltrude.

"No. Most definitely not. I've been here, asleep," said Eldred.

"You had all night to do it. Balian just found him," said Pernet.

Eldred glanced at Balian. "He found both of the bodies."

Balian cocked his head. "Yes, but I had no dispute with either man. I have known them forever."

Pernet scowled. "How about you, prince? Did it make you angry to be stabbed by a commoner?"

Eldred frowned. "I'm not the only person he bothered. What about you, Henreit? Madalulf was always talking back."

Henreit raised his palms. "I would never kill the man."

"He attacked you, prince!" barked Pernet.

Balian cleared his throat. "Madalulf's hand is missing."

Eldred blinked. "His hand?"

Balian straightened his back. "It is missing. I searched all around the cell for it."

"Could he have eaten it?" asked Pernet.

Eldred took a shuddering breath and wagged his finger at the knife. "I threw a dagger like this off the roof during our game of Serpent, Pernet. You could have gotten it. Gervese—you were there. You saw it!"

Balian turned towards Gervese, who nodded.

Pernet shrugged. "The prince cannot throw for shit."

Eldred pointed at the leather case on the table. "The others are all here. It wasn't me."

Balian walked over to the table and unrolled the leather wrap holding

Eldred's knives. Seven blades gleamed in their slots, only one of which had a dark blue grip.

Eldred's mouth fell open.

Pernet sneered. "Did you think we could not count because we are peasants?"

Eldred looked around the room, seeing hard eyes everywhere. "I was sleeping. Anyone could have taken my knife."

Balian set the bloody towel down on the table, wiping off his fingers as he did. "It was you who hated him, prince."

"I had another vision," said Eldred hurriedly. "I was telling Henreit—just before you came in. There was a man in a dark room full of corpses. He had Madalulf's hand. It's not here. You have to look. When you find it, you'll know I'm telling the truth."

"He did mention a room," said Henreit.

"He killed two of us. We should kill him," said Pernet.

Balian shook his head. "Gervese, Raduard—go clean out the cell. Once the prince is secured, we will all look for Madalulf's hand."

Journal Part 2

We set out from Belum with two hundred men at arms—Prince Gaufroi's horsemen along with one hundred of my mounted guardsmen. The twenty camels from the caravan walked behind us, their fancy wares replaced with bags of water and stores from my warehouse. Only two Pergamonese joined us: Zlatan and Gligor. Prince Gaufroi had used his methods to ascertain that Gligor was Zlatan's son. It was a surprise to me as they did not even have the same color eyes.

We made good time traveling up the coast and soon reached the northernmost reach of the Parvus Sea, where we turned east into Pergamon. The road passed through a desolate stretch of land that grew bleaker with each mile. We crossed a few small streams, but most ran with water too brackish to drink— too brackish for men and horses. However, the camels drank their fill.

On the third day into Pergamon, the wind kicked up and blew waves of grit into our faces. I slowed my horse and waited for Zlatan, shielding my eyes as best I could. I asked him if this was one of the dust storms he had been going on about so much. He paused for a moment, standing there with the rope to the lead camel in hand, smiling apologetically. No, this was but a breeze, he said.

HIs words bore out. On the fifth day, a red cloud arose on the horizon. Within an hour, we were caught in a raging torrent of flying sand. We hurriedly set up the caravan tents we had borrowed. I joined Prince Gaufroi and some of his men in a tent with Zlatan. The prince always kept Gligor separate as a check on Zlatan's ambition to escape.

As we huddled there, the sides of the tent dancing in the wind, Prince Gaufroi demanded that Zlatan show him the guiding stone. That was the first time I saw it. The stone was a smooth oval, dark gray in color, and well sized to hold in the palm of your hand. We passed it around, each of us holding it in turn. To the touch, it was just a stone.

Prince Gaufroi told Zlatan to demonstrate the use of the stone. Zlatan argued at first that it made no sense since this was not a standing storm, that we need only wait it out. The prince set his chin—not by much, just a barely visible amount—and Zlatan's tiresome objections dried up. He took the stone and pressed it between both of his hands as he muttered some nonsense prayer to Korrina while moving his hands back and forth in an arc. After sitting still for a minute with his head bowed, he took a breath and raised his eyes. He pointed at the wall of the tent. That is the way east, to Chalcis, he said.

The prince frowned. He could see as I did that only Zlatan could use the cursed stone, presuming it worked. Not that it mattered then; the storm was passing. Afterwards, we packed up and rode onwards, riding late into the evening to make up time.

On the seventh day, we reached the standing storm. We first saw it some miles away, a tumultuous ribbon of dust howling across the sandy desert. The sight of it filled me with dread. Even Zlatan did not smile. I followed after Prince Gaufroi along with the others. We trudged forward, in much worse shape than when we had left Belum. The horses were thirsty and weak, battered by our desert passage. The men wore dazed expressions as they glanced at each other, each waiting for someone else to say it was a joke, that nobody would walk into that infernal storm. But nobody spoke up.

Of course, we had a plan. Zlatan had told us what to expect. Men dismounted, leading their horses, and gripped long ropes tied with bells so that we could stay together. The prince and I followed directly behind Zlatan, our men arrayed behind us. The storm never stopped, but at night it slowed just enough that we could make a ragged camp. The stars were lost to us, even to those like myself whom the Mother had blessed with dark vision. But while the constellations were hidden from us, Zlatan had his guiding stone and could always point the way forward.

On the second night into the storm, the prince and I ate a tasteless dinner with his captains. We allowed ourselves a cup of wine—a fitting indulgence, considering our station—and the prince began to speak oddly. At first, I chose to ignore him, just nodding as he spoke. I focused on enjoying my drink. But he went on and on.

After a spell, his words finally dawned on me. He was disparaging Chalcis. Not just the inhabitants, which would make sense, but the city itself. He had a litany of complaints: the citizens were not worth killing, their jewels were cracked, their crystal was cloudy, their gold was likely blended with copper.

I blinked into my half-empty cup. Why, I asked, why are we in this Mother-

forsaken place if the riches of Chalcis are only so much crap?

I have been telling you, he bellowed. Were you not listening? Chalcis is nothing. Even to Pergamon, it is nothing—a squalid city by the sea. It is no more to this land than, say, Belum is to ours. What would we get if we sacked Belum? A handful of rat skins?

I took offense at that; I wanted to strangle Gaufroi. I felt my hands grow tight as if they already gripped his slender neck. But I sat on my cushion and choked back my words, lest I reveal my thoughts.

Prince Gaufroi's mad eyes sought mine. Rat skins or real treasure, he said. We can make the choice. We have the power to create our own destiny.

I controlled myself with effort. I gulped down the rest of my wine. Do you mean we turn back, I asked.

His face grew dark. Have you heard nothing I said, he demanded. Where are we? He hopped to his feet, waving his hands back and forth. Where are we, he repeated, looking only at me. His clueless captains sat on their rears, staring at me as well.

I lifted my palms. In a storm in Pergamon, I said.

Gaufroi laughed and shook his head. You are the only other educated man here, yet I may as well be alone, he said. Do you suppose a slug that crawls up on a plate has any awareness? Can it tell that it is on a crafted object, built of intention, and not just on some random stone?

I sat, waiting for him to go on with some new conjecture, but he waited for me to answer. His damned captains looked on, bearing vexed expressions, as if they knew the answer to the prince's query.

My mouth felt dry. A slug would not recognize a plate, I said, mustering as much conviction as I could.

The prince cast a disdainful glance across the gathering. Clearly not, he said.

I dropped my cup on the floor, irritated. What is your meaning, I asked.

He raised his arms up to the roof of the tent. A storm that stands is a font of power, he said. A storm that stands endlessly has endless power, unlimited power! That we would waste our ability to pass through such a storm to sack a pathetic city—that would be the surest sign of our stupidity.

Everyone was still looking at me. I took a breath. What must we do, I asked.

His lips spread in a wide toothy smile. We must go to the center, he said.

What is there, I asked.

He pointed towards the wall of the tent and spoke softly. What else could be there, but Korinna's capital, Megara.

JAIL

The banging started around noon, echoing from down the hallway that led to the rest of the lower floor. Eldred set the journal on a table just outside his cell, the table which pressed against the bars. He picked up a small cup of wine that Henreit had left him—a tight squeeze through the bars—and drank, perched up on his cot, leaning against the wall, wearing only his night clothes. They had carried him directly from his bed to this place.

Iron bars set in the ceiling and floor framed the cell in the corner of a large stone-lined cellar. Elaborate glass paned windows ran along the top of the opposite wall, lighting the room. In the cell itself, there was only a small barred window halfway up the wall that opened at ground level, for the entire first floor of the palace was sunk into the ground.

Aside from the cot, Eldred's cell boasted only two buckets near the iron door. One held water for drinking and washing. The other was for waste, though at the moment it only contained Madalulf's excrement. Eldred was putting off that function for as long as he could.

Eldred frowned at the blood that was still drying in the cracks and crannies in the floor. Not only had someone framed him, but the murderer had left a stinking mess. He had requested that they wash it away three times since morning, but they were all too busy hunting for Madalulf's blasted hand.

A half hour into the infernal hammering, Henreit entered the outer room carrying a plate. He shouted over the noise, "Sorry, cousin!"

"Are you, cousin?" asked Eldred.

Henreit took a seat at the table and pushed the plate over to Eldred: a piece of bread and an apple. "What is that smell?"

"Madalulf, though whether you smell his shit or his blood, I don't know," said Eldred.

Henreit glanced over the cell. "Well, it will not be for long, not if your vision is true."

Eldred fished through the bars for the apple. "It's true enough. I saw it. What's with all this racket?"

Henreit gestured back towards the hallway. "They found a bronze trapdoor buried under trash in the far wing. Balian thinks you may have hidden the hand there."

Eldred rolled his eyes. "Really? Why would I do that? Why would I kill the idiot and then leave my knife, but take his blessed hand? Besides, I can't even walk."

Henreit tilted his head. "You know that is not what he thinks."

Eldred took a bite of the apple. "You mean, not what she thinks. She spreads her lies, and I find myself here."

Henreit shrugged. "They are frightened. With two dead already, they are cautious. Once they think it through, they will understand you are no mad killer. And if they find your man from the vision, they will free you— simple as that."

Eldred glanced at the key hanging from a hook below the windows. "Not if he finds me first."

"Oh, of course. I forgot. You asked that Gervese guard you. I fear he is the one swinging the hammer. Perhaps I can get Pernet."

"Pernet, huh," said Eldred. "Perhaps this. Perhaps that. Perhaps you can remember that you lead this expedition."

Henreit stood up stiffly. "Very well. I will rejoin the hunt."

Eldred waved him on. "You do that."

✦

JOURNAL PART 3

We reached the eye of the storm in five days. We stepped out into an oasis of still air filled with bright sunlight. A towering wall of swirling dust—it seemed impossibly high—circled a small sand strewn plain dotted with dwarf palm trees that stretched a few miles across. Everyone rushed to a pond that was near at hand, the most beautiful thing I had ever beheld.

We drank and drank. Some laughed, some cried. I moved away from the camels and our few remaining horses, and sat in the water up to my neck, looking up at the blue sky. I sat there for ten minutes, rocked by the gentle waves of man and beast, before I heard him calling.

The prince stood by the shore of the lake, half-dressed, pointing out into the arid plain. Two dozen narrow towers rose above the sand. I shrugged and half-turned back towards the water. I wanted to resume my bath.

Get some men, demanded Gaufroi.

This proved a challenge as they lacked enthusiasm. I expect the losses weighed on them. Seven of my men had been lost in our travels through the storm, presumed dead. The prince lost even more of his supposedly elite soldiers. Those left stared with intense eyes, but they seemed hollow, shaken. I coaxed a dozen of my guardsmen to join the detail; the prince's captains gathered up a similar number. We formed a ragged line and marched to the nearest tower, nearly a mile away. The heat dried me before we arrived.

The tower stood thirty-five feet high with a diameter of forty feet—no door, no windows. Gaufroi's shouts that someone show themselves went unanswered, Eventually, he bid us climb up. A few men stepped forward, but they found no holds on the smooth walls. Some of my men made a failed bid to form a human pyramid. The prince's men milled around, gathering wood from the stunted trees, creating a useless pile of scrap.

Denisot, one of my men, found the way. He ran back to camp and returned *with a length of rope and a metal bar. He tied the rope to the middle of the bar and heaved it over the tower's crenellations. The bar caught when tugged, and up went Denisot, walking his feet along the smooth wall as he clung to the rope. He was on the top for just a minute before he leaned over and called down that the tower was full of sand.*

The prince made the climb to see for himself, and I went after him. You could see where the stairs went down into the tower from the upper platform, but sand filled the entrance to the lip. Without the gaps in the crenellations, I expect the entire platform would have been buried to the height of the crenels.

His captains came up the rope as we looked out over the rows of towers, encircled by the raging storm. One of his men kneeled by the stairs and started digging them out with his cupped hands.

I pointed at the nearest tower, one of similar height. We can try that one, I suggested.

The prince gestured at the digging man. You are no brighter than him if you think the sand only landed here, he said.

The man continued to dig as if he had not heard.

Then what, I asked.

He nodded at the tallest tower, the one in the center of the formation. It stood one hundred-fifty feet high with no windows. I did not see a door. The wind may not deposit as much sand at that height, he said.

I raised my hands. But how can we, I asked. Nobody could throw the bar that far. I sputtered. Why even should we? What do you want?

He grabbed my shoulders, shouting, his spit flying into my face. I want everything! We are in Megara, you fool! Anything we might wish for is beneath our feet.

He pushed me back and dragged his captain to his feet. You have tonight to figure it out, he said. We climb the tower tomorrow.

BURIAL

To Eldred's relief, the hammering stopped in the late afternoon. The smell combined with the noise was making him sick. As he sat, hoping it was more than a short break, Balian entered the outer room with the others lined up behind him.

Balian approached Eldred and leaned on the table, his face close to Eldred's. "I am ready to bury Madalulf."

Eldred looked them over. Henreit was staring at his boots. Weltrude and Pernet were flushed with anger. Gervese, Raduard and Rollon stood back, looking worried. Eldred waved his hand at the cell. "Good, then you can finally have someone clean up this mess."

Balian kept his eyes trained on Eldred's face. "I am ready to bury Madalulf, but I require his hand. I will not bury him without it."

Eldred gripped a bar with his left hand and pulled his face closer to Balian's. "Then don't bury him. Let him rot, for all I care. Just get this damned cell cleaned. The smell is intolerable. I'm a prince of this realm. You're treating me worse than anyone."

Pernet stepped forward. "Let us kill him. If we kill him, we can all go."

Henreit raised his arms. "Calm down. We said we would ask him about the hand. He says he does not know."

Weltrude shot an angry glance at Henreit. "No, he says he does not care. I believe him for once."

Eldred leaned back against the wall. "What about your door? What was in there?"

Balian rubbed his hands together. "We are still working on it."

Eldred sighed. "Well, that's too bad. And Weltrude, I don't know the whereabouts of Madalulf's hand. I had a vision of it on a table in a room full of cadavers. But whether the vision is true or not, I can't say."

"Last time you knew where the hidden room was," said Balian.

"That time I did. Not now. All I know is that if I had cut off Madalulf's hand, I would have left it on the floor," said Eldred.

Balian clasped his hands and inclined his head in thought. After a moment, he turned to Gervese. "Gervese, I want you to wash down the prince's cell and empty his buckets. The rest of us will stand guard outside while you do. Once you are done, we will move Madalulf's body up to the roof. It should be safe enough from vermin up there for one night."

Pernet shuddered as he walked to the far wall to get the key—only he could work the cell door's lock reliably. "He is going to kill us all."

Balian shook his head. "We have the prince confined."

JOURNAL PART 4

The central tower rose one hundred-fifty feet high, taller than any other. That was the challenge to overcome. But the uniqueness of the tower was our salvation. For upon inspection in the morning, we discovered an ornamental design remained—though weathered—on one side.

None of us could quite decide what all the figures and creatures were intended to convey. Most agreed that the figure of a tall woman with a bow stretching thirty feet high was likely Korinna. As for the shapes arrayed around her, some—including the prince—said these were fish. But who hunts fish with a bow, I maintained. The shapes were dogs. Hunting with dogs makes more sense.

We argued about the design as the prince's man started his ascent with a long rope wrapped over his shoulder. The regular spacing of the dogs was key to the man's strategy. His hands sought the shape of the dog above as his bare toes gripped the narrow indentations of the one below. He started fast, quickly reaching the height of Korinna's sandals, forty feet up the tower, but then he slowed.

It was no help to the climber that the heat of the day increased as the sun climbed higher. We on the ground sought the shade from nearby trees, watching as the penalty for a mistake grew ever more serious. He paused when he came even with Korinna's headdress. Here the pattern changed, the dogs giving way to a new shape. I held these were snakes, twisting up into the air, but I conceded to Prince Gaufroi that this made little sense as a practical matter. I took it as being an artistic liberty, unless Korinna had actually crafted flying snakes. I expect it would have been within her power.

In any case, this is where the man fell to his death. He had appeared uncertain, fishing around with his hand, trying to get a grip on a snake's tail. The next moment, he plummeted to the ground. I half-expected the prince to try next, since he was so keen on reaching the top. But when he did not step forward,

I beckoned Denisot, my man who had seen success the previous day.

Denisot started slower than the prince's man had—a point that the prince noted with some complaint—but he was steady. And when he reached Korinna's feet, he switched over to climb her instead of the dogs. At first, this seemed questionable, since the dogs offered more regular handholds. But his decision was borne out when he climbed up her hair and reached the top of her helmet. He now had a route up the arrows that Korrina was shooting, a route that had been unavailable to the prince's man.

It was a tremendous display from Denisot, who was one of the poorest men in my troop but rich in terms of dexterity. When he hooked his hand on top and pulled himself over, the men jumped up and down, shouting in their excitement. Up to that point, we had only whispered for fear of distracting the stalwart climber.

Denisot lowered the combined rope, combined in that it was, in fact, several ropes that had been tied together. The thin rope ran right down the middle of Korinna's carving and ended fifteen feet above the ground.

The prince strode forward. The lowest portion of the carving was of a giant boar whose legs and lower body were missing, cut off by the ground. He navigated the snout, not so gracefully as Denisot had, but not awkwardly. He reached the rope and pushed out to walk on his feet, swiftly rising above the ground.

How might things have been different if he had slipped—if he had lost his grip and fallen. Of course, I did not know the future. At the time, I watched with some discomfort. At the time, I did not want the prince to fall. Of course not.

The men cheered loudly for the prince when he completed his ascent, though he only pulled himself up the rope Denisot had fastened. After the prince disappeared from view, I found everyone staring at me. It seemed to be my honor to go next.

I admit I hesitated. If—as could surely be the case—the sand filled this tower as well, then what was the sense in me starting up the rope? They would just be coming down in a minute themselves. However, Denisot started waving and calling for me in an indecent display. He should never have presumed to yell out my name.

With this concern in mind, I began my ascent. I confess that I may have taken more time than either the prince or Denisot. I certainly took more care. I believe that, whereas they forgot the long drop below them, I never did and never could. I froze more than once, peering down between my legs, but I tightened my grip and resumed the climb, for my arms were most certainly equal in strength to the prince's.

They cheered for me too when I finished. I could not say whether they were as loud, for it sounded quite different from the top. I can truthfully say that it did not matter to me. I had a smile as wide as my face. I felt ready for anything. I was ready for anything. I stood, marveling at myself for just an instant before the prince poked his head up from the stairs and called me over. The way was clear.

We made our way down in the dark, each of us doubly blessed by the Mother, me no less than him. At first, each stair bore a pile of sand, making them slippery. But as we descended, the stairs disappeared under heaps. I steadied myself against the wall as the small river of sand I kicked up ran on ahead of me.

We had gone down a fair way till we reached the narrowing point. Here the sand nearly blocked the passage but for a small gap with just enough room for a man to slither through.

I eyed the tunnel with some trepidation. How far does it go like this, I asked.

The prince smiled. I do not know; this is as far as I reached before turning back for you, he said.

I kneeled down next to the gap. I could only see twenty feet before it twisted out of sight.

Will you go down forward or backwards, asked Gaufroi. He rubbed his chin. Facing forward is the more optimistic way to proceed, he added. A coward would descend backwards, looking to retreat at the first sign of difficulty.

I agreed, though I did not say it. What of Denisot, I inquired. He has dark vision. Perhaps he can dig as well as he can climb, I suggested.

The prince shook his head. We do not know what riches lie below, he said. Who knows what your man might pocket or swallow?

In my head, I disagreed. I was certain the prince could torture Denisot if it came to that. Besides, Denisot was an honest man, and did he not deserve some fine reward after his brilliant climb? Surely something should be done. The tunnel was tight and the sand unsteady. If I became stuck five feet down, they might pull me out. If I became stuck a hundred feet down, I would be finished.

I was still thinking that as I lowered my right arm into the gap and followed it with my left. I was soon on my belly sliding over the sand, with a small wave of yellow grains bouncing down in front of me as the stones from the roof pressed against my shoulders.

The piles of sand must have been perfectly balanced. For soon, I found myself gaining speed, gliding forward with no motion of my own, unstoppable, or so it seemed. For shortly, I did stop, jammed tight against the ceiling. In a few seconds, the pouring sand filled the space around me, muffling my cries for help.

I was trapped thus for a moment in resigned terror. Whether it was five heartbeats or five minutes, I could not say. As hope was disappearing, my stomach started to sink down into the sand. A new stream had started, flowing with a powerful current, and the sand poured down the stairs as water down a pipe, carrying me with it. I rolled back and forth, battered by the walls. Spun one way and then back to the other. So I flew down a thousand feet until there were stairs under me once again, their stone surface visible under the piles. I continued to tumble, taking a beating, but then I slowed and finally stopped.

I groaned, grabbing at my aching shoulder, my throbbing leg. But my heart still worked, and the way was clear. The only sand on the step where I perched was that as poured out of my tunic. I was sitting there for just a beat before the prince came tumbling down after me. I grabbed his leg, and we both slid a further twenty feet. I bounced along on my rear. The prince took a thrashing on his side.

I helped the prince right himself, and we sat resting for a spell. He gripped the stairs tightly. He was done with tumbling. When he recovered, he put out his hand to me. Together, he said. And on we went.

We may well have been under the ground at that point. I could not be sure with the lack of windows. But we soon came to an unmistakable sign—an empty hallway branched off from the stairs and ran into the distance.

The prince chuckled to see it. We did not miss that outside, did we, he asked. No, I said.

We continued downwards, passing hallways with some regularity, but we did not venture into them. For me, I confess a certain attachment to the stairs filled my thoughts. It was the way out to the sun, to food, to water. We did not leave the stairs, but in a sense the stairs left us.

First, the walls fell away. A stone center remained that the stairs circled around, but the walls ended and space extended in all directions around us. A tightness grabbed my stomach; to fall here and tumble off would mean death. The ceiling of a vast chamber curved down beyond my sight.

Two faint lights illuminated a patch of the floor a hundred feet below. We had to stand right on the edge of the stairs and look straight down to see them. I only took a glance before stepping back. The prince stared for a minute or more. I thought he might fall. His toes were right to the lip of the stairs. But, alas, he did not.

We wound down and down. The ceiling and walls of the great hall were lost from sight. That is when it struck me where we were, our situation. The roof was buried under a mountain of sand. If it should crack, we would have been buried in an instant, flattened into jelly. I made an effort to step lightly, to disturb as little as I could.

We encountered the first remains on the lower stairs just before we reached the ground. Some appeared as you might expect: men's dusty skeletons wrapped in armor with perhaps a shield or sword lying close. Others were odd creatures of all sorts—some much larger than a man—their teeth, bones and feathers strewn about in unfamiliar shapes.

A sword caught the prince's eye; its gold inlaid pommel was studded with jewels. As he picked it up, the blade fell to pieces before our eyes in the same way that a china cup might shatter if tapped by a hammer. He stood dumbfounded with the pommel in hand spouting a few shards of steel.

I motioned him to hand me the broken sword and tested the jewels with my thumbnail. These are sound, I said.

He took it back without comment, but from then on we each stopped from time to time to knock a gem loose from various articles. Unfortunately, neither of us had a bag so we carried our treasures in cupped hands.

The bodies grew thick as we approached the light sources, so tightly packed that we had to walk on them. All metal was corrupted—not with rust, for the ground was dry, but by some other means. As we neared the lights, we need only tap a suit of armor to see it disappear into a cloud of dust.

One light shone brilliant blue; the other shone the deepest black. Such a light only makes sense to one blessed with dark vision. The blue light radiated from a cloven skull bedecked with faded curls of golden hue; inside lay a large sapphire such a might fit in one's palm. The dark light oozed out of a cracked skull with a thin covering of black hair.

The prince pointed to the corpse swathed in darkness. The Son, he said.

I pointed at the skull with golden tresses. Korinna, I said.

We dropped our jewels and gems, worthless baubles that they were, and each claimed a stone of power. I took the full true stone of Korrina. The prince gently rocked back the Son's head to reveal the shard of the Mother's stone. Thus we split the two greatest treasures in all the world, pressing them to our hearts.

DINNER

Eldred sat on his bunk, leaning against the wall, holding an uneaten leg of chicken.

Henreit eyed Eldred from his chair at the table, glass of wine in hand. "Are you well, cousin?"

Eldred looked over with unfocused eyes. "Why do you ask?"

Henreit gestured at Eldred's plate, heaped with cooling chicken parts. "Your appetite. This is not like you."

Eldred reached the chicken leg through the bars to set it back on the plate, and wiped his fingers on a napkin. "What do you think happened to the Son?"

"He marched on Pergamon with his host long ago."

Eldred licked his lips. "And what then?"

Henreit shrugged and sipped his wine. "A battle, I suppose. Who knows? Perhaps he is conquering the Islands of Cassos."

Eldred tapped the journal, sitting next to him on the bed. "The man who wrote this, Duke Philippot of Belum, says the Son is dead."

"Hmph, there is no such man."

"Not now, but I found his family tree in those books. He lived a hundred years ago. He traveled to Pergamon with Prince Gaufroi, a relative of King Acelin and a distant cousin of ours, many times removed," said Eldred.

Henreit scoffed. "That is fanciful. Everyone knows the Son lives."

Eldred scratched his wrist. "They found the body of the Son and of Korinna as well. They took the stones."

"Poppycock! A man may not take the stones. That is forbidden!"

"Well, they did."

Henreit shook his head. "You should not be considering these things.

You have enough troubles here. Pernet—he is crazy enough to kill you."

Eldred grunted. "If only it were just him."

Henreit sighed and took a drink. "This expedition has not gone as I had hoped."

Eldred gripped the bar and leaned closer. "I need my powder. I need hot water. If I'm not walking by tomorrow, they could kill me."

"You think it will work by tomorrow? How can you still believe that?"

"You saw yourself how it healed me. This injury—the one that cripples me—it just goes deeper. It will take more powder. That's all," said Eldred.

Henreit set down his cup, a resigned expression on his face. "Very well."

"And the potion. I need Weltrude to make another potion."

Henreit raised his eyebrows. "I make no promise there, cousin. She is poorly disposed towards you."

Eldred gave a weak smile. "She hates me. Just do what you can."

✦

JOURNAL PART 5

W e celebrated with a grand feast that night, grand considering our circumstances. Zlatan and Gligor trapped a number of jerboas, or rats, that they cooked up in a fine tasting stew. By some miracle, the prince dug out a bottle of wine that I swear perfectly complemented the rich taste of the oil fried rat meat. The prince, myself and the few men of quality with us dined well. I even gave Denisot a cup of wine as a reward for his fine ascent.

Those who ate less well were still filled with a merry spirit, as every man had treasure—some ruby or diamond or sparkling stone. Most had at least a pocketful, each trinket worth more than they would ordinarily earn in their lives. Twenty doubly-blessed men had spent the better part of the afternoon down in the depths of the tower gathering loot. The prince made sure everyone got something.

As the evening passed, men showed off their collections and argued as they swapped their gems. Most did not know the worth of what they had. I witnessed many idiotic trades. Meanwhile, the prince generously held out Bonitus's stone for examination to anyone who would ask, though he would not allow them to touch it. I kept Korinna's stone to myself. Zlatan and his son had gone pale when they learned I possessed it. What could be more sacred to them than their stone bearer's own stone?

As dusk settled and the trades grew less frequent, Prince Gaufroi rose to his feet, holding the Son's stone high over his head. I am the Son now, he said. He repeated himself, turning in a circle, until everyone except for the Pergamonese and myself lay prostrate on the ground.

He continued, you are all rich. Rich enough to buy land, to buy horses, to buy wine, to win wives. The men cheered, shaking their jewels in their fists. The prince pointed at them. Some would find this the right time to run home and buy the sweet life—they would be fools, he said. The men went silent, not sure what he meant. I chewed my lip. I knew it would be trouble.

The prince raised his chin, and his face grew hard as stone. There is a temple, he said. It lies south down the coast from that stinking city, Chalcis. We will pay the priestesses there a visit. And then on to Chalcis itself, for plunder and retribution. We will avenge Bonitus! They will pay!

I looked over. Gligor sank to the ground on his knees. Tears welled in Zlatan's eyes. You had to expect that in the Pergamonese. Of course, our men cheered dutifully, but I sensed some hesitation and felt the same in myself. Had we not already won richer treasure than lay ahead in that lesser city by the sea? If we really needed more, we merely needed to climb the rope that still hung from the tower and scavenge for another day. There must be something still down there.

As for avenging Bonitus, the prince and I had personally looted his corpse. Prince Gaufroi had two rings from the Son and I wore one. We seemed more involved in his degradation than in the restoration of his honor.

Later that night, I visited the prince's tent. He was packing for departure in the morning. He greeted me curtly and continued his work.

I wonder, I said—would it not make more sense to return home? You and I have treasures beyond imagining, relics that should not be risked for whatever trash the Pergamonese have left.

Gaufroi scoffed. You are double blessed by the Mother, but only slightly less simple than the stupidest man in your guard.

I felt a red heat fill my face. My hands itched for the hilt of my dagger. Are we not equals now, I demanded. Do I not carry the stone of Korinna?

The prince laughed an odd laugh, like he was trying to stop, but could not. Finally, he controlled himself and wiped a tear from his eye. You are a stone bearer, oh worthy Duke of Belum, in that you carry about a stone of power in your grubby hand, he said. But a stone bearer, a true stone bearer, carries the stone inside themselves.

I stepped back. Inside ourselves, I asked. Like a Maledictus?

He nodded. Like the Maledicti—those strong willed men who held these stones before the Mother and her sisters cast them down, he said. He held out Bonitus's shard. Held like this, he said, it is easily taken. One need only stab me in the heart and pluck it from my cold hand. But held within me, will I not become a true Maledictus with all the power and strength such a being is said to have? Is that not what the Son truly was? How did he differ from those frightening men of old?

He was the favorite son of the Mother, I said defiantly. I was perplexed, though I did not admit it. Bonitus held a fragment of the Mother's stone, one she had freely given him. How did he differ from a Maledictus, except that they bore the whole stone, like the stone I clutched.

The prince crossed his arms and looked at me with an exasperated air. Do as you wish, Duke, he said. Head home tomorrow with as many men as will follow you. Zlatan and his guiding stone will come with me.

My anger flooded back. And you trust him, I asked. You think he will just lead you to his temple and his city so you can destroy them?

I know he will, said the prince. I will extract a terrible price for their sins, but I will leave some living. If he should defy me, I will take them all.

SLEEP

Henreit was good to his word, bringing down hot water along with the packets of powder—only one packet and a quarter were left. After the treatment, Weltrude had shown up with the potion, though she only set it down and left without comment.

Eldred finished off the potion, as disgusting as ever. As he settled back, the warmth and relaxation flowed up through his torso, up his neck and down his arms. He wondered about the journal and its author, Duke Philippot. How had his journal ended up here? Why hadn't he heard about it if someone was going around pretending to be the Son? Eldred yawned and shut his eyes.

As he lay there, he heard Weltrude's voice as if from quite far away.

"He is a danger," said Weltrude.

"Not now. I have him caged." It was Balian.

She sniffed. "He will worm his way out. Henreit took dinner down there with him. That fool does whatever he is told. It is only a matter of time. When Eldred gets free, it will be me he kills first. You should have seen the look in his eyes when I brought him the potion."

Eldred frowned. He had barely looked up from the journal.

"No, my love. He will never harm you. I will not allow it," said Balian.

"He could choke me to death with one hand."

"If he tried, I would take his head off," said Balian.

"Then do so now—right now. His cot sits against the bars. Go down and drive your sword into his neck and put an end to his pretense," said Weltrude.

Eldred's eyelids fluttered.

After a pause, Balian answered. "He is still a prince."

"People will be saying that right up until he kills us all."

"Then we leave," said Balian. "We leave in the morning. We can say we are going for help. We have two men dead."

"But I make the prince his potion every night. And each treatment must be fresh to be effective," said Weltrude.

"He does not know that, does he?"

Weltrude sighed. "I told him once, but who can say if he listened? He should be able to tell in a few minutes if the brew is more than half a day old. It would have less effect, and it would taste even worse."

"Just leave him something else. We will be gone," said Balian.

"Something else, something else," Weltrude muttered, then continued, her voice rising. "Something to stop that Mercian heart that beats in his chest. Something to close those Maldavian eyes that see everything."

"Oh," said Balian.

"It would have to be potent, a strong brew. You saw how he healed from Madalulf's attack. With three fatum lapides, he is almost supernatural," she whispered.

"What would it take?"

Weltrude took a deep breath. "I saw what I need near the abandoned village—two small trees, both bearing fruit. I can use their seeds to brew an end to Eldred. The way he gulps it down, he will not catch the taste. And it would act quickly, very quickly."

"So, an end to him, then?" asked Balian glumly.

"Oh, do not worry, my love. I already warned Henreit about the danger of mixing my potions with Eldred's Wretched powders. Henreit will not suspect anything. And in his ignorance, he may live. If we act, we all may live, those of us who are innocent."

A thread of drool escaped Eldred's lips as he descended deeper into sleep.

Sometime during the night, like a spark from a flint, a scene suddenly appeared before Eldred: the carcass-scattered room, the table and the seated figure from the previous night. The severed hand had been cleared from the table—Eldred thought he saw the fingers resting on the floor behind a table leg. In its place were eight glittering knives laid out in a row—Eldred's blades. As he watched, the man idly picked up one of the heavier blades, turning it over in his hand before setting it back.

He sat there studying the blades. He was muttering something in a soft voice.

Eldred focused. He wanted to hear what the murderer was saying. As he strained to listen, he heard the man mutter, "Not that one; not that one. He is one of his."

The man shifted and suddenly turned as if looking Eldred in the eye. The man's face was clearly visible—dark sunken eyes and skin as pale as a corpse. A few long strands of greasy black hair hung down in haphazard fashion. But his eyes—they were blessed; Eldred could see that.

The man rose to his feet with a powerful motion, palming one of the daggers as he did. He walked closer to Eldred, waving his unarmed hand in front of him.

He licked his lips. "I know you are there. Show yourself!"

Eldred could only hang there silently in his vision.

The man started to sniff and glanced around the room, but always his eyes returned to where Eldred stood in his dream.

The man probed the space around Eldred's presence with the knife, one of the long blades. After a moment, he stopped and laughed. "Very strange. Very mysterious. I am trying so hard not to kill you. Will this"—the man made a circle around the space with the blade—"will this stay with me when you are dead? I am not sure I will like that." The man showed his teeth in a grimace. "Must I kill you elsewhere? Away?"

As the vision began to fade, the man lowered his knife and nodded. "Tomorrow—when the sun goes down."

FAREWELLS

Eldred woke in a cold sweat as the first rays of light touched the windows across the outer room. He pulled the covers up around his neck and lay there shifting, trying to get warm, waiting for the morning sluggishness from the potion to pass.

It was an hour before the palace started to wake. First, a shuffling noise came down the hall from the kitchen; Rollon was starting to bake. Not long after the faint smell of fresh baked bread wafted to the cell, Henreit appeared, carrying a plate with four slices of toast piled with cheese.

Eldred pulled himself higher against the bars. "I had more visions."

Henreit set the plate down on the table next to Eldred. "The man with the hand?"

Eldred nodded. "Yes. And he saw me. Somehow he knew I was there." He paused. "He is coming for me tonight. That's what he said."

Henreit took a seat at the table across from Eldred. "We will set a guard then—Gervese. We will not leave you down here alone."

Eldred shook his head. "You don't understand. He has a chamber full of the dead. He could kill us all."

Henreit tilted his head. "But he did not. It was a quiet night last night. Nothing amiss."

"I said he's coming tonight!"

"We can set more guards if you wish."

"No. It won't be enough. We have to go with them. Balian and Weltrude are making their escape. We must leave as well."

Henreit narrowed his brows. "How did you know that? Balian just told me this morning."

"My visions! When will you start listening to me?"

Henreit cast a glance at the cell door.

"And not just that. He has the knives. My knives!"

Henreit frowned. "No. I do. I have them up in my room."

"When did you check last? I saw them. He had them laid out on his bloody table."

"I can check them now if you wish."

Eldred nodded vigorously. "Yes. Go check them now. They are in his hands. And he's coming. He's coming tonight!"

Henreit rose and hurried out through the corridor.

Ten minutes later, Balian appeared with Henreit and the men in his wake. Balian approached the cell door and shook it.

"Good morning, prince," said Balian as he continued his inspection of the door.

Eldred glanced at Henreit. "They're missing. Aren't they?"

Henreit clasped his hands before him. "The knives are not where I left them."

"What if he has a key to the cell?" asked Pernet.

Henreit gestured at the key hanging on the far wall. "That is the only key there ever was."

Balian turned his attention to the barred window of the cell. "I do not think he got out," he said softly.

"Why not?" demanded Pernet.

Balian gave Pernet a sideways look. "It was a quiet night."

Eldred scoffed. "Then where are my knives?"

Balian glanced at Eldred. "They are valuable, prince. People have shown an interest in them."

Pernet drew himself up, full of indignation. "Oh. It is on me then? Is it? I only ever wanted to bet with him."

Balian waved his hand lightly. "It is of no consequence. Nobody is accusing anyone of anything. The point to consider is that the prince is secured. Weltrude and I will continue with our mission."

Henreit shifted on his feet. "And we are sure of this?"

Balian gestured at the door. "I just checked it. Now, moving forward, you must always have at least one guard present. While I am gone—this is important—you should only change his buckets once a day. I want everyone here while this is done, ready and armed. Gervese, you go in. You get along with him. Do that for three days—four at the most—and Weltrude and I will bring back two dozen of the king's own soldiers."

"The man from my vision is coming tonight," said Eldred.

Balian frowned. "We just need three more quiet nights. They have been peaceful since you took up your residence here."

Eldred pulled himself up on the bars. "He's coming tonight. He has the knives. He could kill us all. He's not a man. He's a Maledictus!"

Balian raised his eyebrows in disbelief. "A Maledictus? In this building?"

Eldred dropped back on his cot and snatched the journal, holding it up for the men to see. "It's all in here. The Son is dead! They found his shard and the stone of Korrina. And one of them—I don't know who—is hiding here. When the sun goes down, he's coming for me."

Balian nodded slowly. "You will have your guard, prince. We will keep you safe." He turned to Henreit. "We will leave just as soon as Weltrude finishes the potions. Have your letter ready by then."

As the men filed out, leaving a worried-looking Gervese on guard duty, Eldred called after Henreit.

Henreit paused by the door to the corridor. "What is it, cousin?"

"Can you bring me paper and pen as well? I wish to send some letters of my own."

Henreit nodded. "Yes, we can compose our missives together. But we must be quick about it."

LETTERS

Eldred stared at the paper that lay on the board across his lap. It contained only two words: "Dear Mateline." Eldred blew out his breath and noted a patch of light on the floor of the outer room coming from the window. He could not mark the passage of the sun through the sky directly, but he could watch the patch slide forward as the sun took one final arc through the sky. Eldred watched transfixed until scribbling sounds from Henreit broke the spell.

Eldred returned his attention to the page and took a breath. Then he chewed his lip. Then he tapped the pen on the board.

"Please, cousin. I am writing as well. I am sharing our situation with Uncle Julian," said Henreit.

"Sorry," said Eldred. He screwed up his face and, taken with a sudden burst of inspiration, squeezed in the letters 'est', changing his text to 'Dearest Mateline.' He nodded in approval at the change and resumed tapping his pen. Dearest Mateline what?

After a moment, he added, 'I have started to drink. I could share some Dinan Stout with you now quite happily.' He studied his short letter for a minute with a growing tightness in his chest. She hadn't come to him; she had gone to Oudin. Eldred bit his lip. She hadn't really saved him either; she had saved herself—or perhaps Oudin. What ought he say?

He looked over again at Henreit, who was scrawling out some long report to Julian, no doubt going on about all his great works cleaning up the mansion—'Oh, and people died and we locked up Eldred.' Eldred scowled and jotted down 'Thank you for everything. Farewell and best wishes, Eldred.' What else was there to say?

He sealed the letter in an envelope and wrote Mateline's name on the same before taking another sheet of paper. At the top, he wrote, 'Dearest

Mother.' Eldred gripped the pen tightly. The patch of light had slipped another inch closer to the windows and somewhere above Weltrude was no doubt busy at work on her potions. Little time remained. Eldred stole another glance at Henriet and started to write.

Dearest Mother,

Henreit says that neither of us is quite right, and I do not think he is wrong on this matter. It has always been so, as if I were striving to climb a crooked ladder. The Bond, I should have had the Bond and I should only have had but one stone, a proper Deiran stone, and though it pains me to say it, you should never have been my mother. That sounds unkind, but I do not mean it so. You were always more pleasant to me than Father ever was. It's just the truth.

Something will happen soon, and I will be gone. I am not afraid. You should know that. I am ready for whatever happens.

Also know this: I never betrayed Father. What happened to him was not from me. I served my role faithfully, but the Corporians had some deceitful trick. And here too. I never killed these men. I never killed anyone.

Love, Eldred

As Eldred sealed the envelope, Weltrude came out of the corridor holding a tray with three cups, one of which was the treasured silver goblet Henreit had shown him on the roof.

Henreit frowned at the silver cup as he took the letters from Eldred. "Do you need to use that one?"

Weltrude warily set the tray just within Eldred's reach and quickly stepped back. "I need to mark them. Each is for a specific night."

Even from a few feet away, Eldred could smell an overpowering sickly sweet scent—something was off. He stretched out and pulled the tray closer.

Weltrude gestured towards the goblets. "The small bronze cup is for tonight. It has the usual potion. It will not be quite as effective since it will not be fresh. It may also taste slightly more bitter."

Eldred nodded.

Weltrude continued. "The silver cup is for tomorrow night. I had to augment the potion to keep it strong enough to calm you."

"Is that so?" asked Eldred.

"Yes, you may notice a slight change in taste. The large bronze cup is for the third night, but Balian and I should have returned by then. I will make you a fresh potion in that case, but you have this in case we are delayed."

Eldred cast a dour look at the silver goblet. "And this change, this augmentation, is all according to the vows you hold so dearly?"

Weltrude raised her chin. "But of course. It is only what is necessary. Does something worry you, prince?"

Eldred rubbed his chin. "No."

Henreit held out the letters, including his own. "Hand these to any steward at the palace, if you would, dear lady."

Weltrude took them with an air of distraction, keeping her gaze on Eldred. "Of course." Then she turned and left.

Eldred pushed the tray away. "You should go with them, cousin."

Henreit shook his head. "No. You are my charge. I will stay."

Eldred looked sadly at the silver goblet. "You will regret it. She only left enough for me."

Henreit chuckled. "I still have two bottles left, and I prefer my wine to hers."

JOURNAL PART 6

The vast temple complex stretched out before us, much larger than I expected. It spread over a patch of ground near the ocean, whose water was greener than blue waters of the Parvus Sea. White stone buildings hunkered down on a series of mounds rising twenty feet high. The largest building might have been perhaps a hundred feet long and thirty feet tall, lined with columns. A thin carpet of grass with a bluish tinge marked the space between the temples. While the buildings looked to be in perfect repair, the complex appeared deserted.

I had a strange sense that we should not be there. I think the men felt it too, such men as were left. The passage through the storm had taken its due. The last horse died two days into the march. Other casualties included five of my men and four of the prince's, including one of his captains. We were all afoot with our gear packed on the camels.

Gaufroi split our forces into ten squads, each with roughly eighteen warriors. He sent eight squads wide around the temples, to ensure nobody could escape. He and I each led one squad into the center of the complex where Zlatan said we would find the holy women. The prince took Zlatan, and I took Gligor—Gaufroi never let Zlatan out of his sight.

As we walked, I must say I expected a fight. It felt like a situation where one would fight, for the temple was clearly valued and should have been guarded. However, the only men present were caretakers and groundsmen who lamely lined up and sat as we demanded. They did not even cry out.

We found the priestesses in a smaller oval-shaped building near the center of the complex. A splashing fountain covered the sound of our approach, and we caught them kneeling in rows, performing their afternoon prayers. The confusion showed on their faces as we surrounded them, swords drawn, as if they could not comprehend what was happening.

Three priestesses sat at the front of the gathering in a place of honor. The one in the center was a short old woman with blue eyes and gray hair and a bent back. She was the High Priestess, we would learn, named Aigli. The priestess on the right, a middle-aged woman with rose-colored eyes that showed her anger, was named Yiana. The last priestess, the one on the left, was my own dear Kalliopi.

Kalliopi was young and beautiful where the others were not. Even as she frowned at me, I could see that her face more commonly wore a smile. And her eyes—I could have looked into her dark green eyes for days. They were so full of life and knowledge. Looking at her eyes, it was almost as if she were talking to me, sharing a private joke or some poetic observance. They were not blessed eyes, but even so, they were exquisite, somehow even finer.

The prince and I stood in front of the priestesses, our men arrayed around them. I kept staring at Kalliopi, but like the others, she focused her attention on Prince Gaufroi, who was laying out his demands.

But she turned her eyes to me when the prince and I revealed our treasures, holding them up so all could see. The priestesses gasped; some started to kneel again, as if praying to me. Not so for Kalliopi, Aigli and Yiana. They stood frozen, their stone faces breaking into an expression of horror. They had been as calm as a cat curled in its master's lap when we had rounded them up, swords drawn, but the sight of Korrina's stone shattered their reserve.

Yiana started towards me, hands reaching out, as if she might snatch the stone away. In its mild way, this was the first sign of resistance we had from those cowardly people. The prince was fast with his knife and stabbed her through the heart. I watched in surprise as she fell at my feet and died. I blushed in shame at Kalliopi's reproachful gaze, but what could I have done?

I had two of my men take Yiana's body away. The sight of her corpse could only worry the poor ladies. Aigli and Kalliopi took their seats, and the other priestesses crowded around them, as if to make some poor shield with their bodies in the hope of protecting them.

I doubt anyone could see it but me, but I could tell the prince was embarrassed. Of course, he had not needed to stab the middle aged woman, or so it seemed. Though I did wonder, as I am sure he did, what would have happened if she had gotten the stone in her hand.

Everything was clear now, regarding our request. The stones, our treasures, had told the story more clearly than the prince's words.

Aigli stared at the floor for a minute, her lips tight. Then she looked up. You truly wish to join the Maledicti, she asked.

The prince flashed a wolf's grin for his answer. I nodded briefly.

She looked us over, her eyes lingering on my own. You will suffer for it, she said. Few can bear them well. Most go mad—especially men, or so the texts of old would tell us.

The Son wore his stone well, did he not, said the prince. The favorite of the Mother, the guardian of the realm, the slayer of Korinna.

Regula made it so, answered Aigli. She shaped Bonitus in the Caves of Carcerem for fifty years before she gifted him the stone, and even then he was bound to her.

As I will be, said the prince.

Aigli tilted her head and looked at the prince in surprise. Did you not find her too, she asked. Regula should have been there. Korinna had taken her to Megara.

No, said the prince. You, your worthless people, attacked us, he said. You took the Mother and slew our captain, the Son. You will make things right, or I will kill all of you. Then I will continue to Chalcis and kill everyone there. I will drag the babes from their mothers' arms and put them to the sword if you do not serve me.

Aigli sighed. Perhaps we could attach the Stone of Bonitus; it is the weaker stone, only a shard, she said. But no man can contain the full power of Korinna's stone—a full unbroken stone of power. The Maledictus who bore them were greater than any man left alive in this age, this age of decay.

The prince stared at my stone with hungry eyes. No man was ever greater than me, said the prince. I will take her stone.

A cold sense of dread filled me as the prince roughly snatched Korinna's stone from me. He may as well have pulled the heart out of my chest. I was shaken, but then I found something tickling my palm—a smaller thing, a lighter thing, the shard of Bonitus. I gazed into its dark light. It did not warm me as Korinna's sapphire blue stone had, but the shard of Bonitus held strength.

A deal was struck, if demands backed by threats of murder might be considered an agreement. I received the treatment first. They lay me on a flower strewn table set inside a pool of gently running water. Whether this was necessary or not, I could not tell. But the sweet smell of the plants and the soft noise of the water did calm me. They rubbed my forehead with a foul smelling gray tonic, scrubbing me so hard that my skin felt raw. But again, I can not say if that aspect of the treatment was necessary.

The necessary step—I am sure—was the incision from the top of my nose to the middle of my forehead. I could feel the blade scraping over my skull. I cried out in pain as they lifted the knife only to dig it into my flesh and widen the groove. Kalloipi hovered over me and pressed the Mother's shard into the wound, pinching the sides together. I passed out as she withdrew her bloody fingers.

When I woke two days later, I was reborn. No longer the mere Duke Philippot of Belum, I was a god, like the Son himself. I lifted a large stone that not even three men could heft working together. I threw a discus twice as far as the prince's strongest captain could manage. I wrestled five men at once, pushing each man out of the ring in turn.

Most pleasantly, my face was uninjured. All signs of the deep gouge were gone, both to the touch and to the eye, as a mirror confirmed. The prince wasted little time before ordering the start of his own treatment. The stone table was swept clean and covered with fresh blossoms. The prince took his place and Kalliopi ran the ceremony, standing beside the table in water up to her knees.

I was standing next to dour Aigli, admiring Kalliopi's shapely legs, when the old woman spoke.

Now would be the time, said Aigli.

The time for what, I asked.

The time to kill your rival, she whispered.

I did not say anything. I stood there with tense shoulders, staring at Kalliopi, who was clad in a thin white robe that hugged her shape.

Now he sleeps, said Aigli, which was true—like I had, the prince had fallen unconscious. When he wakes, if he wakes, he may rival you in power, continued Aigli. Yours is the child's stone, the baby stone, the shard Regula passed to her defective son. If the prince rises with the full strength of Korinna, you will serve him.

She stepped closer, going on tiptoe to bring her lips near my ear. If you leave us our stone, we will make beautiful things, for that is our way. She nodded at Kalliopi. Do you not value beauty, she asked.

I heard her words. I cannot say they did not interest me. I was a free man with the strength of the Son and—while the prince lay still on the table—I was ruled by no man. I also heard the promise in the old woman's voice. Kalliopi turned, palm wet with Gaufroi's blood, and I looked into her eyes. I felt a passion that numbed my brain.

Nevertheless, I held true to the vows made by the Duke of Belum—my former self—and placed a strong guard on the resting prince. When I retired to my chambers, I found plates piled with grapes and cheese, a crystal carafe filled with wine, a wide bed covered in red cushions and Kalliopi. I had never felt more alive.

A PAUSE

Eldred paused in his reading, distracted by his realization of the silence; the hammering had stopped. The patch of light had disappeared from the outer room. A new block of light, freshly minted, lay below the cell's window with each of the three iron bars etched within it. The journal slipped from his fingers onto the bed. The sun had crossed over and was on its way down.

It was no surprise, no shock. Of course, the sun would rise and set, for that was the nature of things. And it would surely do the same the following day, though Eldred would not be there to see it. He took a strangled breath. It was his turn. The squires had died, the lords had died, his father had died, Hobbie had died, Dreven had died, and others too, many others. Guillotin had died down the hallway. Madalulf had died in the very same cell where Eldred sat. This time it would be Eldred's blood fouling the floor, congealing in the cracks.

He had wanted to be a king. In his childhood, he had dreamed of the Deiran throne, and when that had slipped away, he had contemplated the Mercian throne. But now, it all seemed like a sorry joke. He was destined to die a cripple, a captive of his own people, slaughtered in his cell wearing only his night clothes. How had it come to that?

Eldred glanced through the bars. Henreit sat across the table facing the hallway, gazing vacuously into the distance. Eldred studied his face, slightly heavy with that thin flat mustache. He was a decent man, a kind man, Eldred's own cousin, but he had gone along with the others in locking Eldred up easily enough. They'd all wanted it—Balian, Weltrude, Gervese and Pernet, especially Pernet. And for what? He hadn't hurt anyone, let alone murdered the two men.

All he'd done was to have seen a vision of murder, to have spotted a giant eagle and to have smelled a terrible odor up on the roof. No crime in any of those. They had all proven quite true. But he had been unkind. His eyes shifted to the silver chalice filled with Weltrude's poison. A few hasty words, perhaps a trifle more than a few, had cost him his freedom. Now the man from the vision would finish him, and who would mourn? Mother? Mateline? Or perhaps no one at all. Eldred sighed. Everyone must take their turn.

"You look upset," said Henreit.

Eldred looked up. "I'm just waiting."

Henreit eyed him curiously. "Waiting for the man, the one from your visions?"

Eldred's eyes grew distant. "Yes, he comes for me."

Henreit scratched his chin. "If that were so, why would he not simply kill you now? Why should he wait?"

Eldred gripped the cell bars and pulled himself forward. "Who knows why he does what he does? He's mad. He's like the dead."

Henreit clasped his hands. "We have been here for many days. If there were such a man of danger, a Maledictus even, we would have crossed paths with him by now, would we not?"

"We did. Guillotin met him first, then Madalulf."

A loud bang echoed from the hallway. Gervese was back at work on the trapdoor.

Henreit smiled. "Perhaps."

"You think it was me, don't you?"

"It was a quiet night with you in there. Was it not?"

"Except my knives went missing."

Henreit shrugged. "Pernet might bear away your knives without doing me harm, but why should a Maledictus show me such courtesy? They were bloodthirsty tyrants, were they not, until their defeat at the hands of the Mother and her sisters a thousand years ago. I was sound asleep. I do not like to say it, but any thief could have easily slit my throat."

Eldred held up the journal. "I told you, these men became Maledicti. One was the Duke of Belum; he is nothing to us. But the other was a prince named Gaufroi, and he is our distant cousin."

Henreit furrowed his brow. "So, he fears to kill his kin?"

Eldred nodded. "Apparently."

"Even though you say he lived a hundred years ago?"

"That's right. He has Korinna's stone. You know she was immortal."

Henreit crinkled up his face, a shadow of a grin crossing his face. "Perhaps you are right. Perhaps a Maledictus lies in wait for us, lurking in the shadows, waiting to do us in. But cousin, if he spared me—his kin—last night, will he not show you the same favor tonight?"

Eldred lowered the journal. "No. He will not." He frowned. "Please, don't. Somehow it unsettles me to hear such hopeful words."

"Oh, I am sorry."

"It's fine. It's as it must be. I'll not leave here. Even if you would allow it, he would not," said Eldred. He looked Henreit in the eye. "Do you trust me?"

Henreit started to answer, then caught himself.

After a pause, Eldred continued. "You should. You truly should. My words before were ill-considered. For that, I apologize to you, to everyone, even Pernet. I've been upset by recent events."

"But, of course," said Henreit. "You have faced tragic losses. In such a circumstance, any man might prove difficult."

"I cannot leave, but perhaps you can. If you go now, do not bother with supplies or packing, but run this very moment to the stables. Mount any horse; do not bother saddling it. Just mount and ride. If you do that, you might live. There may be enough daylight left to keep you safe."

Henreit pursed his lips. "So, I would leave you and the others here?"

Eldred shook his head. "No. Take them too. But each of you should choose a different direction: one east, one west, one north, one south. If you do that, some of you will live, perhaps all of you should the Mother grant you fortune."

"Hmm. Well, I promised Roscille to bring you back safe and sound." Henreit smiled. "I think we must stay and keep you company."

"Then you'll die," said Eldred softly.

Henreit's eyes wandered to the cell door. "Do not worry, dear cousin. We are all of us here to help you."

Eldred pressed his lips tight. "I've warned you. I don't know what else I could have said."

JOURNAL PART 7

The prince was less impressive in his recovery than I had been. He opened his eyes after six days and just lay there, staring into space. There was a strange presence about him that suggested he was listening to us though he did not move. The guards looked embarrassed standing about—clutching their weapons—as if they realized it was pointless to protect a dying man.

Kalliopi prepared me for this outcome. A weak-minded man could never bear Korrina's stone, she assured me. He would be lost between the worlds of mind and matter until his deserted body failed.

My thoughts were generous, for I had come to love Kalliopi, she of the gentle smile, the deep green eyes. I planned to bury Prince Gaufroi outside the temple grounds and make haste back to Belum. I saw no need to harry the poor people of Chalcis. My only concern was whether Kalliopi would join me. When I looked into her eyes, I was sure she would, but when she turned away from me and I heard her voice, she sounded like a stranger.

I was shocked when the prince sat up the next day. Of course, the men were happy. They carried him from the stone table to a nearby bedchamber. Food was brought. I watched him struggle to eat—his throat did not work properly. The poor man, he fought to stay upright while I was ready for anything. Still, it was his greed. He had forced the switch. He could have been the Son instead of whatever wretched child he had become of Korrina.

It was a week before he could walk on his own. The men lined up to hear him speak. They had been well behaved over all this time, only a few incidents with the locals to blemish their honor. I expected that Prince Gaufroi would announce our departure for Gauraci and wondered whether he had the strength to make it. He surprised me.

He gestured for the men to come closer—his voice was too weak to carry far. Bring her, he snarled in his rasping voice. Bring me that bitch of a priestess.

My heart started to pound. Who was he talking about? I could not fight them all.

His captains sprang to their orders, marching towards the hall where the priestesses were engaged in their morning prayers. Aigli stood on a dias, leading her sisters in prayer. In the first row knelt Kalliopi, my beloved.

Aigli paused as they stomped into the room, her blue eyes clear and calm. What is the meaning of this, she asked.

Without stopping, one of the prince's captains walked up and grabbed her by the arm, dragging her away after him. The priestesses were all on their feet, shouting their protests. All except for my beautiful Kalliopi; she stood calmly, looking at me. I knew then that the prince must die.

The prince acted out a sad spectacle. One of his men held the old priestess as Gaufroi stabbed her through the neck with a shaky hand. And then they cheered—for that! As if that were some great feat. The spawn of Korrina was feeble beside me, the true Son of the Mother.

He stood over her body, staring down. She lied, he rasped. She lied to all of us. She promised me greatness, power above all others.

She had not, of course. Her words had spoken of caution. She had warned him that his mind was too small for the blue stone. I still remember its warmth. It had been so warm in my hand.

Bring the others, shouted the prince. I have been cheated. I have been tricked. I will have vengeance.

Wait, I said, pushing to the front. Kalliopi is mine. Anyone who goes to harm her must face me.

I surveyed them, looking them over, searching for my men among the pack. I recognized their faces, but they dropped their eyes. Only one or two would stand with me by my count. I was reaching for my sword when the prince spoke.

Let the Duke keep his whore, even though it was she who cut me, said the prince. He is an honorable man. You are all honorable men. We are all honorable men. Set her aside, but kill the rest—every last one.

A brutal slaughter ensued as I struggled to hold Kalliopi, who writhed in my arms as her sisters were put to the sword. Hush, I said. It will soon be over.

You idiot, she said, her back turned to me, her voice harsh. Do you not see? He is the end of everything—everything you hold dear.

No, I whispered in her ear. He was cheated. He would be me, except for the vile trickery of Aigli. I pity him.

When the last priestess lay dead, the prince laughed. His back seemed straighter. His face held more color. A good start, he said. Now, on to Chalcis.

TRAPDOOR

In the late afternoon, the monotonous banging suddenly sounded a different note and was followed by a reverberating crashing noise. Eldred dropped the journal and watched the doorway, grabbing the bars to sit at attention.

When Henreit and Pernet ambled in, he leaned back. "What happened?"

"The big man is finally through the door," said Henreit.

"And?" asked Eldred.

Pernet smiled triumphantly. "There is a deep pit. Once Gervese finds an adequate rope, we will begin the search."

Eldred sniffed the air and made a face. A faint scent of decay was creeping into the room. "I wouldn't go down there."

"Is that so? Are you worried about what we will find?" asked Pernet.

Eldred nodded and glanced at the silver goblet that Weltrude had left. It had been quick for Guillotin, but to all appearances Madalulf had suffered for some time, not that he didn't deserve it. The thing below had no trace of mercy. Of that Eldred was sure.

Henreit noticed Eldred's focus. "Are you preparing for sleep, cousin? The sun is still quite high."

Eldred wet his lips and ran his index finger over the base of the goblet. "Not yet. Soon, but not yet. Could you wait an hour before going down? Just an hour? I want to learn something first."

Henreit shrugged and turned to Pernet. "Tell Gervese to take a rest. What is the hurry?"

Pernet glowered. "Our friend's hand lies down there in the filth."

Henreit laid his hand on Pernet's shoulder. "We will make Madalulf whole again. But first, we will give the prince this interlude, a moment to prepare himself."

Pernet shot a glare at Eldred as he left the room. Henreit stayed behind and took a seat at the table. After a pause, Eldred picked up the journal and resumed.

✠

JOURNAL PART 8

I will not speak of Chalcis. As horribly as things went at the temple, Chalcis was unimaginably worse. We took three days to travel there using horses we seized at the complex. It took four days to carry out our activities in the city. On the fifth day, we rested. A few squads of men searched the ruins looking for more riches. We also buried our dead, having lost thirty or forty men.

The prince was transformed, or I should say, completed his transformation. The weak man who could barely stand was gone. In his place was a warrior who ruthlessly struck down anyone who opposed him. He wielded a battle hammer he had taken from an enemy near the end of the first day. Splattered with blood and brains, his presence struck everyone with terror.

Unsettled as I was, I took solace in the one piece of good news: we were headed home. I had my treasure and my beloved, though Kalliopi was understandably upset. She cried as I packed up my belongings in the eerie silence of the dead city. As she shuddered, she looked more angry than pathetic. I told her she would like Belum, but she would have none of it.

The weather was good as we rode away from the city. The men were harder than they had been at the start of the expedition; wealthier too. Their mood was cheerful, if dangerous. Some spoke of their hopes to catch more Pergamonese. Others eyed my beautiful Kalliopi, though none dared take action.

Of course, the weather turned bad, as it must on that passage. Zlatan led us into the storms with his guiding stone. We were on foot with the camels, having turned the horses loose. We had learned it was pointless to drag them along.

On the sixth night, I was in my tent with Kalliopi, holding her close against me as the wind howled outside.

Do you love your people, she asked.

I stirred and made a face. My men do as they are ordered, I said.

No. Not these animals, she answered. Your people back home in Belum. Do you love them?

I thought about the city, similar in many ways to what Chalcis had been but a few days before. Each boasted deep harbors, sandy beaches and elegant buildings, though the architecture differed. Belum was greener, at least in spring when lush grasses covered the nearby hills and the trees sprouted fresh leaves. I think you will like it, I said.

And your citizens, do you wish them harm, she continued, her voice soft and silky.

No, I said. Like any good duke, I wish them prosperity, in moderation.

She brought her face close, her eyes probing mine. He will kill them all, she said. He will destroy Belum just as he did Chalcis.

I considered her words and shook my head. He is headed to Emon, I said.

She dug her fingernails into my shoulders, and her voice rang in my ears. It seemed I could not hear the roaring sands outside for a moment. He will kill everyone you love, everything you care for, she said.

I could tell she believed it. How could she not after the butchery she had witnessed? I looked up at the roof of the tent, shaking in the wind. No man can oppose the prince—not now, I said. After a pause, I continued, I allow that Aigli was unfairly slain, for she but told the full truth, all the risks and all the rewards he faced. She was right—the power of Korinna's stone is greater. I am more than a man, but I cannot stand against him.

You can—you must, she demanded, pulling my face back to hers. If you cannot kill him, then take his eyes; let him lose his path.

Lose his path—the words rattled in my brain. Out here, it would be easy to lose one's path. And Belum, what would become of it, or Emon? The prince had destroyed Chalcis because of treachery even when there had been none. He had proved as much as he—far more than anyone—slew the Pergamonese. He had started by single-handedly destroying entire squads of their warriors. He finished by hunting down women and children; he had to have seen by then that Aigli's words were true. He had power. She had not cheated him.

I left the tent, taking Kalliopi with me, for she would not stay behind. The prince's tent was the largest from the original caravan, twenty feet across on the narrowest side and sixty feet long on the widest. At no point did the roof rise more than five feet from the ground; it had been crafted to face the storm.

We found the prince reclining on pillows. Zlatan was huddled next to Gligor. They were speaking softly to each other, wearing long faces. The prince waved us to some nearby cushions and beckoned one of his serving men. At least this time we have wine, said the prince.

I nodded as we were each handed a cup of sweet Pergamonese wine. I prefer the tarter taste of Belum wines, but I found the drink refreshing.

To what do I owe this visit, asked the prince. Have you finally grown tired of coupling with your priestess whore?

Kalliopi's face grew tight, but I waved off the comment. No, prince, I said. I was just wondering what will happen when we return. I expect there will be change.

The prince's eyes grew bright. Change, yes—there will be change, he said in an animated tone.

You will be king, I said.

He laughed. Yes. Time grows short for King Acelin, he said. My uncle will soon take his final rest.

I sipped my wine. Naturally, I said. An unfortunate but necessary step.

Why unfortunate, asked Gaufroi. Is it that much more of a tragedy than if I crushed a beetle?

Well, he is your kin, I reminded him.

The prince frowned and swished the wine in his cup. I have no kin, he said. The weak man I was before had kin—mother, father, uncle. I have no kin except perhaps for the two of you: the priestess whore who shoved the stone into my head and you, my lesser brother. Take no offense, Duke. There is nobody closer to being my equal than you.

I bowed my head. You honor me, I said. So your uncle must perish. He alone must be pushed aside?

No, said the prince, glancing at Kalliopi. Aigli spoke true when she said we have diminished. We miss the guidance of the Mother. I will assume her role now. I will clear out the weak. I will remake the Maldavians with strength to match the people of old. My agents must reflect my power. You are worthy, Duke. You will serve me as the Son served the Mother.

You bear the stolen stone of Korrina, not Regula's stone, said Kalliopi in a harsh tone. You are not the Mother, nor do you belong in Guaraci or anywhere. You are a foul Maledictus, a brutal slayer of children, a creature beneath contempt.

I grabbed Kalliopi by the shoulders. Hush, my dear, I said. I turned to the prince. Please excuse her, prince, I said. She is mad with grief.

You cowardly murderer, Kalliopi cried. She wormed her way out of my grip and took a step towards the prince and spat in his face.

I sat, frozen in shock, as the prince grabbed up his hammer and crushed her head in one smooth blow. Her blood flew through the air, striking me in the face. I wiped it from my eyes to see the prince standing over her broken form.

He wore his wolf smile. Goodbye, priestess, he said.

I dashed to the other side of the tent where I took Zlatan's neck in my hand and snapped it. The prince's captains rose to their feet, drawing their weapons. A cry went up, and men started pouring into the tent. The prince stood still, hard faced, watching me as I pulled out the guiding stone from Zlatan's pocket and crushed it into sand.

Gligor grabbed his father's corpse and started to cry. Of course, Zlatan should have died long ago, taking his own life if he had the merest trace of courage—Gligor too. The father and son had paid too dear a price for their meaningless survival.

The prince called off the swarm of men and stood, leaning on his hammer, my beloved's blood still trickling down his arms. Do you serve me, Duke Philippot of Belum? he asked. Consider carefully. You have given me much to forgive this night.

I took a moment to look over the men. They wore angry faces lined with fear. Everyone knew Zlatan's role and our dependence on his guiding stone. My beautiful Kalliopi lay crushed into a bloody pile at Prince Gaufroi's feet. I do not see how I can, I said.

The men raised their swords and shouted for my death, but the prince waved them off. This is not a concern for the likes of you, he said, his voice cold.

As I left his tent with Kalliopi's remains wrapped in a rug, I heard the prince order the long overdue execution of Gligor. Back at my tent, I took a shovel and buried Kalliopi ten feet deep. I did not want the storm to blow my beloved across the sands for eternity.

The next morning I rose to find the prince standing outside with all his men in line behind him. Have you changed your mind, then, I shouted over the wind. You wish to fight me?

No, said the prince. I wish to travel beside you.

I will not lead you from this place, I replied.

Then I shall wait, he said.

We are doomed, you know, I said.

Beings such as we are never doomed, he answered. That is for lesser creatures.

I noticed a ripple of indignation wash over his men. You should not have killed Kalliopi, I said.

He smiled. I gave her everything she wanted, he said.

I ignored him and reentered my tent.

Thus began our game of waiting, our battle of patience. Each day well past midnight, for that was when the storm was most still, I would open the flap of my tent and survey the camp. For the first few days, it remained unchanged, but then the camp began to gradually disappear. Men started to pack tents and supplies and start off in small groups. I would sometimes see them headed off into the darkness. Sometimes I saw the prince by his tent. He might look at me, but we never spoke.

A week into our game there came a major shift. Most of his remaining men—including Denisot, my brilliant climber—struck out into the storm-battered wasteland. The prince did not even turn to watch them go. Instead, he stood at the entrance of his tent and watched me with an unreadable expression.

A few days later, only the two of us were left. The men were gone, the camels were gone, the food was gone and the water was gone. For my part, I did not suffer the way a man might. Make no mistake—I desired a drink and would have gladly eaten a loaf of bread or a fine cut of meat. Fruit—I would have eaten an entire bowl full of fruit if one had been present. Water to drink and bathe in would have given me immense pleasure. But the absence of all these things only touched me on the outermost layer.

Inside, I stayed strong—powerful. I would sit in deepest contemplation thinking through events with such focus that I sometimes forgot to check on the prince. In this state, I passed through a furious episode in the storm that tore at my tent for two days. When I recalled myself and checked on him, his luxurious tent was gone. A small smile cracked across my lips. The prince had become a beggar and remained so for days beyond counting.

Over time, though I was not diminished, I felt something change within me. I wanted to stop moving, to stop breathing. I just wanted to lie still. The only task I would do, the only task I wanted to do, was to check on the prince. I liked to see him sitting there. Some days he might turn his head and look at me, which felt surprisingly good. But that was a rare treat; mostly he just stared up into the swirling clouds of sand.

Now I find myself writing this journal in advance of my final transformation. I learned a few nights ago how to stop everything; I even tried it for a moment. I can stop my heart, my breath, even my thoughts.

So why do I wait? I am waiting for the prince to look at me one last time. I mean to wave to him, to signal what is about to happen. I am certain he will understand. It will only be a few minutes after that.

I wonder what he will do. He must like sitting there, or he would have left by now. Perhaps he will come in the tent. Will he bury me?

FINAL NIGHT

Pernet walked into the outer room from the corridor. "It's been an hour. Gervese is climbing down."

Henreit stirred on the chair. He had been dozing. "Oh, good. We will see what he finds."

Eldred sighed. "You won't like it."

"Even a prince must pay for his crimes," said Pernet.

Eldred glanced at the journal. "Not always."

"This time, then," said Pernet.

A scream rang out from the hallway.

Henriet blinked and rose to his feet. "What was that?"

As the screaming started up again, Eldred stretched his hand out to the silver goblet. Gervese was a good man, very polite, very reasonable. He would certainly never have done anything to offend the man down in the basement—was it truly Prince Gaufroi? But what was the prince doing to him? This is what the prince did to nobody, to anybody. Eldred picked up the goblet, barely lifting it above the table. Weltrude knew how to mix a potion. If she said it would be a quick death, then surely it would be. There was a way out. The screaming stopped.

"What in the Mother's name was that?" asked Henreit.

Eldred set the cup down in place, untasted. "Just what I have been telling you about for the last three days. The Maledictus—Prince Gaufroi here in person to cut us all to pieces."

"You lie," snarled Pernet.

Other voices sounded, rising into screams—Rollon and Raduard. Henreit and Pernet drew their swords and faced the hallway.

Eldred pulled himself up on the bars. "I need a weapon. Henreit, toss me your dagger." The men ignored him, remaining fixated on the hallway.

It wouldn't make a difference, not if he had all his knives. The potion, then. He gazed upon the silver goblet, considering it. He had to take the potion, but he couldn't bring himself to do it.

Eldred looked up as he caught scent of an unnatural odor, the same he had smelled that night on the roof. The man from the vision stood in the hallway, staring at Pernet with a long bloody dagger in hand, one of Eldred's dark blue handled knives. To his credit, Pernet charged the thin old man, swinging his sword down in a long arc. But the man—if he was still a man— caught Pernet's arm and stabbed him six times in rapid succession, leaving the blade lodged in Pernet's chest on the final blow. It happened with unbelievable speed.

Henreit dropped his sword and retreated back towards the cell. "No, I beg you. Mercy!"

The man's face was stone, but his blessed eyes twinkled at Henreit's plea. "Mercy—for a wretch like you?"

Henreit dropped to his knees, bowing his head forward. "If—if Eldred is correct, we are kin. I am your kin—your cousin."

The man drew another of Eldred's daggers from under his cloak. "A man with farmer's eyes should make no such claim."

"Please!" shouted Henreit as the man pulled him up by his hair and stabbed him over and over. Henreit's screams filled the room.

Eldred slumped back against the wall, too terrified to move, suffocated by the stench radiating off the man. The man drove the knife into Henreit's heart and let him drop to the ground. Eldred watched as the man walked over and retrieved Henreit's sword, swinging it through the air a few times.

"It's not a good sword," muttered Eldred.

The man paused, midswing. "You should never have mentioned me to them. Now, this is the best I can do for you. I tried to have them do it. I truly did. I could get in trouble—a prize bull gone lame." He gave a strange high-pitched laugh and pointed the sword at Eldred. "You visited me. Now, I visit you."

"A final drink?" croaked Eldred. He gestured at the three cups.

The man rapped the table with his sword. "You would waste it. You will be dead before you could even feel its effects."

"For the taste, then," said Eldred.

"You have a taste for other people's things, thief." The man sat on the table and picked up the small, weathered notebook that contained the tallies. "This is mine."

Eldred dropped his eyes. "I'm sorry."

The man put the sword under Eldred's chin and made him raise his eyes. "How did you find my hideaway? How did you know?" He narrowed his eyes. "And how did you visit me last night?"

"I take a medicine. It gives me visions," said Eldred quietly.

"Show me."

Eldred tugged out the small clear bag that he had tied around his waist. The two packets of powder were visible within—one full, the other down to its last quarter. "The Sun People gave this to me."

The man retracted his sword. "It has been a long time since I heard anyone call them by that name."

Eldred glanced at the notebook in the man's hand. "What does seven hundred sixty-seven mean?"

The man grinned. "You counted it up. Very good. As for its meaning…" He gestured at Henreit's body, then Pernent's and finally—with his smile growing wider—at Eldred. "I keep track of my guests."

Eldred gazed despondently at Henreit's bloody corpse for a moment. This man—this Maledictus—was unstoppable. It was time to take the poison, if he still could. Eldred licked his lips. "Where are your manners, prince? If I'm your guest, you should let me drink."

The man slowly tilted his head and placed his sword down on the table. "You have a point, pup. And are you not a prince yourself, even if only a lame one? You may drink."

Eldred's hand trembled as he reached past the bronze cup for the silver goblet, only to watch in surprise as the man snatched it away.

"Greedy, greedy pup. Any man of manners would be satisfied with the nearest drink," said the man, who downed the contents in one gulp.

Eldred stared at the man with his mouth agape.

"Take that drink," said the man, pointing at the cup nearest Eldred. "Are you simple?"

Eldred took the cup and cradled it against his chest.

The man glared. "Well, what are you waiting for? Finish up before I change my mind."

Eldred took a small sip from the goblet, grimacing as he recognized the foul taste of his nightly potion. How could the prince have taken the drink for normal wine? Had he lost his sense of smell down in his foul pit? Or had Weltrude changed her mind and not poisoned the silver goblet? Whatever had happened, the prince was standing well at ease. "Why—why are you here?" stuttered Eldred.

The man's shoulders tightened. "Why am I here? Why, this is where I live." He stepped over and kicked Henreit's corpse in the side, sliding it closer to the cell. "I did not invite you or your idiot cousin, yet you made yourselves quite at home." As he turned back towards Eldred, he froze for a second, a flash of concern crossed his face. Then his left leg spasmed. He balanced for a moment on his right leg, until that trembled and he lost his balance. He fell forward towards the table, grabbing it with his hands as he spit out curses. The table slid under the impact, knocking over the last remaining cup and several of the books piled there.

Eldred dropped off the cot and scrambled back towards the far wall of the cell. She had poisoned the potion, after all.

The man grabbed Henreit's sword and stepped up to the cell bars, but Eldred was out of reach. The man hung there for a moment, loosely gripping the bars with clouded eyes. "You are a wily devil, pup—wily. But I will teach you a lesson. You will die much worse than any of them, worse than anyone ever has."

Then he grabbed his head and staggered back, sitting down abruptly on his rear in the middle of the room. His arms and legs twitched and jerked, but he kept his back straight. "This will take a moment, only a moment." He gave a long exhale as his torso shuddered.

"Just die!" shouted Eldred.

Behind the man, the windows exploded. The golden eagle, the giant bird that Eldred had fed on the roof, burst through the window and set upon the man in a frenzied attack, ripping into his back with its talons and tearing at his shoulder with its beak. The man gave way under the assault. He'd lost the sword, but spun around and slashed at the eagle's leg with one of Eldred's daggers. The eagle came on, undaunted, and stomped the man to the floor. As the man struggled, the eagle raked his forehead with its beak.

Before the eagle could strike again, the man stabbed its leg multiple times with startling speed. The bird coiled up in pain and withdrew.

The man laughed and slid back across the floor. "All your stupid patience is wasted! You came too soon, you craven vulture. I will carve you for my dinner!"

It came to Eldred that the man looked less shaky and his wounds, the deep gouges in his back, weren't bleeding. He wasn't dying. Eldred felt a sinking sensation in his stomach. Eldred scanned the room. Henreit's body lay a few feet beyond the bars, his head angled towards the cell, a dagger thrust through his heart.

Dragging himself forward, Eldred thrust out his hand, jamming his shoulder as far in between the bars as it would go. He could just reach the ends of Henreit's hair, squeezing the strands between his fingers as the battle raged between man and bird. But Eldred couldn't get a firm enough grip to pull the corpse closer.

The man was back on his feet now, moving deftly. The towering eagle was a pillar of feathers and menace, and outweighed the man by hundreds of pounds, but it was screeching loudly and giving ground. Eldred paused his desperate effort and brought his arm back. He tore off his thin belt and set the sample bag with the packets on the floor. He stuck his arm out again and used the belt to hook Henreit's neck, catching it on the second try.

The man had backed the eagle all the way to the far wall. Its outstretched wings covered almost the entire length of the room. The man darted in and stabbed the eagle in the chest. The eagle gave a piercing shriek that momentarily stunned Eldred. The man was frozen as well, and the bird struck him on the top of his head with a powerful blow.

As the man reeled back, Eldred pulled the corpse closer in a jerking fashion. The belt lifted up Henreit's chin and pressed the back of his head into the floor as he slid forward. When it was close enough, Eldred seized his late cousin's hair and yanked him over. He snatched his knife out of Henreit's chest—perhaps now he could do something.

The bird advanced. The man retreated, wiping blood from his face. Eldred gripped the knife in his right hand as he held himself up with the left, watching the fight. The man twisted and dodged the eagle's attacks, moving fluidly now. His shaking had abated. He moved in and stuck the bird twice in the chest, and ducked away before the bird could retaliate.

The bird shuffled back and thrust out its wings. It emitted the loudest scream yet, seemingly shaking Eldred's eyeballs, and flapped its wings, rising into the air with both talons reaching out in front of it to catch the man even as he stabbed the eagle furiously. He fell back, continuing to strike the enraged bird as he pushed himself back across the floor in the eagle's grip.

The instant the man came within reach, Eldred was upon him—stabbing, stabbing, stabbing. Not so swiftly as the man might, but deep damaging wounds. The man went limp as the eagle struck the man's forehead, its enormous beak not two feet from Eldred's nose. Eldred paused.

Was the man dead? As he considered, the eagle grabbed the man's feet and pulled him away.

While the man's body limply slid away, Eldred saw it, or seemed to see it. The wound—the terrible wound the eagle had dug in the man's forehead—emitted a faint trace of light. But instead of being the brilliant blue light of a sapphire, the light was cool and dark, a light that only blessed eyes could see. The Mother's shard, the stone of the Son was there—right in front of him. "No!' shouted Eldred. He grabbed the man, barely catching his wrist before the eagle got him away.

They fought, tugging and pulling. The bird had enormous power, but Eldred's arms were its match. He shuddered; he sweated; but he would not let go of that slippery wrist. Suddenly the eagle released the man and struck Eldred's left hand with its beak, shattering the bones. Eldred screamed in pain.

The eagle advanced to the bars bent low, looking for some way to get at Eldred. Eldred took a deep breath and willed the pain away. He snatched up his knife and struck the vicious bird in the eye. The eagle shrieked, almost splitting Eldred's eardrums. Eldred struck the eye again and the bird staggered back, waddling across the floor, finally leaning against the far wall on unsteady feet. It turned its destroyed eye away from Eldred, glowering at him with the one it had left.

As Eldred studied the bird, knife in hand, the body of the man twitched. Eldred raised his eyebrows in disbelief as the man moved his hand and started lifting his head. With a shuddering groan, Eldred weakly pushed the man down with his broken left hand and stabbed the man over and over. The bird watched impassively, not moving from its spot. After thirty rending strikes, the man's hand lowered to the ground.

Eldred paused, choking on his spit. After a moment, the man's hand floated up again, moving blindly. Eldred considered the bird, whose deep red eye stared hatefully at him. It had known its business. Eldred wet his lips and gingerly dragged the man's body closer. There was only one way to finish this.

The knife scraped along the man's forehead as if Eldred was digging through stone. Hard, rock hard, but Eldred chiseled away at it. The blade from Uncle Julian held up as Eldred dug his way in. The dark light shone clearer and brighter until finally it was in reach. Eldred pried out a dark mass encrusted with bits of bone and brain and held it in the palm of his hand, a look of disgust on his face.

The man finally lay still. Who was he? Not Prince Gaufroi, if the journal was to be believed, for this was surely the shard of the Mother. Had Duke Philippot changed his mind—was this him? Eldred shook his head. No, it was someone else. The shard, that is why the prince waited so courteously until the Duke killed himself, waiting so he could claim both treasures. The family trees in the dusty books mentioned the prince's brother, a man named Magner. This could be him. If so, Magner was dead.

Across the room, the eagle stirred. Eldred looked up and grimaced, feeling the pain in his left hand. "It's mine. It's properly mine. I don't know what you are or who sent you, but this shard belongs to me."

The bird squeezed its neck down and seemed to register a look of disapproval. It was then that Eldred noticed the feeling of warmth in his torso, just a hint of it, and cursed. He had merely taken a sip of the potion. Was that all it took?

He examined the crusted mass in his hand with heavy eyelids. It felt solid. It felt strong. He had to do it. He took his dagger, the packets and his treasure in his right hand, his working hand, and crawled to his water bucket. He worked the grit and filth off the stone which shone with dark brilliance as the warmth in his chest spread to his neck and down his arms. Time was short; soon he would sleep.

"It's not the proper preparation," he muttered as he settled on his back against the far side of the cell, as far away from the bars as he could get. The floor was cold and hard. He reached up and rested the knife against the top of his nose. He could feel it pressing against his skin as he stifled a yawn.

"Please, Mother," said Eldred and he made the first cut. He knew it was too shallow. This had to work. He worked the blade through again. Deep, painfully deep, and yet the pain was distant to his numbed senses. He was floating on the edge of sleep.

"I know it's not right," he said dreamily. He sprinkled the full packet of powder into the cut. He pressed the stone in the wound and rested his hand over it. Would it take, he wondered as he drifted away.

AWAKENING

Something was probing; something was pushing. Eldred yawned loud and wide. Something poked his foot. Eldred sat up sluggishly, trying to remember where he was. A metal tipped spear prodded his heel. It struck Eldred as very odd. Then he turned and saw them.

A dozen or more men in armor, Maldavians from the look of them, were moving around in the outer room. He was in the cell. The shard! As he reached up, he caught sight of his hand and paused. His left hand was unharmed and unscarred. Unscarred! He quickly checked his right hand in his confusion, but his hands bore neither the mark of the dead dragon nor the furious eagle. He gingerly touched his forehead and found it smooth to the touch, no trace of the stone or any wound.

"This one is alive!" shouted the man holding the spear.

The others lined up along the cell. Four more men stuck their spears through the bars, their tips hovering a few feet away from Eldred's face. Eldred staggered up to his feet. He was standing. He could stand. A smile broke across his face. How long had it been since he stood up?

Eldred turned to the soldiers. Two more had thrust their spears into the cell, threatening Eldred. "What is the meaning of this?" asked Eldred as he searched their faces. As he turned his head, he became aware of long strands of hair hanging down over his shoulders. He grabbed a lock of it in his hands. His hair had been short when he had lain down. It had grown half a year's worth as he slept.

"He is a fiend and a liar," said someone, a woman's voice. And there she was, Weltrude, standing behind one of the soldiers. Balian stood next to her, eyes wide in disbelief.

"I didn't do anything," said Eldred.

One of the soldiers murmured a curse. They held their spears threateningly. Their eyes brimming with fear.

Eldred glanced down. He was half naked with long wild hair and covered in dried blood. Magner's blood, but they didn't know that.

Weltrude pushed past the soldier, coming up to the bars. "We found your daggers stuck in each one of them, except Henreit. But you killed him too, did you not? Kinslayer!"

"Kinslayer," muttered one of the soldiers.

Eldred looked down and saw his fatum lapides lying on the floor next to the sample bag. Shocked, he ran his hand over his left temple and found nothing. They had fallen off! Without a thought, he knelt sharply to stuff the stones into the sample bag just as a spear stabbed at him. On instinct, he grabbed the shaft and shoved it back, knocking its wielder across the outer room. The others started striking at him. A few managed a hit before Eldred ripped the last spear from out of their hands.

He glared at the men as they unsheathed their swords. "I'm innocent!"

"You can walk!" shouted Weltrude, her beautiful eyes dark with hate. "You were pretending the whole time, and I knew it. You sneaked down to the kitchen and killed Guillotin. You killed Madalulf in this very cell, cutting him to pieces. Now you have butchered your own cousin as well as our friends. You stand there covered in their blood and falsely proclaim your innocence. You lie! You are a liar! Kill him before the kinslayer kills again."

Behind her, Balian walked to the far wall where the key to the cell hung. More men were running out of the hallway into the room, two dozen of the king's best. Balian had been good as his word.

A groan escaped Eldred. "I didn't." He pointed at Magner's corpse. "He did it. He murdered all of them!"

One man glanced at the bloody corpse. The rest seemed not to hear. Across the room, Balian retrieved the key. Eldred looked around the cell: a dagger, two buckets, a flimsy cot and a few scattered spears. Eldred picked up a spear and a yell went up from the men—Weltrude and several of the soldiers backed away from the bars. Balian was running back from across the room. Eldred sighed. Twenty men set to attack, and he was wearing rags.

He turned and looked out the window on a sunny day. Freedom was right there, just behind three rusty bars. Eldred gripped the rightmost bar. Balian was already working the lock, but only Pernet could open it quickly. With a cry of desperation, Eldred yanked on the bar, and it gave. He stepped back, staring in surprise at the bar in his hand with two chunks of stone stuck on either end.

Balian was through the cell door with a stream of soldiers jostling behind him. "You will never harm her!" he shouted, raising his sword.

Eldred threw the iron bar, catching Balian in the chest, knocking him down. The next two fell to the floor alongside Weltrude's would-be defender. Eldred pulled out the center bar as one might pull a weed from the dirt on a rainy day. There was room enough. Eldred squeezed through the opening. One of the men charged forward and landed a blow on his leg, but Eldred shook it off. He was out.

He glanced back in the cell, packed with angry soldiers. Weltrude cradled Balian's head, but he looked well enough, considering. His eyes were open, and she was a good healer when she cared to be. For a moment, Eldred was at loss as to what to do, and he just stood there in the bright sunlight. But as the first soldier clambered out of the cell window, Eldred came to his senses. He turned and ran.

His feet felt alive as he ran across the grassy field beside the manor. The sensation of the ground against his toes was delicious. His legs moved faster and faster, more sure and steady with each step. The palace was gone, falling back into the distance along with all the shouting men. He sprinted silently through the trees faster than he had ever run in his life, his breath easy, his heart steady. He was alive. They thought him a murderer, a kinslayer, but he was alive. And then he realized he was something new—a Maledictus.

First Entry

I am Eldred, son of Alfred, fallen king of the Deirans. I am the fourth to bear the Shard of the Mother, following after the Son and two lesser men. The shard has brought me new life, new strength. It rescued me from prison and healed my wounds. It severed my past gifts, my fatum lapides, which I cast into an overgrown pond, draped in green slime.

I am a hidden man, though unlike the one who came before me, I roam the world. The love I had in my past life, little as it was, is lost to me. Such is the lot of a kinslayer, which I am, though not as they believe.

But if love is barred to me, such is not the case with hate. So, I walk my way, a borrowed sword in one hand, a pilfered dagger in the other. Those who have wronged me will feel my touch.

THANKS

Thanks for taking the time to read The Crooked Ladder. For those who are interested, the story does not end here. In many ways, it is just getting started. The upcoming book, The Corporian Dilemma, was actually the first book for which I completed a draft. I went back and wrote The Dragon of Turicum and The Crooked Ladder to set up the events yet to come. But, of course, just because I am invested in the upcoming story does not mean you are of the same mind.

Speaking of your mind, I am very curious to learn about your thoughts regarding The Crooked Ladder. If you can take a minute to leave a rating, I would be most appreciative. If you can take a few minutes to leave a short review, you will find me to be a most attentive reader.

In any case, best wishes to you in all of your honorable endeavors.

ACKNOWLEDGMENTS

My deepest thanks to my friends and family who suffered through many conversations regarding this book. These noble individuals include: R. Bracher, A. Bracher, J. Etow, and K. Roberts.

This book benefitted from great professional contributions, including the cover art, illustrations, editing and beta reading. My thanks and appreciation to each of these individuals.

Cover by Jeff Brown, jeffbrowngraphics.com

Map Illustration by FictiveDesigns

Line Editing/Proofreading by Kit Duncan

Interior Book Design by Lorna Reid

Guerilla Marketing by C. Schelstraete